"LOOK O...
SHOUTED ON THE RADIO!

□ □ □

Suddenly, two stinging shocks. *Bang! Bang!* The first, distant, smashed us sideways, accompanied by agonizing screaming on the intercom; must have been in the main hull. The second exploded right beside me: raw energy roaring through the hullmetal plates, a sudden mist in the flight bridge that disappeared as our atmosphere escaped.

Decompression! My faithful instruments were . . . gone. Smashed crystal and dark displays mocked me from the smashed panel. But it was my leg that caught my attention. Felt blood pumping in my left leg before my battlesuit sealed itself like a tourniquet just above my knee. This one was serious—hurt like fire! The screaming continued on the intercom, it was all I could do to keep from joining the poor devils.

"Damage report!" I shouted through clenched teeth. "Give me a damage report!"

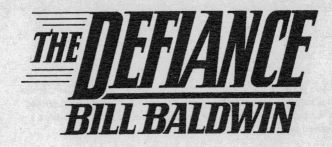

THE DEFIANCE
BILL BALDWIN

ASPECT®

WARNER BOOKS

A Time Warner Company

WARNER BOOKS EDITION

Copyright © 1996 by Merl Baldwin
All rights reserved.

Aspect® is a registered trademark of Warner Books, Inc.

Cover design by Don Puckey
Cover illustration by Chris Moore

Warner Books, Inc.
1271 Avenue of the Americas
New York, NY 10020

Visit our web site at
http://pathfinder.com/twep

Ⓦ A Time Warner Company

Printed in the United States of America

First Printing: November, 1996

10 9 8 7 6 5 4 3 2 1

Mk V Starfury killer ships destined for the defense of Ata-lanta, the colossal Imperial Fleet Base on Hador-Haelic. Until moments ago—just short of the halfway point from Braltar, the Empire's space citadel in a neighboring sector of the galaxy—we'd faced little more than the boredom of an uneventful, three-day trip. Then the head and shoulders of Yin-Hardwyck, our Systems Officer, materialized in one of my globular displays with bad news. Other starships were approaching—and out here, they could hardly be from our side of the war. "Dampiers, Lieutenant?" I surmised.

"Both proximity systems indicate the enemy ships are Dampier DA-79s, Admiral Brim," she replied.

"Give me the whole thing."

"Aye, sir. Eight DA-79s bearing two seventy-five degrees true, point nineteen light-years, on course three fifty-five de-grees true; speed twenty-five M LightSpeed, and closing fast."

"Got you," I said, absently scanning the flowing, con-stantly altering colors and hues of my readouts. Odors of a new starship everywhere: hot metal, sealants, logics, polish, food, people. Too new. We weren't ready to put up much of a fight today. Of course, the Dampiers over there didn't know that . . . maybe *wouldn't*—if I could be clever enough.

In these perilous days, all of Emperor Onrad V's subjects needed to be clever—because cleverness was nearly all we had to fight with. Our ancient Empire stood defiant, but nearly alone and friendless in the Home Galaxy, with only the Great Federation of Sodeskayan States—herself under at-tack—to help counter the onslaught of Nergol Triannic's League of Dark Stars. One by one, I'd watched the great al-lied star domains capitulate before these lightning attacks: A'zurn, then Gannet, then Lamintir, then Korbu, then even powerful Effer'wyck, the latter in concert with a final, humiliating retreat from old Dankir by General Hagbut's Imperial Expeditionary Forces. Now, fully half the galaxy lay prostrate beneath Triannic's jackbooted feet.

As the League advanced, other would-be tyrants followed its success with great interest. One, Grand Duke Rogan LaKarn of The Torond, had quickly determined he could likewise extend his own empire beyond certain portions of the Dominion of Fluvanna he had seized previously. But he would need help. To this end, he'd ingratiated himself with the dictator Triannic until, ultimately, he, too had declared war on the Empire, thus placing all remaining free Fluvannian planetary systems in deepest jeopardy, along with some of the Empire's most precious, and critical, resources.

In my new assignment, I was supposed to do something about all that . . . somehow.

Glanced through the forward Hyperscreens—after nearly half a standard day on the repair list, they were once more translating Hyperspeed-jumbled photons to comprehensible vision. Nothing yet. The Dampiers were still too far away. Nearer at hand, the other Starfuries had already opened from our normal, long-distance ferry formation into four groups of four ships—"quads," two-by-two combat formations on which we'd recently standardized. "Red" quad—the only four ships with activated disruptor cannon—was mine.

"Red One from Blue One: got a visual on four unknowns at Blue Apex. Thirty c'lenyts and closing fast."

Squinted through the Hyperscreens over my left shoulder. Gradually, a formation of faint sparks emerged in the distance high to port, moving at an angle to the stars rushing past in the "spaceman's tunnel." "Got them, Blue One, bogies at Blue Apex." I acknowledged, edging the ship right for a better tracking position while I considered my next move. Even though The Torond's fleets were mostly manned by ill-trained bullies drawn from the ranks of gangsters—talent at a helm wasn't necessarily linked to honesty: look at our own great Fleet—the ships they flew were good, *very* well armed. Underestimating their capabilities might well be fatal because it only took one lucky hit and . . . *pfft,* good-bye buttocks. Needed to face these ships down right away. "We'd better go see what they're up to, " I said, turning our half-armed Starfuries to the attack. Made me nervous when I thought about it! But no more than a few clicks after we changed course, the six Dampiers abruptly set me at ease by veering away onto a parallel track with the convoy—well out of disruptor range. I could have cheered!

Continued on course a few moments more to make them sweat. Then I, too, turned, aligning my quad on a course separating the two groups, relieved—but not at all surprised by the Toronders' reaction. Our tri-hulled Sherrington Starfuries were graceful, 330-iral-long killer ships that could top 75M LightSpeed and tussle with anything the galaxy could throw at them. They were reduced in size by nearly half from the Mark 1C Starfury "pocket battlecruisers" that were their immediate ancestors, yet they retained the identical main battery of twelve 406-mmi disruptor cannon and required a crew of only fifteen. In their intended role as short-range interceptors, they were renowned—and feared—throughout the galaxy. Most likely, the enemy commanders out there had no idea that eight of our convoy were not armed. Or for that matter, that the four of us—the so-called escort—carried only a partial suite of disruptors.

Our regrettable lack of firepower was a sad fact of life. The very success of these Sherrington interceptors was also an undoing—at least for some roles. In spite of the finest 'Grav and Drive systems in existence, their atmospheric-sleek, tri-hulled spaceframes and power generators had been optimized from the start for short missions of less than a Standard Day's duration.

My sixteen ships had already been in continuous flight more than two Standard Days, and it had been necessary to disable numerous ancillary systems in order to make even *that* possible. The *additional* one and a half Standard Day's flight from our present position to Atalanta had required either disconnecting all the disruptors or many of the control systems. We'd come to a tricky compromise with the four ships that would be manned exclusively by Fleet personnel—*six* active disruptors (out of twelve) per ship and only the most basic control systems. Nobody, especially *me*, was very happy with the result, but the squadrons posted to Atalanta would need reinforcement within a very short time. So I'd agreed to lead a convoy; I was on my way there in any case. After this trip, however, replacements would have to come by transport, at last until someone on our side invented a good long-range interceptor.

Decided to re-form into one unit. Increasing the size and apparent firepower of our little flotilla was nothing but pure fakery, but even *looking* more capable than we were could be worth something. Broadcast "join me" orders to the other Starfuries by KA'PPA communications—in the clear so the Toronders would read it aboard the Dampiers, too. KA'PPA transmitters instantaneously deliver information "packets" to all "listening" receiver nodes in the known Universe. In turn, the receivers ordinarily ignore packets addressed elsewhere, but I knew the Toronders couldn't resist scanning everything that came their way. If nothing else, my little ruse might mean a moment's hesitation over an attack. And I'd been saved by a moment any number of times during my career as a combat Helmsman.

As the others took up station, I kept a wary eye on the six

Dampiers, imagining their messages to and from some Sector Headquarters as they KA'PPAed with Controllers. Not much for independent action, those Toronders. It was a flaw I intended to exploit, both now and during the battles that were certain to come, if, of course, I got to Atalanta in the first place.

My new assignment: take command of the military base on Atalanta's Grand Harbor, including the Starfuries of 71 Group—primary Sector Space Defense for the planet Haelic. The present commander, Rear Admiral W. Groton Summers, a known Triannic sympathizer and member of the League-sponsored Congress for Intra-Galactic Accord (CIGA), had deliberately allowed the base to deteriorate. I'd been briefed that he was protected from indictment by powerful, League-leaning CIGA politicians in the Imperial Parliament.

For a number of years now, Grand Harbor had been under dual management: a Military Commandment responsible for operation of the Fleet Base and a civilian Harbor Master who operated the commercial port. Both offices—in theory, if not in practice—reported to the largely ceremonial office of Port Governor, appointed directly from our distant Imperial capital on the planet Avalon. However, that tradition was about to change—at least for the duration. The last civilian Governor, Photius I. Grünwald, an elderly, disinterested academic, had passed away some weeks hence in office. He would not be replaced. Instead, the Military Commandant and Harbor Master would both report directly to Avalon. In this manner, the Admiralty would be more directly in charge of both civilian and military operations during this rather difficult interval in history.

My first task: restore the base to a wartime state of affairs in the shortest possible time. *Summers has let things reach an exceptionally miserable state there*, they'd told me, chuckling—all of them chuckling—*so it's not going to be a plum assignment. But then, you've never had a plum assignment, Brim, so you're more or less the best man for the job, eh?* They'd relented after that—only for a moment. *We think you'll like the second part of the job a lot better,* they'd added, *even though it will be infinitely more difficult—and dangerous.* But until I got the first one accomplished, they'd refused me any more information about it—only something about a rapidly ticking clock and the code word *Sapphire.* . . .

It was food for *a lot* of thought. So far, Negrol Triannic's plans for his League of Dark Stars had been focused on a largely unsuccessful attack against our five Imperial capital planets—now known as the Battle of Avalon—followed by his invasion of Sodeskaya, an enterprise that was also slowly running into trouble as the Great Sodeskayan Bears, commanded by my old friend Marshal Nikolas Yanuarievich Ursis, gained the necessary strength and confidence to defend their homeland.

Meanwhile, half a galaxy distant, the sprawling base at Atalanta—despite its tremendous size and strategic location—had been allowed to become little more than a backwater in the fast-expanding Second Great War. It wasn't as if our War Cabinet in Avalon considered Atalanta unimportant; but Imperial resources were low after years of League-backed opposition to defense spending by powerful CIGA interest groups. Until home production caught up with demand, our limited forces would necessarily be concentrated in locations that were under active attack.

According to our best intelligence, the planet of Hador-Haelic was next on Triannic's schedule of conquest, although no one had yet been able to determine precisely *when*. I personally suspected this dearth of information wasn't so much a failing of our intelligence services as the fact that Triannic had assigned *this* particular enterprise to his flunky from The Torond, Grand Duke Rogan LaKarn and the slipshod, unprofessional military organization he had put in place since his ascension to—call it "theft of"—The Torond's throne.

Perring out the Hyperscreens, I was about to risk another feint with all sixteen ships, when the Dampiers suddenly turned tail and disappeared among the stars. Probably, they were heading to The Torond's big Fleet base at Otnar'at, less than half a day distant from Atalanta. I shrugged, my little deception had worked well enough, but the xaxtdamned Toronders could easily guess where we were going. It was a foregone conclusion that—sooner or later—I would encounter them again . . . and again and again.

Chapter 1

Entirely New Management

15–16 Heptad, 52014

Interplanetary Space, near Hador-Haelic

The star Hador had grown from a flickering pinpoint of light to the dazzling jasmine star presently looming in the blackness off to port. Ahead, Haelic's planetary disk occupied most of the forward Hyperscreens as my haggard ferry crew prepared the Starfury for landfall. KA'PPA channels were filled with traffic from ships entering and leaving the colossal port of Atalanta and its sprawling Fleet Base. "All hands to stations for landfall! All hands man your landfall stations." I called into the blower. "Secure from HyperLight Operations. . . ."

From below, the Starfury's cramped navigation bridge

filled again with the distant *thuds* of airtight doors and hatches, crewmen dashing to their stations, and the semi-ordered confusion associated with securing a starship from deep space.

Waiting for the Transition, I glanced forward as the ship slowed toward LightSpeed. Presently, all 'Screens were still projecting their HyperLight simulation of the view outside. But there . . . even as I watched, they got more and more transparent while our big Wizard 60 Drives fought the terrific momentum that had taken us a quarter of the way across the galaxy from the great Imperial space citadel of Braltar.

As we passed through LightSpeed, I switched to the six powerful Admiralty-391 gravity generators the ship used when flying HypoLight, then shut down the Drive. Presently, photons began to arrive at speeds my human eyes could translate, and the 'Screens came over to full transparent, revealing an ocher planet with overtones of ultramarine cloaked here and there by filmy white cloud banks. I'd first seen that panorama something like a thousand eons ago, it seemed—during an altogether different war.

Tried to force the past aside while I went through the rigmarole of securing approach clearance from Planetary Center. Got the clearance; the other didn't work. A woman with long brown hair I'd known then—face had never gone completely from my memory. She was still there—I'd made it my business to check. Would she remember me after all these years? Or would she even care to? Shouldn't think about her just now, but . . .

I'd always found Atalanta fascinating, and not just because of *her*. The city had been a vital anchorage of one sort or another since time immemorial—long before the Age of Star Flight, when only seaborne ships called at her already age-blackened stone jetties and piers. HyperLight travel changed the very warp and woof of civilization on Haelic, and gradually, Atalanta's identity merged with that of the whole planet. Advent of the militant Gradgroat-Norchelite Order and, later, their huge, hilltop monastery with its orbital forts gave the city-planet yet another identity—one that would ultimately save the Empire itself during the final battle of the First Great War. That clash effectively destroyed much of the ancient city as well as the League's fleet, the latter causing Emperor Nergol Triannic to sue for amity with his double-dealing armistice and subsequent Treaty of Garak. Now: another war had come, with Atalanta once more slated for the pain and misery associated with a major strategic role.

Ahead—actually, *below*, now—Haelic had taken on added dimension. My Starfuries were descending through ever-thickening atmosphere like meteors while they beamed directed-energy plasma torches out ahead to shield their hulls from the heat of reentry. At the edge of vision, I checked my other quads—all keeping perfect station in echelon to port.

Down we swept toward shapeless, smoothed-over cloud banks that quickly became moving, grayish masses fringed with color as the horizon lost its curve and I made my personal transition from navigating the vast emptiness of deep space to flying in crowded, controlled airspace. Glancing at an altimeter, I keyed the radio, "Atalanta Center," I sent, "Fleet ST-337F with Convoy ART-19 requests approach clearance."

"Fleet ST-337F," a civilian controller responded promptly, "Convoy ART-19 is cleared to Orbital Buoy nine nine one, Frequency seven eight four three. On arrival, continue descent to two five zero c'lenyts and decelerate to velocity twenty-five zero zero."

"Fleet FA-337 acknowledges direct routing to HoverBuoy

nine nine one. Convoy is presently at five fifty c'lenyts and thirty-one zero zero velocity. Decelerating to velocity of two five five zero."

Within twenty cycles, I had the HoverBuoy in sight to starboard, radiating a coded pattern in flashes of ruby light. We were now well within Haelic's atmosphere and measuring altitude in irals rather than c'lenyts. Out ahead, a departing merchantman crossed our path on the way to outer space. As the Starfury bounced through its churning gravity wakes, the head and shoulders of a young woman appeared in a globular display over my right-hand console. "Fleet FA-337," she said, "Convoy ART-19 may descend and maintain flight level three hundred."

"Convoy ART-19 will continue descent to flight level three hundred," I acknowledged, checking the Hyperscreens for local traffic. From long experience, I understood that the Center's traffic controllers were severely overworked—and used equipment that was rarely uprated. Been around long enough to understand that one of the *first* items to be rationed during wartime was safety, with every commander on both sides—including myself—deceitfully preaching some brand of safety gospel as if we actually believed a word of it.

Came through a solid bank of clouds nearly as large as the continent it covered. Only a few hundred irals below, I picked out at least four more layers of dirty, gray-looking clouds—detritus of a frontal system moving slowly down from the polar regions of the planet.

"Fleet FA-337 with Convoy ART-19, descend and maintain one zero thousand irals with a heading of three one five to join the Blue-five radial inbound," a new controller directed. She had pretty blue eyes.

"Many thanks," I replied. "Convoy ART-19 descending to one thousand irals and a heading of three one five for radial

Blue." I listened to the steady beat of the 'Gravs thundering in the Starfury's lower two hulls—"pontoons" was the builder's term—on either side of the Starfury's main fuselage. Thought about the ferry crew, at least as anxious to be down as I was.

I set the lift augmentors, listening to the 'Gravs spooling up as they shouldered the extra load. Clicks later, the ship trembled as finned cooling radiators deployed from either side of the main fuselage and roared in the slipstream.

"Fleet FA-337 with Convoy ART-19: proceed direct to intercept Blue beacon on the three nine three radial," the blue-eyed controller intoned. "Cross the threshold at eight five thousand and maintain altitude."

"Convoy ART-19 flying direct to Blue radial three nine three to cross threshold at eight five thousand and maintain altitude." Eyeballed the altimeters and turned on the landing lights just as the autopilot disconnected. It was the only automatic system still on line in the Starfury; actually I often flew with the automatic systems disconnected, especially during lift-offs and landfalls. Wasn't alone, either, at least among the better Helmsmen. . . .

During the next minutes, the controller reduced our speed to 200 cpm (c'lenyts per metacycle), then 150 before turning us onto an instrument vector for landing. Silhouetted ahead in the evening light was an unmistakable cityscape and glowing harbor—Atalanta! My eyes followed the great upsweep of City Mount Hill as fading daylight illuminated the Gradgroat-Norchelite's reconstruction of their colossal monastery. In spite of myself, I felt a growing sense of excitement. Twice before this legendary city had assumed critical importance in my life. It was clear a third instance had already commenced. . . .

A different controller appeared in my globular display:

this time a young man with short, fiery red hair. "Fleet FA-337 with Convoy ART-19," he advised, "your ships are cleared for landfall by quads line abeam; vector ninety-eight left. Wind from three hundred at four six with gusts to five nine."

"Thank you, Atalanta Tower," I replied. "Convoy ART-19 is cleared for landfall by quads line abeam: vector ninety-eight left." He switched to the convoy frequency. "Quad leaders—you noted all that?"

"Affirmative, Admiral," three voices replied in unison.

"Good," I said. "I'll take my four ships in first. Harris, you make a circuit and follow with Blue quad, next Kimple with Yellow, and finally Bell with Green. Any questions?"

"None, Admiral."

"See you on the surface," I said as a solid ruby light flashed out of the evening magenta ahead. A gust of wind pushed the ship to port, and the light began to dissociate into horizontal lines. As I corrected to starboard, the ruby lines converged, then separated again, this time to vertical lines. One last correction and they coalesced again—on centerline. Increased the lift augmentors and fed in ten degrees more power to take up the load.

More landing checklist. Continuous boost ON; radio nav switches set on RADIOS; flight panels checked. The other three ships in my quad had now moved into line-ahead formation behind me, each ship slightly offset to the left. It was time I got everyone belowdecks down in their seats. "All hands secure personal stations. All hands secure personal stations . . ."

Altimeter, flight, and nav instruments set and cross-checked; airspeed EPR bugs reduced to one thirty nine and cross-checked, speed brake levers LOCKED. The starship began to sink as I reined in the power. Off to starboard, a virtual forest of shipyard cranes slid by my Hyperscreens, then huge rounded towers, darkened globes, and a maze of tall crystalline structures catching the last of Hador's failing light. Three thousand irals to my left a veritable city of darkened goods houses and wharves materialized out of the night, most of the latter occupied by one sort of starship or another.

Only a hundred irals' altitude, now—the part that separates Helmsmen from wannabes. Walked the steering engines carefully, concentrating on the ranks of waves glittering out ahead in the landing lights. Glide path . . . descent rate . . . speed . . . angle of attack. None perfect, but close enough at this altitude, especially with a human at the helm. Called up a little more thrust—should be 3–4 cpms fast—then eased off the steering engines. The bow swung to windward, then I slanted the deck a little for drift. Nose up ever so slightly. Judging the wave troughs . . . held her off . . . deftly leveling the trihull only an instant before cascades of dark water shot skyward past the side Hyperscreens, diminished as we slid through a trough, then shot skyward once more as I gently plastered the pontoons to the surface. We sliced through two more of the big rollers before I pulsed the gravity brakes gently, sending long streams of gravitons out ahead to flatten the waves and slow the ship. Moments later, we were stopped, rolling gently on the surface of Grand Harbor while I switched to local gravity (as always, nearly losing the contents of my stomach), then configured the controls for surface running. In the overhead 'Screens, the clouds had passed, and stars from the galactic center shimmered like a great canopy of lights to set the water glittering with a million-odd colors and hues. After a number of momentous years, I had again returned to Hador-Haelic's Atalanta—and perhaps a middle-aged woman with long brown hair who had never been far from my mind during thirteen long years. Focused on the ship again—no time to think about *her* now!

We'd scarcely cleared the landing vector when a harbor controller with an axious look appeared in my globular display.

"Harbor Control to all quads of Convoy ART-19 . . . Harbor Control to all quads of Convoy ART-19," she said. "Slave your ships to individual blue taxi vectors with all haste. I repeat—*with all haste*. Enemy raids are imminent."

"Red quad scanning for vectors," I responded—not at all surprised. The zukeeds had us nailed! Configured for surface running, our Starfuries were much too far behind the energy curve for quick lift-offs—especially in the face of an attack. As I spoke, Red Four turned hard to port, followed by Red Three, then Red Two. Abruptly, a blue harbor vector gleamed in my own port Hyperscreen. Pointed an acquisition tube at it until three blue lights converged in my nav panel, then it was up to the Starfury. Now, remotely steered from somewhere in the darkness ahead, we headed straight for the vector. Rising from the helm, I peered aft through the darkness, where Blue quad was skimming to a landing in clouds of spray no more than a thousand irals behind us.

By the time Yellow quad reported they were down, I could sense rather than see a large opening in the massive seawall ahead, where the water's reflection ended in the darkness. My taxi vector was beamed from it. "Docking and mooring details to stations," I ordered on the blower. Moments later, hatches popped open atop the pontoons and soon crews of starsailors dressed in attractor boots, sea slickers, and big insulated mittens were scurrying along the wet, dimly lighted surfaces to open our optical mooring cleats.

As our four ships approached the massive entrance, a searing flash lighted the sky and dimmed the Hyperscreens, almost as if a nearby star had exploded. Startled, I jumped in my seat, then steadied myself. Of course—the Gradgroat-Norchelite orbital forts! They'd be the first to fire on an attack from space.

Another blinding flash. Then another, and another until the darkness was turned to a throbbing, toneless blue-white daylight. Then . . . darkness again—darker still for the contrast.

I knew the attackers were now either past the forts or destroyed as I listened to the ships of Green quad report their landing runs, then make an abrupt turn shoreward. Breathed a little easier. All of Convoy ART-19 was at least safely *down*—if not yet safely sheltered.

Suddenly our four ships were safe inside the darkened cavern, running four abreast along what appeared to be a wide canal. From her position at the extreme right of the quad, my Starfury seemed to be speeding along only a few irals from a *very* solid-looking seawall—with nobody at the helm!

Abruptly, we came to an halt with the 'Gravs idling, and I glanced aft again—just in time to hear the ships of Blue quad report themselves safely through the entrance, four dim white wakes against the near darkness. Then the unmistakable flashing of disruptors lighted the sky outside of the hangar, bathing Yellow quad in brilliant strobes of light as the four ships raced for shelter through a veritable forest of glowing, yellow-green waterspouts just short of the entrance.

I watched—horrified—as the rightmost Starfury lifted from the water atop a glowing, coruscating eruption of greenish energy and water. While its luckless Helmsman struggled with the controls, the Starfury's nose reared higher and higher, then fell off sharply to starboard—just as it managed to reach the hangar entrance. Next moment, the speeding ship slammed broadside against a solid-rock column, then broke in two and exploded, spewing glittering clouds of hullmetal sparks as it sideswiped its closest neighbor. More disruptor flashes outside, these much brighter. The Fleet Base was *finally* shooting back—just as the doors began to close.

But where was Green quad?

Another tremendous explosion—followed by an angular-looking starship tumbling into the mouth of the hangar, aflame from stern to Drive tubes. One of The Torond's new Dampiers! The stricken ship erupted in a blinding sheet of pure energy while the massive doors continued to slide shut. Without warning, a Starfury burst through the incandescent rubble, followed by a second . . . then a third, only *just* squeezing through the narrow opening that remained. Then a secondary explosion and the doors finally slammed together.

Moments later, when the hangar's internal lighting came on, a glance around revealed that we were in a huge, arched tunnel carved from solid rock—at least two hundred irals high and perhaps five times that in width. The "canal" I'd sensed in the darkness was actually the ends of piers lining either side of the underground passage, which appeared to extend for nearly a quarter c'lenyt in either direction. Wreckage fom the downed Dampier still smoldered just inside the massive doors, and the six survivors from Yellow and Green quads were idling in two ranks behind the four ships of Blue quad—all apparently undamaged, as were my own Starfury and the three other ships of Red quad.

I'd lost two of the sixteen Starfuries in my charge—better than twelve percent. Not a record to be proud of, especially since the ships *had* come all that way safely. They'd be missed; no doubt about that. From my position on the canal, I could count twenty-nine other Starfuries moored in three groups along the tunnel. Fifteen older Defiant-class attack ships were clustered into two additional groups. The remainder of the occupied wharves nearby were taken up by various utility and transport starships as well as three biazarre-looking "benders" that could "bend" nearly all radiation around their hulls, rendering them virtually invisible to all known receptors.

Clearly, the defending squadrons of 71 Group had been caught with their collective pants down. Why? With the sophisticated, late-model KA'PPA-based BKAEW early-warning systems that had been shipped here only Standard Months earlier, they should easily have been spaceborne in plenty of time to blunt—or even completely foil—the assault that had destroyed two brand-new attack ships and their crews. Yet none of the ships appeared even to be manned, although a few maintenance crews could be seen working on their hulls.

Well, by Voot, I'd been warned. What a state of affairs! With a fast-growing sense of indignation, I promised myself that tomorrow—first thing—I would start rooting out the bastards who were responsible, starting with the present, outgoing commander, one Rear Admiral (the Hon.) W. Groton Summers, who would soon be on his way to a comfortable staff job in Avalon. My angry musings were interrupted by a surface-traffic controller who appeared in his globular display with a mooring assignment at one of the empty piers. . . .

I was roused at Dawn plus one twenty-five by a chime from my timepiece. Frowning, I sat up in the bunk and glanced around. The message screen on the wall of my temporary cubicle in the Bachelor Officer's Quarters indicated three messages waiting. I hadn't even checked the previous night; I'd been too ragged out from the trip for anything but a desperately needed shower, immediately followed by a bed. Shrugging, I took a battered Remote from the night table and displayed the first message:

14 Heptad 52014, Brightness:3:30

TO: Wilf A Brim, RADM, I.F.

From: Hathaway Cottshall, Administrator

For: W. Groton Summers, RADM, I.F.

Admiral Brim: RADM Summers sends compliments, and directs me to convey that it will be his pleasure to receive you in his private Headquarters office at Morning:00:00 sharp for Transfer of Command Ceremonies to be held promptly at noon. Formal uniform recommended.

Formal uniform, eh? So *that's* the sort of thing that concerned Summers. Certainly didn't seem worried much about his base being attacked—or about safe arrival for badly needed reinforcements to its defense. Except for a few dockside mooring squads, no one had even bothered to meet my tired ferry crews as they stiffly piled out of their Starfuries at pierside. And it couldn't be that they'd mistaken our arrival time; the message had been forwarded here to the VOQ late yesterday afternoon.

Later yesterday, when I'd personally inquired about what sort of defenses had been aloft when the Dampiers arrived for their attacker, I was informed that only the orbiting space forts and the harbor's fixed disruptor batteries had been put on full alert. Yet even in worst case, many of those twenty-nine Starfuries I counted *had* to be operational. So where in xaxt were their thraggling crews? And why hadn't at least a few of the zukeeds been flying a Combat Space Patrol? Maybe Summers was a CIGA, but he certainly couldn't have effected damage on this scale without a lot of help.

The Ops Officer was responsible for much of the way the base appeared. But first responsibility lay with Summers and his Executive Officer; that's where I'd start. After that, I'd root out the decay so that this kind of treason would never happen again—ever.

The next message was from Master Chief Petty Officer Utrillo Barbousse, highest-ranking noncom in the Imperial Fleet and a trusted personal associate since our days together aboard I.F.S. *Truculent* during the First Great War. Barbousse and I had formed such an effective team that for years Emperor Onrad insisted the two of us be stationed together. According to the him, it was the most damaging thing he could do to the League.

WO9FGU7BVJW405967HGJQ0W9E8RG
[TOP SECRET]

FROM:
U. BARBOUSSE, MCPO, VPOQ, IFB, AVALON, AVALON-ASTERIOUS

TO:
WILF A BRIM, RADM, VOQ, IFB, ATALANTA, HADOR-HAELIC

HAVE TRANSPORTATION ORDERS IN HAND FOR I.S.S. SWANNERLAND DEPARTING HERE 26 HEPTAD AND ARRIVING ATALANTA 32 HEPTAD. ALREADY PACKED NUMEROUS CASES OF VINTAGE LOGISH MEEM YOU MAY FIND INTERESTING AS WELL AS DELICIOUS. KA'PPA OTHER "NECESSITIES" I SHOULD PICK UP FOR

YOU IN AVALON. SEEN MUCH OF YOUR DAUGHTER,
HOPE, IN LAST FEW DAYS. SHE IS ABUNDANTLY
HEALTHY AND FILLED WITH THE SAME WONDERFUL
SUNSHINE AS HER LATE MOTHER. SHE CONSTANTLY
ASKS ABOUT YOU, IN SPITE OF NEARLY PERPETUAL
OVERINDULGENCE BY EMPEROR ONRAD—WHO SENDS
PERSONAL REGARDS, AS DOES NURSE COSA TUTTI.
HAVE LATEST HOLOPICS IN HAND SO YOU CAN SHOW
HER OFF TO EVERYONE IN ATALANTA.

[END TOP SECRET]

WO9FGU7BVJW405967HGJQ0W9E8RG

I grinned. My tiny daughter Hope did seem to have some
internal source of sunshine—on those all-too-few occasions I
got to see her. Officially, the little girl's father was Mustafa
Eyren, the Nabob of Fluvanna; her mother, Raddisma, a
singularly gifted and beautiful woman as well as Eyren's
most favored courtesan. But I was the little girl's *actual* father—after a single, extraordinary night with the beautiful
courtesan aboard a crippled starship. Sadly, we saw each
other only twice more after that.

Little Hope had come a long, treacherous route to her present fortuitous state of affairs. Just before the fall of Fluvanna,
Emperor Onrad granted asylum in Avalon to the Fluvannian
court—including Raddisma, who delivered little Hope
shortly after her arrival in Avalon. And, upon Raddisma's
death from a stray disruptor burst during the Battle of
Avalon, Onrad further made the little girl his personal
ward—some whispered as a courtesy to me when he acci-
dentally discovered her actual derivation. At all events, Hope
now resided in the Imperial Palace, cared for by Raddisma's
faithful retainer, Cosa Tutti, although elderly Nabob Eyren

still visited faithfully in the belief that the little girl was his true daughter.

My third message was from the Base Housing Office, informing me in the most incoherent bureaucratese possible that my base housing authorization was denied because a form had been misfiled in Atalanta. Shrugging phlegmatically, I made a note to let Barbousse handle *that* item, then fetched my tote bag from the shelf over my bunk. Clearly, I had plenty of work in store—and very little time to do it.

At Dawn plus two, roughly five metacycles remained until my "ceremony" with Summers; I resolved to use it productively. I dressed from my duffel bag in worn blue flight overalls, soft leather boots, a battered black leather Helmsman's jacket, and a garrison cap with two small stars as the only indication of my flag rank. Then—just in case—I buckled on my Wenning .985 blaster in its leather holster. Grabbed a steaming, sweet cup of cvceese' on my way through the VOQ lobby, then strode out into the early morning duskiness—where the star Hador was already clearing Atalanta's spinward horizon with a swollen streak of burnt orange—and caught a grimy freight tram to the underground hangar.

Below, I found the vast gloomy cavern much the way I had left it the previous evening, redolent of seawater, overheated logics, solvents, hot metals, sealants, lubricants, and the other smells common to a starship anchorage. It was also *still* mostly unpopulated, with only a minimum of activity going on—although a few more vehicles were moving within my purview. Here and there, I could hear the staccato *t-zaapt* of collapsium welders, reflecting their wobbling glare on the jagged rock of the ceiling. An overhead crane hummed along a track over the main canal carrying a crated Drive crystal, and from somewhere far inside came the lonely chime of a communicator. But the giant facility was virtually abandoned. Where in the name of Voot was every-body?

Behind me, the doors to the harbor had been rolled open again while a floating crane noisily dredged up the tangled wreckage of the Dampier and my Yellow-quad Starfury that had crashed during the previous evening's attack. Farther out in the harbor, a second salvage crane had just turned off its working lights, raising, I assumed, the wreckage of the missing Starfury from Green quad. I ground my teeth. Neither Starfury needed to have been lost—certainly not pissed away without opposition as they had been. Without even a fight. Starfuries themselves were hard enough to replace; but their crews could *never* be replaced—either aboard ship or among their families. Especially the civilians. Bad enough to sacrifice StarSailors; possible death was written into their job descriptions. But the civilians—*that* was murder.

I strode along a section of the broad concourse that paralleled the left-hand wall of the tunnel. The surface was littered and stained by puddles of spilled lubricant slippery enough to cause an accident. Yet I could see no sign of a maintenance detail anywhere. Many of the stains looked as if they had been around for a long time.

I checked one of the piers that jutted out from that side of the great subterranean hangar. Hardly a Karlssohn lamp was burning with a full array of illuminators. Dockside gear was carelessly adrift everywhere; some even blocking access to the N-ray mains—in spite of flashing fire-lane indicators built into the surface. On the second pier, a number of optical bollards were weak and clearly out of adjustment, allowing both Starfuries moored there to drift dangerously close to the piers.

Except for the ships I'd delivered myself, the Starfuries and the Defiants I could see appeared to be *anything* but ready for battle, or even flight. Especially the more complex Starfuries. Many had access hatches open as if they were waiting for maintenance of one kind or another. Thick cables fed into them here and there, but nobody seemed to be doing much work—at least nobody in a hurry. Here and there crews of mechanics stood in little groups talking and smoking the spicy local mu'occo cigarettes. None of them one paid me the slightest attention as I strode along the concourse—a complete stranger. Where in the name of Voot was Security? Where was thraggling *anybody*?

I grew more disgusted with each pier I passed, especially when I remember how things had *once* been at this magnificent Fleet Base—even during peacetime. But in those days, some of the best minds in the Empire had been in charge. Clearly, that had changed drastically.

I stopped for a moment to take stock. Things were deeply wrong in the Ops, Engineering, and even the Space Divisions of the base. I checked my timepiece. Still three metacycles until my appointment with Summers. Used a portable Holo-Phone to pass a few quick orders to the three quad leaders who'd flown in with me, then caught a nearby lift to the surface and cadged a ride to the transport pool.

More smells of lubricants and solvents as I opened the door to the office, but with a strong overtone of . . . *polish*. Nothing wrong with that! Peered through an open door into the main garage; spied a lone rating energetically shining a large, elegant limousine skimmer. The last time I'd been stationed in Atalanta, the base didn't even *have* a limousine skimmer.

"Can I help you, sir?" the young StarSailor called through the door with his sweaty back to the checkout counter. Young, in his early twenties, he was stripped to the waist and flexing muscles in the manner of someone who likes to keep himself in shape.

"I need a gravcycle, Mister," I said, glad to see at least someone hard at work.

'D you mind just takin' one, sir?" he puffed over his shoulder. "I've got to have this thing shined for the big doings at Headquarters, and I don't have much more time."

"What's going on at Headquarters?" I asked—as if I didn't know.

"New military commander checkin' in, sir," the StarSailor explained, still with his back to me. "Guess they're going to show him around."

"They need a *limousine skimmer* to show him around?"

"I don't ask questions, sir," the StarSailor said, grunting as he reached across the top of the big machine to polish a recalcitrant spot, "I just take orders and spread wax."

Grinned in spite of myself. "I see," I said, stepping through the doorway into the garage—which on first sight appeared to hold some of nearly every type of vehicle known to civilization. Toward the rear of the huge room, a group of mechanics were grouped around a heavy lorry, their tools and voices echoing distantly in the vastness. I turned to the rating. "Isn't anybody around to help you out?" I demanded.

"Oh yes, sir," he replied, still not turning around. "But they're a bit late this mornin'. Usually I can handle it myself, but today Headquarters wanted the Admiral's limo all shined up—and nobody got around to tellin' me about it till I got here about Dawn plus two twenty-five." He shook his head. "Awful lucky I was early, or I'd be in a real pickle."

"I see," I said. "Very well. How do I get myself a 'cycle?"

"Just sign the tubulator back there on the office counter, sir, then go pick one out," the StarSailor said, pointing to a large collection of gravcycles nearby. He climbed down to move the ladder. "When you ride past, call out the number, and I'll note it down for you, er . . ." Suddenly, his gaze fell on my garrison cap. "*Admiral*, sir!" he said with a stricken look.

"At ease, StarSailor," I answered, raising a hand to check him. "What's your name?"

"Er, Russo, sir. Joe Russo, Petty Officer, Third Class—sir."

"Who's your boss, Russo?"

"Er, Chief Petty Officer Lorton Tambourne, sir."

"Where is he?"

"I, er, don't know, sir."

I looked at him carefully. "Is he on leave, or something?"

"No, sir."

"He *supposed* to be here, then?"

"Well, er . . ."

"Yes or no, Russo."

"Yes, sir."

"Who's *his* boss?"

"Chief Tambourne works direct for the Base Transportation Officer, Commander Baily, sir."

"I assume Baily reports to the Ops Officer?"

"Yes, sir. Captain Harper."

"All right, Russo," I said, making a quick decision. "Three items for you. First: park the limousine; it won't be needed today. Second: at Brightness on the dot, I take over from Admiral Summers as Base Commander and you're promoted to Petty Officer, First Class—call it a battlefield commission for obvious reasons. Third: at that moment, you're *also* in temporary command of the transport pool. Can you handle it?"

"Command . . . *me*?" He only hesitated a moment. "You bet I can handle it, sir, b-but . . ."

"The name's *Brim*, Mister. If anybody gives you trouble, refer him—or her—to me at the Base Commander's office. I'll take care of it personally."

"Aye *aye*, Admiral Brim."

"Good. Now stow that polish and go sign me out one of those gravcycles—a good one. On a permanent basis. . . ."

Cycles later, I was astride a powerful, deliciously balanced new RSB gravcycle, wind whistling past my helmet as I sped around the base making a quick private inspection.

Didn't like much of what I saw.

Some parts of the huge complex were immaculately kept—in certain cases, even better maintained than I remembered they were years ago. But these were maintained by the civilian Harbor Master's Office—except the Officer's Club, which appeared to be *very* crowded for this time of the morning. Warehouses, power networks, communications centers, buildings, supplies—all were clearly in order and to the book. Better than the book. They made the military portions look . . . *neglected* was an accurate term. Clearly, the Harbor Master had the situation well in hand. And she was just as clearly working without much help from her counterpart in uniform. Also, I knew who she was. Knew her *well*. . . .

The farther I went, the more my ire grew until—with still nearly a metacycle and a half before Summer's ceremony— neither I nor the base could wait any longer. Pulling up to the ostentatious new Fleet Headquarters Building (the original had been destroyed during the First Great War), I parked the gravcycle in an empty "RESERVED FOR COMMAND STAFF" slot near the door. All but two of the similarly marked slots were empty as I strode into the lobby, trying my damnedest to stay calm.

What a lobby! I quickly took in the rich, polished-wood floors, the expensive lighting fixtures, the lavish furnishings, the theaterlike entrance to the briefing auditorium—all a far cry from the squalid, unkempt operational zones I'd known during most of my career. True, it was important to keep up appearances at the Atalanta Fleet Base. Important people from all over the known Universe passed through this lobby. But this extravagantly furnished room would have served well in most houses of state—even embassies.

The whole thing appeared empty, except for a lone Chief Petty Officer sitting engrossed in a HoloNews magazine behind an information counter. He didn't even look up as I came through the door.

Took a moment to get my bearings, then strode to a wall directory and selected COMMANDER'S SUITE from the menu. The display changed to a three-dimensional holographic corridor map of the first floor with a path to the suite flowing in radiant green. Nice toy. I looked around, found the corridor, then started across the polished floor.

"You're on course for the Commander's suite, sir," the Petty Officer observed without looking up. "Need some help?"

I continued past without stopping. "Next time, Chief," I said.

Two glass doors at the far end of the corridor; the great seal of the Imperial Fleet etched on the left door; "Commander, 71st Group, Imperial Fleet," in old-fashioned ciphers on the right. Keeping a close rein on my temper, I set course.

"Hey, wait, sir!" someone called after me. "The Commander's Office is off-limits this morning. Admiral Summers's orders."

"Not anymore," I said, continuing on without turning. Presently, there were footfalls behind me. "Just a cycle, sir," the Petty Officer called. "You can't go in there. It's off-limits!"

I turned so he could see the two stars on my garrison cap. "I've placed it back *on* limits, Mister," I said.

The Petty Officer stopped in his tracks. "Er, w-who are you . . . A-Admiral?"

"Brim—Admiral Brim to you, Mister," I said. "I'm the new 71st Commander. And why didn't you ask that when I came in?"

"I . . . ah . . ." the Petty Officer stammered.

"Here's my ID," I said, handing over my card. "Check this at your lobby station, then return it to me in the Commander's office."

"Y-yes, Admiral."

"And Chief. . . ."

"Admiral?"

"You are now a Petty Officer, First Class. I'll expect that rocker to be off your rating badge as soon as you've returned my ID. Understood?"

"Er . . . y-yes, Admiral. . . ."

I continued along the corridor, then pushed open the right-hand glass door and strode into a second lobby, more lavish—if that were possible—than the first. Everything here laden with overstuffed pillows—all elegantly color-coordinated, in the most feminine of pastels. I'd learned a little about decoring years ago at this same base from one of the most stunning women I've ever encountered—but she kept it all at home, where things were *supposed* to be soft and color-coordinated. I ground my teeth, gazing from couch to couch. Voot's beard! Military people were supposed to kill people and break things, not lounge around on thraggling pastel pillows.

"May I be of service?" a low-pitched, deferential voice demanded.

Startled, I whirled around to confront a tall, gaunt civilian,

elegantly dressed in an old-fashioned formal business suit.
He was sitting behind a graceful antique rosewood desk, so
placed to make entry impossible without crossing its enfilad-
ing field, much like a well-sited blaster nest. When his eyes
fell on my two stars, he rose on long legs and held himself to
what might be regarded as a civilian's version of attention.
He had a long, aristocratic nose and large, puffy brown eyes
that peered out from age-creased sockets above gaunt cheeks
and hirsute brows. Funeral director. Wondered if he'd ever
smiled—decided not often.

"May I be of service, Admiral Brim?" he repeated.

"Didn't catch the name," I said, offering my hand.

"Hathaway Cottshall, the Commander's private secretary,
Admiral," he said, taking my hand in a tentative grip.

"You mean *Summers's* private secretary," I corrected,
venting some of the anger that had been building within
me—and instantly regretting it.

"Er . . . yes," Cottshall replied, his eyes acknowledging
my meaning.

"Good," I said. "You can keep the job temporarily. We'll
see what we can work out on a long-range basis later." I nodded toward the room's only other door. "The Commander's
suite?"

"It is, Admiral."

"Where's Summers?"

"At the Officer's Club, Admiral," Cottshall replied. "A
farewell breakfast with a few of his staff."

"Get him here," I ordered, as the ex-Chief returned my ID
card.

"Admiral?"

"I want that worthless son of a capcloth here within fifteen
cycles—before I see anybody else. Understand?"

"B-but, I c-can't summon Admiral . . ."

"Tell him it's an emergency. You won't be lying, trust me."

"Y-yes, Admiral."

"I suppose the Executive Officer's at the Club, too?"

"Er, no Admiral. He wasn't invited."

Interesting. "Why not?" I asked.

"I have no idea, Admiral?"

I'll bet, I thought. "Where's his office?"

"Captain Williams's office is on the next floor up."

"After you've got Summers on his way, tell Williams I want *him* in here with me—in the Commander's office—exactly one cycle after Summers exits—whenever that might be. Understand?"

"Er, yes, Admiral."

Oh yeah," I added, "and cancel any special base functions that might have been scheduled for this transfer of command—reviews, assemblies, and the like. I'll take care of them later, myself."

"Yes, Admiral. No assemblies."

"Get busy, then," I said, striding through the doors into Summers's office. It was so lavishly overfurished, I nearly gagged. *More* soft, overstuffed, understated furniture. I closed my eyes a moment. This was a place one might sleep in—better yet, make love in. But in *no* way was it a place from which to run a military operation. Turning on my heel, I stormed back into the lobby, just as Cottshall was breaking a HoloPhone connection. "Was that Summers?" I demanded.

"Captain Williams, Admiral. He's standing by."

"Very well. Is Summers on his way?"

"The Admiral assured me he is, Admiral."

"Good. Then I suggest you go get yourself a cup of cvceese' while he and I meet. Just don't be gone too long. I doubt if I'll need much time with Summers at all. Understand?"

"I understand, Admiral."

"Finally," I added, "before you go, bring up the month's Day Books on your display."

"T-the Day Books, Admiral?"

"The Day Books," I repeated. "Get 'em, then take your break."

"Immediately, Admiral," he said, bringing to his primary display the rows of daily transactions that made up the base's Day Book. Then he silently exited the office like a tall, gray wraith.

I sat at the ornate desk to concentrate on Ops, Engineering, and Space entries . . . while I waited.

Nearly thirty cycles later, a heavyset Rear Admiral dressed in a white-and-gold formal uniform burst angrily through the doors, on course for the inner office. "What's the meaning of this, Cottshall?" he demanded over his shoulder.

"Cottshall isn't here," I said, looking up from the console. Instantly, I knew it would take every measure of restraint I could bring to bear just speaking with the man.

"And who in vargt are you?"

"Brim's the name."

Summers stopped in his tracks and turned while his eyes fastened on my garrison cap. I remembered those mean eyes from the Helmsman's Academy. He was a senior during that awful first year of mine—and quite active in the less-than-furtive activies to make me quit.

Prior to the First Great War, the Fleet had been mostly a preserve for scions of the Empire's wealthy families—like Summers, heir to the giant Summers & Vincent, Ltd., Asteroid Mining Engineers. However, the tremendous slaughter had forced Training Command to open admissions to competition—*after*, of course, all political admissions had been satisfied.

I'd managed to break into the first so-called open class—a dirt-poor Carescrian, and they'd hated me for it. Probably a major reason that I'd endured was just to prove to *them* that I could. . . .

"Well, well," he said with cynical little smile. "Brim the guttersnipe Carescrian. And now *Admiral* Brim, of all things. How remarkable."

"Better be *Admiral* Brim," I answered, frowning in spite of myself. "Otherwise, there are *two* people pretending to be Admirals in this room right now."

"Why aren't you dressed as I ordered?" Summers demanded, then my words seemed to register ". . . And just what did you mean by *that*?"

"What I *do* mean by that," I said, ignoring his remark about my uniform, "is that critical sections of this base look like hammered shit and don't function at all. If you're in charge—as I am led to believe—then you're only pretending to be an officer. *Or* a commander."

Summers's eyes opened wide, showing a combination of anger and surprise. He started to speak, but I cut him off.

"Where was the Combat Space Patrol last night when my ferry squadron arrived?"

"What?"

"Where was the thraggling CSP last night when my ferry squadron arrived?" I repeated, my ire increasing by the moment.

"I don't have to answer *any* of your questions, Brim," Summers stated indignantly.

"Is that right?" I asked, vaulting from behind the desk and striding rapidly across the floor until less than an iral separated our noses. "One more time, Summers. Where was the CSP last night when my ferry squadron arrived?"

Though he was a large man, my sudden proximity seemed to deprive Summers of his aggression; years ago at the Academy, he'd been quite intimidating, especially to an habitually beggared underclassman. But his size was now gone to a fleshiness that transformed his bullying to little more than bluster. He hesitated for a split click, then got a look of defensiveness. "All ships were moored in the cavern, where they *should* have been," he declared.

"*Should have been*?" I demanded in surprise. "During a thraggling attack?"

"The GradyGroat orbital forts are quite sufficient protection from attack," he explained as if he were lecturing a first-year cadet.

"Sufficient? What in xaxt's *your* definition of 'sufficient'?"

"The forts accounted for six of the fifteen attackers last night—and our own ground batteries shot down two more."

"I lost two ships and their crews to the remaining seven. That probably wouldn't have happened had even a few of our ships been out there," I growled.

"Nonsense," Summers exclaimed indignantly. "The losses might even have been significantly higher, had there been dogfights. Besides, I had the city to consider, as well."

"You weren't doing much to protect the city that *I* could see."

"Shows how low the Fleet sank when it allowed trash commoners into the officer corps," Summers sniffed. "People like you *never* seem to understand the ways of peace—only war." He glowered and shook a finger at me—but came no closer. "Were I to project us as a more powerful, belligerent force here at the base, those Toronders might just begin to attack the city itself.

"So, you simply let those zukeeds open fire on Imperial ships?"

"Of course I did," Summers said defensively. "I didn't want to stir them up any more than I had to. They've been increasing their attacks for weeks now. Why should the Atalantans suffer for a war that we have already lost?" he demanded loftily. "What little remains of our—Onrad's—failing Empire stumbles along friendless in the Home Galaxy. Only the Great Federation of Sodeskayan States are disposed to help us these days, but the Sodeskayans themselves are under attack. How can we possibly hope to counter Nergol Triannic's League of Dark Stars?"

"Mother of Voot," I growled in mock surprise. "So you've noticed there's a war's on, then, have you?"

"Of course I've noticed, Brim. And I've handled things realistically—delicately, too. What can this base possibly do against a whole star domain like The Torond? They're not that far away, you know."

"I've consulted a few HoloMaps," I growled.

"Then, what did you expect me to do? Provoke a major attack on the base—and the city?"

"I expected you to be Fleet commander, Summers. I expected you to protect my ships. If you kept in touch with your Intelligence Bulletins, you'd have seen that the war's hotting up on this side of the galaxy, no matter how much you try to cool it down. Nergol Triannic wants *all* of Fluvanna in the hands of his toady Rogan LaKarn—not just that part the bastard's managed to take so far. He wants to, *needs* to, cut off our last supply of Drive crystal seeds. And he'll have to put this base out of action to do it—*city or no city*. That's why I'm going to need every killer ship I can get my hands on. And soon. That's why I needed you to protect my ships last night!"

"Well, I *did* protect them, so far as I can see," he said with the same arrogant laugh I'd *so* hated years ago. "In fact, your little convoy had quite substantial support, despite any misguided sentiments of dissatisfaction you may have experienced. Besides," he added haughtily, "what did *those* two particular ships mean to you? *Your* Starfury arrived in perfect safety, didn't it?"

Those words were the last straw. In spite of his size, I grabbed him by his lapels and shook him the way a terrier shakes a rat. "Summers, you cowardly murderer," I growled, "I want you—and anything that might remind me of you—out of this office in the next metacycle. Do you understand?"

"How dare you touch my uniform like that?" Summers demanded.

"How dare you *wear* that uniform, traitor?" I growled, pushing him backward into his private suite. "Now, clear everything of yours from this office. You've got something less than a metacycle, at the moment."

"You're mad," Summers said, diving for his HoloPhone.

"Not mad—*angry*," I said, pulling the suddenly wide-eyed man back to the center of the room. "Now get busy."

"And if I don't?" Summers asked, summoning up a few remaining shreds of affront.

I calmly drew the big Wenning from its holster, "If you don't," I said, "I'm going to personally kill you for the cowardly murder of the men in my ferry squadron."

"Y-you wouldn't!" Summers shrieked, diving for the HoloPhone once more.

Before he could touch it, I fired the blaster four times in quick succession, melting the HoloPhone itself and a corner of the desk. Then—for effect—I transformed a trio of ornate chairs that faced the man's desk to charred matchsticks.

In the swirling smoke, Summers shrank into a corner of

the room as if he were facing a madman—which by this time, I suppose I was. "D-don't kill me, Brim," he whispered.

I considered for a moment, then holstered the blaster. "You've got what remains of your original metacycle to clear out of here," I said. "Every trace. I don't want anything left to remind me of you—and how low an officer can crawl." Then I strode into the hall, grinding my teeth in anger and looking for the cvceese' shop.

I sat down at one of the tables with a mug of cvceese' but didn't drink it because my nerves were already in an uproar, and what I wanted to do was calm down. Especially if Summers decided to tough things out and was still in his office when I returned. I suspected that I probably would kill him as I'd threatened. And although I wanted him to *think* I would, actually doing so would cause all sorts of problems at a time when I really wanted only to get on with the job of revitalizing the base. Not only didn't I have much time to do that—a lot less time than they'd thought in Avalon when they'd briefed me—but I was presently working alone, with no idea of how deeply the CIGA rot had gone here nor to whom I could turn for help.

A lot hinged on this man Williams, who was my Executive Officer. If, as I hoped, he and Summers had been at loggerheads, then—given the native ability he'd need to qualify for the job in the first place—I might rely on him for much of the operational work. Actually, if he were any good at all, I'd *have* to rely on him. Executive Officers are people who *carry out* the Commander's objectives through various division heads: Operations, Space Flight, Medicine, all the rest. If I went around him—for any reason at all—I'd seriously undermine his ability to get things done. And at the same time

I'd tie myself in knots trying to do his work while I neglected my own.

Watching the timepiece on the wall, I waited while two eons and an epoch passed in slow motion. Then it was time to go upstairs and face whatever the near future held in store.

To my utter delight, the zukeed Summers was nowhere to be seen and Cottshall was back at his desk with a small, muscular Fleet officer standing beside him. The latter was dressed in the traditional, workaday duty uniform: dark blue, double-breasted "money jacket," or reefer, matching trousers, white shirt, black necktie, and black space boots. Four gold rings on each cuff denoted his rank. Didn't tell me anything about him. "Captain Jim Williams, Executive Officer, reporting as ordered, Admiral," he said, coming to attention.

"At ease, Captain," I said, staring into his eyes for some indication of who—what—he was. "Appreciate your coming at such short notice."

Williams returned a humorless gaze from above round cheeks and a pug nose that was so offset from the center of his face that it must have been broken a hundred times over. He was a clearly a tough son of a capcloth, but the wrinkle lines around his eyes indicated a man whose customary aspect was a smile. It didn't take a Drive scientist to tell that the smile hadn't been exercised very much lately. "Wasn't much else to keep me in my office, Admiral," he replied. "I've been mostly out of the loop since I got here, as Cottshall may have told you."

"Cottshall hasn't had a chance to say much about anything, Captain," I replied, "nor has he offered to. So let's you and me break in my new office while you catch me up with things."

"You may not like what you'll hear," Williams warned as we strode toward the inner office. Then he hesitated and frowned. "Er, Admiral," he observed, "is that *smoke* I smell?"

"Yeah," I said—casually as possible—as I ushered him through the door. "Nothing to worry about. Summers and I didn't much see eye-to-eye."

"Er, I see," he said, following me through the door. The office looked as if a Sodeskayan land battle had recently been fought there. In addition to the three carbonized chairs and burned carpeting beneath them, the desk—with its blackened corner and melted HoloPhone—had been thoroughly rifled. Scraps of documents littered the floor everywhere, and most of the pictures were gone, leaving clean rectangles on the soot-blackened walls.

"Mother of Voot," Williams commented under his breath, "I, ah, guess you and Summers *didn't* see eye-to-eye, did you?"

I righted two chairs and set them facing one another. "Sit down, Number One," I said. "I've got a strong feeling that you aren't any happier than I about the condition of this base."

"You've got *that* right, Admiral," he replied quietly, never taking his from mine—a man who had come through some *difficult* times. "But I take full responsibility for everything you see here, because no matter how hard I tried, I wasn't able to countermand Summers's orders, not even behind his back."

"I believe you," I said. "I'm going to ask a lot of hard questions—and I don't want you to pull any punches, 'cause I'm going to verify in person everything you tell me. After that, all I'm interested in hearing is how we're going to put things to rights in a minimum time frame—and what I can do to help."

Williams watched me carefully, then closed his eyes for a moment. "I think," he said with a faint smile, "that I've finally been let out of the base sewer. All right, Admiral, here goes. I've been waiting a long time for this. . . ."

Williams and I spent the remainder of the day in conference. Cottshall brought sandwiches for us about midday, then catered a heartier meal himself on the wreckage of Summers's desk late in the evening. By the end of Twilight Watch, it was reasonably clear to me that Williams could stay as my Executive Officer as long as he wished. Not once had the man attempted to besmirch the reputation of his subordinates at division level; instead, I learned about hundreds of attempts, at all levels of rank, to circumvent Summers and his underlings—attempts that invariably resulted in punishments and even incarceration. Additionally, my questions corroborated a number of my earliest suspicions, especially about the Ops, Engineering, and Space Divisions, each dominated at their highest levels by close friends and onetime schoolmates of Rear Admiral W. Groton Summers, I.F. All of them, of course, had been deeply involved with the Congress for Intra-Galactic Accord. Ultimately, CIGA power had been on the wane since the Battle of Avalon, and most who still believed in the cause were now underground. But CIGA spirit still riddled portions of the Imperial military and—like Summers—posed a definite threat to the war effort through either native incompetence or outright sedition.

Ultimately—well into the Dawn Watch—I looked at my tired Executive Officer and felt I understood him: where he'd been, where he wanted to go. I nodded. "So that's your strategy, eh?"

"It is, Admiral," he said.

"Pretty complete," I remarked, dividing the last of the cold cvceese' between our badly stained mugs. "You must have been working on it for a long time."

"Since the day Summers put me in the brig for a week, Admiral," Williams said. "I figured nothing this bad could last forever—and when it was over, I'd be ready, just in case anybody was interested in hearing what I had to say about things afterward."

I nodded. "Did I sound interested enough?" I asked.

"Enough for me, Admiral," he replied. "Just say the word, and I'll put it all into action—immediately."

"Going to surprise a lot of people," I commented. "You're sure those replacements you picked can handle their new jobs?"

"You saw their files too, Admiral," Williams said. "Was there anything you didn't like."

I shut up. "No," I said, "There wasn't."

"Good," said Williams. "I spent a lot of time studyin' those folders, Admiral." He thumped a personal display Cottshall had brought in earlier. "I'm betting whatever career I have left on these people," he said. "And I'm nowhere near to being ready for retirement."

Nodded. "What will you do about the people you plan to get rid of?"

"They're powerful, those zukeeds," he said. "Best way to handle 'em is to offer a one-way trip home—if they go quietly. Otherwise, it's the brig for the duration."

Sounded good to me. "And the rest," I asked, "—the ones who will have to mend their ways starting with Dawn Watch. How do you plan to handle them?"

"Firmly, Admiral," Williams said. "Every one of us here at the base is ripe for a courts-martial because we couldn't—

or didn't—do anything about Summers. And none of us was so stupid that he couldn't see what was going on. We're all responsible for the pickle we're in, and we're going to have to work our butts off to put things right. Either people are with us, or they're not part of the Fleet. It's as simple as giving and taking direct orders. Most of them are professionals—and just as unsatisfied about the place as you or I. When they know what sort of a job's expected of them, they'll do it. Voot's beard, Admiral, they'll *exceed* it. You know Blue Capes."

That was why William's plan sounded so promising. In the end, it was based on people and the professionalism that was the very basis of the Imperial Fleet. "Captain," I said, "you've a lot of dirt to move before the next Dawn Watch. Is there anything else you need from me."

Williams grinned. "Only orders to get started, Admiral."

"You've got 'em, Captain."

"Then, Admiral, with your kind permission, I'll get back to m' office. I mean to start movin' that dirt immediately— middle of the night's best for some jobs. With a little luck, you'll see a few early improvements on your way to work in the morning."

"I'll look for 'em," I said, ushering the man into the lobby . . . where Cottshall was sleeping, head on his arms, at his desk. "And it appears as if we're not the only ones putting in a late night," I added.

"Old Hathaway's all right, Admiral," Williams replied, looking directly into my eyes. "Neither of us will ever know what he had to put up with working for Summers. The Admiral could be pretty hard on people when he had 'em in his power."

"I never thought of that," I said with a wince.

"Cottshall would never admit it," he said. "In his own

civilian way, he's a tough son of a capcloth, too. And if anybody knows the ins and outs of this base—in all their subtleties—it's him."

"Glad you told me that," I said, quietly kicking myself.

"Figured you'd want to know," he replied. Then donning his peaked cap with its single row of gold oak leaves, he nodded. "I'll be available for anything—whenever you need it, Admiral." With that, he turned and strode quietly past Cottshall's desk into the hall.

I returned to my inner office for nearly half a metacycle, again using a portable HoloPhone to check in with the three quad leaders—they were ready, just in case. Then I walked quietly to Cottshall's desk and touched him gently on the elbow.

"S-sorry, Admiral," he said, raising himself groggily. "I must have dozed off."

"Nothing to be sorry about that I can see," I said. "I'm mighty glad you stuck around. You didn't have to."

Cottshall straightened his old-fashioned tie and shrugged. "No, Admiral, you're wrong there. I *did* have to: I just happened to make the call myself."

Time for another quick decision—maybe too late for this one. "Mr. Cottshall," I asked, "is it possible that you'd overlook my statement about your being Admiral Summers's private secretary?"

Cottshall smiled. "I should be most happy to do that, Admiral Brim."

"Thank you," I said. "If you'll stay on, then, I'll attempt to minimize that kind of mistake—especially when I'm irritated, as I was this afternoon."

"I shall be quite proud to stay on, Admiral," Cottshall replied.

"Thanks twice, then," I said. "And call me Wilf."

Cottshall's eyes lighted. "Thank you, er, Wilf," he said, grasping my hand in a warm, firm grip. "I shall do everything I can to make that decision worth your while."

"You're already off to a good start," I replied. "Now let's wind things up around here for tonight. Before you leave, detail somebody to clean up the mess in my so-called office. Then I'll want to speak to all the base officers—no excuses. Make it Brightness three, on the dot in the main auditorium—coordinate it with Williams. After that, we'll see what happens next. Right?"

"Excellent, Admiral, er, Wilf," he said. "It promises to be another busy day indeed. I shall look forward to every cycle. . . ."

"So will I," I said, but I wasn't certain I hadn't just told a lie. . . .

Chapter 2

◆

When You're Outnumbered . . .

16–31 Heptad, 52014

Imperial Fleet Base, Atalanta, Hador-Haelic

Managed less than a metacycle of sleep that night—I was roused from my bunk just after Dawn Watch by alarms and sirens . . . and the deadened, ground-shaking *thump-a thump-a* of rapid-fire disruptors. Struggling into my battlesuit, I raced into the hall and fought my way to the front door against a half-panicked throng heading for assault shelters in the opposite direction. As I leapfrogged onto my gravcycle—wet with Atalanta's xaxtdamned COLD dew!—the attackers still appeared to be battling their way past the orbital forts. I rode off at top speed for the hangar elevator.

In the cavern, I gunned the gravcycle from the lift through

barely open doors and howled along a littered concourse, headed for the pier where our four, more-or-less-battleworthy Starfuries were moored; they hadn't been touched since we'd landed. As I'd arranged earlier with the other quad commanders, the ships were manned, the 'Gravs were running, and the mooring beams were already singled up.

"Button her up!" I yelled at a rating as I dived into the lead Starfury, kicked away the brow, and pulled the hatch shut after me.

"We're going to take 'em on, Admiral?" a grinning Gunners Mate called after me as I took the bridge companionway two rungs at a time.

"You better believe it," I shouted over my shoulder.

"Everyone's at battle stations, Admiral, and ready for liftoff," Talbert reported from the gunnery console. At the helm, three globular displays had already materialized over my COMM console as I strapped on a LifeGlobe pack and climbed into the Helmsman's seat. "Red Two checking in, Admiral," Harris reported.

"Red Three's ready, Admiral," Kimple said.

"Red Four, Admiral." Bell never used more words than he absolutely *had* to.

I strapped myself in and ran a quick console drill—it was all I had time for. Most of the indicators were green, and Voot knew I'd rarely had the pleasure of flying a perfectly operational Starfury during these early war years. "All right," I radioed to the other three Helmsmen. "Red One's ready, too. Let's roll!" I switched to the internal blower. "Fore and aft mooring cupolas—cast off all mooring beams, *now*!"

Instantly, four green tractor beams that secured the Starfury to optical bollards on the wharf winked out, and I used differential power on the 'Gravs to ease carefully around the end of the pier and into the portside canal—followed closely by the other three killer ships—all running dark. I could feel myself tense as adrenaline began to flow, my pulse rate elevated; it was always like that before a combat lift-off.

"Stand by for local gravity," I warned over the blower, then—as always—nearly threw up when I hit the switch. Forcing my sour, half-digested stomach contents back where they belonged, I focused on the next task at hand—ahead, the massive blast doors were still closed. I'd expected it; Williams couldn't change things *that* fast.

Keyed the COMM unit to a Harbor Control band I remembered from the night before, then bellowed at a startled Commander who appeared in a display. "Open the harbor door, Commander!" I ordered, calmly as possible. "We're under attack!"

"My orders say those doors remain closed during attacks," the Commander said firmly.

"Orders from whom?"

"Captain Harper, Operations."

"The name Brim mean anything to you?" I asked, forcing myself to relax—at least outwardly. Everything was poised for combat; focused; all the hormones were in place—and I wanted to kill *him*!

"*Admiral* Brim?" he asked. "The new base Commandant?"

"That's right, Commander," I said. "As of now, Summers's operational directives are countermanded—and you, Mister, will open those doors immediately."

"Sorry, Admiral. I'll need *written* orders to countermand an operational directive."

I nodded—I'd see this bastard's testicles hanging over the base gate like mistletoe if Williams didn't get rid of him first. "Your decision, Commander," I growled. "I'll be forced to blast 'em out of the way on takeoff. You certain you want me to do that?"

"How d-do I know you're Admiral Brim?"

"You don't," I said, spying a small blockhouse to the right of the massive doors; a light shone from its single window. "But . . . is that *your* station down there to the right of the doors?"

"It is," he said. "And coming here will do you no good. I simply won't let you in!"

"Very well," I replied, keeping my galloping temper just under control—this misbegotten, effete zukeed was more child than professional StarSailor. "However," I added, "you may just want to leave that blockhouse on your own. I doubt if you'll want to be quite so close to the target area when we fire our 406s at the doors."

"Your 406s?" he gasped. "You're planning to . . ?"

"Fire them," I said gently. "At the doors. As I'm certain you know, 406s are meant for outer space use, and the concussion lobes they generate are pretty violent close in like this." I turned on the landing lights as if better illuminating the target.

The Commander's face abruptly took on a strange look. "Holy mother of Voot!" he gasped in a suddenly high-pitched voice. "You wouldn't . . . would you?"

"You've got three clicks to clear the area," I growled, advancing the thrust dampers. "Either open those doors yourself—or don't—it's up to you. One way or another, we're taking off!" I activated the blower again—without turning off the COMM. "Gunnery Officer," I called to Talbert.

"Aye, Admiral Brim."

"Talbert, you'll take out those doors at my command," I

growled. Then I pushed the thrust dampers to takeoff power and the Starfury bellowed forward along the canal. . . .

I peered down through a completely cloudless sky at Atalanta, her magnificent harbor, and the ten circular canals that ringed City Mount Hill already c'lenyts below—an extraordinary picture in washed-out light and shadow from two of Haelic's brightest natural satellites, Moncrief and Laicour. Glanced at an altimeter: 280,000 irals and climbing. Even diminished by ferry rig, Starfuries were astonishing interceptors.

"Tallyho!" Kimple's voice came over the helmet speakers. "Multiple ships approaching on bearing Blue Apex."

"Got you," I replied, then turned to Talbert. "Rob," I said, "you are cleared to fire at will." From his console behind me, Talbert controlled a single disruptor in the belly turret and two in the ventral turret. Between the two of us, we still could use only half the Starfury's normal complement of twelve 406-mmi disruptors; it would have to do. But this time, I had a strong feeling we would need to use them.

"Acknowledge clearance, Admiral," Talbert replied a little stiffly. I'd heard it was his first time in combat and hoped he'd get over his shakes quickly. Shorthanded as we were, everyone had to pull like a veteran.

Switched power to my gunsight and initiated self-test routines on the three forward-firing disruptors I controlled from the helm. Each ran to TEST SUCCESSFUL.

"Look out, Red ships," I sent, keeping an eye on the approaching enemy. "Prepare to break port." I went into a slightly left-handed turn and looked through the upper Hyperscreens. A mass of perhaps twenty ships was emerging from the GradyGroat barrage into Hador's light some 30,000 irals above my little pickup squadron. I couldn't identify particular types yet, but I assumed Dampier DA-79 IIs or the newer Oiggaip 912s. Definitely Toronders—their formations were wobbling all over the sky. From instinct, I tightened the restraint beams for my seat, hunched down, and shifted the steering controls to EXTRA FINE. We were badly outnumbered, but I personally felt ready for them—at the very top of my form. When the GradyGroat barrage faded to nothing, excitement keyed my muscles to even a higher pitch than before—tonight's battle would be fought close to the surface at HypoLight speeds. It was the ultimate test of a combat Helmsman. Above Hyperspeed, a great deal more depended on the ship and its computing powers. Below, it was pretty much crew-to-crew combat. I grinned as latent nervousness evaporated into a flat, unemotional calm. I was ready. Out to port, Mat Harris had tucked his Starfury in close to my left pontoon. High and trailing to starboard, Kimple led Bell in the same manner.

I began to climb in a wide, easy spiral. Now! The first group of some ten Toronders was fanning out and diving toward us. "Break port," I ordered, "climbing!" I eased the thrust dampers fully forward, and the Starfury responded like the thoroughbred she was—with a hefty kick in the seat back.

The first attackers were Oiggaips, perhaps the best attack ships The Torond built—*nearly* good enough to be Leaguer ships, but not quite. My Starfury was climbing almost vertically, hoist on her own petard, as it were, when I intercepted the first group in the act of diving on Atalanta in line—evidently still unaware of our fast-approaching opposition.

Didn't the idiots have proximity indicators—or did they even bother to look at them? Reminded myself they were still dangerous—and *we* were badly outgunned.

When the first Oiggaips came into range, I managed to get

in a burst on the leader, whose fuselage lighted up with hits. Surprise! As we hurtled past, Talbert further raked him with a turret shot, blowing off a number of panels and sending a thin tongue of radiation fire into his wake.

Two more Oiggaips—*finally* alert—did a tight turn, bringing them head-on to me, their 326-mmi Breda-SAFATs making rapid-fire bursts that formed long, glittering tentacles snaking toward me and curling down just under my pontoons. From that point on, the sky was a whirling confusion of ships—mostly with Toronder insignia—black triangles edged with yellow—on their sides.

At least there was no dearth of targets! So many, in fact, I relied on sensing them rather than actually seeing the presence of individual ships circling 'round—until suddenly my eyes would fix on one of them.

Like now.

This time, a Dampier, circling and wiggling while its Helmsman anxiously looked for a target. I felt myself grin; as I'd planned, surprise was clearly augmenting the apparent size of our tiny squadron and nervousness was already taking its toll of the Toronders. I framed the Dampier in my forward sights, but Talbert fired obliquely at another Oiggaips at the same time.

Even a jumpy Toronder couldn't fail to notice *that*—and didn't. He fell off into a tight turn, then began a vertical climb straight out toward space. But in his haste, he'd clearly neglected all gravity management dicta, allowing his power chambers no time to build up to such a maneuver, and suddenly the big ship spun along its pitch axis, completely out of control while momentum bled off as if it were spilling from a bucket. This time, Talbert was watching; we fired at the same time, raking the enemy ship from stem to Drive with direct hits from all six disruptors. Abruptly, the

Dampier's clear image shook, then began to crumble. Its bridge Hyperscreens burst into fragments. Moments later, the Drive section and power chambers disappeared in a roiling, flickering puffball—blindingly white in the center, dirty red toward the outside—filled with speeding, white-hot shrapnel. I had to put the helm hard over to get out of the way. and as he flicked past, I had a last vision of the Dampier trailing a long ribbon of radiation fire and diving like a comet toward the dark ocean below. No bobbing LifeGlobes floated down in its fiery wake.

The whole thing had lasted no more than a couple of clicks—with lots more Toronders to go! To the right, a Starfury broke off and dived toward another Oiggaip. Quickly foiling several determined attacks, I went into a tight spiral dive to cover him. The Starfury fired: six throbbing, gleaming streams of disruptor energy—at the same time a shadow formed over my Hyperscreens. I glanced up—less than a hundred irals overhead, a Dampier's enormous, heat-streaked belly passed like a streak. He'd missed me, and was now getting ready to fire on a secondary target.

Instinctively, I retarded the thrust dampers, pulled gently on the steering engine to align the Dampier in my sights, then opened fire with my three disruptors at point-blank range, obtaining direct hits just ahead of the power chambers. The Dampier staggered, skidded violently to the left while the fuselage broke cleanly in half with a shower of sparks, then whizzed past in a hail of fragments.

I'd scarcely recovered from *this* surprise when six Dampiers appeared on my tail in perfect close echelon, each surrounded by a halo of white-hot graviton exhaust. Coming for me at top speed. While Talbot blasted away aft with his three turret-mounted 406s, I found myself maneuvering more from instinct than anything else. With one movement, I

pushed the thrust damper all the way forward to FULL MIL-
ITARY, clicked it back into the RESTRICTED detent, then
rammed forward again to EMERGENCY power. I had been
forced to use this flight regime a number of times, yet the effect was still extraordinary—and it was immediate. My Starfury veritably leaped forward with a mighty roar from the
'Gravs that shook the very spaceframe and—in spite of the
gravity system's best efforts—plastered me against the back
of my recliner. Within clicks, I had doubled my speed and
left my pursuers behind as if they'd suddenly run into a brick
wall. Even so, it was *still* going to be close . . .

Clang! The ship jumped violently, then swung left as if it
had been sideswiped by a large meteor. I could hear a gar-
gling scream on the intercom, cut off abruptly by—*Wham!*—
a second hit.

Blinding explosions just in front of my helmet threw me
backward in my seat, breaking the restraint beams and nearly
bursting my eardrums during the millisecond before the control bridge lost all atmosphere. The gravity system pulsed,
and I let go everything, instinctively trying to cover my face
with my arms . . . but my left shoulder wouldn't move, at
least without a dazzling eruption of fiery pain, and I heard
my battlesuit seal off a whistling leak that made a glittering
red cloud of frozen blood crystals—*mine!*

Tried to reach the controls, but the pain blazed up again—
a fragment of hullmetal shrapnel had clearly lodged in my
shoulder; there was no strength in my left arm—only the
dripping sensation of blood draining inside my battlesuit and
puddling in the glove. Wondered how long it would be until
the bleeding started to affect me. Nothing I could do about it.
Jostled about, heart in my mouth, hanging upside down in
the wrecked gravity system, I ignored the pain and reached
for the controls again—my left arm weighed a milston!—but

I got them. Or what was left of them. One of the smashed instruments on the flight panel was hanging on the end of its wiring, and I could see blue sparks behind it while static crackled from my helmet earphones. Below, the 'Gravs were still running—some of them—but they were barely able to keep us aloft and didn't sound exactly right, either. Tried the controls—the Starfury responded, at least.

Panting, I somehow got us righted, then glanced aft . . . everyone all right and staring back as if they'd seen a ghost. Primary intercom was out of whack, damage most likely localized in my panel. Needed decisions fast—with no information. Bad time to hesitate with the Toronders shooting at anything that moves. A bright light overhead, then a shower of fragments glowing with radiation fire and heading for the surface. Only two or three insubstantial-looking Life-Globes floating down in their wake—a lot of people died in that one. A Starfury or a Dampier?

Fortuitously for us, the Toronders abruptly decided they'd had enough and began to fade into the starry sky. Time to make landfall while I could do so under my own power. Only Voot knew where the other three ships were. Cycles passed as I let down, scanning for a landmark, and periodically blacking out from loss of blood. At ten thousand irals, I had City Mount Hill on the horizon. Looked good . . . right up to the moment when what remained of the 'Gravs pulsed violently, and I noticed a shower of sparks blasting out into the wake from either side of our power chambers—followed by a long, thin tongue of radiation fire. The hullmetal collapsium was beginning to un-collapse again. *Bad* sign. I turned to engergize the N-ray generators there—a lot of them in that part of the ship because of the tremendous energy hazard. But before I could touch the switches, they turned yellow, flashing ENERGIZED. Karen Kelly, the Engineering Officer, had gotten to them first and was now on my secondary intercom.

"Radiation Fire! Radiation Fire in power chambers one and two! Damage team three to the site on the double!" Presently, the blaze died back for a moment or two, then reappeared. At least one of the power chambers was clearly ruptured! Too much risk. I needed to get everyone out immediately.

"Belay the damage team," I bellowed. "This is the captain—all hands abandon ship immediately! I repeat: all hands abandon ship immediately." I glanced at the pole indicator. "Nearest land bears directly Red, three hundred c'lentys." I looked back at the bridge crew—with my shoulder aflame. They were staring back in fright. "Out, xaxtdamnit!," I bellowed. "Everybody knows how to use a LifeGlobe. Somebody'll be by to pick you up within the metacycle."

Nobody moved.

"GO!"

They got up and ran for the aft companionway. Soon, there were fourteen LifeGlobes bobbing down toward the ocean in my wake.

Rang up Atalanta to summon a rescue flotilla; they gave me a true course to the base. Good . . . *if* I could make it. After ten anxious cycles, during which I swayed in and out of awareness and controllers from the base mothered my fast-settling Starfury like anxious hens, I finally made out a vector. Two green flares came snaking up almost immediately, clearing me all the way down with the base in emergency mode. Now I had a decision. Should I bail out and let the salvage people pick up the Starfury for scrap? Or should I try to ride her down. The latter case *could* result in a repairable Starfury, which was desperately needed. Unfortunately, it could *also* result in scrap regardless—but with *me* as part of the scrap. . . .

Bailing out appealed to my cringing inner self. But stronger than that was the old Helmsman's instinctive reluctance to sacrifice the machine—especially since I'd gone to all the trouble of bringing this one here in the first place.

Took inventory as I continued to descend—the power system was certainly almost gone—that's where the fire was. And the 'Gravs were only partially operational. But we *were* moving with nearly a thousand irals under us—and the steering engine was still in fine shape.

Passing over the base, I dithered only a moment when one of the controllers made up my mind for me.

"Those flames are getting worse, Admiral. You've got to do something *quick!*"

Yeah. On top of that, the 'Gravs were cutting out more and more frequently—and I couldn't do much about controlling anything because I had no working instruments.

"Fleet FA 337 landing now," I assured them. Probably my voice didn't sound very steady—thank Voot the video was gone; I'd have scared them to death! Willing myself conscious in spite of what my head wanted to do, I made a very gentle approach, curving around until I got the vector, then fixed the emergency seat restraints in MAXIMUM and set the Starfury down—at the same moment the 'Gravs cut out for good.

Lost control . . . terrific uproar! Towering geysers on either side . . . jerks, jolts . . . pandemonium. Certain the restraints would fail two or three times—once wished they *would!* After nearly a c'lenyt of skidding and bouncing, we stopped, bobbing in the gentle swell of the harbor and listing to the right, but safe—except for black, acrid smoke that was beginning to fill the bridge. I'd just switched off the restraints and climbed from my seat when the whole cabin seemed to turn upside down and I felt my helmet strike something hard—the deck.

My last conscious thoughts were about our hurried lift-off and the amazing way massive hangar doors that size could open—a major engineering accomplishment, when one thought about it. But at the time, I hadn't been afforded much opportunity to consider technical details; my Starfury had been already more than forty irals off the surface as we streaked through the hangar entrance—followed in close order by three more killer ships on a direct heading in harm's way. . . .

Kneeling astride me naked, head back, long dark brown hair flowing to the waist—most beautiful woman ever—can't quite believe she's with me like this. Wide-set eyes, closed now—squeezed shut. Long eyelashes, pug nose, dauntless chin. Beautiful. Beautiful. Beautiful. Hands on hips—sucking her lower lip as she thrusts faster and faster . . . almost there. Both of us. Great rounded breasts bobbing, jerking up and down in spastic rhythm. Mouth opening now. Cheeks glowing. Panting. Animal sound starting deep in her belly.

Throbbing. . . .

"I think he's coming out of it now." Male voice? Throbbing.

Fading. . . .

"Bit of a close thing. Lost a *lot* of blood." Another male voice—Williams? Throbbing.

Face fading. . . .

". . . tougher than any of you know. He'll make it." *Her* voice! Throbbing.

"No! Don't go! Finish!"

"What was that? He's trying to say something." First male voice. Throbbing.

"I'd better be on my way." *Her* voice again. Throbbing.

"For Voot's sake, don't go!" I yelled. "Not *now*!"

"Are you in pain, Admiral?" First male voice again. Throbbing.

"Where is she, xaxtdamnit?"

"Admiral?" Throbbing.

Gone. . . .

Throbbing. Throbbing. Very fuzzy overhead—man looking like a doctor peering at me, wiping my brow. Sterile white ceiling, blinding lights. Smells of antiseptic. Hospital!

Can't move anything. Throbbing beside me. Turn head slightly—burns! Move eyes. Healing machine, sure. Left shoulder engulfed in throbbing proto-tissues.

"Nearly finished. How do you feel, Admiral?"

"Just WON-der-ful, Doctor."

"That good, eh, sir?"

Terribly young and handsome, blond hair, blue yes, and the thin, narrow face and nose that fairly shouted *aristocrat*. Nervous, too. Wondered idly if he was one of Summers's cadre of CIGAs. "That good," I promised him. "What time is it?"

"A little after Brightness two, Admiral," he replied.

"Sixteenth Heptad?"

"All day long, Admiral."

Young smart-ass. But *there was still time*. "Thanks," I said. "You said this is almost finished?" Throbbing abruptly stopped. Felt the tissues withdraw.

"As of *right now*, Admiral."

"Good. Get me out of here. I've got to be in the Auditorium at Brightness plus three, Doctor—on the dot."

"You must be kidding me, sir."

"Let me assure you, Doctor: I am *not*."

"But you can't. You're in no shape to . . ."

"Open the thraggling machine, Doctor," I interrupted.

"Admiral, that's against regulations. I simply won't be responsible for . . ."

"*I'll* take responsiblility, Doctor," that other voice said from across the room—definitely Williams!

"B-but Captain."

"How bad is it going to hurt him?"

"Depends on how tough he is, sir."

"You heard what she said, just like I did," Williams growled.

She?

"Er, yessir, Captain."

Long, dark brown hair, I'd bet. Find out later. Got to pay attention *now*. . . .

"Then you know as much as I do, Commander. Now open the machine or show me how to open it. If the Admiral can physically make it, he's going."

"Y-you'll have to take responsibility for him, Captain Williams."

"I'll thraggling take it. Admiral—you're *really* all right with this?"

"Try me."

"Doctor, I order you to open the machine."

"Aye, Captain Williams."

Wasn't all *that* much pain, but felt as if I weighed a milston or more. Struggled to sit up. Couldn't. Weak as a Halacian Rothkitten. "Help me up," I said.

Hands at my right shoulder, back, pushing. Dizzy. Room whirling. Back down in the machine.

"What did I tell you?" the smart-ass doctor asked.

"Again," I said. Must have sounded like I meant it. This

time, I could stay up—with a little help from Williams. The room was cold. Bright. Cleaner than clean. Smelled of antiseptics. Hated hospitals.

"Anything hurt?"

"Just the shoulder, Doctor. Thirsty, though."

Got a drink. Gulped it down. "More."

Another drink; paused for breath. "Jim, how long do we have?" Noticed he was dressed in fatigues, garrison cap, and brogans—*he* got the message.

"About half a metacycle, sir."

"Admiral, you're not going to make it!" The doctor's voice had a tenor of reprisal to it.

"Gorksroar." Before he could do anything about it, I slipped my legs to the floor, but a table came up and hit me on the head. Soon, *everything* was on the floor.

Instantly, Williams had his hands under my arms and set me on the bed again. "No. Gotta stand!" Back on my feet, Williams holding on as if *he* needed *me* for support. Knees trembling. "Let go."

This time, one of the walls tumbled over, smacked me.

Back on my feet. Closer to the wall, now. "Let go."

When the wall came over to hit me, I was ready for it. Tried to push it back with my left arm. Mother of Boot! *Searing* pain in shoulder. No strength. Back on the floor.

"Again!"

Pushing the wall back with right arm now. Knees more steady. Gonna make it this time. Peer around room—a bloody pile of dead tissues in a kidney pan beside the healing machine. On top, a ragged fragment of hullmetal, bigger than my thumb, but not much. "That what got me?"

"Yessir."

Not very impressive.

"Want it, Admiral?"

"All yours, Doctor."

"How much time now, Jim?"

"About ten cycles, Admiral."

"Gotta get going. Where's my battlesuit?"

"It's gone, Admiral," the doctor said. "Shredded and full of blood."

"I brought your duffel bag, Admiral," Williams said. "Figured you might need some clean duds."

"Coveralls, Jim."

"Got 'em."

Gulped down a cup of warm protein mix while he brought my leather jacket, boots, and garrison cap, too. Good man. Helped me struggle into everything. Jacket *hurt*, but got it on—arm in a sling, only throbbing now. Boots. Cap. "How long, Jim?"

"Got about six cycles, Admiral."

"Let's go." Hung on to Williams; hobbled out to a skimmer—no limousine.

"Go!" he ordered.

"Aye, Captain!"

Grinned: driver was Russo. Why was I not surprised?

One cycle to go. Getting a little lift from the cup of protein. Thinking how lucky I'd been that the Base Rescue Service had been out and ready for me. The little cooling unit of my battlesuit had saved me from the radiation fire gnawing away at the Starfury right below the helm, but it was almost exhausted when they got me off the ship and raced me to the Base Hospital. Another few cycles and *pfft*—good-bye buttocks. . . .

Russo drove right up the walk and through the doors into the lobby. "Give 'em heck, Admiral!" he whispered, as Williams helped me from the backseat.

"Do my best, Chief," I assured him shakily.

Moving slowly across lobby toward the center doors. Wall tried to hit me again. Williams grabbed right arm. Steadied. Started again. Head up. Look normal . . . no, look *stern*. Laughed to myself. Be lucky to look *alive*.

A tall, blond captain I hadn't met saluted and stepped into the auditorium in front of us. "The Commander," she shouted.

Sounds of shuffling feet, then silence. Leaned on Williams all the way down the aisle. Felt his hands tighten on the way up the two stairs to the stage. Got me to the podium. I grabbed and hung on tight as I started to black out again.

"Want me here?" Williams whispered.

Took a deep breath. "Don't go too far away," I mumbled from the side of my mouth. Felt his hands release my arm.

"Give 'em hell, Admiral," he whispered, then stepped back.

I switched on the microphone. "Seats," I said, feeling a bit stronger as the protein began kicking in. I paused to let the room quiet down—more energy coming on by the moment. Head clearing. Ready. . . .   "The name's Brim," I began, "—Rear Admiral Brim. I'm the new Commander here, and for those of you who haven't heard, this base is under *entirely* new management."

Undercurrent of hushed voices swept the room.

"I don't much like speeches or assemblies," I continued presently, "—especially ceremonies like this. They take time away from the job we have to do—which, in case anyone doesn't quite have the picture yet, is waging *war*."

More hushed undercurrent—longer. I paused again to let my words sink in. Some of those people out there wouldn't agree. It was *they* who would have to be rooted out and sent home during the next couple of weeks.

"That means from this moment on, we have three basic

tasks here at Atalanta," I continued, counting them off on my fingers, "—breaking things, killing people, and spending as much time as possible in harm's way. From this very moment, *all* base activity, at *all* levels, will center on promoting and supporting these tasks—in the most pragmatic, efficient manner possible, regardless of the consequences. I've got a rule I've always lived with—it'll be the basis for everything we do. And it's so simple, none of you should *ever* have trouble comprehending. Simply, put: when you're outnumbered, the only choice you have is to attack."

This caused a *big* rustle in the crowded auditorium.

I wondered how many of them were with me—and how many weren't. "For the few of you out there who have a problem with this," I continued when the noise had died down some, "I suggest you carefully reread the Imperial oath of allegiance you took when you were commissioned. Read it immediately following this assembly. If after that you *still* have a problem, you'll have until Darkness sharp to resign your commission in the Fleet and clear the base. We'll try to ship you home on a nonpriority basis—when we can. Starting immediately, however, *any* dereliction of duty—in any form—will result in courts-martial and the heaviest penalties applicable during wartime."

That got their attention; the room went stone quiet.

But I was finished speaking; I'd said what I needed to say. Only one more point to make. "I'll try to get around to meeting each of you in person," I said, "soon as I'm able. Meantime, I suggest you all get to know Captain Williams, your Executive Officer. He'll be speaking for me, and can resolve most every problem you may have. If he can't—there'll be times when that happens—then you can always come talk to me. Each of you knows where my office is. But be warned. One of my primary jobs here is to be obstinate. And I intend to pursue that with everything I can muster." Getting weaker again. I turned to Williams and nodded.

"Ten-HUT!" Williams boomed, then was at my side instantly. "You all right, Admiral?"

Little weak, but I thought I could make it to the skimmer. "Just grab me if I start going over," I said.

"Right behind you, Admiral."

He was, and I made it—all the way to the skimmer under my own power. Spent the next few hours in sick bay getting more strength back. Then I was off to the office, with a hell of a lot of work to do. So much that Williams had already gone to his quarters before I thought to ask him who the woman was in the hospital. But by that time, I was so tired I wasn't even certain I'd heard a woman at all.

On the doctor's recommendation, took the morning off and allowed myself an extra metacycle of sleep—my timepiece read Dawn plus two and a half when it woke me. A lot of action going on in the hallway outside. Good! Action overhead, too. I'd been woken even earlier—middle of the Dawn Watch—by the sound of Admiralty 'Gravs overhead at takeoff power. Clearly, Williams had restored a CSP over the base and the city as his first priority.

I shaved and pulled on a clean set of flight overalls, chuckling while I picutred Williams taking names and kicking rear ends. Truth to tell, I'd hate to be on the wrong side of Jim Williams, myself. . . .

Outside, old Haelic was treating Atalanta to its most beautiful weather—deep blue skies, occasional puffy clouds, and perfect temperature. Hador was well along her morning climb from the Gulf of Atalanta, lighting a path of ocher flame across the calm water. Even the breeze was fragrant, coming from the land laden with the smells of conifer, flowers, herbs, and wet earth mixed with chance aromas of baking bread and hot cooking oils from the city itself. Only a sore shoulder suggested my little space battle scarcely more than a local day ago. And somehow, in the enchantment of the bright morning, those short moments of peril seemed relatively unimportant. Atalanta was storehouse for some of my most pleasant memories; I could no more stifle the great smile that escaped my lips than I could stop breathing.

Completely taken by the moment, I strolled leisurely to my gravcycle, complying utterly with the doctor's instructions to stay out of skimmers and starships for at least a day or more, if possible. The RSB was, after all, not even faintly like a skimmer, and today it was recumbent beneath a beautifully fitted cover embroidered with "W.A. Brim, RADM, Base Commander." I simply *had* to look. A strong redolence of polish when I removed the cover—and stowed it in one of the custom saddlebags that had also miraculously appeared on the gleaming machine—made me strongly suspect Petty Officer First Class Russo. I nodded in appreciation. He'd had done it correctly, never showing his face for direct recognition, but anonymously returning favor for favor. It was a sign I'd made a right decision concerning the man.

Back to the glorious morning! No more decisions until I'd escaped the base for a few metacycles on this beguiling gravcycle. If I were any good at all predicting the future, it would be the last free time for me in a long while.

Hunkering beside the 'Grav compartment, I activated the powerful graviton generator, then peered through a tiny porthole into its ion chamber, while I listened for flaws in its silken growl. None. Unlike the ancient and often unreliable gravcycle I'd owned during my second stay in the city as a beggared laborer, this extraordinary machine had *four* plasma beams; all in pluperfect sync and looking as if they'd stay that way through a planetary explosion.

Grinning like a little boy with a new plaything, I threw my leg over the purring 'cycle, eased into hover, and moved carefully into the kind of incoming morning traffic that told me Williams was making significant progress everywhere. While I cruised over the familiar stone arches of Harbor Causeway, the occupant of an open-air skimmer in the opposing lane beeped and waved as she passed. It happened so quickly, I nearly missed her, but in the rearview mirrors, I could see long brown hair streaming in the wind as the skimmer sped toward the base. Instinctively my heart leaped—I knew who she was, and clearly she recognized me. I almost turned in pursuit, but held back. *Now* was not the time to renew a relationship with that kind of potential for emotion. Until the base was solidly on its way to recovery, I'd need every ounce of concentration on the job I could muster. But once things were even a *little bit* under control, we'd meet— *have* to meet. And then I'd find out if hers was the voice in the hospital. Even though I already knew it was. . . .

Approaching the main gate at the end of the causeway, I forced the half-seen woman and her long tresses back to where they'd dwelled in my mind for nearly thirteen years, then slowed and stopped at the guardhouse. Got a rather overdone salute there—and a *carefully* checked ID card. More evidence of Williams's efforts. Then I was on my way into the ancient city of Atalanta.

On the mainland side of the causeway, the Grand Canal— outermost of ten concentric watercourses ringing City Mount Hill—was fronted by unending blocks of ancient government warehouses and office complexes—interrupted here and there by much newer buildings from the period of furious reconstruction at the end of the First Great War. I well recalled the great, foul-smelling mountains of fire-blackened debris they replaced. But in that section, I found little of more than passing interest and drove considerably faster along the wide thoroughfares, buzzing across canal after canal until the huge, faceless buildings grew smaller and began to thin in number. As I sped onward, the office precincts gave away to light industrial complexes, then to tall, ages-old bedroom neighborhoods built of stone, brick, and mortar. Just short of the final canal bridge, I skirted the port's gaudy pleasure district, its streets swarming with painted, raucous crowds even at this early hour.

Presently, I bumped over the last, steep canal bridge and pulled to a stop at the gate to Atalanta's historic, walled Rocotzian Section. The long-haired woman once told me it was so named because the wall traced the uniquely suggestive outlines of a male rocotzio bud. It was here, she'd said—behind these very bulwarks—that this mighty city had actually seen its beginnings, tens of centuries in the past.

Predictably, the course of civic evolution had been neither smooth nor peaceful. Long after the walls retained only symbolic meaning—Omot warriors from space had overrun Hador's entire planetary system, and for nearly three hundred years enslaved the civilization that had developed there. Only when warlike priests from the ancient Gradgroat-Norchelite order appealed to a newly confederated Galactic Empire for help were the Omotian conquerors ultimately overthrown. After which the priests mercilessly hunted them down throughout the Home Galaxy until it was certain that no living creature carried their genes.

During subsequent years, the Gradgroat-Norchelites constructed a great monastery at the summit of City Mount Hill—and shortly afterward orbited their thirteen renowned forts. The latter insured against a threat of invasion from the warlike confederation of star-states that nearly half a millennium later coalesced into the League of Dark Stars under the ruthless leadership of their great chancellor, Kramsib'nov Otto.

The invasion never came, but the forts' huge energy projectors endured as the most devastating defensive weapons ever devised. During the hundreds of intervening peaceful decades, however, they fell into disuse as the Order assumed a more serene purpose in the galaxy. Ultimately, even the external source of energy that once powered them was lost from memory, and the forts became mere objects of historic interest—tourist attractions. Nevertheless, the GradyGroats, as the Order was by now almost universally nicknamed, continued to maintain them in pristine condition as if they still housed first-line weapons systems. And as a result, the term GradyGroat became an analog for "ridiculous" in almost every galactic tongue—until the priests and their space forts actually saved the Empire from invasion at the end of the First Great War by destroying a large part of the League's battle fleet. The priests accomplished this miracle by powering the mammoth cannon directly from Hador's radiation—after launching their entire hilltop monastery at the star to stimulate its output. . . .

I closed my eyes a moment, lost in memory. The monastery's cataclysmic lift-off had taken place nearly fifteen Standard Years ago, but it seemed more like eons. I only missed seeing it with my own eyes by little more than a day, but that's another story, entirely.

A new, even grander edifice now stood on the melted, glasslike summit of City Mount Hill. And even though this one was *not* designed to launch itself into space, it had quickly become a major tourist destination, attracting travelers from all over the galaxy, while the sleepy old Rocotzian Section endured quietly, largely forgotten in the bustle of intragalactic trade—and war. But it had *all* started here, in this tiny, antiquated compound.

It was also here in the Rocotzian Section that *she* lived— or at least *once* lived years ago.

Feeling a bit drained—probably the morning's ride had been a bit premature—I shrugged and eased my gravcycle back out into traffic, then headed back to the base. The precise location of her residence didn't matter anymore—we'd seen each other. I knew she'd risen in rank over the years to the office of Harbor Master, directing all civilian activities on the base. That was enough for now—and all I'd have time for in the immediate future.

During the next week and a half, I spent nearly every waking hour at work, even then barely keeping up with the tasks at hand. However, with Williams apparently working in ten different locations at the same time, the base at last started looking and acting like a military installation again.

We lost perhaps fifty CIGAs officers in the purge; luckily only six were Helmsmen—CIGAs tended to specialize in fields that had little to do with combat.

The only thing that Williams and I *didn't* change was the Officers' Club; Summers had set up a good one and it remained open 'round the clock. I took advantage of that whenever I had the energy to do so, both because I simply needed a place to sit down and have a drink every once in a while and because it was a good place to meet the other officers. The job of Base Commander is much like being Skipper of a large starship. You've an Executive Officer who pretty much carries out the day-to-day work while you make policy and take responsibility for everything. It can be an ivory-tower existence if you let it. But the best Skippers keep in touch with the pulse of their "ships" by mingling, gently, often in the wardroom or the Club. The trick is never talking *directly* about anything, but mostly listening, absorbing the mood, the very atmosphere. It's that ability—listening gently—that makes the difference. Tonight—long metacycles after everyone but the Night Watch had turned in—I was alone at the bar, drinking a decent enough Logish Meem when I sensed someone behind me. Before I could turn, a hand touched my arm, and I got a trace of half-familiar, mostly forgotten perfume, with the spicy scent of a mu'occo cigarette.

"Hello, Wilf Brim," a soft, warm voice purred like Halacian sunlight itself.

I turned; my heart skipped a beat. Beside me in the half-lighted room stood a startlingly beautiful woman—neither young nor old—whose countenance instantly released a flood of memories I had struggled to suppress for years. As if we were completely alone, I stood and took her hands, staring at her as if she was a vision—which, entirely, she was. Petite and utterly feminine, she still wore her dark brown hair almost to her waist in gently flowing waves that had never been far from my mind's surface in the eighteen or so years since we'd first met not far from this very spot. Her wide-set brown eyes—soft and intelligent—were now graced by a network of tiny crow's-feet, but the long eyelashes, the same almost (but not quite) pug nose, the generous lips that had often brought me to the heights of passion, and the intrepid chin that revealed the true woman behind this dazzling beauty—all were truly untouched by age, only heightened by maturity. I glanced at her ample bust—as always boldly flaunted in a snug-fitting, fashionably short native Atalantan pleisse that revealed a modest waist—perhaps *slightly* increased in perimeter over the years (but then, whose wasn't?)—the same slim legs, and the same tiny feet in the timeless high-heeled sandals she favored. Characteristically, she was looking me directly in the face with the half smile of a woman who is quite accustomed to having a substantial impact on men. "Claudia Valemont," I whispered as if I were speaking in a dream.

"You're staring," she said with a little smile.

"Do you mind?"

Same wonderful smile. "Do I mind? For a moment, I was afraid you might not remember me," she said almost shyly.

"Some memories are so wonderful they don't go away," I replied, feeling my cheeks burn after all these years.

"Thanks, Wilf," she said. "I guess I needed that."

Found myself without adequate words to express my emotions; I could only shake my head in amazement.

"Quite a show you put on for us the other night," she said at length. "I knew who was leading that fight without even asking. Lots of us in town have waited a long time for something like that to happen—fighting back, of course, not having you wounded."

"Nice of you," I said with a grin—then frowned. "That was *your* voice I heard in the hospital, wasn't it?"

She nodded.

"Why did you leave? I was coming around."

"Because I know *you*, Wilf Brim."

Raised an eyebrow.

"Even if you'd been conscious, Wilf," she said, "it wasn't time—you had too much on your mind. This base had gone to hell in a handbasket, and I wanted more of you than would be left over in the early stages."

"Touché."

She smiled and shrugged.

"You said the people in town had been waiting for us to fight back," I noted, changing the subject. "According to Summers, the city people are dead set against resistance this go-around. What gives?"

"Summers never asked me," she said. "Nor any of the people I run around with."

I nodded. "I kind of thought that might be the case. Of course, I haven't been here all that long, either."

"About two weeks," Claudia said, glancing at me out of the corner of an eye with a little smile. "But then, who's keeping track?"

"Can a fellow buy you a Meem?" I asked, suddenly realizing that we were still standing.

"Thought you were never going to ask," she said with an expression of relief.

Helped her onto a barstool beside me. The skirt opened, revealing her leg all the way to the thigh, and I couldn't help looking. "Sorry," I said, feeling my cheeks burn.

"About what?" she asked.

"Well . . . staring. . . ."

"Did you like what you saw?"

"Of course."

"As much as you used to?"

"More, probably."

"Then don't be sorry. If I hadn't wanted you to look, it wouldn't have happened."

Same Claudia—thank Voot! "Meem?"

"Of course. The Avignon oh-eight is good."

Swung my leg back over the barstool and sat beside her, pointing to my goblet of Logish Meem. "Another one of these for the lady, please," I said to the bartender.

She laughed. "Ought to have known you'd find the best all by yourself."

"No," I replied, looking into her brown eyes, "the best found *me* this evening." Without thinking, I put my arm around her waist and gently drew her to my side. "I tried to keep my mind clear of you—all the way from Sodeskaya," I blurted out. "And it didn't work worth a xaxtdamn." I closed my eyes. "Still married to Nesterio?" I asked, mentally bracing myself for her reply. That was something I purposely hadn't checked on before I left Atalanta—needed to hear it from her.

She nodded after a long silence.

Dropped my arm from her waist; felt my cheeks burn. Embarrassed. "H-how is he?" I asked for lack of anything else to say.

Another long silence. "Gorgas is fine," she said in a barely audible whisper. "Still tends his cabaret . . . it's . . . much bigger now. He's expanded it." Abruptly, she seemed to run out of words.

We sipped our meem in silence for at least two hundred Standard Years . . . perhaps three hundred. "And you, Wilf?" she asked at length, breaking the awful silence without looking up. "I guess you and your princess never got together, did you?"

Margot. . . . "No," I replied. "We never got together."

"Sorry," she said. "I shouldn't have asked."

"Why not?" I demanded. "I wanted to know about Nesterio."

"I guess we both . . ."

"*Needed* to know," I finished for her. Stared into her face. "You haven't changed much," I blurted out. "you're still the most beautiful woman in the Home Galaxy."

"And you, Wilf Brim, are still the most charming liar in the same place."

"Look at you," I protested, gesturing with my goblet. "Some fabulous hair, same beautiful face . . . same great shape. If you've changed any, it's to become even more beautiful."

"Oh, Wilf Brim," she said with a little smile, "I *know*

you're full of Gorksroar, but I love to hear it anyway." Suddenly she frowned. "You *are* still single, aren't you?"

"Nobody would ever have me," I said. "Women are just too xaxtdamned wary and intelligent these days. Besides, nobody knows how to cook anymore—not like you do, anyway."

She smiled a little, looking at me carefully. After a long time: "I'd *love* to cook for you again. Anytime you wanted. Would you come?"

Felt myself frown. "Do you suppose your husband would mind?"

"Mind?" she asked. "He'd *love* to see you—remembers what you did in the first war. Probably even bring him home for a change."

Raised an eyebrow.

"It's pretty much the custom with native Atalantans," she explained self-consciously. "Probably you didn't notice when you were here, but men here spend most of their evenings in taverns with their cronies."

"And that's what Nesterio does?"

She nodded. "It's *his* tavern, too."

"Poor zukeed—doesn't know what he's missing," I said before I could stop myself. Then, lamely, "Sorry."

"Nothing to be sorry about," she said, blushing again. "It's quite a compliment."

Took her hand and to hell with convention. Remembered our last meeting years ago, when I watched her little skimmer disappear around a corner. Suddenly, I desperately wondered why I'd *ever* allowed a magnificent woman like her slip through my fingers. I wanted to say something now, but ran out of words and just sat there mute, looking at a face I'd dreamed about for years. "I'd love to have supper with you, Claudia," I whispered.

A tear ran along her cheek. She quickly wiped it away. "You name the time, Wilf Brim," she said with a self-conscious little sniffle.

"If I'm any judge," I replied, "that job of yours—congratulations, by the way—doesn't give you much opportunity to entertain."

"Not much," she said, brightening at last. "But by the love of Voot, I'll be free any night you can make it, even if I've got to close down my part of the base—and the sooner, the better."

"It may take me a while to get free for a whole evening," I said.

"I understand," she said, nodding earnestly. "I know you've got an enormous job on your hands. I had to deal personally with Summers sometimes."

"What was he like?" I asked.

She shook her head and laughed. "God, what a pompous ass. Couldn't keep his hands to himself—even in the office. Can you imagine a CIGA trying to talk *me* into bed?"

"Oh, I can," I said, surprised. "Did he?"

"You really want to know?"

Frowned. "Well, it's clearly none of my business," I mumbled, a little ashamed of myself. "But . . ."

She giggled. "I never mentioned this to a soul before, but actually, he did—*once*," she said, glancing at me from the corner of her eyes. "That particular night, though, was an inappropriate time of the month; I planned it that way." She grinned a little guiltily. "After a *very* expensive supper and enough vacant flattery to sink a barge, I let him find out for himself." Blushing now, she suddenly giggled. "Didn't think he'd go for it, and I was right. Watching the look on his face was worth everything."

"Then," I said, "he really *didn't*, did he?"

She grinned. "He got me in bed—that's what you asked."

"Valemont," I said with genuine admiration, "you are an evil woman."

"Thank you, Admiral," she said with a little smile. "I always attempt to do my best."

"Clearly," I said. "And, as I also remember from at least eighteen years past, at least *part* of your 'best' includes cooking in the manner of a professional chef. I'll want to take you up on that invitation . . . as soon as I can."

"I hope so," she said. "It's been a *long* time."

Lost it completely, after that. Blurted out, "How about tomorrow?"

"Strange," she replied with a little smile. "I was hoping you'd say that."

"What time?" I asked.

"You tell me—tomorrow, when you know" she said. "Call me. Cottshall has my number."

"What if I'm late?"

"Then we'll dine late. . . ."

We left soon after that. I suppose people were staring at us as we went out the door. Didn't particularly care. Walked to the parking lot and helped her into the skimmer. Touched her arm—felt excited and guilty at the same time. "G-good to see you," I blurted out.

"Good to see you, Wilf."

I stood there dumbly in the dusky, early-morning stillness, staring. Lost all track of time.

I thought I spied a tear on her cheek when she reached out and touched my hand. "Tomorrow night," she whispered, then started the skimmer.

"Tomorrow night," I gulped, so filled with emotion I could hardly speak. Watched her drive away until she was completely gone. Except the perfume. . . .

Chapter 3

Sapphire

32 Heptad, 52014

Imperial Fleet Base, Atalanta, Hador-Haelic

Familiar voice talking to Cottshall in the outer office; made me grin. "Barbousse!" I yelled. March yourself in this office—on the double!"

Huge man—nearly seven irals tall, broad shoulders, muscles everywhere. Looked as if he weighed a solid milston; walked with the catlike grace of a dancer. Totally bald with no eyebrows. Gentle—intelligent—eyes. Pug nose, round face, strong chin. Big hands, strong enough to bend the barrel of a blast pike. Perfect uniform, perfect salute. "Master Chief Petty Officer Utrillo Barbousse reporting for duty, Admiral Brim."

I stood, returned the salute, then extended my hand. "Awfully good to have you here, Chief," I said. "You're needed."

"Hope so, Admiral," he said. Grasped my hand in a warm, strong grip.

"You'll wish you'd stayed put in Sodeskaya," I warned him.

"Heard it's a mess here."

"You should have seen it when I got here," I said. "Williams has worked miracles already."

"Your Exec?"

"Yeah. I think you'll like him. He's good."

"So I've heard. Checked him out with some of the old-time Chiefs in Avalon. They say you've got yourself a prize."

"Two of 'em now that you're here."

He grinned. "Thanks, Admiral," he said. "But by my count, it's *three*."

I don't keep guest chairs in my office. Makes the meetings short. "Buy you breakfast in the buffet?" I asked.

"Best offer I've had since I got here," he said.

For the next metacycle, Barbousse caught me up on all of the scuttlebutt from Avalon, handed over at least fifty HoloPics of Hope . . . on Emperor Onrad's lap . . . on Grand Admiral Calhoun's lap . . . on Admiral Gallsworthy's lap . . . on General Drummond's lap. . . . Clearly, she had conquered most of Onrad's General Staff. Afterward, I filled him in on as much background about the base as I'd been able to absorb. Then we met Williams in a conference room and got down to business—completing the task of returning the base to full operational status.

Just before midday, got a call from Cottshall. Said someone was in the office to discuss what he called "important matters." Name of Deighton Ambrose, from Avalon. Arrived on the same starship as Barbousse.

I hit the MUTE button; turned to Barbousse. "What do you know about a fellow named Deighton Ambrose?"

"Had a Deighton Ambrose on the ship with me, Admiral," he said. "I'd guess he's a government man of some sort— maybe a courier. Carried a black briefcase secured to his wrist. Never saw him talking to anybody except the captain and a couple of stewards."

"That's all you know?"

"That's it, Admiral."

Nodded. Canceled the MUTE. "Ask him what sort of 'important matters.' "

"I shall do so, Admiral."

Heard him ask; didn't catch the answer.

Presently: "Mr. Ambrose asked me to mention the word *Sapphire*."

"Cottshall," I said, "put a guest chair in my office and tell him I'm on the way. . . ."

A big man in a dark business suit, sitting there in my office, briefcase secured to his left wrist. "Mr. Ambrose," I said, extending my hand, "Wilf Brim."

He stood, gripped my hand, fixed me with a powerful gaze. "Glad to meet you, Admiral," he said in a deep, quiet voice, looking and sounding more like a Sodeskayan Bear than anything else. Massive forehead and jaw, deep-set eyes, straight-line features. Big hands, perfectly manicured. Placed his briefcase on my desk. "If you'll put a thumb here," he said, pointing to an Imperial seal near the top, "I've some items for you from Avalon."

Touched my thumb to the seal. Warm.

"Keep it there a moment, please."

"Sorry."

Presently, the seal became cold and the briefcase opened. Ambrose reached inside, removed a thick, secure-looking pouch with "Sapphire" printed on the outside. "Left index finger here, please," he said, indicating an ID frame near the top.

This time, I let my finger remain. The security strip at the top of the pouch disappeared with a quiet *zip*.

"You'll want to look these over while I'm here." Ambrose said, closing his briefcase.

After struggling with the pouch for a moment—the outside catches were often stubborn the first few times they were used—I opened it up and spread its contents before me on the desk: two navigational charts, an old-fashioned, illustrated book—Voot knew how long ago it had been published—and a Personal HoloScreen displaying: PRE-LOADED WITH IN-FORMATION FROM THE IMPERIAL MUSEUM AND THE COLLEGE OF SPACE ANTIQUITIES, IMPERI UNI-VERSITY. "You meen they sent a courier all the way out here to bring me *this*?" I demanded.

"The remainder comes from here," Ambrose said, pointing to his forehead with a smile. "But not in your office. Outside, somewhere in the open air—away from the base. I've rented a skimmer." He handed me a small leather folder.

I opened the folder, felt my eyebrows rise as I looked at the gold emblem inside. No mere courier, this Ambrose—one of perhaps fifteen senior Consuls in the Empire called Travelers. Carry flag rank, at minimum. Put the Sapphire pouch under my arm, followed him out of the office. "Be 'in conference' till I get back," I said to Cottshall on the way past his desk.

"I shall place a 'Do Not Disturb' sign on your office door," Cottshall said with a smile.

Ambrose's rented civilian skimmer in the parking lot was a

nondescript Nordan 223 four-door. He silently drove us out in the country a distance, checking constantly in the rearview mirror. We stopped on a hilltop beside an unkempt olive grove with high, uncut grass and, beyond, a great stone tub surrounded by overgrown hedges.

I peered around for a moment—two elderly looking farmers scything grass at a leisurely pace in the distance—then relaxed, turned to Ambrose.

"A bit sudden, this," he said. "Sorry—but we're about to treat Rogan LaKarn and his friends in The Torond to a nasty surprise. We don't want them to catch wind of things until there's little they can do to prevent it."

I nodded that I understood.

"Right, then," he said. "The ultimate objective of *Sapphire* is the invasion and ultimate liberation of all planets in the domain of Fluvanna."

Felt my eyebrows rise at that, especially since we seemed to be on the *defensive* nearly everywhere else in the galaxy. A million questions sprang to mind, but principal among the ones that didn't pertain to troops and material was what the liberation of Fluvanna had to do with *me*—and Atalanta. The city would be bombed to smithereens if we tried to assemble an invasion fleet in the harbor. Nodded again, but shifted my eyes to the farmers, who were still slowly working their way toward us.

"You're not saying much," Ambrose commented.

"I don't know enough, yet," I said, returning my gaze to him.

"Ever hear of Gontor?" he asked.

That brought a frown; I had . . . somewhere. Yes. "The old space fortress in Sector Nineteen?" I asked.

"That's it," he said. "What do you know about it?"

"Not much," I admitted. "Just that something's there that must look like a fortress."

"*Is* a fortress," Ambrose corrected gently. "Actually, a tremendous asteroid orbiting a little dwarf star called star Cyjix-19. Been vacant for a millennium or more. Hundreds of Standard Years before that, someone with a lot of talent and power to spare—nobody remembers who anymore—life-formed the monster into a nearly impregnable fortress, so large and spacious it can accommodate a sizeable invasion force in safety."

That started the bells ringing. "Where?" I asked. "I know it's not on any of the established space routes."

"Wasn't always the case," Ambrose said. "Fifteen hundred, two thousand years ago—give or take a few—Cyjix-19 lay astride the main commercial thoroughfare between the old Mornay Star Empire and an up-and-coming star domain that called itself the Vann Group."

"Never heard of it," I said.

"I'll bet you've heard of the Flu'wicz Empire," Ambrose said.

"I think so," I said. "But I can't place it."

"They conquered the Vannians to form . . ."

"Fluvanna?"

"You've got it," Ambrose said. "Give you some idea of how handy old Gontor is to the Fluvannian star systems? It's less than a Standard Day's flight distant."

"Mother of Voot!"

"Right."

"Don't you think The Torond has thought about that, too?" I asked.

"Probably," Ambrose said. "But they aren't doing anything about it. After all, they've already taken half the country."

More pieces of the puzzle in place—getting a strange feeling about . . . "And, so far," I said warily, "they see us doing very little to change the situation."

"Suggest anything to you, Admiral?"

Winced. "Mother of Voot," I groaned. "Is *that* why Summers and his CIGA colleagues got away with letting the base go to xaxt?"

Ambrose nodded. "It's also why you and Williams have to be *very* careful how rapidly you put your improvements into place—or at least how much you let them show. You're already moving a lot faster than we'd hoped. *A lot* faster." He laughed quietly for a moment—first time I'd seen him smile. "A number of us didn't want you—or your sidekick Barbousse—within light-years of this place. No offense intended."

My head was whirling. "None taken," I said. "But why did you . . . ?"

"Horns of a dilemma, Admiral. We *also* couldn't turn such a ticklish operation over to anybody without a reputation like yours."

"Reputation?"

"Of digging in and getting things done—against bad odds," he said.

"Luck," I said. Regretted it instantly.

"That too." His second smile.

Looked at him carefully while the last few pieces fell into place . . . and sent icy chills along my spine. "So where does Gontor enter the picture?" I asked, but I already knew.

"As you've guessed," Ambrose said, "your assignment to 'clean up' the base here was only a cover. The *actual* reason you find yourself in Atalanta for a second tour—project *Sapphire*—concerns only Gontor. You are first to occupy and secure it, then provision it—after which the Imperial Expeditionary Forces will use it as a staging area for the men and material of Operation Spark—the liberation of Occupied Fluvanna."

"Into the bargain," I added, almost to myself, "I've got to keep the lid on the base here at Atalanta—and the Toronders unsuspecting—until we've got Gontor so secure that it's too late for them to drive us out."

"In a nutshell," he said with an apologetic little smile.

The zukeeds never *did* trouble themselves laying on the work, did they? Frowned. Outside, the elderly farmers had been joined by six much younger ones. Big, husky men, I noticed idly. Ought to make the work go *much* quicker. "What sort of resources do I get?" I demanded.

"You've already got pretty much everything we can spare," Ambrose said. The little smile, again. "You of all people know we're pushed to the limit everywhere," he said. "And the Sodeskayans . . . well, it was *you* who sold the War Cabinet on the importance of supplying the Sodeskayans with all our surplus."

I could only nod my rueful agreement.

"Sorry," he said.

Didn't think he *really* meant it. I took a moment to think it over. Probably I could use part of the base's excellent military police force. It was one thing Summers hadn't got his hands on: bigwigs like that consider themselves *above* police. Remembered a couple of small, fast transports in the hangar—not enough, but maybe I could commandeer a few civilian ships in the harbor. The three benders I'd seen the night I landed; they'd come in handy—somewhere. Forty-odd flyable Starfury interceptors—excellent protection for the base and the city. Not much in the way of spares, but we'd take care of that somehow—always had. Biggest trouble would be getting the troops and supplies across to Gontor. Even without a starmap, I knew it was a long-distance haul. A lot farther than Starfuries could fly—at least Starfuries with all their disruptors enabled. That meant that the convoys, such as they might be, would have to go unescorted. . . .

"There *is* some extra help we intend to provide." Ambrose broke into my thoughts.

"Love to hear about it," I replied—all ears.

He looked at me carefully. "Well," he said with a little hesitation, it's got to do with your home province of Carescria."

That got my attention. I raised an eyebrow.

"You certainly must know that we Imperials—actually past Emperor Greyffin IV—opened a number of production plants there just after the first war. And Onrad's kept up the support as if he'd had 'em built himself. Carescria's become *very* important to the war effort in the last few years."

I nodded, with a somewhat guilty sense of pride for the people of my own section of the Empire, though I'd selfishly forsaken everything Carescrian most of my adult life. Even *before* the first factories were complete, Carescrians back home were turning out the extra Starfuries that made the difference during our Battle of Avalon. I'd flown a number of them. *Those people out there broke their backs making starships that saved our Triad.* Onrad had once said to me. *They're important: we're going to need them a lot more before we finally whip the Tyrant and his bloody League.*

"Every one of those factories is in full production now," Ambrose continued, "turning out new, unique designs that appear to be very promising."

Raised an eyebrow. "Like, what?" I asked.

"Like a whole new breed of ships they call Basilisks, hunter-killers," he replied—as if he'd been reading my mind. "Big, tough, oversize killer ships with the kind of range that Mark Valerian never even considered when he designed our vaunted Starfuries. There's also a fast, rugged medium attack ship that's nearly the equal in firepower of those new Sode-skayan Ro'stovik crawler killers, but they carry a belly full of HyperTorps as well."

Sounded too good to be true. *Far* too good. "But . . . ?" I prompted.

Ambrose nodded. "The 'but' is that none has ever been tested in actual combat. Nor have the all-Carescrian crews who man them. *That's* why we thought of you, Admiral Brim."

Didn't like the sound of that. I'd spent years making certain I got assignments *in spite* of my Carescrian background—didn't want to get one now *because* of it. "*What's* why you thought of me?" I demanded.

"The work you just finished with the Sodeskayans," he replied. "Right now, our Carescrians are just about where the Bears were a year ago: ready to send plenty of promising new people and equipment into the field—with no experience. And you've been through it all before—including the *very* difficult job of directing the operations of people who don't even report to your organization. A job that few people *ever* get right, especially the first time."

"Thanks," I said, mollified. Noticed the extra farmers had *really* sped things up. They'd more than halved the distance to our skimmer.

"And, of course, you are a Carescrian," Ambrose added.

Nothing ever changes, does it? Looked him in the eye with the coldest stare I could muster. "First and foremost," I said pointedly, "I am an *Imperial Citizen*—as is everyone who hails from Carescria."

His face reddened. "Um . . . yes . . . terribly sorry, Admiral Brim," He said. "Figure of speech."

Ignored the apology. "So how many can I get?" I demanded.

"How many what?" Ambrose asked.

"Hunter-killers. Medium attack ships," I said. "How many can you send me and *when*?"

Ambrose's face brightened with relief. "You *want* them?" he asked.

"Of course," I said. "There's something wrong with 'em?"

"If you mean other than a lack of combat experience, then nothing."

"No disease? Insanity? Infirmity?"

The little smile again. "Just normal people like you or me, Admiral Brim," he said.

Back on track. "Then how many and when?" I repeated.

Ambrose thought a moment. "The 'how many' is easy," he said. "I can have the first pair of squadrons—sixteen Basilisks, by the way—here in a little less than two months. Replacements for casualties will start two or three weeks after that."

"Sounds good to me," I said. "And the mediums?"

"I'll send a squadron of twelve around the first of the year."

Wished it were sooner, but . . . "What about maintenance and spares?"

"Package deal," Ambrose explained. "They bring everything with them. All you've got to do is house the ships and feed the crews."

"And train 'em to fight," I added.

"Best we can do," Ambrose said. "Sorry."

"No criticism implied," I assured him. "A little guts does wonders for the fighting spirit. Ask the Bears. I saw some of them stop motorized attacks with little more than blast pikes and mines."

"And you wondered why we thought *you* were the right man to help 'em into combat," Ambrose said with a chuckle.

Absently glanced out the window at the farmers for a moment—no more than a hundred irals from our skimmer by this time. Young ones were working as if there were no tomorrow. "You've got to be a little crazy, I guess," I said.

"A prime qualification," Ambrose observed, "especially when you hear our deadline for securing the old fort."

Steadied myself. I'd been waiting for *that* shoe to fall, wondering why it hadn't. "Bad?" I asked.

"Bad," Ambrose declared.

"Give it to me."

"Twelve weeks—starting *yesterday*," he said. The first convoy lifts in eighteen days to prove out the route. You can expect it at Atalanta by seventeen Octad."

Closed my eyes. "Voot's beard," I groused, "you people don't mind laying on the work, do you?"

"I know," he agreed. "But there's not much anybody can do about it. With the Toronders gearing up for their own invasion, twelve weeks is cutting things awfully thin as it is. Best information says they'll start moving reinforcements into Occupied Fluvanna within the next few Standard Days; you'll need to put a crimp in that directly—along with everything else you're tasked with."

Nodded. Made sense—nothing's easy when it comes to waging war. I sat for another couple of moments in silence. "Anything else?" I asked warily.

"That's it, Admiral," he said.

"All right," I said, reaching into the backseat to rummage into the Sapphire pouch. "Let's spend a couple of cycles looking over the stuff you brought." The catch, of course, chose that moment to stick again.

"Good idea," he said. "I think you'll find them interesting as well as . . ."

While I struggled in the backseat with the catch, I suddenly felt a searing blast of heat on the back of my neck, and when I glanced up . . . I nearly screamed! Ambrose's head had simply, well *cooked* to a char—while he was talking—cut him off in mid-sentence. Lidless eyes stared at me in agonized consternation, mouth open for the next word. Stench like roasted pork. I ducked my head in alarm—just as a second blast of searing heat missed me by no more than a hair, ripping his door away from the skimmer's body and hurling it to the other side of the road. For a moment, the entire Universe erupted in blinding light, concussion, and flying glass. Instinctively, I dived for the floor, only a split click before the upper half of my door exploded inward and I felt the skimmer sink heavily to the roadbed. Stunned senseless, I scrambled over Ambrose's flaccid legs and threw myself outside, fumbling for my holster. Grasped the Wenning just as someone leaped around the front of the skimmer, bringing up a blaster in a two-handed grip. Fired the big .985 almost blindly—full power. Heard a grating howl as his chest exploded. Someone coming from the rear. Whirled around . . . *too late*. His blaster was already aimed. Braced—good-bye, Brim. Expected the *zappfft*, but instead, he simply got a surprised look, slowly dropped the blaster, then cumpled facedown on the dirt with a huge dagger buried halfway to the hilt in the back of his neck.

Barbousse!

More shots. Screams of pain. Sounds of running boots. Only an iral behind me, the skimmer was burning furiously—scorching my back. But I didn't dare leave its shelter.

Then Barbousse's voice. "Admiral! Admiral Brim! Are you all right!"

"Chief!" I yelled back. "I'm all right. Where the xaxt *are* you?"

"Coming round the rear end, Admiral. Got the situation in hand. Don't shoot me."

Rolled away from the skimmer. Knees so wobbly, didn't know if I could stand. Saw Barbousse sprinting toward me—how can someone so big move so *fast*? Dragged me to my feet, roaring orders like a Sodeskayan at a detachment of Space Police.

Hardly heard him. In the field, one of the younger "farmers" was on his knees with his hands up, eyes big as saucers as he peered into the barrels of five powerful blast pikes. Another man sprawled beside him . . . wasn't moving. Farther out, more SPs were running the two "older" farmers to ground like hounds after a fox.

The man I'd managed to shoot had been thrown backward ten irals by the force of my blaster. Nothing left of his chest except a blackened hole. Felt my gorge rise. At least the searing effect cut down on puddled blood.

Clearly Barbousse's work there at the back of the skimmer. Nobody else in the known Universe throws a knife like that.

Glanced inside the burning passenger compartment . . . wanted to throw up. Turned away. Nothing anybody could do for Ambrose. I stiffened—the pouch! Ran to the skimmer, pulled it out of the backseat moments before the upholstery went up with a terrific *whump* that nearly knocked me from my feet again. Barbousse caught me. "Er . . . Sorry, Admiral," I heard him say as he gently set me on my feet. Shaking his head. Angry at himself.

"You merely saved my *thraggling* life, Chief," I protested, trying my shaky legs. "*I'm* not sorry, believe me. What if this had happened before you arrived this morning?"

Barbousse knelt to pull his knife from the unfortunate assassin's neck. "Don't even want to think about such a thing, Admiral," he said, carefully wiping the blade on his victim's sleeve.

I put my hand on his shoulder. "Fact is, you *were* here,

though, Chief," I said. "Just as you always have been in the past." Then I frowned. "What *was* it that made you follow me in the first place?"

"The man Ambrose," he replied, standing to replace his knife in its scabbard strapped inside his left trouser leg. "Somethin' about 'im I couldn't put my finger on. An' I couldn't learn anythin' about 'im on the Chiefs' network. So I decided it wouldn't hurt to put on a little protection." He looked troubled. "I kept my distance 'cause I figured it was none of my business. That's why we were so long getting here once the trouble started."

I took the hint. "I'll be a lot more careful in the future, Chief," I promised. "And it *is* your business, believe me. But it's *really* sensitive stuff. Can't talk about it here—I'll have to fill you in once you get me back to the base."

Barbousse nodded, looked relieved. "Thanks, Admiral," he said, then strode toward the SPs and took charge. Within moments, he'd commandeered the skimmer they'd come in and we were on our way, passing five armored personnel carriers headed the opposite direction. For me, the war had just entered a much uglier—deadlier—phase.

On the way in, I briefed Barbousse with what he needed to know, then clamped a MOST SECRET classification on the whole thing and turned it over to him. The old farmers would be sworn to secrecy—they'd be more than happy to trade a year's wages for bragging rights to the yarn—and the surviving prisoner would go to the SPs for interrogation, although I didn't expect to learn all that much when he finally cracked. Looked to me as if the *real* perpetrators had contracted the job to local thugs—Voot knew there was no dearth of *those*—who couldn't reveal much if they failed to make an escape.

With Barbousse making fur fly, I went back to my office

and began to sort things out. Ambrose had been just about finished with my briefing when he died, so I already had my marching orders. Those, a couple of starmaps, an ancient book, and a HoloScreen. Just thraggling wonderful! Oh yes, and a xaxtdamned near impossible deadline of twelve Standard Weeks. But all that was in my hands now.

The Carescrians, however, were *not*. They were critical to the mission, and my only link to them was dead—murdered. Now what? Suddenly, I remembered the HoloPics of Hope—especially the one with her sitting on . . . . "Cottshall," I said to the intercom, "get me a secure KA'PPA channel to Fleet Headquarters, Avalon, flash priority. I want to speak to General Harry Drummond at the Admiralty."

Took nearly half a metacycle, but at last Cottshall signaled he'd made the connection. Because of the tremendous traffic load, wartime KA'PPA communication was made using old-fashioned ciphers instead of normal holographic images. A little clumsy, but it worked. Enabled my HoloPhone, which immediately displayed:

ADMIRALTY: PLEASE SIGNAL WHEN READY FOR GENERAL
DRUMMOND.

"Ready," I said. The HoloPhone translated my voice to ciphers, then scrambled them before transfer to the base's KA'PPA transmitter.

DRUMMOND: HELLO, WILF. HEARD ABOUT DEIGHTON—BAD
NEWS INDEED. EXPECTED YOUR CALL. WHAT HAP-
PENED?

Told him in the fewest, *most gentle* words possible; figured they might know each other. Then: "I'm ready to tackle everything he and I discussed, but don't know how to contact the Carescrians—or who to talk to. Can you help me?"

> DRUMMOND: YEAH, YOU CAME TO THE RIGHT PLACE; FIG-
> URED YOU WOULD. I WAS ABOUT TO KA'PPA YOU, BUT
> YOU GOT HERE FIRST. CAN'T TELL YOU MORE THAN
> THAT. SORRY. CAN I TAKE IT YOU AGREED TO AVAIL
> YOURSELF OF THE CARESCRIANS?

"Absolutely, General," I said. "No way to complete Sapphire without them."

> DRUMMOND: FIGURED THAT, TOO. GOOD! WISH THEY HAD A
> LITTLE MORE EXPERIENCE, BUT NOTHING'S PERFECT.
> I'LL SET UP THE SAME DIRECT CONTACT DEIGHTON ES-
> TABLISHED. A COLONEL, NAME OF ANDERSON; HE'LL
> CONTACT YOU WITHIN THE NEXT SIX WEEKS.

Figured I'd have to wait. Fleet time and actual time have very little in common. "What sort of clearances will he have?" I asked.

> DRUMMOND: CLEARED AS HIGH AS YOU ARE, BUT HAS NO
> NEED-TO-KNOW YET. YOU DECIDE WHO LEARNS
> WHAT—AND WHEN. WHOLE THING'S YOUR BABY
> NOW, YOU LUCKY ZUKEED.

"My joy is unbounded," I sent.

> DRUMMOND: SAME TO YOU, BRIM.

I chuckled. That was about it, then. "Great pictures of you with Hope," I sent.

DRUMMOND: GONNA BREAK A LOT OF HEARTS, THAT KID OF YOURS. DAMN LUCKY SHE LOOKS LIKE HER MOTHER.

"Agreed. Anything else you can tell me?"

DRUMMOND: YOU'VE GOT EVERYTHING I KNOW. BEST OF LUCK AND ALL THAT.

"Thanks," I sent. "Signing off." I touched DISCONNECT, and the display faded. Sat there staring at a wall for a little while, head spinning. Where to start? Needed to get an SP detachment formed right away so they could have some sort of training before they occupied Gontor. Of course, first someone would have to learn enough about the old fort to do the training. And they'd need weapons—not just the usual side arms and blast pikes. If for any reason the Toronders discovered what was going on, the SPs would need to defend themselves from *heavy* attack, even though they were holed up in a pretty impregnable place. Then there was the question of transportation. *That* whole matter would have to be coordinated with the civilian Harbor Master . . . who had invited me to supper!

Glanced at my timepiece. Nearly Evening plus three—damn! Where had the day gone? "Cottshall! Put a call through to the Harbor Master's office. On the double, please!"

"At once, Admiral. To whom do you wish to speak?"

"Sorry," I said. "Claudia Nesterio, please. If she's still there." Grimaced while I waited. Simply *hated* to forget personal commitments. Damn! Watched the 'Phone materialize a miniature of her head and shoulders . . . smiling, at least.

"Understand you had a busy day," she said, so beautiful I wanted to reach out and touch her.

"Oh?" frowning in spite of myself. "What'd you hear?" Thought I'd made everything Top Secret.

"Only scuttlebutt."

"Like . . . ?"

"Bit of a shoot-up inland," she said, looking a little concerned. "Heard you were involved."

Nodded. Couldn't put that TOP SECRET lid on things until I got back to the base, and word had clearly gotten out. "Yeah," I said, chuckling. "Only thing that goes faster than HyperDrive is scuttlebutt."

"You all right?" she asked.

"Only embarrassed," I said.

"Embarrassed?" she asked. "About a shoot-up?"

"About supper tonight. The shoot-out's not important anymore."

She rolled her eyes. "Wilf Brim," she said, "you haven't changed one iota in all these years. You are still totally and completely impossible."

"Does that mean I get no supper?" I asked. "I know I'm late."

"Told you we'd dine late if we had to," she said. "Can you still make it?"

"Of course," I said. "I was just afraid I might be *too* late."

"Give me till"—she glanced off to the side—"Twilight and a half." Then her eyebrows rose. "Belay that," she said. "You don't know where I live anymore."

"I can take directions," I said.

"Easier if I just pick you up on my way home. See you in fifteen cycles outside Headquarters."

"How'll I get back?"

"Same way," she said. "It's not that far. All right?"

"Fifteen cycles," I promised. "Front door." Sat there like a log realizing how much seeing her meant to me—even after the day I'd just put in. Needed to tone those feelings down some, I reminded myself. She *was* married, after all. And though I'd seldom let that bother me with other women over the years, Claudia Valemont-Nesterio was a *very* special case.

Shook my head.

Back to business. Tomorrow was another day! Grabbed my garrison cap and left the desk the way it was. Stopped at Cottshall's desk. "I'll need to see Williams in the small conference room first thing tomorrow," I said. "Morning and a half sharp. Tell him I apologize for what that does to his schedule, but he'll understand when he hears." Thought for a moment. "I'll need Chief Barbousse there, too. And, yeah, better arrange for a substitute at this desk, because I'll want you in on all of this, too. Got that?"

"Got it, Admiral."

Glanced at my timepiece; started for the door when . . .

"Er, Admiral?" Embarrassed look on Cottshall's *very* serious countenance.

"What's up?"

"These," he said, nodding to a box of native flowers that looked as if they had just been delivered. "Thought you might want to take these with you."

Frowned. "Don't know what you mean," I said. But I did.

"In that case, Admiral," Cottshall said, quickly placing the box beneath his desk, "please ignore my words. Clearly, I erred."

Felt prickly; *hate* anyone's nose in my personal business—and Valemont-Nesterio was about as personal as things got with me. Wanted to tell him off, then reined in my galloping temper. "Just why would I be interested in those flowers?" I demanded.

Cottshall looked at me as if I had just inquired about the weather. "Because," he said matter-of-factly, "by the hour of the call I placed for you, I assumed you are dining with our Madame Harbor Master this evening for the first time since your arrival. And since at one time you two were known to be, er, close friends, I also assumed flowers might be in order. Clearly, Admiral, you have had no time to purchase them."

Stood there flabbergasted. He was completely right, of course, his actions well within the limits of a personal secretary. I'd never had a real secretary before. Shook my head while the anger changed to gratitude. "Damned thoughtful of you, Cottshall," I said, holding out my hand. "I really do appreciate those flowers. What do I owe you?"

Cottshall looked at his timepiece as he handed me the box of flowers. "You're running a bit short of time, Admiral," he said. "I shall bill you in the morning."

Claudia pulled up to the curb just as one of the guards saluted and opened the door for me. She *loved* the flowers, for which I shamelessly took credit all the way to her new home. . . .

Gorgas Nesterio, Claudia's husband of nearly ten years, was waiting at the door of their new home with his grandest smile. "Welcome to our humble home, Admiral!" he boomed in a voice deep enough to rattle the furniture. Dressed in bright, traditional Atalantan garb, he hadn't changed appreciably since I'd last seen him, some fifteen years ago. Huge, swarthy, and heavily bearded, he wore an embroidered red tunic with shiny brass buttons in two rows that extended from a high lace collar to a short tapestry skirt woven in brightly colored patterns. A broad, elaborately jeweled leather belt draped over his hips, placing a long silver dagger close to his right hand—and made me wonder uncomfortably if he had *any* idea about the fun things his wife and I used to do to each other. Long pointed shoes that curled into coils and blue tights over powerful, muscular legs completed his costume. He smelled of perfumed oils, leather, and musk—and looked as if he could throw me bodily all the way back to the base in the event I stared at his wife too much. Didn't take much speculation to guess what had kept Claudia's juices flowing so well all these years. "Er, thank you, Gorgas," I said, feeling rather small, shriveled, and impotent. "It is a distinct honor to be here."

"A libation, my friend?" Nesterio asked.

"Love one," I said. "Meem will be great."

"But of course," Nesterio said as he stepped behind a magnificently inlaid bar and opened a wall panel to reveal a large meem rack. Slipped an ancient-looking glass bottle from a wall safe and peered at it proprietarily. "I think you will find this interesting, Admiral—a Cantrell, vintage 5205; Logish, of course. Slightly sweet, fruity. It is said one can taste the age."

Nodded expectantly; watched him expertly open the ancient container and fill a single crystal goblet.

Then he placed two long-stemmed flutes beside it and filled them with clear liquid from a magnificent carved-crystal decanter. "E'lande," he explained, as if I might have forgotton the fiery, powerful native Atalantan liqueur.

Nodded again. Remembered now that was what Claudia drank at home; wondered why I'd forgotten at the Officers' Club and ordered meem for her. Just then, she returned from the kitchen with the flowers, now charmingly arranged in a tall vase, and placed them on the bar.

"I propose a toast to honored guests and old friendships," Nesterio said, lifting his flute.

Claudia raised hers. "To honored guests and *renewed* friendships."

Thinking quickly, got to my feet and raised my goblet. "To

the Nesterios," I saluted. "Old friends: long may you delight in the glow of happiness!"

Both Nesterios drained their flutes in a single draught before I had even finished a sip of the magnificent old Logish Meem.

I laughed. "No way am I going to bolt *this* treasure," I protested with a grin. "Don't care what the local customs call for."

"Then, it is we who are doubly honored," Nesterio replied, filling both their flutes again. "I propose a second toast—this time to old friends who appreciate Logish Meem!"

Claudia glanced at me for a moment, her eyes striving to say something mine couldn't understand. "To enduring friends who appreciate Logish Meem," she echoed, downing her second flute of E'lande.

I got to my feet again, raised my goblet. "To enduring friends and remarkable Logish Meem." Savored another taste of the spendid meem, then, as I raised the goblet to my nose for the bouquet, Nesterio filled their flutes a *third* time. Noticed Claudia no longer met my eyes.

"I propose a toast to the Emperor!" Nesterio announced, raising his flute and looking expectantly at Claudia.

"To Onrad the Fifth," she said, raising her flute but still averting her eyes from me, "Grand Galactic Emperor, Prince of the Reggio Star Cluster, and Rightful Protector of the Heavens."

"To Onrad," I said simply—while the two Nesterios drained their third flute of E'lande in less than fifteen cycles. Completely at sea by now, I took another sip of meem to see what came next.

"And now," Nesterio said, abruptly, "the cabaret beckons me." He put his arm around Claudia's shoulders and drew her to him, planting a wet, noisy kiss on her lips. Then, turning her like some sort of life-sized mannequin, he . . . well, seemed to *present* her to me. "You will provide Admiral Brim with all hospitality that I would bestow myself, had I no prior commitments, tonight," he said.

"Er, y-yes, I shall, Gorgas," she said, a blush appearing high on her cheeks.

He laughed. "Do not let him leave until he has finished the meem. Few here in the city can appreciate its vintage." He next turned to me and bowed. "Perhaps another night for the three of us, Admiral," he said, looking me directly—*knowingly* was a better word—in the eye. "It is my understanding that you and my wife have long been friends; therefore, I trust you will have much to revisit." Without another word, he grasped a dark green cloak and strode to the door, opened it, and with a low, graceful bow to Claudia, simply . . . departed.

The two of us stood in silence for a long interval—looking *anywhere* except at each other—before Claudia turned to me with a stricken look. "I am *so* sorry, Wilf," she said. "I didn't think he'd do this to me tonight."

Walked to her side; touched her arm gently. "Sorry for what, Claudia?"

"Wilf, Wilf, Wilf," she said. "You never did learn about Atalanta, did you?"

"I don't know what you mean," I said, suddenly worried . . . about what, I had no idea.

Her voice had begun to slur now, and I helped her to a chair, put my hand on her shoulder. Couldn't imagine someone so petite drinking all that E'lande so quickly—in so little time. "What didn't I learn?" I asked gently.

Staring at the floor. She touched my hand, shook her head. "Nothing, Wilf," she said. "S-shouldn't have said anything. Forget I opened my mouth."

"Of course, Claudia," I said. Probably not a good time to disagree.

Looked up at me after a few moments. Eyes were wet, but she'd got *that* part of her under control, at least. "Still hungry?" she asked.

Surprised. "Are you?"

"A-asked you first."

"Well, as a matter of fact, I am," I said.

She smiled a little uncomfortably. "So'm I," she said. "And I *did* offer you supper, if I remember."

"You did, but . . ."

"But *nothing*, Wilf Brim," she said. "May be drunk—devil take it—but think can still cook . . . if you'll assist."

"Whatever I can do."

"Help me into the kitchen," she said, giving me her arm. "By all that's holy, nobody—not even Nesterio nor all his cronies—can do me out of my supper with you, Wilf Brim. I've waited for this more than twelve years!"

Put her arm over my shoulder; had to half carry her to the kitchen. Clearly, the E'lande was still coming on, but she was fighting it.

"In the c-chair, there, Wilf," she said. "Prop myself on the table. It'll wear off."

Did that. Her eyes were half-closed.

"Goddamn him," she mumbled. "*Goddamn* him and every man ever born of Haelic!" Suddenly, she slumped facedown on the table.

Got one arm behind her shoulder, the other beneath her knees. Lifted gently, laid her on the couch beneath a superb native coverlet I remembered from the old days. Hair like a brown halo on the cushions—remember *that*, too.

"Don't leave me, Wilf," she whispered breathlessly. "It'll wear off, I promise."

"I won't leave," I said, drawing up a chair. Gently caressed her hand.

"God, I'm, sorry," she groaned suddenly.

"Sh-h-h."

"I'm not like this," she said fervently. "*Not like this.*"

"It's all right," I said, anxious to calm her.

"*Please* don't leave me, Wilf. . . ." Suddenly, she was asleep, breathing deeply.

Checked her pulse. A little fast, but not unusual. Went to the end of the couch, pulled up the coverlet, took off her sandals. Tiny, beautiful feet . . . ticklish, once, I remembered. Returned to my chair, noticed the open meem bottle. Got up and corked it. Somehow, drink had lost its appeal. In the kitchen cooler, thick butter and sharp cheese; crusty bread on the counter. I'd made many a meal of those in my lifetime—good meals, too. Loaded a plate and took it to the drawing room where I could keep an eye on her. Changed my mind about the meem. Filled the goblet. Nothing like the supper I'd hoped for, but then I *was* here alone with her—admitted that's what I came for in the first place. And even if she wasn't presently aware of my presence, it was a damned sight better than my office. Another goblet of that *unforgettable* meem, then I settled back in the chair, kicked off my boots, and listened to what could only be a flight of Starfuries lifting off from the hrbor. Had been a *long* day indeed. Momentarily closed my eyes to rest 'em . . .

"Wilf?"

Opened my eyes. Startled for a moment, then remembered. She was kneeling beside my chair with a troubled look, hand on my arm. "How do you feel?" I asked.

"Humiliated," she said quietly.

"Don't."

Closed her eyes for a moment. "What kind of person *wouldn't* be humiliated?" she asked.

Didn't have an answer for that. Covered her hand with mine.

"Let's forget it," I said. Glanced at an expensive-looking time-piece on the mantel: Darkness plus two.

She caught my glance. "Guess it's too late for supper," she said.

"You still hungry?" I asked.

Gave me a doubtful look. "Yes," she said, "I suppose I still am."

"How do you feel, then?"

"Well, all right. Little bit woozy, but . . ."

"But something to eat ought to fix everything up."

"That's what I was thinking."

"Like some company?"

"Are you serious? After . . . ?"

"Of course I'm serious." I pointed to the crumbs on my empty plate. "All I had was an appetizer. Great cheese, but, well, I did come for something a bit more substantial."

"How about eggs and bacon?"

"An Imperial feast," I said, gesturing with my arms, "If I am permitted to cook."

"W-wilf, I can't let you do . . ."

"Tell it to Voot," I said with a chuckle. "Unless, of course, Nesterio would have a problem with me puttering around in his kitchen."

"In the first place," she growled, "it is *my* kitchen. And in the second, he won't be home till sometime tomorrow afternoon, believe me."

"You're serious?"

A vitriolic look passed her eyes. "Serious," she said. "Trust me."

Got to my feet; helped her up. We walked *carefully* to the kitchen. "Over there," I said, pointing to the chair in which she'd passed out earlier.

She sat.

Hadn't noticed the kitchen the first time. Like everything else I'd seen of their house, it was all expensive and hard-edged. Not at all like the soft, feminine retreat I remembered from her days as a bachelor girl. "You'll need to tell me where *everything* is," I said. "Eggs and bacon first."

"Cooler," she said, "middle shelf."

Found them. "Fry pan?"

Pointed to a cabinet. "There," she said. "Middle drawer."

Found the fry pan. Rooted in a couple of drawers near the stove and discovered everything else on my own. Took the bread to her with a knife and a bread board. "Here," I said. "Make yourself useful." I had the bacon snapping in no time and was beating the eggs when: "I can't believe you haven't walked out on me," she said.

Put down the egss; turned a slice of bacon. "Guess I'm like you," I said. "I've waited damn near thirteen years for this, too."

"Not *this*."

"Well, for *seeing you*, " I amended.

"You don't care that I got so drunk I couldn't . . . ?"

Turned more bacon. "Of course I care," I said. "But, well, somehow, I don't think that was the *normal* Claudia I saw tonight. It wasn't, was it?"

"One of the Claudias," she said, slicing bread with the over-careful movements of someone who is still considerably under the weather.

"I see," I said, vigilantly judging the bacon . . . within a click or two of perfection. "And just how many Claudias *are* there?"

"There are *two* Claudias," she said. "You've met only one— Claudia the professional."

Perfection! Took the fry pan from the heat, began forking the bacon onto a towel. "Think I've been in love with *that* Claudia much of my adult life," I said. Drained the grease;

turned down the heat while I looked at her. "Who's the other Claudia?" I asked. "The one I've never met."

"Never met her until *tonight*," she corrected.

I let the skillet cool another few moments while I thought about that. Wasn't as if she'd never been drunk with me. In the old days, we were often . . . pretty tipsy, I remembered. But *never* senseless, as she was tonight. Never. We had much better uses for our nights together than sleeping. Put the skillet back on the heat; looked at her. "Want to tell me about it?" I asked.

"You sure you want to hear?" she asked.

Nodded. "Yeah," I said. It was pretty clear she needed to tell me about it.

"You know I'm a native of Haelic here, don't you," she asked, "that I grew up right here in Atalanta?"

Poured the eggs into the fry pan, listened a moment—just right. "You told me, once," I said.

"Well, there's a lot of difference between life in Atalanta—especially *native* Atalanta—and life behind the base enclosures. More than you ever dreamed."

Thought about that while the eggs slowly cooked. *Wilf, Wilf, Wilf—you never did learn about Atalanta, did you?* Glanced at her and frowned, as if I was meeting her for the first time—again. "Tell me," I said.

"Customs," she said, "—sometimes thousands of years old."

Rarely had I seen anyone *this* serious outside of combat.

"I live in two worlds, Wilf," she said quickly, "with two sets of customs, each as foreign to the other as oil and water. And until tonight, I never tried to mix them. Thought after all these years I could get away with it smoothly. But, as you can see, I failed." She rose a little, peered into the fry pan. "You'll need to flip that," she said. "I'll wait."

She was right; the omelet was nearly ready for turning . . . *There*—now or never! Held my breath; gently raised the pan from the heat. Balanced myself. Focused everything on that pan. *This* separated the wannabes from the *true* omelet artists. Drew my arm in. Steady . . . Flipped it, while the Universe slowed and the omelet glided from the fry pan . . . rose majestically, curling end over end until . . . Caught it! Steadied it! Gentled it! Then set the fry pan back onto the heat. Kissed my fingers. Magnificent! Relaxed a moment. "I guess I don't understand what you failed this evening." I said, attempting to continue our previous conversation, "or what you tried to mix. You might have had a little too much E'lande, but, well, it isn't as if we haven't been drunk together before."

"Oh Wilf," she said. "You've never really seen native Atalanta, have you?"

"Seen what?" I asked. "Atalanta?" Couldn't figure what she was getting at.

"*Native* Atalanta," she corrected. "I've never met a real Imperial who has."

"I thought," I said, looking up, "I'd seen a lot of native Atalanta. Remember how we used to meet at Nesterios? If that's not native Atalantan, I don't know what is."

She smiled. "Have you learned to speak Atalantan?"

"You know I haven't," I said.

"Then you've missed all the substance of what you saw—and sensed," she said. "Good as you are at sensing, Wilf Brim, our native culture is so far removed from Avalon's that you never got more than a hint." She peered into the fry pan again. "I'm steady enough to bring the dishes, now," she said, getting up and moving gingerly to a large cabinet. "Use the platter next to you."

Gently placed the finished—*perfected*—omelet on the platter, incredible stoneware thing. Expensive like everything else. Arranged the bacon strips, garnished with sprigs from native millen herbs growing in a window box. Laid the platter with a flourish between two places she'd set at the table.

"It's *beautiful*!" she said, clapping her hands with a bewildered little smile. "You know, Wilf Brim," she said, elbow on the table while she propped her head with a single manicured finger, "you really *are* impossible." Then she closed her eyes. "And wonderful."

"Better not decide which till you taste the omelet," I cautioned, loading her plate before I served myself. Odd how quickly bread and cheese abandon one's stomach when something else presents itself.

She dug in, quite ladylike—but clearly very hungry.

Not much I can cook for myself. But eggs? Best in the thraggling known Universe. I dug in, too. Everything except a single crust of bread disappeared in a hurry.

At length, Claudia touched her mouth with a napkin and settled back in her chair—clearly much revived. "I don't suppose you need much telling that I enjoyed that," she said.

"All compliments are accepted with gratitude," I prompted.

She grinned. "It was absolutely magnificent."

"Thanks," I said, grinning pompously. "I thought so, too." Then I took her hand. "How are you holding up?"

"Better every moment," she said.

"I mean, time-wise," I said, carrying some of the dishes to the dishwasher.

Took my hand. "I've already had my beauty sleep," she said. "And Nesterio won't be back for a long time, so-o-o . . ."

"So-o-o?" I asked, listening to a number of Starfuries thunder over the house.

She got to her feet. "Leave the dishes," she said, leading the way back into the drawing room. "The first night we've gotten together after all those years has been a disaster—with the exception of your omelet. So I need a little time to explain. All right?"

"Well . . ."

"Listen, Wilf," she said. "I know you well enough that if you didn't feel something for me, you'd have been out of here the first click you knew I wasn't going to die. Right?"

Startled for a moment—but it was the old Claudia. "Yeah," I admitted, "probably I would have."

"Then, we'll be seeing more of each other, won't we?"

Nodded. "I hope so," I said.

"Count on it," she said. "But where years ago you saw only one side of me—a reasonably normal 'Imperial Claudia'—tonight, you got your first look at the 'Atalantan Claudia,' who sometimes acts completely outside the bounds of Imperial decorum." She looked at me carefully. "Understand, Wilf, that years ago when you and I were lovers, there was no reason for me to be anything but an 'Imperial Person' when we were together. Made things easy—normal—for you and, well, simpler for me; it's the person I still use when I'm on the base. But when I went out with Atalantans like Gorgas, I reverted to my native side, a very comfortable persona, too . . . most of the time." She paused a moment, placed her hand on mine while more Starfuries thundered overhead—clearly on takeoff power. "Probably had you and I become . . . well, a bit more . . . permanent, I should have eventually discarded that native side of me. But for one reason or another, we didn't—and I haven't. Which brings me to Gorgas Nesterio, who is one hundred percent native Atalantan—a man whose entire existence is oriented toward the Atalantan way of life. When I married him, I peripherally made a commitment to observing Atalantan conventions and social values in my home life. Not a bad commitment for a native Halacian—It's comfortable, as I've said. But quite the opposite for Imperials, I'm afraid. You got a taste tonight."

I shook my head. "You've lost me," I said.

"I'm almost finished," she said. "And unless I can make you understand about tonight—and any future evenings we may share as well—we're in for trouble."

"Never," I said.

She smiled. "Never—ever—say 'never,' my Avalonian friend. What you say tonight—my getting so drunk that any normal Imperial would have walked out on me—was quite acceptable in Atalantan society."

I started to remonstrate; she stopped me with a warning hand.

"You see, Wilf," she continued, "I made an error tonight. For the first time in all these years, I risked mixing the two cultures and got disastrous results. Somehow, I had expected that Gorgas would adhere to Imperial mores in honor of your presence tonight. Unfortunately, I misjudged. He is so in awe of you, that he could only react as an Atalantan. And believe me, Wilf Brim, *you have been honored.*"

"I don't understand," I said for the eleven millionth time.

"I know," she said. "That's why our continuing friendship will probably depend heavily on how tolerant you can be when our two cultures intersect—as they clearly will. Gorgas is a fine man, Wilf, and a wonderful, caring husband who loves me deeply. He is not a sophisticated intergalactic traveler, of course, but . . ." She shrugged. "I could have done a lot worse."

"I'm certain," I said helplessly.

"Probably you are wondering what all that has to do with three quick—large—shots of E'lande taken quickly."

Nodded.

"Wilf, Gorgas Nesterio is so impressed with you—an Admiral in the Imperial Fleet—that he couldn't handle it. At the last moment, he reverted—maybe retreated is a better term—to Atalantan male behavior, and I couldn't bear to rebuff him in front of you. He'd have lost so much face, it would have destroyed him, so I went along."

"But what was he trying to do?" I asked.

"Honor you the best way he knew how," she said.

"Honor me?" I asked. "By making you so tipsy you couldn't cook supper?"

She grimaced. "You bet," she explained. "You see, Gorgas was offering me—my body. I'm the one treasure he can extend to someone like you who, in his eyes, must be sated with things that he cannot even imagine. So far as he's concerned, we are having sex right now, and I am doing everything in my power to make it a memorable occasion for you." She smiled a little. "You should feel exceptionally honored, Wilf. He's done that only twice before."

Rolled my eyes. "Only twice?" I asked as more Starfuries thundered overhead—hardly heard them. "For the love of Voot, Claudia, how did you manage to . . . ?"

"I managed very nicely," she said, looking me directly in the eye. "Very nicely. One of them made a point of complimenting Gorgas afterward. Don't forget, I was the other Claudia, and I really did everything I could think of—including," she said with a little blush, "some of the things you and I invented together, Wilf Brim."

"My God," I gasped, completely flabbergasted.

"I was being a good wife," she said, "as I was tonight. It made Gorgas very happy and proud—and that was the point of the whole thing, wasn't it?"

Squeezed my eyes closed a moment. "I suppose I should have taken advantage of the opportunity, then," I groaned.

"You'd have devastated me, had you done that," she said.

Then she smiled ironically. "However, if Gorgas ever discovers we *didn't,* it'll be he who is devastated."

"You mean," I said, grimacing, "I've got to make a fuss about . . ."

"Please," she said. "Make up anything you like. Remember some of the things we did years ago, if you don't want to lie to him."

Was about to say something about that when suddenly blinding lights strobed through the windows, startling me out of a year's growth.

"The space forts!" Claudia cried out. "We're under attack!" Moments later, the strobing doubled, then redoubled, as local surface-based disruptors began to fire accompanied by ground-shaking thunder.

Through the din, I head the HoloPhone chiming.

Claudia grabbed it, hit the ENABLE . . . globular display came up dark—in PRIVATE mode. Barbousse's voice over the din: "Admiral Brim, are you there?"

"Yeah—I'm here!"

"I've got a skimmer for you two, Admiral," he yelled. "Downstairs at the door!"

Then—quite abruptly—the windows came bursting into the drawing room while the world around us exploded in an impossible burst of light and noise . . .

Chapter 4

GONTOR

33 Heptad, 52014

Imperial Fleet Base, Atalanta, Hador-Haelic

Looked around the conference table again. "Any questions?" I asked. "Anybody not sure what's expected of us?"

No one opened his or her mouth. They still looked stunned. My little Morning and a half meeting had gradually grown in size until by Brightness it included Lt. Commander Jill Tompkins, the new Chief of Operations; Commander Burton LaSalle, Space Officer; Lt. Terry Westover, SP Commandant; and Claudia as Harbor Master; plus our original cast of four. None looked as if they'd had enough sleep, especially Claudia, who was clearly fighting a headache, as well as sharing the others' surprise at the base's secret new mission.

"Right, then," I said by way of dismissal, "let's be at it. We've got a lot of work to do and very little time to do it."

"As well as doing it in secret," Williams added. Plainly, clandestine projects weren't his cup of cvceese', but he'd signed on like the good StarSailor he was.

Claudia furtively rolled bloodshot eyes at me as everyone filed out. Clearly, our "friendship" was well-known throughout the base, so I took her aside. "You're all right, now?" I asked.

She smiled ruefully. "Except for a monumental hangover," she said, shaking her head. "That and having a Dampier crash into the house next door."

"I was thinking more about the latter," I said, trying my best to avoid taking her hand. We'd had a close call as I carried her bodily to the skimmer, but that was part and parcel of living in a war zone. She and Nesterio—I supposed I'd always call him by his surname—would have to replace some glazing in the new house, but it was at least standing—with both its occupants among the living—which was a lot more than could be said for their late neighbor's house next door.

She reached out for a moment, then withdrew her hand with a little brush of embarrassment. "You'll forgive me, then?" she asked.

"There's nothing to forgive," I said, *"unless* we can do it again soon."

"Voot's beard," she whispered with a bogus look of alarm, "you mean I've got to go through *that* again?"

"Well," I said with a little smile, "perhaps your husband won't want to share you so soon."

"That wasn't nice," she said with a little smile.

"Damn straight, it wasn't," I said.

"Now, Wilf," she averred, "remember the two Claudias."

"I've remembered one for a lot of years, now," I said.

"I shall try to ensure you see the other as little as possible," she promised. She looked around—the room was empty now—kissed me on the cheek. "Take care on your trip, Wilf," she whispered, then left before I could say another word.

After that, Barbousse and I had approximately two metacycles to pack and board the bender that would take us for our first look at Gontor.

Three days of cramped, uncomfortable travel aboard a cloaked bender, and we were there. In spite of what I'd learned from Ambrose's book, I was still taken aback by the sheer size of the huge, perfectly spherical asteroid hanging over me in the starry darkness of space—and its incredible, smooth-rock surface dimly reflecting the harsh rays of Cyjix-19. The ancient fortress—at the edge of an immense asteroid shoal—looked as if it had been *cast* rather than formed. I'd read that originally the great rock had been more than ten c'lenyts in diameter. The builders, whoever they were, had studded the surface—apparently at random—with enormous, jet black metallic structures, most of them circumscribed by high, circular walls and ringed with what certainly looked like colossal disruptor cannon emplacements—great crystalline spheres plated over for nearly a hemisphere where they were pierced by two slender, finned rods that must have reached two hundred irals in length. All of these surface features were apparently connected by c'lenyts-long channels of what appeared to be armored cable, broken here and there by fields of extravagant antenna arrays. The channel networks met at opposite poles in giant, towering structures—one white, the other crimson—constructed of odd-sized boxes inset with glazed apertures and bristling at the top with articulated arms of various length. Each tower appeared to be built on a large black disk, raised from the rocky surface on white pillars that looked for all the galaxy as if they were some sort of energy insulators. And each disk was surrounded by five concentric circles of the spherical "disruptor emplacements." Fascinating place, if totally baffling and totally without power. As far as the eye could see, nothing moved; nothing glowed—anywhere.

I was at the controls of the bender's launch with Barbousse in the right seat. Aft, five of our twenty SPs peered through the canopy in awe.

"Wow!"

"Will ya look't *that!*"

"Voot's beard—'j ever see one of those before?"

Chuckling, I let them prattle on. Actually, the view *was* pretty exciting; even Barbousse's eyebrows were raised behind the visor of his battlesuit. According to my old book—actually some of its excellent holographic illustrations—one of the citadel's four main portals was located within the circular structure I was fast approaching. Looked like it. From close up, it took the form of a large, circular building—call it a pillbox—topped by more of the complex antenna arrays. An angular tower jutted vertically from one side to an altitude of perhaps sixty irals. The latter was topped by a large, glassed-in room. As I circled, it became apparent that nearly a quarter of the building's circumference was fronted by a section of lighter-hued materials that accommodated some thirty massive doors of various sizes. The complex was surrounded by more "disruptor emplacements" that also enclosed an area blackened and pitted as if it had been the sole target of a terrific attack. I guessed it was a landing field for the ancient fusion "propulsors" in almost universal use prior to Sheldon Travis's renowned discovery of the HyperDrive.

"What do you say we set down over there by that collection of smaller doors?" I asked.

"Looks good to me, Admiral," Barbousse said, his voice hollow in my headset. "From what I read in the book, that should be some sort of entrance for people or at least manned vehicles." He flipped through the ancient plastic pages. "Says here some of them's been jacked open."

Checked the gravity below—registered .19 Standard Imperial Gravity Units (SIGUs) on the meter—no more than normal for this sort of mass. Nodded, slowed the launch, and brought us to a near-vertical touchdown some fifty irals from an almost-whimsical collection of spherical objects on slender masts that fronted this quadrant of the building. Switched the 'Gravs to LOW IDLE and set the entry hatch to OPEN—don't know why I had a feeling we might need to leave in a hurry. Clambered out—more like "floated out"—first, followed by Barbousse and the SPs, two of them hauling a five-day survival pack. The others were burdened by new MK-9A MRMs, microradiation meters that could detect the slightest occurrence of biological life—or anything else with similar emissions for that matter—through five hundred irals of solid mass.

We peered about to get our surface bearings, then set off, loping past the spheres-on-sticks almost as if we were in flight. As advertised, a number of the doors had been crudely jacked open over the years by archaeological expeditions. Blackened and gouged sections attested to numerous—completely unsuccessful—attempts to burn them open.

"Looks like the ancients knew a thing or two about armor plating," I observed. Wondered why the explorers didn't concentrate on discovering how to *open* the doors before spending so much time trying to burn them through, but then, I was only a simple Helmsman. . . .

"Strong, those, Admiral," Barbousse agreed with a chuckle. "They must have left the place unlocked when they vacated, 'cause I can't see tryin' to pick their locks would do much good, either,"

We stopped for a moment while the men checked their MRMs—nearly zero levels—then switched our helmet lights to BRIGHT and stepped under the door into what appeared to be a colossal receiving room for goods. Huge trams hung cold and dead from an overhead network of switches and guide ways that disappeared into circular tunnels clearly designed for other than human transit. Barbousse and I checked the book.

"Next one," Barbousse said.

I nodded agreement.

The next door—actually a *row* of human-sized doors behind a long, panel of sliding, overlapping armor places that had long ago been forced open by some sort of hydraulic ram—led into a spacious, human-sized, human-appointed lobby. A fleet of smaller, spindle-shaped trams waited in mechanical patience for passengers who had departed the galaxy millennia in the past. The overhead network of tramways from which they hung also exited into tunnels, but evidently, these had been more attractive to archaeologists, for they had been at least partially diagrammed. Ambrose had given me an excellent set of maps. On the way over from Atalanta, I'd downloaded the information in everyone's battlesuit, so it could be projected on the inside of our helmet visors.

We parleyed for a few moments, then the three SPs with MRMs bounded into the tunnels that seemed to pass through the most area. The other two SPs remained on guard at the surface, while Barbousse and I made our way through the tunnel leading to a station near the site of the "power chambers."

Took us nearly two metacycles to get there, walking single

file along the amazingly smooth bore of the tunnel. The guide-way—a complex extrusion with a cross section that must have resembled a five-pointed star—was suspended only a few irals above our heads on peglike stanchions imbedded into the rock itself. At a point I estimated was nearly halfway to our destination, we passed a blackened section of tunnel that bore deep gouges and marks of a major wreck, perhaps a head-on collision. Clearly, the ancients were no more pro-tected from cock-ups than we "moderns." Somehow, I never shook the ridiculous feeling that the next moment we'd see a fast-approaching headlight from one of those trams back at the surface terminal and . . . *pfft*, good-bye buttocks.

As advertised, the fifth station we came to matched the hologram I projected on the inside of my faceplate—complete with door that had been forced open by some sort of hy-draulic jack. Archaeologists—at least *these* archaeologists—I decided, seemed a lot better at ruining things than preserving them for history. But then, what did I, a simple Helmsman, know about archaeology? Still, the damage irritated me.

Following a series of images projected on our helmet vi-sors, we made our way through a complex maze of corridors and ramps to three cavernous vaulted rooms—so high that the powerful beams of our headlamps scarcely lighted their great domes. The rooms had been hollowed out at the apexes of a right triangle and were connected by great excavated passages big enough to accommodate an extensive distribu-tion grid. Everything was completely empty, stripped (in my estimation) of the generators that once powered the huge citadel, but the connecting grid passages contained what I took to be attachment points that would serve replacement power sources—as if the departing engineers expected to re-turn some day with newer, better equipment.

A great deal more interesting than these—except for

size—was what appeared to be a whole section of connected rooms dedicated to energy management. In one of them, three rows of double-sided consoles looked as though they'd received little attention at all from intruders (archaeological or otherwise) during the millennia since they'd last been shut down. The few manual controls, such as they were, appeared to be made for humanlike hands, but since most of the console's surfaces were made up of a dark crystalline substance, I could discover no readouts. Probably, they had been generated externally by the vast array of logic engines I'd read were located elsewhere in the fort.

Found Barbousse studying a wall chart so large that his helmet light illuminated only small sections at a time. I remembered it in the background of a HoloPic in the book Ambrose had given me. "What d'you make of that?" I asked, joining him.

"Don't rightly know, Admiral," the Chief said. "Looks like some sort of flowchart."

"How about a network diagram?" I suggested, adding my helmet light to his.

"Something like that," he agreed, distractedly. "Energy *distribution,* maybe." He pointed to a large, central node—represented by three circles joined into a triangle—from which all the major trunks emanated, then spread out to become the network. "I'll bet this stands for the three rooms we came through back there."

I nodded.

"Got a hunch, then," Barbousse said thoughtfully, "that a team of half-decent power engineers could return energy to this whole fort without much trouble at all. After that, getting a lot of this old equipment back in service oughtn't to be too difficult." He put his hands on his hips and nodded to himself as if he were giving a lecture. "Except for what the archaeologists touched, nothing much has been disturbed since the place was abandoned. And clearly this dark, airless environment hasn't supported much deterioration anywhere."

Made sense to me, although I didn't consider myself much of an engineer. Oh, I could understand everything I needed to know about the starships I flew—probably a little *more* than I needed to know after all these years of flying. But Barbousse was another story indeed. He'd studied under some of the greatest Sodeskayan professors alive and had become a pretty good systems engineer. I watched him put his gloves on his hips and scan the ancient diagram again and again, passing his helmet light repeatedly over parts of the surface as if he were brushing on a coat of glaze. Finally, he activated his suit's recorder pack. "Think I'll send some HoloPics to our boffins at the PARC Memorial Power Labs on Asturious-Proteus," he said. "If I'm right, we might be able to get this place humming with a lot less effort than anyone thinks."

Metacycles later, the seven of us rejoined on the surface as planned, pronouncing the great space fort as benign as the MRMs could discern after an initial scan. Reports from the orbiting bender indicated that nothing on the surface had changed—or moved—while we were below, either. So far, so good, I thought—keeping in mind an important corollary to Voot's Law stating that the rate of things going disastrously wrong increase in direct proportion to the apparent ease of the job.

Straightaway we began a shuttle service with the bender's other launches, off-loading the fifteen SPs, who would remain behind as the advance party. While this was going on, the rest of us began an inspection of the citadel's surface facilities, which turned out to be just as impressive as the ones buried deep beneath our feet. We found vast hangars and storage rooms everywhere, all clearly constructed to cache large items—and protect them with staggeringly massive armor. None were locked from the outside: however, all inside doors leading below the surface *from* them were firmly secured. I had no idea what these huge spaces were originally created to house, but they were perfect for items like Starfuries and battle crawlers—to name only a few—that could never fit through the underground tunnels.

Those of us who were returning to Avalon in the bender spent the night aboard, then got an early start for the surface to see how the others had fared. I had to chuckle: the hardy souls who'd volunteered for this crazy duty seemed to love it! They'd already connected their little survival globes into a tent city of sorts and were serving up a delicious brew of cvceese' as we stepped through one of the airlocks. I was just about to lope over and investigate one of the big disruptor emplacements when a call came through on the guard channel from the ship's COMM center.

"Eyes-only KA'PPA message for Admiral Brim—Flash priority."

"Thanks," I sent to the ship. "I'm on my way back right now." Turned to Barbousse. "Coming up?" I asked.

"Think I'll look around a little more, Admiral," he said.

"See you aboard, then," I said, loping off for our launch. Twenty cycles later, I was in the ship's KA'PPA room.

2IVEQHG14YUYKLWNJV E32UY85215FC
[TOP SECRET * SAPPHIRE*]

FROM: J. WILLIAMS, CAPTAIN, ATALANTA FLEET BASE

TO: W. A. BRIM, RADM, ABOARD BENDER B-908

1. AVALON INTELLIGENCE INDICATES TOROND CONVOY OF 8 FAST TRANSPORTS (TROOPS AND

EQUIPMENT) PLUS ESCORT WILL LIFT FOR OCCUPIED
FLUVANNA IN 12 STANDARD DAYS.

2. ADMIRALTY MESSAGE TODAY "SUGGESTS"
INTERCEPTION FROM ATALANTA.

3. REQUEST INSTRUCTIONS.

[END TOP SECRET * SAPPHIRE*]
21VEQHG14YUYKLWNJV E32UY85215FC

It was the most polite "get-your-butt-back-here-and-take-charge" message I'd ever received. Pretty clear the Chief's network was right on the money—Jim Williams was an absolute jewel. I KA'PPAed him to tell his new Space Officer about our latest "challenge" from Headquarters Avalon, then ordered everyone on the return flight to board immediately.

Barbousse was on the last launch from the surface. Said he'd been back to the mysterious power chambers to record more data. Good to see the Chief so absorbed in this kind of work; he'd labored mightily for his education.

Same uneventful return trip Atalanta—with one worrisome exception. We sighted fully *eight* long-range patrol ships from The Torond along the middle third of our supposedly unused route. Far too many, in my way of thinking, to be where they were by mere happenstance. Clearly, they weren't looking for benders running in cloaked mode. None was transmitting the N-rays that—I'd earlier explained to one of the SPs—could smother our ship's computational ability to detect incoming radiation anywhere on the hull, then duplicate and broadcast it from an obverse position in precisely the same direction as received.

But the very fact that so many ships were patrolling an area of space containing so little of *normal* interest reminded me how tenuous information security becomes in wartime. I had little doubt that the Toronders and Leaguers both had a pretty good idea about our plans for Gontor; after all, why else would they have done away with Deighton? Gave me real problems about how I was supposed to secure the ancient fort, or, for that matter, how we'd transport a whole invasion force to it. Certainly we'd never accomplish the latter by moving twenty or twenty-five SPs at a time in benders!

But one thing at a time. I'd at least *started* the securing process, which would now proceed at its own speed, no matter how hard I pushed. Meanwhile, I still had to worry about the first convoy that would lift from Avalon in eight Standard Days, bound for Braltar, then Atalanta, and then Gontor. As usual, they'd given me a secondary job whose priority seemed to exceed any of the primaries. Ah, for life in the Fleet! So say the recruiters. . . .

"Figured you might not have enough to keep you busy out there," Williams shouted as I stepped from the bender's brow, breathing fresh air for the first time in more than a Standard Week. "I sent that message so you wouldn't be bored, Admiral." He chuckled. "Bet you couldn't wait to get home."

"Wouldn't wager too much on *that* particular bet," I replied with a wry grin as I watched Barbousse running to catch a tram for the KA'PPA center with his data. "We've got some real problems." I hadn't the foggiest notion how to secure a space lane between Atalanta and Gontor. Figured I'd base a flight or two of Starfuries on Gontor, itself—if I could get 'em there. But even then I'd still be faced with an awful full-day span in the middle of the trip when the transports would travel without escort—or at least any kind of killer-ship escort. And of course, there was The Torond's supply convoy we were supposed to destroy in our spare time. Thank Voot I had people like LaSalle who could take care of small details like that.

Climbed into a skimmer with Williams, and we headed back toward Headquarters.

"What was it like out there?" he asked.

"Pretty impressive," I replied. "Perfect place to collect an invasion force. And launch it. But that's not the problem."

"Getting it there?" Williams suggested.

"Getting it there *in one piece,*" I amended with a grimace. "Our bender took three days traveling to Gontor moving roughly at the same speed as those convoys coming from Avalon. If we don't come up with some long-range escorts before then, they'll be traveling two full days without escorts at the far end—not only between here and Gontor but between Braltar and here. They'll be thraggling shredded."

Williams nodded agreement. "What about those Carescrians we were promised?"

"Even if they got here today, they've no combat experience." I shrugged. First things first—and what I had to do before anything else could happen was fortify Gontor. "Have any luck lining up some transport to Gontor?" I asked.

"I haven't," he said with a grin, "but I think maybe your friend the Harbor Master has," he said. "Looks as if she's scored a real find."

"Tell me."

"Fella name of Delacroix—Cameron Delacroix, I think. Comes from one of those little one-and-two planet 'parishes' that used to belong to Effer'wyck. Claims he has a hot ship with plenty of cargo space and a crew that can get in and out of just about anywhere."

I raised an eyebrow; claims like that were pretty common anywhere independent crews gathered. Especially in major ports like Atalanta. Still, Claudia had been around for nearly as long as I—and had *a lot* more experience with civilian space operations. At the moment, we were passing the civilian Headquarters building, so . . . "Jim, why don't we stop off here and ask if she can see us?"

He grinned again. "Timed it perfectly, I did," he said, pulling to a halt in a VISITORS ONLY parking place close to the door.

We arrived outside Claudia's office at the same time a meeting seemed to be breaking up. "Admiral Brim, Captain Williams," a secretary asked as if she'd known us for years—I supposed Cottshall could perform the same magic— "what can I do for you?"

"Admiral," Williams said, "this is Adele Hough, who runs Ms. Valemont-Nesterio's life during duty hours."

She stood. "Admiral," she said, offering her hand. "I've heard such excellent things about you for years. What a pleasure."

Flustered, I felt myself blush. "Er, thank you," I stammered. "Claudia always was too kind."

"Somehow, I doubt that, Admiral," she said, seating herself primly. "I take it you'd like to see her."

"If she's got a few moments."

Adele nodded, glanced at a display. "Somehow, I'd bet she does." She touched her display. "Two military gentlemen to see you, Ms. Harbor Master." She listened to a hidden earpiece, then smiled. "Yes, ma'am," she said with a chuckle. "They *appear* to be gentlemen, at any rate."

Momentarily, Claudia appeared at the door to her office. "Well," she said to Adele, rubbing her chin as if deliberating, "close enough. I'll vouch for Captain Williams, at any rate."

Williams took my arm. "I'll personally vouch for the Admiral," he asserted.

"Please come in, then," she said, motioning us inside. "No visitors, please," in an aside to Adele.

Her office was absolutely businesslike—a place for serious commerce—yet somehow it was *also* thoroughly feminine. A lot like the Claudia I'd known over the years—or, I supposed, the "Imperial Claudia" she'd described to me. "Jim tells me you've got a ship for us," I said, pulling up a chair while Adele poured steaming mugs of cvceese'.

"Never *were* a big one for small talk, were you, Admiral?" she admonished.

Felt my cheeks burn. "Sorry Cla . . . er, Ms. Harbor Master," I stammered.

She laughed. "Claudia's fine, Wilf," she said. "And you're simply being Wilf Brim, so that's fine, too." She glanced at Williams. "I assume, Captain, you've noticed he becomes rather focused at times."

"Never noticed a thing, Ms. Claudia," Williams said in his best down-home decorum.

Shook my head. "I think I may be sick," I groaned.

"Not when you see the ship I've located," Claudia said.

"The one you told Jim about?"

She nodded.

"Sounds too good to be true," I suggested.

"Possibly," she said with a shrug, "but the ship's brochure certainly looks promising. And there's something about her master that says, well . . . 'daring.' It's a look in his eye, I guess." She shrugged. "Something you'd have to see for yourself. Interested?"

Didn't have to think long about that. "You bet," I said. "I'll go look at anything you think looks promising. Where is it?"

"If you'd like some company," she said, "I'll help you find it myself."

"When?" I asked.

"Right now," she said. "I've just had a long project review postponed."

"Now?" I asked doubtfully. "I don't know. I haven't even *seen* my desk in nearly a week.

"Talked with Cottshall as you landed, Admiral," Williams interjected. "*He* assures me he's checked with Chief Barbousse, who agrees finding a transport is a lot hotter than anything waiting in your queue."

"All right," I said, "I'm game. You coming along?"

"Well," he asserted, "since you and Ms. Claudia know a lot more about starships—and their drivers—than I'll ever learn at this age, I think I may just mosey back to Fleet Headquarters, where I can be at least marginally useful." He turned to Claudia. "I assume you can supply transportation for the Admiral, Ms. Harbor Master."

"Probably can scare up a spare skimmer somewhere," she assured him.

"I'm on, then," I said—as if they'd left me a choice.

"Good," Williams said, getting to his feet. "Myself, I've got more work than I can handle already, so I'll be on my way directly. See you when you're finished."

"Put out a 'grab call' on your summoner if you need me," I called to his fast-receding back, then glanced at Claudia. "Does it seem to you that we've been railroaded, or something?" I asked.

She blushed a little and nodded.

"Why?" I asked. "It's almost as if . . ."

"I don't think we were, well . . . *discreet* as we might have been all those years ago," she interrupted.

"I don't believe it," I said.

"Unfortunately, it's true," she replied. "According to Adele, we're *still* seen as an item by a lot of old-timers."

I laughed, blushed a little myself. "Yeah," I whispered. "I suppose that *could* happen." Suddenly I was struck by a memory I simply couldn't keep to myself. "Claudia," I whispered, "will you ever forget the night we got caught on a mat in that experimental LifeGlobe?"

She reddened and touched my arm. "Wilf Brim," she said with an embarrassed little laugh, "I was thinking about the same thing myself." She shook her head, then got the damnedest smile. "How I ever let you talk me out of *all* my clothes. . . . My God, I think the whole base got a good look at me—absolutely in flagrante delicto—with damn near everything they wanted to see pointed right out the hatch."

"Well, I was pointed the same way, if you'll remember," I whispered in mock reproach.

"Oh sure," she replied. "But the part of *you* they wanted to see was quite well hidden most of the time. I can vouch for that." She rolled her eyes as she laughed. "Little thraggling wonder people still think of us as lovers."

"Bet that makes Gorgas happy," I observed.

She shrugged. "I doubt that he gives it much thought—or credence, for that matter," she said. "This base and all that goes with it are, well, not very *real* to him. Besides," she added, "it *did* happen a few years ago."

"Yeah," I said, quashing a number of conflicting emotions that were rearing their various heads when they shouldn't. "Ancient history."

"Yes," she echoed, "ancient . . ." Suddenly, she shook her head vigorously. "Adele," she called without using the intercom. "Check on Captain Delacroix for me, please. See if he's on board that *Yellow Bird* of his."

"Yes *ma'am!*"—through the door again.

We stood in embarrassed silence until Adele replied, "He's aboard. Shall I tell him you're on your way?"

Claudia glanced at me and raised her perfect eyebrows.

I nodded.

"Tell him fifteen cycles," she ordered. Before we left her office, she stopped me and took my hand. "We *did* have a good time those days, didn't we?" she whispered, still blushing.

"The best," I assured her. "The very best—*ever.*" I meant it. . . .

Claudia could find her way most anywhere in Atalanta, but we'd twice found ourselves at odds with an official map before we finally drew up beside *Yellow Bird.* The ship was moored at the end of a polluted, odoriferous backwater canal, practically hidden from any distant glance by destitute groups of goods houses in one of the meanest sections of the harbor. Close on, though, she stood out like a sore thumb among her near-derelict neighbors. Long, powerful-looking, and sleek as a game fish, she'd clearly been built for high-speed, atmospheric work—in short, the smuggling trades. Her builder had placed huge Drive and SpinGrav units in slim, teardrop nacelles mounted at the ends of short, radically swept 'midships sponsons. Two small, razor-thin fins rose in a wide "vee" near the ship's stinglike tail. Overall, she looked less like a transport than one of the racing ships I'd flown between wars for the Mitchell Trophy. But her sheer size—at least fifteen hundred irals overall, I estimated—put her forever outside that arcane class of spacecraft. Smoothest design I'd seen in years; even the vaunted hulls of our Starfuries were disfigured by turrets and disruptors. Some third of the way aft, an angry-looking bridge rose glaring from the needlelike bow, then fared back into the smooth circular cross section of the hull as it reached its widest point. To me, this particular yellow bird was more of a raptor than any other breed.

"You haven't uttered a word since we turned onto the wharf," Claudia said, breaking into my fascinated reverie. "Can I take it you're interested?"

"You bet," I assured her, still scanning the ship's long, elegant lines as I opened the door. "Never seen anything like her anywhere." Helped her down from the driver's seat. Hot afternoon sun was nearly blinding. "What's the owner like?" I asked.

She laughed a little. "Not sure how to describe him," she admitted. "But he seems to fit the ship pretty well."

"Must be quite a guy," I offered.

"That, Wilf Brim," she said, "may be the greatest understatement you've ever uttered."

As I spoke, a tall, painfully slim figure—dressed in a white linen suit and clamping a sinuous, black cigarette in the corner of his mouth—appeared in the shade of the boarding hatch, arms reflectively folded, regarding us as if we were a pair of domestics he might deign to engage. Clearly, he'd paired us with Adele's call, for he motioned us to approach—with all the aplomb of a sovereign bidding mendicants approach his throne. Beneath a high forehead and black hair that grayed at the temples, his face was slim, as was his long, patrician nose and the thin, black mustache he wore. He had sensitive lips and a pointed jaw embellished by a sharply trimmed goatee. As we advanced, I saw his gray eyes—far out of proportion with the rest of his features—sparkle with intellect and perhaps a certain deprecating humor. Here, I considered, was a gentleman who could fit himself into any epoch—or *no* epoch. He was the living embodiment of every wily space gambler I'd ever encountered, in fact *or* in fiction.

I took Claudia's arm and we stopped a few irals short of the end of the brow. "Captain Delacroix?" I asked as a rogue breeze carried the aromatic bouquet of his cigarette past my nose.

"At your service, Admiral Brim," he said in a deep, musical voice, and made a slight bow.

I nodded in return—we of the Imperial Fleet are forbidden to bow under any circumstances. "This is Harbor Master Valemont-Nesterio," I said. "We'd like permission to board your ship."

Delacroix nodded. "I shall count it as an honor," he said, offering his arm to Claudia, then leading the way to the ship's small lobby.

Felt myself smile as I followed them through the hatch—I'd never been deprived of a woman's arm so smoothly in my life. Inside, the boarding lobby was small, very small actually, but lavishly appointed, smelling of wood polish and the rich carpeting that cushioned my steps. It was a place where large sums of money might change hands in return for risky, and dangerous missions, most of which would be on the far side of "legal." In the background, I could hear— "feel" was a better word—the faint bass thunder of what promised to be huge power chambers. Clearly, Delacroix kept his ship ready for swift—unplanned—lift-offs. Two huge, bearded men with the enormous biceps of professional k'ito wrestlers stood watchfully on either side of the door that led to the interior of the ship. They were dressed as stewards, but never took their eyes from their captain. Delacroix offered us seats on a very expensive-looking couch; Claudia shook her head. "The cargo compartments first, please, Mr. Delacroix," she said, disengaging her arm from his. "Then, I think Admiral Brim will want to see the bridge."

"But of course," Delacroix said, glancing at me with an almost-invisible nod of abdication. "Please follow me," he said, leading us through an inner hatch and into a busy corridor.

After a considerable excursion forward, during which we were shadowed at a respectful distance by two men who appeared to be ship's officers, Delacroix led us through a hatch and into . . . "Wow!" I exclaimed . . . a perfectly cavernous cargo compartment—large enough to stow three pairs of Starfuries loaded nose to stern plus a tremendous amount of miscellaneous cargo packed among them.

Delacroix nodded proudly as his footsteps echoed hollowly in the vast chamber. "I take it you approve, Admiral," he said quietly.

"If she'll lift all the cargo a space like this can hold, she's quite a ship," I said, peering around in admiration.

"She has her limits," Delacroix replied, "but I trust you will find she can lift ample mass for your purposes."

I looked into his eyes—he met my gaze honestly. "I think I believe you, Mr. Delacroix," I said.

"Thank you, Admiral," he said with a strange little smile. "A mutual friend recently assured me you would have no trouble deducing *Yellow Bird*'s capabilities. She referred to you as a . . ." he frowned momentarily, " 'natural spaceman,' I believe."

"A mutual friend?" I asked, wondering where this Effer'wyckean might have run into a mutual friend. I'd spent so much time in the Fleet, it often seemed as if I had no other acquaintances outside its rather narrow confines. At that moment, a small woman dressed in a flight suit appeared in a doorway and made a signal to Delacroix.

He winced. "A thousand pardons, Admiral, Ms. Harbor Master," he said with a little bow, "but I must immediately tend to an important situation." He quickly turned to our escorts. "Engles, Carthin," he ordered, "you will please escort the Admiral and Ms. Harbor Master to the flight bridge." Then, without another word, he turned on his heel and disappeared down a companionway.

Frowning, Claudia and I followed the two men onto an ascending companionway. The spacious flight bridge, which we reached only after more protracted walking, was nothing like the cramped warships to which I'd grown accustomed. It was at least twenty irals wide, with two roomy, comfortable-looking helms and a navigator's station situated directly behind the forward Hyperscreens. Aft of those were a massive systems station and two communications consoles, backed by three consoles that Carthin asserted were configured for cargo control. Clearly, *Bird* was equipped with the latest in autoloading and unloading. Made sense. She probably didn't spend much time in large, metropolitan harbors like Atalanta.

After a short time, Delacroix rejoined us at a small, round table that—by edict, to all appearances—inhabits the aft bridge of every civilian starship in existence. "Well, Admiral, Ms. Harbor Master," he asked with obvious pride, "what do you think of my *Yellow Bird* now?"

"Most impressive, Captain," I remarked—and I meant it.

"Thank you, Admiral," he said, his nod summoning a small, powerfully built steward. "Ms. Harbor Master, may I offer a libation, perhaps?" he asked.

"Er, cvceese', thank you," Claudia replied with a blush that told me volumes about what she thought of Delacroix.

"Admiral?" he asked solicitously.

"I'll have the same, Captain," I said—somehow liking the man before I'd even got a chance to know him. Something told me we'd been cut from the same cloth. For a moment, I wondered who our mutual friend might be, but left the question to another time when I wasn't so pressed with things to do.

Clearly, Delacroix picked up on my sense of urgency, for he got right down to business. "Admiral," he began, glancing rather fondly at Claudia, "Harbor Master Valemont-Nesterio has been kind enough to inform me that you are in the market for some high-speed transportation."

"Looks as if I've come to the right place, doesn't it?" I replied.

"Then you like the appearance of *Yellow Bird* too," he said with a flicker of pride in his eyes—*deserved* pride, in my opinion.

"Of course," I replied. "She looks magnificent. If she flies that way, you've got a masterpiece on your hands."

He smiled, glancing appraisingly at Claudia for a moment. "She flies much better," he said.

Somehow I wasn't surprised.

"I assume," he added, "you and perhaps the Harbor Master will want to prove this for yourself by flying her."

I shook my head and glanced at Claudia—who looked as if she'd *love* to go aloft. Wasn't certain whether the attraction was *Yellow Bird* or Delacroix, but I strongly suspected the latter. "Claudia?" I asked.

Suddenly, she blushed. "Oh, no, er, Mr. Delacroix," she stammered. "I only located your ship for Admiral Brim. I am no Helmsman."

"Perhaps you would enjoy a ride?" he persisted.

"Thank you, Captain, but . . ." she hesitated a moment, "no. I simply won't have time." Now, she was *really* blushing.

I wondered what it must be like to have quite *that* much masculine charisma to manifest. *Godlike*, I termed it, with a twinge of jealousy. Claudia was as worldly a woman as they made, yet this Delacroix had her flustered as a schoolgirl.

"A pity," he replied, then turned to me.

"And you, Admiral," he asked. "Will you fly with me?"

"Much as I'd love that," I said, "I simply have no time, either. Besides, I don't plan to be aboard any of the flights you may undertake for us. And at this point I emphasize the word *may.*"

"How will you evaluate us, then?" he asked in obvious surprise.

"I'm willing to pay for one or two short, local flights," I said, "during which you and your crew will demonstrate your capabilities in conditions that simulate actual mission parameters—at least the important ones."

"But *you* will not be aboard?"

"That is correct," I said. "However, I shall be quite adequately represented by people who can evaluate your overall performance as well as I—probably even better, because I'm already so impressed with your ship. *Yellow Bird,* herself, is only *part* of my needs. It's an ability to accomplish the *whole* mission that interests me, not just piloting a sweet-flying starship."

Delacroix held his cigarette between his thumb and first three fingers, staring at it in silence for a considerable time. Once, he looked up at Claudia and smiled. Then he seemed to reach a conclusion and nodded with a curious little smile. "Admiral," he said, "bring on your experts . . ."

Once Barbousse briefed me on the current situation at the base—everything "urgent," nothing unusual—I set him to working out a demonstration schedule with Delacroix. Then I began worrying about a strike force to counter The Torond's reinforcement convoy, scheduled to lift in some eleven Standard Days, according to our best intelligence estimates.

Luckily, Burt LaSalle, Williams's new Space Officer, hadn't been sitting on his hands since he got my KA'PPA message from Gontor three days ago. After studying the situation, he had determined that the Toronders' convoy would almost certainly pass well within range of our Atalanta Starfuries. Clearly, if they suspected trouble, it would be a simple matter for them to detour out of our range, but since we had only just begun getting the base back on a military footing after Admiral Summers's disastrous reign, they'd feel no particular threat coming from what was still nearly an inactive base. Additionally, Avalon's intelligence indicated they were in a hurry to land this large force on Fluvanna before they lost the initiative.

Therefore, with great caution, LaSalle had immediately started carrying out what he simply called "defensive exercises" in full view of anyone who wanted to observe—especially the disguised reconnaissance ships from The Torond that showed up nearly every day.

He'd quickly cobbled together a makeshift "convoy" from the few small transports assigned to the base, then bolstered it with a number of itinerant civilian cargo ships stuck in the harbor since the beginning of hostilities. The latter were more than glad to have some income. Next, he'd designated twenty of our Starfuries as "attackers" and five more Starfuries plus eight of our older—nonetheless potent—Defiants as "defenders." After this, he announced in secret (depending on it quickly leaking back to The Torond through the cargo-ship crews) that he was training the latter for a role as convoy escorts. In reality, his primary purpose was exercising the twenty Starfury "attackers" in preparation for their assault on the Toronders' Fluvanna-bound convoy.

Relieved that someone was attending to at least one of my immediate problems, I turned what remained of my energies to the apparently near-hopeless problem of *really* escorting our own convoys. Realistically, the word "hopeless" was little more than a euphemism for "impossible." Our Starfuries and Defiants simply hadn't the range to escort much farther than a Standard Day out from the base. Oh, we *could* get more range from them by disabling most of their offensive systems, as we had done ferrying them from Braltar to Atalanta. But the very first dogfight following our arrival—the one I'd rashly led with our ships still rigged for ferrying— proved that under really determined attack, we'd likely lose the convoy ships *as well as* the Starfury escorts. They'd be sacrifices rather than battle losses. And I didn't believe in sacrifices of any kind, especially where Imperial Star-Sailors—or my own highly cherished hide—were concerned.

Unfortunately, I still had a responsibility to do what I could for the convoys . . . something. Found myself pacing back and forth in my office. Thought about attacks on convoys—the kind LaSalle was practicing even as I helplessly paced my office. Since he couldn't very well shoot down the friendly transports in his cobbled "convoy," what he was *really* practicing out there was the destruction of *escorts*. Without them, the transport could move freely. Something there, but what? I scratched my head. . . .

Suddenly it all came to me in a rush. Of course! If I couldn't knock out The Torond's attack ships *while* they were going after the convoys, perhaps I ought to concentrate on doing something about them *before* the convoys actually passed. That had definite possibilities—for the Toronders' base from which all their attacks would be launched when our convoys were in mid-transit was the big base they'd established at Otnar'at, only planet of a large star that was within range of both our Starfuries *and* Defiants. At the extreme *limits* of their range, perhaps. But a well-planned attack oughtn't to need all that much time over the target, I considered.

Besides, farfetched as it might have been, it was the only possible plan I could think of.

LaSalle's "defensive exercises" left me with the sixteen Starfuries of 614 Squadron and eight of 510 Squadron's older Defiants for my mission. Of course, these ships *also* constituted our alleged CSP, but they were all I had to work with. Hadn't been all *that* long ago that the base put up no CSP at all. And following Ambrose's admonition to go slowly in restoring the base's apparent readiness, we'd been *very* careful in our responses to any Toronder provocations. So I decided to take a bit of a chance.

Years ago, long before the current war was much more than a gleam in Nergol Triannic's eye, I'd been closely associated with Sherrington Limited, and the company's principal designer, Mark Valerian—father of the Starfury. In fact, I'd spent countless hours aboard the prototype, I.F.S. *Starfury*—old "K5054," as she was called. This association gave me considerable, fortuitous insight into the design of the graceful ships, including "hardpoints," as Valerian called them, for the attachment of HyperTorps. When it was later decided that Starfuries should carry HyperTorps internally— as did all early "light cruiser" models of the ship—the hardpoints were "skinned over" with hullmetal and forgotten. However, to my knowledge, the stiffeners and bracing that supported them *also* buttressed other important structures on the ships, and had been carried through each successive model to the most modern MK V-B marks, although no frontline Starfuries had carried HyperTorps anywhere for nearly two years.

Given a little luck, I intended to make use of those nearly forgotten, out-of-sight hardpoints—and a store of some two hundred HyperTorps that had been languishing in one of the base magazines since before the war began. "Cottshall," I said into the intercom, "see if you can scare up Jim Williams for me."

At Dawn plus one and thirty the next morning, the two of us were seated in a crowded conference room with Commander Tom Carpenter, Base Engineering Officer for Space (one of the few key officers retained from Summers's reign) and Commander Burt LaSalle, who was flanked by representatives of his reserve starships: Lt. Commander Tip O'Hara, Leader of 614 Squadron with its sixteen Starfuries, and Lt. Cap Lindamann, a Flight Leader in charge of the eight remaining Defiants from 510 Squadron.

Briefly told them what I wanted to do, then watched mouths drop open with surprise.

"We're going to *what?*" LaSalle demanded through a wide grin.

"While you're out shooting up the Toronders' invasion fleet," I repeated with a shrug, "I'm going to use the rest of our ships to attack their base at Otnar'at—see if we can't chew up some of their attack ships before they get a chance to use 'em on our convoys."

"And we're *finally* going to use those old HyperTorps, Admiral," Carpenter said with a bemused look. "You've got no idea how long I've tried to get rid of those things. Been taking up space in the magazines for years. Never could get authorization to scrap 'em."

"You've got it now," I said. "We'll scrap 'em for you. All you've got to do is mount 'em on our Starfuries and we'll even cart 'em away—free of charge. Think you can do it?"

Carpenter frowned. "If the structure for hardpoints is in place as you say it is, then absolutely I can—or *we* can."

"Here," I said, handing him a KA'PPA address for the city of Bromwich on the planet Rhodor, "get in touch directly with the Sherrington plant. They'll tell you all you need to know. Ask for Mark Valerian; say I told you to call."

Suddenly, Carpenter's eyes narrowed. "Mark Valerian," he whispered as if he were speaking the name of some ancient god. "Voot's beard, Admiral, then you're the Wilf Brim who used to fly those Sherrington racers before the war, aren't you?"

Felt myself blush; suddenly, all eyes were on me. "Yeah," I admitted. Seemed like a thousand years ago, yet a lot of people were still fascinated by the Mitchell Trophy races. Before he could derail the meeting, I stopped him. "Call him now," I said firmly. "Right now. We have only a short time to bring this off, and every cycle's going to count." I softened. "Let me know what he has to say," I added with a wink, then turned to LaSalle and his deputies. "All right, gentlemen," I said, "let's plan a mission to Otnar'at. When Brother Carpenter's finished with his modifications, your Starfuries will carry eight HyperTorps each—a pair on either side of your pontoons—and fly like overloaded quarry barges until you get rid of them. You won't have much time over the target, but each HyperTorp will give you the destructive power of a battleship's broadside. And, oh yes, I plan to fly the lead ship. . . ."

Never escaped from headquarters that day till Twilight plus one. It had just become dark, and the warm evening—somehow tranquil in spite of a bustling garrison around me—smelled of the nearby harbor. Difficult at the moment to imagine war raging throughout the galaxy around me. I was wearily uncovering my gravcycle—as always, newly polished in my absence—when a skimmer bustled past on the street, came to an abrupt halt, then reversed and pulled to a hover at the curb beside me.

"Buy you dr-e-e-nk, StarSailor?" someone with Claudia's voice inquired from the driver's seat.

Laughed. "Sounds like a line to me, lady," I said.

"You've had a better line tonight?" she demanded.

"Absolutely not—probably never in my life," I replied, climbing into the passenger seat—and the faint, seductive incense of her perfume. "How about a drink *and* supper?"

She laughed. "I almost asked you the same question, but I was a little afraid that after the other night . . ."

"Great omelet, that time," I replied quickly. "Your chef is magnificent. Handsome, too."

"Awfully nice of you, Wilf," she said.

"What's awfully nice is your stopping," I said. "And you haven't answered me yet. How about some food with those drinks? The Officers' Club serves all night. Doesn't exactly rival Avalon's best, but it's not all that bad, either."

"Sounds wonderful," she said, skidding through a one-eighty turn and heading for the Club.

Hesitated a moment, then had to ask. "Where's Gorgas tonight?"

"At the Cabaret as usual," she said.

Glanced at my timepiece. "You're certainly a bit late tonight," I commented.

"Can't blame me," she said, pulling into a parking place. "It's that new Base Commandant. Keeps things stirred up so much I'm *usually* late these days. Took up a good chunk of my afternoon—just to go see somebody's transport ship, would you believe?"

"Hmm," I said, unsuccessfully attempting to ignore the

way her dress rode up when she slipped out of the seat. Wondered idly how much of it was on purpose . . . if any. "You wouldn't have volunteered this afternoon for that duty or anything, would you . . . or enjoyed yourself once you got there?"

"Why, Wilf Brim," she exclaimed, "how *ever* could you imagine something like that?"

"Oh-o-o, nothing much," I said with what must have been an enormous grin, "but you sure seemed fascinated by Captain Delacroix." Ushered her into the Club lobby—smelled comfortably of food, spirits, and mu'occo cigarettes—then signaled the chief steward for a booth. Noticed idly that I got a lot quicker service as an Admiral than I'd derived years ago as a Lieutenant.

"By Voot he *was* sexy, wasn't he?" she said with an iniquitous little chuckle.

"I couldn't tell," I replied, "but I'll take your word for it."

"Expected you'd say that," she murmured.

We ordered from the small, late-evening menu—this time I remembered her E'lande, but instead she opted to share a bottle of meem. The Club's dining room was only partially filled at that hour, a pleasant, quiet place to talk. Dim lights; candles on the tables. Nice music—a local group playing softly. Romantic. One of the most beautiful women I'd ever known sitting on the other side of the table—and married to someone else. Had to break the spell or I was going to say—suggest—something silly. "S-so what did you think of him?" I asked desperately.

"Who, Delacroix?" she asked as if she'd expected something else from me.

"Yeah," I replied. "What do you think he'll be like to work with?"

She thought a moment, sipped her meem. "I suppose you

mean with his clothes on," she said with a theatrical look of disappointment.

"With his clothes on," I replied, nodding vigorously. "It's important."

She set down her goblet, looked at me with that little smile she got when she *really* knew what I was thinking, then frowned. "Interesting man," she said, playing my game. "Something about him I liked, but I don't particularly know what it was. I kind of got the impression you felt the same way, too. Maybe it was the way the crew looked at him—as if they, well, really appreciated him. Like a father, almost, though he's not all that old."

"That could be good *or* bad," I observed, gesturing with a piece of bread. "What if he's a pirate czar and they all admire him because he's murdered so many people?"

She rolled her eyes. "Be serious, Wilf," she admonished.

"I am serious," I protested—then relented. "Couldn't help noticing the same thing you did, Claudia," I admitted at length. "I've met damned few men who keep a happy crew and can't be trusted. Starships, no matter what their size, are too small for secrets. So that's a big point in his favor."

"I also liked the way he kept the ship, herself," she added as stewards brought our suppers. "I know it's new, but with a crew that size, it doesn't keep clean all by itself."

"Good point."

"But," Claudia said, gesturing with her raised goblet, "none of that means a hill of these beans compared to what impression he makes on Chief Utrillo Barbousse, does it?"

I grinned. "You know me well," I said. "Doesn't much matter whether or not I like him as a person—it all depends on how well I think he can do the job."

"When do you find out?"

"Already *found* out," I said, pouring the dregs into our goblets.

"Thanks . . . You mean this afternoon?"

"Delacroix had *Yellow Bird* ready to lift by the time Barbousse arrived at the wharf to set up a demonstration. Surprised even the Chief. The whole thing was over a couple of metacycles ago."

"And?" she asked, peering up from her meem.

"Barbousse was plenty impressed," I told her. "Delacroix put him in a jump seat right behind the helm, then took the controls himself and ran through one of those tricky asteroid shoals off Nartin-11 as if he'd practiced the course for a month. We'd only mapped it out this afternoon."

"Why am I not surprised?" Claudia asked with a smile.

"Same reason I wasn't," I replied. "He *looked* good to begin with."

"He's got the job, then?" she asked.

"Not yet," I said.

Claudia looked up again and raised her eyebrows. "What's wrong with him, then?" she asked. "Thought Barbousse said he was so good."

"He did," I replied. "But Delacroix is clearly no fool either. He knows good and well he's got the best crew and ship available in this part of the galaxy. And I told Barbousse to make certain he understood the risks involved. Couldn't keep that from him. So naturally he wants a bloody fortune to do the job."

"Is he worth it?" she asked, finishing her meem.

"Yeah," I said. "I'm pretty sure he is."

"Then what's holding you back?"

I laughed. "Wanted him to stew about his price a while tonight. He'll have the job tomorrow, but he shouldn't know how easily he got it. Otherwise, he might be tempted to demand more for the next trip, and there's no sense paying more than a fair price, is there?"

She smiled. "Yeah," she said. Then, suddenly, conversation lapsed again; we were once more alone together with the dim lights, the music, and now a half bottle of meem each.

I, for one, was feeling very, well, *relaxed*. And having a terrible time keeping my eyes from Claudia's bosom, wondering guiltily if those ample breasts had changed much in the nearly fifteen years that had elapsed since I'd enjoyed looking at them without the distraction of clothing.

"You're staring again," she whispered with that soft look in her eyes she got when she was happy. "Just the way you used to . . ."

"Guilty as charged," I said.

She lit one of her mu'occo cigarettes. "What were you thinking about them?" she asked with a little smile, exhaling a tiny cloud of spiced smoke.

"You really want to know?" I asked.

She nodded, looked at me through half-closed eyes. Drew on her cigarette again.

"I was thinking . . . well"—felt myself blush—"*wondering* if they'd changed much since I'd last looked at them."

"You did, eh?" Another puff of spiced smoke.

"Yeah, I did."

"Well," she said, glancing at herself circumspectly, "they probably droop a bit by now. They're a little larger, too, of course—along with the rest of me, Voot take it." Then she looked up with a little smile. "Otherwise, though," she added, "I think they're pretty much the same as they were when . . . well, when we enjoyed them together."

Her small, perfectly manicured hand was near mine on the cushion between us and I wanted to feel its warmth and softness. Of course, I couldn't. For a moment, my mind's eye glided into the past to glimpse great, heavy breasts, tipped by large, dark aureoles and taut, swollen nipples . . . "Claudia, Claudia, Claudia," I swore softly through clenched teeth, "you were—you *are*—so god-awfully beautiful!"

Suddenly, I felt her hand on mine, warm and soft as I imagined. "Wilf," she whispered breathlessly, "I'm losing it. I shouldn't have drunk all that meem. . . ."

"You're sick?" I asked, grabbing my napkin in momentary panic.

"Not sick, you awful boob," she hissed in a desperate voice, looking at me through nearly closed eyes. *"Horny, sexually aroused, libidinous, carnal. Turned on,* Wilf Brim—the way no other man has turned me on before I met you—or since."

I looked into that beautiful—now thoroughly blushed— face and felt a familiar, terribly urgent surge in my loins. The whole Universe had suddenly dissolved around us, and I was desperately thrashing around for the right words, when . . .

"Er, Madame Harbor Master," a sotto voice announced hesitantly, "there's a Mr. Nesterio on the phone for you."

Chapter 5

◆

Otnar'at

13 Octad, 52014

Imperial Fleet Base, Atalanta, Hador-Haelic

Couldn't sleep, so toward morning I made my way to the underground hangar, where preparations for our mission were filling the huge room with echoes of every kind. LaSalle and his squadrons had sortied for the Toronder invasion fleet only a few metacycles earlier. The overworked starship fitters and riggers at the base had been working 'round the clock to put *that* mission into space, then somehow managed to prepare our Starfuries and Defiants—with their special HyperTorp mounts—as well. I still didn't know quite how—certainly, no one associated with the maintenance crews had managed to cadge much sleep during the last few nights before the raid. At least we'd had minimal incursions from The Torond. What with our carefully slowed series of "operational improvements," they seemed satisfied to deliver occasional reminders of their presence, which we fought off with a great deal less enthusiasm than we might have—or would in the near future. Today, we would show our hand in a big way—with no time at all to spare. The first convoy from Avalon was scheduled to arrive in four days, and it was time to deprive our enemies of as many offensive units as we could possibly destroy.

Off in one corner of the cavern, our special "ground attack" Starfuries and Defiants were moored by themselves, fairly bristling with HyperTorps. The first time I'd seen one of our lean interceptors with eight evil-looking torpedoes hanging off its slender pontoons, I decided I was not going to like this phase of the work at all—short-lived as it might be. The Starfuries looked intolerably burdened with their loads, and the monstrous, warty HyperTorps were a basic contradiction of all the intrinsic beauty and symmetry of the starships themselves. Perhaps I had become unduly sensitive after flying these elegant starships for such a long time. To me, it was one thing to attack ground targets in a heavy starship designed specifically for the purpose like one of the Sodeskayans' Ro'stoviks that could destroy battle crawlers from the air *like* a crawler, but it was quite another matter to force these relatively light, sensitive starships into the same role.

The night before, I'd stood on a wharf with Marsha Kelly, one of the Helmsmen on the mission, as together, we inspected one of the torped-up Starfuries. "What do you think of running a mission with them, Marsha?" I'd asked.

"Not much, Admiral," she'd answered. Redheaded, almost painfully slim, and amply freckled, she had a serious countenance that lighted up like fireworks when she laughed. She *also* had a record of nineteen Leaguer and Torond victories to her credit and was a veteran of the Battle of Avalon. She'd been unhappy with the conversion from the beginning. Like most of her compatriots, however, she'd gone along with only a bit of grousing to let us know she didn't wholly approve. "If we'd got some decent range-extenders to hang on the pontoons instead of those ugly things, we might be able to do some decent escort work instead of pretending we were flying some sort of goods lorries filled with rocks. . . ."

Unfortunately, the whole thing had been my idea in the first place, and I would have to see it through.

Volunteers from each firing crew had been slaving night and day in simulators to perfect their aiming skills. To my way of thinking, they were developing into deadly marksmen, but of course, no simulator can really fabricate the terrors—and opportunities to blunder—that are created by actual combat conditions. Until one places the actual flesh of his or her buttocks at deadly risk, everything is little more than harmless theory. And most of these interceptor crews had never experienced anything like close ground support in their lives.

Checked my timepiece—a little nervously, perhaps. The final mission briefing was scheduled in less than a metacycle. I'd seen enough combat in my lifetime to use up at least eight and a half of the fanciful nine lives ascribed to sable Rothcats—Haelic's own *Felis Rothbartis*. But I'd never gotten used to it—only hardened, maybe.

On the bridge of my own Starfury, technicians were still at the consoles, making last-cycle checks and adjustments. The power chambers had been rumbling deep in the main hull all night as maintenance crews tweaked them—and the wave guides they supplied with specially prepared energy—to *exceed* their already-celebrated rated efficiency.

Stepped out onto the pier again. Briefing in one metacycle. Made my way to the huge, noisy hangar cafeteria—always smelled a *little* of the dishwashers. Grabbed a steaming mug of cvceese' while a sleepy-looking, motherly woman dropped a jellied mass of eggs and a couple of Atalanta's famous Rocotzian sausages onto a thick wedge of toast, then pushed the lot onto a plate and handed it to me. I carried it to an unoccupied table, dripping hot cvceese' over my cringing fingers and avoiding eye contact with anybody who looked as if he might like to talk. Wanted to savor the last moments of peace before my life went crazy again—as it seemed accustomed to doing every day since I'd arrived. Today, however, promised to be a lot crazier than most others.

Idly thought about Delacroix and his *Yellow Bird,* blasting toward Gontor with six partially disassembled Starfuries even while I sipped my cvceese'. Today marked his second run; only a few more and the Toronders would begin to get suspicious of his ship making repeated trips so far off the beaten path. Then he would begin to really earn the tremendous fees he was charging. Made me pause and wonder. I was banking a lot on my gut feeling about the man's good character. A lot of people I'd met over the years would simply cut and run, jettisoning my cargo at the first sign of trouble. That's why I was packing every cubic iral of *Yellow Bird* with goods. Until I got to know Cameron Delacroix a whole lot better, I could only predict that the first few trips would have a good chance of arriving at their destination.

At last, it was nearly Dawn plus one. "Mission briefing in five cycles—mission briefing in five cycles," someone called over the blower. "Mission briefing in five cycles—mission briefing in five cycles." *Enough!*

A lot of people from all over the huge room got up at the announcement—most, like me, had been sitting alone. We moved singly or in small, silent groups into the corridor that led to the Intelligence Room. Helmsmen, Gunnery Officers, Navigators, all mostly still alone with our thoughts. In a few cycles, we would either coalesce into the tight-knit team we'd envisioned during the last few arduous days of practice—or we could fail in what might well turn out to be one of the pivotal battles of the war.

The foyer—a small, comfortable reading room—was cluttered with HoloGraphs, starmaps, technical information, and confidential Fleet publications. In a corner, a small door—secured today by two armed guards standing at attention with blast pikes at their sides—gave access to the actual briefing room. I didn't for a moment think there was any reason at all for armed guards to be there. But people from the base's Psych Warfare Office weren't above such staged tricks to, "put the right mood on things," in the words of their commander, Lieutenant Brewster—a plump, overserious, overeducated, and according to popular scuttlebutt, oversexed young woman from one of the large universities in Avalon. So long as she didn't put herself *too* much in the way of normal operations, Williams pretty well let her operate as she pleased.

Instead of entering straightaway, I joined an equally silent Barbousse in a smaller anteroom and poured myself a mug of cvceese'. As the commanding officer, I would be "announced" by Jim Williams once everyone else was seated. Watched the briefing room through a one-way glass and shuddered. The atmosphere was purposely designed to snag people's attention—by the throat—the moment they stepped through the entrance. If they weren't serious about things before they arrived, they were soon afterward. The first thing anyone saw was the wall-sized HoloMap of the target sector. Otnar'at and its small star, Keggi, were centered in one side, Hador-Haelic in the other. A directionally pulsing ruby thread joined Hador with a point in space a few Standard Light-Years short of Galvone-19 (around which orbited a long-abandoned marshaling center), feinted left and outward into the room until it skirted the Contirn asteroid shoals, then turned abruptly and drilled straight inward for the target, after which it returned to Hador via the Velter/Epsilon space hole, whose fierce gravity we would use to stretch our range home. It was a ticklish route—downright dangerous at Velter/Epsilon. But this was wartime, after all, and the advantages far outweighed the risks, even though many lives hung in the balance.

The crews pushed through the doors with flickering note takers under their arms and sloshing cups of cvceese' in their hands, finding themselves somewhere to sit amid the muffled stamping of space boots and scratching of cigarette lighters. Sweet, spicy smoke began to curl up from camarge cigarettes held in nervous fingers. Models of starships from both sides of the war hung from the ceiling: Starfuries, Defiants, Oiggaips, Gorn-Hoffs, Dampiers, ZBL-4s, QF-2s, Gantheissers, Zachtwagers—I'd fought 'em all and more. On the walls were HoloPics of Dampiers and Oiggaips, the kind we most expected to encounter this mission. They were taken from every angle, with diagrams giving the corresponding aiming deflections for varying marks of disruptors. Someone had posted battle slogans everywhere.

"Beware the Leaguer in the light."

"Never go after a ship you've already hit. Another will get you for certain."

> "It's better to come home with a 'probable' than to be shot down with the one you've confirmed."

> "Look out! It's the one you don't see that gets you."

> "Silence on the Short Range KA'PPA. Don't jam your channel!"

> "If you're brought down in enemy territory, escape. If you're caught, keep your trap shut."

As the last two or three latecomers hurried to their seats, sloshing even more cvceese' than the others, Williams nodded to me and I stepped into the room. "The Commander!" he announced amid a scraping and whacking of chairs as everyone stood.

"Sit down, people," I said—briskly, I hoped—and stepped to the platform. Didn't need any notes for the first part, so I started in immediately. "It's about time I let you in on what we've been practicing for," I said, "and why we've bunged up your pretty Starfuries with HyperTorps. This morning, we're going after the Toronders' base at Otnar'at with the express purpose of destroying as many of their killer ships as we can while they're still moored on the surface. The more you take care of now as sitting ducks, the fewer you'll have to fight out in space when their disruptors are firing."

A rustle passed through the room; I noticed quite a few nods of approval. Wondered what their reactions would be if I could let them in on the whole story. That was impossible, of course. If any of them were captured—and broke under the torture they could expect from their captors—they could jeopardize the whole Sapphire operation, whose existence we understood was still unknown to The Torond.

"The enemy order of battle relative to this operation puts some 160 Dampiers at the base itself," I continued after waiting for the inevitable shuffling and clearing of throats. "A few may have scrambled into space by the time you get there, but most will still be on the surface, unless their long-range BKAEW is a lot better than we think. However, by the time you've been there a while, another 60 to 120 Dampiers and Oiggaips might be on their way from the base at E'cnerolf, but if you go about your business quickly and efficiently, you should be on your way home in plenty of time to miss them, so don't dawdle. Questions about any of that?" I asked.

There were none.

"Flying instructions, then," I continued, pausing again while everyone got his note taker ready. Why in xaxt they couldn't do it *before* they sat down has always been beyond me—but then I never professed to understand people. And never will. "I'll lead 614 Squadron myself," I continued. "Our call sign will be Hammer. Cap Lindamann will lead the eight Defiants from 510 Squadron, call sign Drill. My personal call sign will be Tempo. We'll lift in squadron formation from Vectors Nineteen and Twenty-four in the spinward harbor. 'Grav start-up for Hammer will be Dawn plus three, for Drill Dawn plus three and two. We'll take off at Dawn plus three and ten. I'll circle at ten thousand irals so you can form up and synchronize zenith orientation; at Dawn plus three and twenty, I shall set course. You've all got that?"

They had. At least no one put up a hand.

Nodded. "Good, then," I said. "We'll fly in the shadow of Hador until Brightness plus one, when we shall take up course for Contirn shoals. If all goes well, we should arrive there at Brightness plus two and five, making our final thirty-cycle leg to Otnar'at. On the way out to Galvone, Drill will fly a c'lenyt to my right, then take up a position one c'lenyt overhead and slightly to the rear. As we round the shoals, I'll wiggle my pontoons as a signal to assume battle formation and straightaway slow to attack speed. Everyone with me?"

Again, no hands. Waited till they stopped making notes. "I know I've been on this again and again since the first practice," I began again, "but I cannot overstress that KA'PPA silence, even short-range, ship-to-ship KA'PPA or radio silence, is compulsory until long after we're below Light-Speed, when I give my signal to attack—which, I remind you once more, will be my voice on your HypoLight radio sets, bursting in with the very novel word 'ATTACK.' At that point, we'll make our strike as practiced."

I paused for a moment to ensure that everyone was with me. No questions. Then, "We've gone to a lot of trouble disguising this whole exercise as part of something else," I said in conclusion. "And we'll be flying in uncomfortably close formation for nearly three disagreeable metacycles so we aren't picked up by The Torond's BKAEW sets. Therefore, we don't want some clod wrecking the whole show by shooting off his or her mouth unnecessarily. It goes without saying that you will constantly have your KA'PPAs in RECEIVE mode so you can hear me in the first place.

"If you have trouble and want to return to base, waggle your pontoons—or fishtail a bit if you're in a Defiant—then switch over to the emergency KA'PPA channel. But don't use it even then unless you are in *serious* trouble. Otherwise, for Voot's sake, keep your mouths shut or you'll cause a hotter reception for the rest of us."

Noticed a number of embarrassed faces among my audience, but no one seemed terribly put out by my curt words.

"Now," I added, "a final bit of advice. Once you're under way, if even one of your HyperTorps checks out hot—as in 'armed' before *you* actually arm it—then warn your leader and go home to jettison all of them properly. We don't want the things lolling around space waiting for the odd traveler to bump 'em by accident. And never forget that if you *do* blow yourself up, KA'PPA energy from your exploding Drive segments will get to our target before we do—and could alert the very people we need to surprise."

Noticed surprised looks here and there among the crew members. Strange how we take instantaneous KA'PPA communications for granted these days—KA'PPA waves arriving everywhere in the Universe at the same instant they are sent. KA'PPA's so common—and so necessary to the pangalactic civilization we live in—we rarely think of it, or the danger it can bring in wartime.

I continued. "We'll be well within the atmosphere during most of our mission, and that means possible dogfighting. Don't forget to give clear indications of the whereabouts of suspicious starships in relation to me—speaking slowly and clearly—and giving your call sign. If there are dogfights, keep together, and if things get very sticky, keep in pairs at least. That's essential. Number Twos must never forget that they are responsible for covering their Number Ones. Always break toward the enemy—and mind your energy management every moment, or you'll find a Dampier you can't shake off crowding your tail."

Almost done. Only the details left. Gave them the direct course home, emergency KA'PPA channels: one if they could make it home, the other if they couldn't and were taking to their LifeGlobes. Remotely synchronized our timepieces to the base master clock. Then, "Keep your eyes open and good luck!" Moments later, we rushed for our lockers.

Carefully emptied my pockets, replacing personal articles
with survival assets: Torond currency, fake papers, packaged
rations, miniature transceivers. Not much, but enough to give
downed starsailors a fighting chance at survival if they have
to make landfall on enemy territory. Pulled my battlesuit
over my fatigues, plugged myself in, and zipped the whole
thing up. Donned thick woolen stockings, then attractor
boots, sealing them to the battlesuit. Slipped a hunting knife
into a scabbard at my left shank, then ran a self-test on my
ancient Wenning blaster—completed successfully with a full
charge. Dropped it into a holster at my right thigh, clipped
the lanyard through a loop in my suit. Donned my helmet
and gloves, ran self-checks on the whole battlesuit: seals,
communications, environmental; ALL TESTS SUCCESS-
FUL appeared on the inside of my visor. Two fitters came
over to help me into my LifeGlobe harness, pulled the straps
tight and checked the systems. Hoped I wouldn't have to use
it. Checked the locker for forgotten items—none I could
see—then made my way out into the hangar and Starfury NL
19.

Dawn plus two and forty-five: I was seated at the helm,
firmly fixed to my recliner by a set of retainer beams and a
separate set of mechanical straps. I'd run my own tests on
the flight and power systems while I watched Cindy Robinson, the Systems Officer, do the same; never hurt to double-
check, although sometimes my rechecking wasn't all that
much appreciated. Tough.

Weapons Officer checked in—all killing systems healthy,
including my three. Navigator checked in—everything fine.
Systems Officer the same. Outside, the last few technicians
were wandering around the hull and pontoons, checking panels and hatches, looking for leaks, making one last visual of
the HyperTorps. Ugly-looking damn things, I thought glanc-

ing out the side Hyperscreens; if they did even half as much damage as their *appearance* promised, the Toronders were in for a royal drubbing.

Glanced back along the line of Starfuries, singled up at the pier behind me and ready to fly. Latecomers were dashing to their ships carrying forgotten starmaps and flight gear. Fire skimmers and emergency lorries rumbled along the pier, hovering in place near their assigned ships. The hour was approaching.

Dawn plus two and forty-eight: Movement all but ceased in the hangar; I suspected things were pretty silent out there, too.

Dawn plus three: I glanced around at the parts of the hangar I could see; the wharf was clear of people. "Ready to start 'em up, Cindy?" I asked, turning to my left. At this, the entire bridge fell silent, as if everyone had been furtively listening for the words.

"Ready, Skipper," Robinson replied tersely, placing her fingers over a glowing red STB. MAIN button on her console.

"Power starboard," I ordered.

As Robinson's fingers touched the button, its color changed to yellow for a moment, then green. "Power to starboard," she echoed.

"Clear to starboard?" I asked, more from habit than anything else. I *knew* the pier was clear.

"Clear to starboard," she repeated.

"Here we go," I said, with the rush of exultation that had never deserted me in all the years I'd spent in starships. Enabled the controls for Number One SpinGrav in the starboard pontoon. When they completed their million and one self-test routines, I moved the gravitation/energy control to IDLE CUT-OFF, and pressed the direction control to NEUTRAL.

Then, from a million years' experience, I opened the right-hand thrust damper slightly, selected the PRIMARY energy feed and INTERNAL energy source, switched the gravitation boost to ON, and touched three of the five primer switches. Power panel revealed a healthy ninety-one quardos on the gauge—the 'Grav was ready! Pressed the starter. Outside on the starboard pontoon a tensioner strobed once . . . twice . . . three times . . . a fourth . . . then the big machine woke, shaking the whole starship and hazing the wharf area in a sparkling, blearing cloud of gravitons.

"Don't see any flames," Robinson joked through an ear-to-ear grin. Back in sorts again.

"Always a good sign," I yelled while the big SpinGrav settled to a smooth, masculine rumble. Shook my head. Systems people—couldn't live with 'em, couldn't live without 'em, either. Xaxt of a quandray.

The other five SpinGravs thundered to life with nearly the same ease, and all the vehemence. Had to laugh. Summers would have died had he seen what we'd done with his starship maintenance organization in just a few short weeks.

Out of nowhere, the wharf became crowded again with helmeted starship fitters dressed in silvery protective clothing and huge mittens as they scurried around, closing panels, dragging cables out of the way, manning the bollards. "Attention all hands," I cautioned over the blower. "Changing now to local gravity." Held my breath while I set the switches, and . . . didn't lose my breakfast. Hurrah! "Docking cupolas," I ordered, "cast off, fore and aft!"

Instantly, the last mooring beams winked out, and I gingerly moved the thrust dampers forward, easing the ship away from the wharf and into the main channel. Ahead, beyond the open hangar doors, the weather was superb; for three days running, Hador had been unusually bright for this time of year. Aft, the other fifteen Starfuries were forming a line.

Dawn plus three and nine: 614 Squadron was lined up behind me two-by-two along Nineteen Vector, 'Gravs rumbling in clouds of spray. To our left, the eight Defiants glinted wetly in the late-morning light. Everything looked ready to me. Checked my timepiece, squirmed in my seat . . .

Dawn plus three and ten: a white rocket rose from hangar entrance at the same time a green indicator lit in my OPS panel. I eased the thrust damper all the way forward and started along the vector. A glance aft and to the side assured me that all twenty-four starships—Defiants and Starfuries— were skimming along the surface as a single unit.

Nearing lift-off speed, NK 19 began to skitter over the wave tops. Towering wakes on either side of our pontoons subsided while the passing rollers coalesced to a glistening blur—we were off!

Turning sharply, our twenty-four starships swept over the base like a whirlwind. I could see startled people on the ground shading their eyes to stare up at us. Some waved. Wondered for a moment if Claudia were looking as we thundered past the Civilian Headquarters and over the Austral limits of the base. We continued in this direction at tree and rooftop level in a thunderous roar, halting people below in their tracks and—I am certain—rattling every window in that part of Atalanta. Suddenly, we cleared a wooded hill, and I began a slow climb over water again, deep blue waves edged by foam and dominated by a long curve of sandy beach. Farther out on the water, a small boat of some sort—probably a rescue vessel—rocked on the swell, surrounded by a swarm of gulls. The far horizon was only a blue, hazy line. Moments later, I got departure clearance and climbed almost vertically to ten thousand irals, where I circled until everyone got the formations sorted out and set zenith orientation to my ship—that way, we'd all share the same vertical reference, no matter where we went. Then, at Dawn plus three and twenty—sharp—I pulled into another vertical climb, scrambling upward into the starry blackness of deep space.

Only cycles later, we'd passed through Hyperspeed and were heading in harm's way. Felt good to be in the saddle again . . . more or less.

Everyone who has ever written about war—or has *attempted* to write about war—eventually has remarked about brief moments of absolute terror interspersed with extended periods of boredom. The flight to Otnar'at was no exception so far as boredom was concerned. While I kept my own tense lookout for enemy starships—both on my proximity panel *and* through the Hyperscreens—most of the time I sat on my backside attempting to occupy my mind with thoughts other than those of my own demise. . . .

"Er, Madame Harbor Master," the steward had broken in on us, *"there's a Mr. Nesterio on the phone for you."* Days later I could still hear that steward's hesitant, sotto voice as if he were speaking beside my recliner. And, if nothing else, he had certainly shattered our spell. The crimson blush had quickly drained from Claudia's face; her eyes had become open and alert, and she was once again all business. Grinding out her cigarette in a shower of spice-scented sparks, she'd passed me an apologetic glance, then nodded calmly. "Thank you, steward," she'd said barely above a whisper. "I'll take it here at the table."

I'd gotten up so she could talk privately, but she'd signaled me to stay. When the steward delivered the 'Phone, it had come to life with the globular display blank. Nesterio—a true gentleman's gentleman—had politely placed the call in *private* mode. She'd clearly expected that he would. They'd spoken only a few, brief words in the local tongue before she'd switched off and smiled sadly at me.

"He wanted to know if I could join him at some sort of local Halacian festivity that's going on in his cabaret," she'd said, pushing the 'Phone aside with a faraway, empty sort of look. "I said I'd come."

"I understand," I'd said, in lieu of any words more meaningful. "Did he know you were with me?"

She'd shrugged. "I don't know," she'd said, then made a little snort of disdain. "Probably never entered his mind." She'd closed her eyes for a moment and put her hand on mine. "Maybe it's all for the best," she'd said with a little quaver in her voice. "But right now, I'd be damned hard to convince. . . ."

Within cycles, I'd found myself back at headquarters watching the taillights of her skimmer speeding out of sight along the causeway. And now, even days later, I still couldn't make up my mind whether I'd been relieved or disappointed. Both, probably.

Over the years, I've certainly never attempted to deny how I feel toward Claudia. At some level, I've retained—virtually intact—all the feelings I'd developed when we were lovers in the true sense of the word. I'd be lying if I tried to convince myself that the man in me didn't dearly want to make love to her again. She was, after all, one of the two or three most beautiful women I'd ever encountered—perhaps the nicest, too. Not only that, but pretty clearly, she'd also retained a few of those selfsame passions toward me—which made the direction our conversation had been taking us at the time a thousand times more compelling. So to say I was disappointed? The understatement of the century!

I scanned the instruments and made a quick check of our

other ships through the Hyperscreens. Good formation flying, if nothing more. Soon, we'd see if they were fighters as well. . . .

Chuckled to myself as I mulled the feelings of relief I'd also experienced during Nesterio's call, great he-man that I am. Like it or not, Claudia and I did have a professional relationship—one that was critical to an important part of the war effort, no less. And professional relationships seldom survive massive infusions of love or sex, no matter how sophisticated the lovers are—or think they are. . . .

About twenty cycles out from our first checkpoint—with Galvone-19 already bright among the stars ahead—Norton, the Gunnery Officer, brought around steaming cups of cvceese'.

Nodded my thanks over the quiet rumble of the Drive. "Did you know," I inquired with my best professorial look, "that you may well be responsible for saving this entire starship with that cup of cvceese'?"

She got a theatrical look of horror in her eyes. "Crikie, Admiral," she said, "I din't put nuffin' in it but cvceese'. I swears!"

"Rats," I grouched.

She rolled her eyes. "None of those in there, either, I'll warrant," and started back to her workstation while I returned my thoughts to reflections of Claudia.

Her disconcerting, long-standing status as "married woman,"—to a man I basically respected—also had its effect on my feelings. Not that I hadn't guiltily, but quite willingly, dabbled with a number of active and not-so-active wives over the years. Nevertheless, to me, Claudia was somehow different—above such things as common infidelity. Her wifely status had pestered me ever since my arrival at the base. And it still did, though not enough to arrest my feelings of wanting her. Sorry, Nesterio!

Finally, I suppose the ghost of that previous—near-perfect—relationship we'd shared some fifteen years ago haunted me more than I liked to admit. Would today's Wilf Brim measure up to her memories of a thirty-one-year-old version? Somehow, I recalled, I had no problem with thinking that *she* would have little trouble in the same department.

Changed course—out from the protection of Hador's brilliance—approximately half a Standard Light-Year short of Galvone-19, precisely on schedule at Brightness plus one and twenty. Our proximity systems sensed no watchers, active or passive—another unwitting present from the turncoat Admiral Summers and his henchmen, who had made the base so nonthreatening that the Toronders *still* gave it only minimal attention while they prepared to launch their own invasion. Twenty cycles to go before raising the Contirn asteroid shoals to begin our final run.

To be truthful, I hated drawn-out attacks like this. I'd been an interceptor Helmsman for too many years to feel comfortable in the role of a ground-attack commander. Even during my stay in Sodeskaya, I'd concentrated mostly on flying their latest ship killers—more than happy to bequeath the job of flying Ro'stoviks against ground targets to those very special Bears known as the Wild Ones.

Reminded me. I'd received a special HoloGram recently from old friend Nik Ursis, Grand Marshal of the G.F.S.S. It pictured a heroic statue recently dedicated as a memorial to the Wild Ones from the K'cassoc tribes who had fallen defending their Mother Country. Rendered in black-veined, alabaster granite and erected near the center of Gromcow—the Sodeskayan capital—this special new memorial depicted a Great Bear with its mouth opened in song while it played one of those horrible-sounding little accordions so beloved in the K'cassoc star sector. Fitting tribute, I thought, for some of the bravest individuals in all the galaxy.

Glanced through the Hyperscreens at the ships I was leading into battle, crewed by humans, but fighting essentially the same enemy as the Bears. Toronders were nothing but second-class Leaguers, after all. Someday, I thought with a lump in my throat, all of us—humans, Bears, flighted Azurnians alike—would meet in the final battle against the League and its toadies. And we would triumph! For a moment, I thought about my own chances of seeing that battle, then shook my head and returned to the business of flying the Starfury. Some things were better off not considered.

Brightness plus two and two: the Contrin asteroid shoals glowed ghostlike ahead like early-morning clouds just before the horizon begins to lighten. They quickly grew to dominate the entire view ahead and to starboard. At the speed we were traveling, our turn around the colossal aggregation of rocks—many large as planets—traversed nearly a quarter Standard Light-Year. Halfway around, I waggled my pontoons, and the ships behind me dispersed smoothly into battle formation: a flat arrangement of six quads—four with Starfuries, two with Defiants.

Target coming up in thirty cycles! Already the star Keggi had become a small, growing disk among the background of stars.

Called for battle stations, then judiciously applied our gravity brakes in preparation for entering Otnar'at's atmosphere. Were I ham-handed with the brakes at these speeds, I would over-ride our local gravity systems and reduce our Starfury to a fused mass about the size of a cvceese' mug. Wouldn't be the first time it had happened; not to me, thank Voot. Glanced ahead; Keggi was now as big as a footgoal ball, and I could already pick out some of the features I'd located on the Holo-Charts. We'd soon be picked up by the base's many BKAEW sites on Otnar'at, but by the time they identified what they were looking at and attempted to put up extra interceptors, we'd be on them. Not that it made our job *that much* easier. Ground attacks were always terribly dangerous, especially in ships that were not designed for that kind of mission. But *any* little advantage was a big help, especially with one's precious buttocks in the balance!

We'd timed our arrival to approach from the dark side of the planet opposite Otnar'at, just as the base was being rotated into daylight. Fewer BKAEW sites in that hemisphere, too. It was a good strategy, for we were well into the atmosphere before the Toronder's BKAEW beams registered on the passive side of our proximity displays. They hadn't even been scanning! Half-laughing to myself, I momentarily wondered if LaKarn had his own versions of Admiral Summers to contend with!

From local broadcasts, we knew the weather over the target was controlled by a huge area of low pressure, with storms and basically miserable atmospheric conditions everywhere. It would make difficult flying, but it would also add slightly to our margin of safety, which could most generously be described as minimal. We dived immediately to five hundred irals altitude and headed for the base at about thirty-five hundred c'lenyts per metacycle—cpm, in Avalonian. Low altitude was our best defense against ground fire, and there would be plenty of *that* to go around once we were at the target. The Toronders might be a bunch of gangsters and bullies, but that didn't mean they couldn't protect themselves. Only clicks distant from Lake Garza, the landmark for my command to attack. Steadied myself. Without any cover from above, we were in for a rough time, and I knew it—though I hadn't made much about it during my briefing. The rest would find out for themselves soon enough. A sizable lake appeared ahead, a picturesque village situated off to our left. Got a glance of ancient steeples and glazed roof tiles as we sped past. The villagers would be running for their 'Phones even as we passed, but by the time they got through to anyone, they'd be too late.

In the brightening light, the lake flashed for a moment beneath us. Time to kick it all off. Slowed to about 550 cpm—attack speed—and went all the way to the deck, dodging around hills and especially high trees. Cindy Robinson, the Systems Officer, ran her last diagnostics on the HyperTorps—all checked out perfectly. I powered up the radio, switched to the proper channel, then touched TALK and waited till my panel timer counted to zero. "Attack!" I shouted with the volume at full. "Target straight ahead in fifty clicks. All ships attack!"

Instantly, our quads flattened to line-abreast formations, then assembled into two ranks, the eight Defiants of Drill about a c'lenyt ahead of Hammer's sixteen Starfuries—and my own Starfury at the center of the second rank. Figured the older Defiants ought to have the benefit of at least one run where surprise was completely on their side. Besides, our Starfuries could take a bit more punishment, when it came to that, and I *was,* after all, responsible for everyone's safety. Such as that might be. . . .

We streaked over the countryside, almost brushing the tops of trees, easing the controls to thunder down into valleys. Climbing parallel to the slopes of the ground rising—and swerving gently to avoid The Torond's ubiquitous twisting towers and high chimneys. Here and there, we bored through belts of opaque mist, forcing us into some tricky instrument flying a few irals above the ground—which, of course, we could not see. Now and again, we overflew the camouflaged flanks of military vehicles crawling over the roads, but we ignored them. We were after much bigger game today—if all went well, their turn would come later in the war.

Under a dark overcast, we approached a thickly populated area—the city of Otnar'at, with the turrets and minarets of Sokol, the old University town, in the hazy distance to the left. Dead ahead—the base. Our last reconnaissance HoloGraphs—nearly a week old; we hadn't wanted to tip our hand—indicated the harbor portion of the base was protected by five mobile antispace platforms (each armed with four quadruple-mount, automatic 20-mmi disruptor emplacements), six heavily armed fortifications ringing the base firing either four 90-mmi or eight 37-mmi disruptors aimed through automatic controls, and nearly two hundred reinforced light antiair disruptors scattered everywhere. Momentarily the fog thickened, then rain started pelting down by the bucket.

"Look out Drill Section Two," someone yelled on the radio. "Disruptor platform, one o'clock!"

Suddenly, terrific explosions erupted ahead, sending clouds of black smoke and whirling debris skyward—including the slowly spinning remains of a 20-mmi quad-mount. The Defiants were scoring.

More explosions ahead, punctuated by cries of "Got 'im fair and square!" and "Scratch a pair of Dampiers!" Then, abruptly, the harbor was ahead—our turn, now. To my right, the twisted remains of an upturned mobile platform, burning furiously. People running wildly from the conflagration—many of them aflame as well—falling on their faces as we thundered only a few feet overhead. And off to the left, another mobile platform opened up at us. Saw one of the Starfuries go up in a roiling cloud of flame and black smoke—not a sound from the crew, thank Voot. Then we, too, were past the first forts in the ring and perfectly centered in what looked like a giant spiderweb—made up of disruptor beams! Unbelievable antispace barrage!

The entire center of the harbor seemed to light up with flashes from 20-mmi and 37-mmi disruptors. There must have been forty of them firing at me alone! Scared! Sweating despite the ministrations of my battlesuit.

Explosions and disruptor beams to the left and right, crossing over and under us. Thunderous explosions—heard clearly even through my battlesuit. Dazzling flashes. Ahead, the broad expanse of water, carved by long lines of taxiway buoys. Doing better than 450 cpm now. First a floating repair hangar . . . a long walkway—people running wildly, jumping into the water. Then the Dampiers, floating clumsily above their narrow touch skids. About thirty of them, with people crouching behind any shelter they could find or diving pell-mell into the water. Too far left for my disruptors, but Norton sprayed them from all the steerable turrets. Ribbons of explosions intertwining among the big starships—and wherever they touched—annihilation. A great light from behind—followed by a considerable shock wave. Glanced aft as the hangar we'd passed went up from a direct HyperTorp hit.

A group of Oiggaips loomed up in my personal sights. I fired, fingers jammed on the buttons. More ribbons of explosions—climbing the hulls and 'Grav nacelles. Smoke . . . flames . . . one exploded just as I flashed over it. Tossed my Starfury like a leaf in a windstorm. Watched a Defiant touch the water. The hull bounced up in a shower of fragments and antennas, then exploded.

More hangars in front of us. Two HyperTorps lazily wiggled out from beneath our hull and drilled toward them, waiting for us to pass before reducing the whole floating complex to blazing debris in our wake.

A tremendous blast somewhere close to port nearly threw our Starfury on its side. Fought the controls to level out. Getting ready to fire when . . . "Look out Tempo!" someone yelled

over the radio. I jumped, glanced around. Sweet mother of
Voot! My number two Starfury, was edging toward me at terrific speed, completely out of control, its bridge a twisted mass
of hullmetal, Macmillan, the Helmsman, obviously dead. I
dodged precariously and he went straight into one of the mobile platforms, erupting in a terrific flash of light, followed by
two huge, expanding puffballs of flame, smoke, and whirling
debris. The armored platform itself flew into the air between,
its firing crew hanging on to a disruptor even as Norton destroyed another line of Oiggaips from our own movable turrets.

I'd hardly even gotten to know Macmillan. . . .

First pass was nearly over. Disruptor tracks were pursuing us
from every direction. Instinctively, I lowered my head and
hunched my shoulders—for all the good *that* might do. A salvo
of 37-mmi burst so close, it nearly batted us out of the sky—all
but deafened by the time I got the ship under control again.

Ahead, one of the outer fortifications—squat, dark, repul-
sive, like a huge, bloated roach—half in flames, but two of its
big 90-mmi disruptors blasting away at us as fast as they could
recharge. Two more of our HyperTorps streaked out ahead of
us—no loitering this time, their target was a bigger danger to us
than the explosion they'd cause. Moments before the missiles
hit, I maxed the 'Gravs and pulled back on the controls. The
spaceframe groaned under the strain—so did everyone in the
crew—but like the thoroughbred she was, our Starfury climbed
vertically toward the overcast, only just clearing a tremendous
double explosion of our HyperTorps as they tore the heart from
the remainder of the fortification.

I glanced back at the base, just visible behind us in the haze.
A thousand irals below, a Defiant was climbing in zigzags, the
disruptor beams stubbornly pursuing him, but at least reduced
in number from what we'd faced before. Much of the base was
already in ruins, with columns of greasy smoke rising every-

where, and delayed explosions still sending up great jets of flame and debris. But NL 19 still had half her HyperTorps, and there were still a *lot* of undamaged killer ships remaining in the harbor below—some of which were beginning to move out toward the lift-off vectors!

No strategy for second passes over the harbor, just get in there fast as possible and demolish as much as we could in the shortest possible time. With my Number Two gone, I simply leveled out just below the clouds and got ready to make the run alone. Below, I glimpsed three of the surviving Defiants making their second run before I dived for the deck, turned, and made for the base at the highest speed our ground-target aiming systems could manage. This time, I'd have to work fast; the antiair disruptor crews would be fully woken and working at peak efficiency.

Skimmed past a ruined fortification—somebody else's work—and caught sight of a Dampier skimming along a lift-off vector. Turned slightly left to bisect his path. To one side, about twenty new Oiggaip 912s—closely packed into what looked like a receiving area—were starting up. People leaped off the hulls into the water as we approached . . . too late. Norton covered the entire area in heavy disruptor fire, turning the tract into what could only be described as a giant fire pit, as exploding ships set their neighbors alight in a massive chain reaction of destruction and death. Farther along, more Dampiers moored to a row of buoys. Norton only got one or two of those as we barreled past.

Now, it was my chance for the escaping Dampier—didn't want him airborne if possible; Fleet training frowns on competition during attacks. Getting close now, but he was off the water and turning left. I turned too, and climbed to 150 irals—attracting the attention of every disruptor on the thraggling planet!

Suddenly, I found myself coming up on still another Dampier I hadn't seen, also on lift-off. Too late to shoot; none of the movable turrets would bear. His fuselage was gray-green, with big, black triangles on either side. I passed within irals of him. He had just lifted and was doing about 160 cpm—I was doing close to six hundred. The Helmsman must have had apoplexy, for he spun away, lost control, then cartwheeled for the water.

I didn't see him hit. I was gaining on the other at an amazing speed. The antiair disruptor crews—probably half-crazed by this time—let fly with everything they had at *both* of us. The Toronder must have wondered what was going on, but he wasn't looking around properly. I got him in my sights just as he started to dodge, but he was too late. At fifteen hundred irals, I coupled all three of my disruptors and hit the buttons. Twelve hundred irals—I went on firing. Seventy-five irals. Before breaking off, I had time to see three hits register: one directly into the bridge, another near the tail section, just forward of the Drive outlets, and the third in that small bulge Dampiers have near their steering engine. The last did him in! I just avoided the stricken ship in time—as I cleared, I saw him turn over on his back and stumble into a spin. From that altitude, he'd never recover—if, indeed, anyone on the bridge was still alive from my first hit.

Back to the business of breaking things on the ground! Swung around hard and dived for the deck again—as much to get away from the antiair fire as finding new targets for our remaining four HyperTorps. Checked the area ahead—nothing but smoke and destruction everywhere. In the distance, I could see Starfuries and a Defiant climbing for deep space, their HyperTorps clearly expended. The only structure that was still relatively intact was a huge tower I recognized from HoloGraphs as the one from which the Toronders controlled flight operations. It was ringed by a number of mobile platforms still relatively intact because it simply hadn't been a designated target . . . until *now,* that is. Probably, it was one of the last targets around worth a couple of HyperTorps.

Got right down on the deck until we were throwing a wake of seawater several hundred irals into the air. The tower was dead ahead, but first we had to get past one of the platforms. A gray, rolling mass in the water, bristling with fire-control antennas like a fat, hairy spider. Suddenly, it lit up with rapid staccato flashes all along its superstructure. I pulled in my head and kept on going; they would either hit us or they wouldn't. Clusters of red-and-green disruptor beams started up in every direction, one of which fell short and sprayed the Hyperscreens with boiling water. I aimed at the control house, between a damaged quad-mount and a high director mast, fired a long, continuous burst from all three of my disruptors—nobody else had a shot. I was short! Raised the nose and watched my powerful disruptor beams explode through the black-striped platform, then climb to the handrails and armor plating, which melted like candy. A fire-director tower crashed down; a spurt of shimmering gravitons escaped from somewhere—probably some sort of power source. Off to one side, five figures in battlesuits hurled themselves on their faces. Closer and closer. The barrels of a 20-mmi disruptor quad-mount were now pointing directly between my eyes. My own rapid-firing disruptors melted the deck all around it, burning one of the aimers in half and throwing his legs into the water. All four barrels fired once more—missed by less than an iral as I bunted over the whole collapsing structure, clipping one of our pontoons on a director mast as it toppled over like a great, top-heavy tree.

Abruptly the whole massive control tower was before us . . . rushing at us. We'd have to fire quickly or we'd do as much damage with our fuselage as the HyperTorps. . . .

Glanced to the right as four Starfuries passed behind the structure like a school of leaping fish, bearing down on the hapless occupants of a half-ruined hangar perched beside a huge concrete ramp filled with burning wreckage—Dampiers, I guessed. But when were *we* going to fire those torpedoes? In a moment, it would be too late.

Then, without warning, all four of our remaining Hyper-Torps streaked out ahead of us, and I banked violently till the pontoons were nearly vertical, clawing my way skyward away from the terrific eruption I knew would follow. Years ago at a Helmsman's Academy refresher course, we'd been taught the best escape strategy from a close-on HyperTorp launch was to fly at about a seventy-degree angle to the detonation point—while pouring on all the velocity you could muster. With the spaceframe protesting like an old man on a ski slope and the 'Gravs howling at EMERGENCY THRUST, I was "mustering" for all my Starfury was worth. Four blinding flashes in quick succession tripped the Hyperscreen AutoShades and I flew blind for nearly a click before I could see anything again. Then I glanced behind us, where the massive tower was settling slowly into a roiling, swelling fireball that was expanding in our direction like an all-consuming vision of doom. In vain, I urged the 'Gravs for more speed, but to no avail—slowly, inexorably, the blast was overtaking us. Closer and closer the roiling bubble of destruction came to our tail empennage. At what must have been the last *possible* moment—I could feel the reflected heat through my battlesuit visor—its advance slowed, then fell behind rapidly, and we were hammered about by four separate shock waves as if we had no more heft than a toothpick. After that, I managed to fight things back under control.

We turned back toward the harbor as the monumental structure began to tilt, then toppled slowly out of the fire pit that was once its foundation, crashing down on the headquarters complex in which it was centered and sending visible shock waves out for nearly half a c'lenyt on either side. Voot's greasy beard, *no wonder* they never recommended launching more than two HyperTorps at a time at any single target. Probably want to have a talk with our launch crew down in the hull when—if—we got back in one piece. But then, we *did* survive after all, and at the same time probably slaughtered half The Torond's command structure in this sector of the galaxy. Definitely would be a great hindrance to their operations for a while. . . .

Dived for one last pass over the base; came out over the harbor, now a jumble of wrecked, half-sunken starships—many still on fire—sticking out of the water in pathetic groups around the collapsed wreckage of their hangars. The weather seemed to have cleared a little. I kept an eye out for enemy ships that might have managed to get airborne from the wreck-strewn lift-off vectors. They'd be around—I'd already proved that. The air was still crisscrossed with antiair disruptor fire. No targets worth going after.

Nearly time to go. Reinforcements would certainly be on the way by now—such as they might be—and I had no idea how many of my own ships had survived their own holocaust. To the rear, the fallen control tower dominated the landward horizon, surrounded by explosions, flames, and clouds of black smoke, thickening as they drifted downwind. As I flashed past, one of the enormous harbor cranes was crashing down like some overgrown animal that had just been shot. . . .

"Look out, Tempo," somebody yelled on the radio, "—antiair!"

Mother of Voot! I was blundering over what I had *thought* was a wrecked mobile platform—that had just come back to life! They couldn't miss. I pulled up and headed for the sky in a vertical climb, jinking for all I was worth. A second or two passed, glowing disruptor beams flashed past the Starfury—

closer than I'd ever experienced. But they didn't hit! Perhaps I was going to be lucky for the ten millionth time. Kept climbing—jinking.

Suddenly, two stinging shocks. *Bang! Bang!* The first, distant, smashed us sideways accompanied by agonized screaming on the intercom; must have been in the main hull. The second exploded right beside me. Raw energy roaring through the hullmetal plates, a sudden mist in the flight bridge that disappeared as our atmosphere escaped. Decompression! My faithful instruments were . . . gone. Smashed crystal and dark displays mocked me from the smashed panel. But it was my leg that caught my attention. Felt blood pumping in my left leg before my battlesuit sealed itself like a tourniquet just above the knee. This one was serious—hurt like fire! The screaming continued on the intercom; all I could do to keep from joining the poor devils.

"Damage report!" I shouted through clenched teeth. "Give me a damage report!"

"Can't tell, Admiral," someone said in a tight voice. "Bad fire 'midships. Pretty sure it's near the Drive section, but we can't tell till we get there."

"Very well," I said, steadily as I could. "Keep me posted."

"Aye, Admiral."

Bad. The ship's four Krasni-Peych Wizard-45 Drive units with their all-important Hyperspeed crystals were awfully near the fire—maybe part of it. But we were light-years from home, so either the Drives worked, or we were stuck—a nice word for waiting until your LifeGlobe's resources expire or you become a prisoner.

"Cindy!" I demanded. "What's your estimate?"

"Can't tell, Admiral," Robinson responded in a tight voice. "All four Drives check out beautifully, but they always do *before* they're in operation."

"Yeah," I replied. "I know. Thanks." Sick with funk, I focused myself on flying the ship and continued out into space. Next check point, the Velter/Epsilon space hole. Starfury NL19 had caught a packet herself, and it was time to go home. *If* she'd go! Glanced around the bridge. Everyone else seemed to be functioning. Listened to the sound of the 'Gravs as we accelerated toward LightSpeed. Definitely ragged, but still doing their job—most of 'em, anyway.

"LightSpeed zero point eight," Cindy Robinson intoned. "Switching power to the Drive mains."

"Power to the Drive mains at zero point eight," I acknowledged. To be on the safe side, I'd power all four simultaneously just after zero point nine five LightSpeed—then . . . well, then we'd know for certain. Switched on the blower. "All hands secure for HyperFlight operations. All hands secure for Hyper-Flight operations." The ship was quiet as an empty hulk. Everybody had gone to their stations immediately after we were hit. I felt very tired. . . .

"LightSpeed zero point eight five. . . ."

"Point eight five."

"LightSpeed zero point nine zero. . . ."

"Point nine zero."

"LightSpeed zero point nine four. . . ."

"Point nine four; ready to fire 'em."

"LightSpeed zero point nine five. . . ."

Clenched my teeth. Listened to the 'Gravs—maxed out. They'd be ruined at this speed. "Point nine five," I acknowledged. Switched on the blower. Now or never! "Attention all hands. We are now switching to HyperFlight. Power to Drive Number One," I announced, and connected the crystals to the mains. . . .

Blinding flash . . . poor old NL19!

In spite of her thirty-four thousand milstons, the Starfury

was like a nut smashed by a gigantic hammer. First, a *terrific*
shock—in *total* silence; the deck bounced up hurtling me
against the side of my recliner with the strap restraints cutting
into me like great, dull knives. Hyperscreens shattered into glittering fragments—this close to LightSpeed, everything outside
had turned to a jumbled, whirling kaleidoscope of random reds.
Saw what looked like one of the pontoons tear off, go shooting
out ahead, then explode in a paroxysm of radiation fire,
whirling shards of hullmetal, hatch covers, and spinning 'Gravs
torn loose from their beddings. I vainly crossed my arms in
front of my face while what was left of the flight bridge was
jerked sideways with such frightful violence that my strap restraints snapped—felt like they broke every bone in my body
before I spun out of my seat. Hurtled forward next—whatever
in xaxt "forward" meant anymore. My helmet faceplate
smashed into something I didn't have time to see, then I helplessly watched myself carom upward, caught a leg on one of
the Hyperscreen frames; felt the battlesuit fabric give, *tear*.
PRESSURE DROP appeared in crimson on the inside of my
half-shattered faceplate as I tumbled free of the hull—sweet
mother of Voot, the Starfury had blown in half! Battlesuit unsuccessfully trying to seal, but PRESSURE DROP starting to
blink. No go—struggling to breathe! With my last shreds of
consciousness, I smacked the LifeGlobe's activator and saw
the diaphanous globe start to surround me . . . only hope now.
Lungs bursting! Then everything went very comfortably
black. . . .

Chapter 6

◆

First Convoy

16–17 Octad, 52014

Under Way aboard *Yellow Bird*,
Interdominion Space, En Route to Atalanta

Yellow Bird's flight bridge was smaller than I'd remembered from my first visit. Probably that was because there was a full flight crew inside now; that and one of my eyes was still swollen nearly shut, too. I was in a jump seat they'd rigged between the two helms, Barbousse standing beside me, urging still *another* glass of fruit juice on my full stomach—giving no quarter, as he did from time to time when it became necessary to keep me alive in spite of my half-witted resistance. Winking thanks, I found room for the nourishing liquid. Hadn't been that long ago I'd despaired of drinking *anything* again.

Delacroix lounged in the left seat, idly watching the flight instruments; the right seat was occupied by a tiny, dark-skinned woman, who was presently flying the huge starship with the light touch of a lifelong veteran—in spite of the gravity storm outside that was causing rough passages for everything in this sector of the galaxy. Through the Hyper-screens, I watched our four-Starfury escort making heavy weather in what I judged (from the apparent motion of the spaceman's tunnel) would be power settings of at least "fast cruise." *Yellow Bird* was one speedy transport!

And quiet! I've spent most of my life in military starships or, in my earliest years, worn-out space barges. None of them was designed for quiet operation inside. At least, not this quiet. I could hardly hear the rumble of the ship's *eight* big Hyperlight Drives, buried deep in her narrow hull.

"You *certain* you won't let the Medical Mate bring you something for those bruises, Admiral?" Delacroix interrupted, staring at me as if I were a little crazy.

Shook my head—painfully. But then, I couldn't find anywhere on my body that *didn't* hurt. "Thanks, Skipper," I said appreciatively. "But with all the excitement about LaSalle's raid on the Toronder supply fleet, I'll need to use what's left of my alleged brain soon as we make landfall. Can't take a chance on being sleepy." From early reports, LaSalle had been wildly successful, with more than half the enemy convoy destroyed and the remainder in full flight home.

Delacroix nodded. "I understand, Admiral," he said in a quiet voice. Stared thoughtfully while I sipped my juice. "Much responsibility, I suppose?"

"Much," I acknowledged, moving painfully to a new position in the jump seat; Barbousse was at my side in an instant, adjusting cushions, "and an awful lot of things to do."

"You have delegated some of your duties, one assumes?"

"As many as possible," I said. "But like you and *Yellow Bird,* if anything goes wrong with the base, I have full responsibility."

"Lives and all?"

Closed my eyes. "Yeah," I replied, thinking about how many Imperial lives I'd forfeited in my own little raid, alone. According to Barbousse, the toll was eight of our twenty-four ships, and only thirty-one of the 320 missing crew members had been recovered—including myself and two ratings from NL 19. The three of us would *never* have gotten out alive had it not been for Delacroix and his crew—and their ability to move stealthily in space near a planet. For nearly ten full watches, they'd searched for us at less than three Standard Light-Days' distant from Otnar'at. Probably the only thing that saved our bacon was the hornet's nest of confusion LaSalle and I had stirred up throughout The Torond— and *very possibly* the quiet, but nonetheless convincing, efforts of Master Chief Barbousse and the party of nineteen heavily-armed SPs who came aboard *Yellow Bird* with him in the dark morning they set out to search for survivors.

"A heavy burden," Delacroix observed, bringing me back to the present. "I was not aware of that."

"I was," I said, then shook my head to clear it—couldn't tell what hurt worse, my neck or my headache. "How many trips have you taken, now?" I asked, reckoning I'd been absent from the base a little less than four Standard Days.

"Eight, now," Delacroix replied. "I had just returned and was preparing for my next load when this giant of yours commandeered my ship." He scowled at Barbousse momentarily. "You *should* pay dearly for this trip, Admiral," he said.

I could only shrug—responsibility for the base included accepting ultimate blame for someone like Barbousse taking the situation in his own hands. Oh, I'd hear about it from Avalon! No doubt about that, especially since ultimately my own worthless neck had been saved by the effort. Probably, I estimated, before the heartless credit counters in BU. FLEET FINANCE were finished with me, I might well wish Delacroix *hadn't* found me. We survivors of NL 19 were the final three rescued, and the search for us required nearly a Standard Day extra. Took a deep breath. "How much?" I asked, looking him square in the eye.

Delacroix smiled a little: a strange smile, mostly with his dark eyes. "Nothing, Admiral," he said, shaking his head as if he couldn't quite believe what he was saying. "Not a credit."

"How many credits?" I asked. "I didn't quite hear you."

The strange little smile came again. "None, Admiral," he said. "Zero credits."

"You're not charging me?" I gasped. "I don't understand."

He shrugged. "This rescue flight has nothing to do with commerce," he explained, pointing to Barbousse, who had taken station to my right. "Rather," he continued, "it has to do with loyalty—and persons like your Chief Barbousse, who were willing to sacrifice me, themselves, and my ship for a chance to save you, Admiral." He laughed a little. "It is what I hope members of my own crew would do in a similar situation."

"But . . ."

"Think about it a while, Admiral," he said. "Men and women with that kind of loyalty are so terribly rare as to be virtually nonexistent. So, I reward them for that rare loyalty, as well as you, Admiral, for creating it."

I looked up at Barbousse—who was suddenly studying the instruments on a console behind him—then returned my gaze to Delacroix. "I don't know what to say," I muttered, nearly mute with emotion.

"Say nothing," Delacroix said, his smile slipping into its normal cynicism. "I acted only incidentally in your interest."

I nodded. "Well," I said through my own smile, "then my incidental thanks to you, Captain. I shall remember your kind favor to Chief Barbousse as long as I live. . . ."

Jim Williams was waiting at pierside as *Yellow Bird* thundered to a stop in Atalanta's monstrous Civilian Terminal. Was glad to spot Claudia farther back in the crowd. Somehow, I'd hoped she'd be there. Embarrassed me nearly to death, but I needed Barbousse's help as I limped along the brow. Guess I nearly *had* bought it in that LifeGlobe. I'd gone into a cold sweat by the time I reached the pier.

"Are all missions this tough on you, Admiral?" Williams asked, saluting with a grin as I stepped to the boards. "Don't believe I've seen you come back in one piece from one yet."

Returned his salute. "Well," I said, "I suppose I ought to be a little more careful, oughtn't I?"

"Mother of Voot," he said, rolling his eyes. "You look like . . . I don't know what you look like. Great shiner, though!"

"Thanks."

"I suppose you've heard the reports about the mission."

"Which one?" I asked with a grin. "From everything I've read so far, LaSalle and his people stopped the Toronders in their tracks."

"Stopped them cold," Williams said. "Not one of the Toronder ships made it to Occupied Fluvanna, and now it's looking like more than half were destroyed outright. People are trying to sort out the claims and confirmations as we speak."

"What about the ones that got away?" I asked.

"A number of them were heavily damaged," he said. "LaSalle's still busy chasing down the strays, but even if some make it back to port, the cargoes they carry won't be in the right place at the right time—and that counts big in this sort of war."

"You've got that right," I said. "So it looks as if we have a triumph on our hands, then."

"*Two* triumphs," Williams corrected. "You didn't exactly leave their base at Otnar'at in mint condition."

I grinned. "Yeah," I said. "Sounds as if we won't need to go back for a couple of days."

Williams grinned. "Probably not," he said. "Our newest damage assessments are incredible—they estimate Otnar'at won't field another effectual raid for as much as six Standard Weeks. You shut them down, Admiral."

"Thanks, Jim," I said with real emotion. "They'd better *stay* shut down a while, for what it cost us in lives and ships."

"Those people won't be the first we've lost in this war," Williams said grimly. "They won't be the last, either. And while you're busy beating yourself about casualties, Wilf Brim, keep in mind that you very nearly became one yourself." Then, before I could say anything more, I caught a breath of perfume and Claudia was at my side, shaking her head in clear amazement.

"Voot's beard but you're a mess, Admiral Brim," she said, extending a very professional hand.

"And a jolly good day to you, too, Ms. Harbor Master," I replied with a wry grin. It was when I touched her hand that reality finally hit me: I *was* alive. I hadn't died in that lonely, lonely LifeGlobe. "G-good to see you, Claudia," I stammered, my emotions completely running away with themselves.

"You're shaking," she said, taking my arm with a very real look of concern on her face.

Fighting back a flood of irrational tears, I ground my teeth until I'd regained a little control. "S'all right," I whispered. "Just a little weak for a moment."

"Could I give you a ride back to . . . ?" she asked, glancing at Barbousse, who was standing a few irals away, very clearly waiting to catch me if I fell.

"He's going to the Base Hospital," Williams said firmly.

Shook my head. "No, I'm all right, Jim," I said. "Really. Just need to sit a little while. Headquarters is fine."

"Well, my skimmer is right over there," Claudia declared adamantly, pointing to a civilian skimmer parked nearby in the center of a red-painted NO PARKING ZONE. "Cm'on, Chief, let's get him into a seat, then he can make up his mind where he's going."

Caught a broad grin on Barbousse as he grabbed my arm; before I knew it, I was in the passenger seat of Claudia's skimmer. "Thanks, Chief," I said.

"Admiral," he whispered, "how *do* you feel?"

"Like hammered shit, my friend," I muttered back. "But the Harbor Master's a lot better looking than either you or Williams. All right?"

Barbousse grinned again. "How about the sick bay?" he asked.

"I'll need you to drive me there later," I said. "But right now, I've got to get back and catch up at Headquarters. I know that first convoy's due in from Avalon tomorrow, even if neither of you have mentioned it."

Barbousse saluted with a wink. "Beggin' the Admiral's pardon, but even so, it probably wouldn't hurt if Ms. Harbor Master were to drive you slowly . . . pick out only the best roads on your way back."

I glanced at Claudia. "You in a hurry?"

"I plan to be *awfully* careful of you," she said.

Williams grinned. "Chief," he asked, "could I offer *you* a ride to Headquarters?"

"You wouldn't take *me* to the sick bay, would you, Captain?" Barbousse asked with a spurious look of concern.

"See what I mean, Admiral?" Williams asked, rolling his eyes skyward. "Discipline's simply collapsed in your absence."

"I'll work on that when I have time," I promised.

"I hope so," Williams said. "Cm'on, Chief, let's see if we can get some real work done before he gets back to Headquarters."

"Scuttlebutt had it that you were dead," Claudia said, her skirt riding halfway up her thigh the way I simply *loved*. Wondered idly if she let that happen on purpose. "The crews of two Starfuries climbing out behind you saw the whole thing," she continued. "Claimed your ship broke apart."

"Stupid zukeeds missed our LifeGlobes," I growled. "We train people to *look for* things like that. Would have saved a lot of trouble if they'd . . ." I ran out of words.

"It only matters that you're back," she said, pressing my hand. She glanced at me—caught me looking—and grinned. "Who would I have to stare at my legs if anything happened to you, Wilf Brim?"

"Probably every male in the galaxy," I suggested.

She shook her head. "I only let it slide up when you're around," she said with a little sidelong glance.

"I'll bet," I said.

"No, really," she said. "I've done it ever since the day I met you. Remember that ride I gave you back from the warehouse? I do."

"How could I forget?"

"I've hoped you hadn't."

"And you *still* don't mind my staring?" I asked, but I thought I really knew the answer.

"I'd be awfully hurt if you didn't," she said.

Took her hand again—warm, small, and soft. "I'd be awfully hurt if *you* didn't want me to," I said. Then I shook my head and stared at the floorboards for a moment, fighting myself.

"You all right?" she asked.

"Yeah," I replied, "I'm all right. It's *us* I'm worried about. I don't think this is turning out the way either of us had expected, is it?" I mumbled.

She glanced at me, dropped her eyes for a moment, then smoothed her skirt back over her knees as we headed toward the base's main gate. "I'm not sure what I expected," she said. "Probably I should have known myself better." She pursed her lips for a moment. "I'm still where I was all those years ago, so far as you're concerned. . . ."

"That's good to hear, Claudia," I admitted. "I never did get over you, either."

"So here we are," she said, shaking her head, "a couple of middle-aged, would-be lovers, tiptoeing around the subject like teenagers who want to sneak a kiss behind their parents' back."

"At least this time we're tiptoeing," I said, showing my pass as we slowed for the guard-shack scanners. "I wanted to get back together with you my second time in Atalanta when I came as a stowaway—before I got caught up in the Mitchell Trophy races. But you'd only just married Nesterio in those days, and we didn't even talk about . . . an *us.*"

"Wonder what would have happened if the Bears hadn't

spirited you off to fly those new Sherrington racers," she said, starting off as the signals turned green ahead.

"I've often wondered the same thing," I said, returning the guard's salute. "Another of those zillion or so paths we're never permitted to take in a single lifetime—so it probably doesn't matter much anyway."

"What *does* matter," she said, pulling up at the Base Headquarters building, "is that you and I have a big job to do professionally, and we've got to do it together. So . . . well, I simply plan to go on living day-by-day, calmly as possible, and let whatever happens between us happen. I'm simply through running away."

"Thanks," I managed to say. "I'm pretty tired of running myself," I could have hugged her, but I didn't dare—too many people around.

We sat without speaking for another couple of moments. Then Claudia broke the silence, her face as calm as if we were discussing operational plans. "If you don't get out of this skimmer immediately, Wilf Brim," she said, "what may happen in the next few moments will be embarrassing to both of us—and very probably will further reinforce those things people started saying after they caught us in that experimental LifeGlobe."

"I was thinking the same sort of thoughts," I admitted.

"In that case, good-bye, Admiral," she said firmly, "—for now."

Yeah. I opened the door and—oh, *painfully!*—worked myself to the pavement, where my knees buckled and I had to grab the skimmer's door. Must have groaned a bit, for she reached over for my arm.

"Can you make it?" she asked. "Should we go to the hospital instead?"

Shook my head. "I'll make it," I said. "Just need a little start."

"You look like you need a lot more than that, Wilf Brim," she observed quietly.

"I know I do," I agreed. "But look what happened after the LifeGlobe."

"Wilf Brim, you are impossible!"

"I've heard *that* before, too," I said with a wink, then marshaling what remained of my stength, I hobbled off for my office. The Marines were nearly a whole click behind in their timing, but the fact that I stumbled twice on my way to the doors probably threw them off considerably. . . .

For the remainder of the day, Williams had me set up to meet with more people than I could keep track of. Resurrection of the base was in full swing, now, with our improvement programs all coming to realization swiftly in full view of the Toronders—if they hadn't caught on by now, they weren't going to. Rapid, high-level decisions were the order of the day; Williams had carefully cut through all the nonsense so that when I had to resolve issues, the pertinent facts—and personalities—were immediately at my fingertips.

By evening, the docket was empty—including most potential problems concerning arrival of the first Gontor convoy from Avalon. They'd been safe under the protection of our patrolling Starfuries for the last Standard Day, and would only stop for supplies maintenance before getting under way again within two days of their arrival. The sheer job of servicing all those ships could only be described as massive, but thanks to Jim and Claudia working things out in advance, the anchorage was ready for them. Every resource available—military and civilian—was standing by.

The only possible hitch I could see came from the convoy's commander, Admiral Zakharoff, actually Count (the Hon.) Basal Zakharoff, Vice Admiral, I.F. He intended to throw a formal ball the night everyone was in harbor—right in the middle of a thraggling war we weren't exactly winning yet! But when someone with Zakharoff's influence wanted something, no matter how outlandish it might be, he got it. We *would* have a formal ball the following night. Thank Voot and all his minions for Cottshall! I'd turned the whole thing over to him, and he'd been busy all afternoon, with more people coming and going at his desk than mine. The man had seemed *delighted* with the assignment. . . .

I was damned well ready to accept the ride to my quarters Jim had graciously offered—couldn't ride my gravcycle for at least two Standard Weeks, according to Dr. Lazar, the Spaceflight Surgeon. However, before I could get up from my desk, the HoloPhone in my office came to life, with KA'PPA TRANSMISSION and EYES ONLY—IMMEDIATE emblazoned on the display. "Can you give me a couple of minutes to see about this?" I yelled out the door.

"I'll be here in the anteroom jawing with Cotshall when you're ready," Williams replied. "Take your time."

Nodded my thanks, then "signed" for the transmission and enabled my HoloPhone, which immediately displayed:

ADMIRALTY: PLEASE SIGNAL WHEN READY FOR GENERAL
    DRUMMOND.

Wonderful, I thought. *Just thraggling wonderful.* Now what? "Ready," I said.

DRUMMOND: HELLO, WILF. HEARD THEY'D FOUND YOU
    THIS MORNING! LOTS OF PEOPLE HERE IN AVALON ARE

DRINKING UP QUITE A CELEBRATION——ONRAD EVEN THREW A PARTY. SAID IT WAS TOO BAD YOU'RE NOT HERE TO ENJOY IT, BUT HE'D DRINK YOUR MEEM FOR YOU. DAMN THOUGHTFUL FOR AN EMPEROR, I'D SAY. HOW DO YOU FEEL?

"About Onrad or physically?"

DRUMMOND: SMART-ASS. ARE YOU ALL RIGHT?

"A few aches here and there, but pretty much alive, thanks."

DRUMMOND: WHAT DOES DR. LAZAR SAY?

"He says I'm killing myself."

DRUMMOND: LAZAR THINKS EVERYBODY IS KILLING HIM-
SELF. ARE YOU ABLE TO FLY A STARSHIP?

"According to Lazar?"

DRUMMOND: OF COURSE NOT——I ALREADY KNOW WHAT HE
THINKS. ACCORDING TO Y-O-U.

Thought about that for a moment. "Yes," I answered. "If I had to, sure."

DRUMMOND: DOES THAT MEAN YOU'D BE AS GOOD AS YOU
WERE BEFORE YOU GOT YOUR ASS HALF SHOT OFF?

Thought about that, too——something told me I'd better believe what I said. Drummond wouldn't be asking unless he

was thinking about putting me to the test. Decided I could. *"Better,"* I said.

DRUMMOND: TOOK YOU A WHILE.

"I meant it."

DRUMMOND: I'LL GIVE YOU ONE MORE CHANCE TO TAKE
THAT BACK.

"I pass."

DRUMMOND: YOUR FUNERAL, BRIM.

"What do you want me to do?"

DRUMMOND: I'LL HAVE TO TELL YOU IN AVALON.

"That's crazy," I said. "This set just spelled out something about your telling me in Avalon."

DRUMMOND: THE SET'S WORKING FINE, THEN.

"You mean you want me in Avalon?" I couldn't thraggling believe it!

DRUMMOND: ABSOLUTELY.

Voot's greasy, flea-infested, diseased, mangy beard. "When?"

DRUMMOND: SOON AS WE CAN GET YOU HERE.

"General," I said in exasperation, "this may come as a shock to you, but I'm a little *busy* here right now. Remember that Gontor thing you wanted me to take care of?"

> DRUMMOND: OF COURSE I REMEMBER. YOU'VE DONE A SU-
> PERB JOB GETTING EVERYTHING STARTED. AND THAT
> RAID YOU PULLED OFF AGAINST OTNAR'AT WAS A
> MASTER STROKE. IT WILL PROBABLY GO DOWN AS
> THE SINGLE MOST IMPORTANT ELEMENT IN SECURING
> GONTOR. IN FACT, BRIM, YOU MAY HAVE BEEN EN-
> TIRELY TOO SUCCESSFUL WITH BOTH THOSE RAIDS
> YOU PULLED OFF, BUT WE'LL TALK ABOUT THAT
> LATER.

Too successful? Shook my head. Where the xaxt was Drummond's head? "Glad you like my work," I argued, "but for Voot's sake, how can I just up and come to Avalon? I've now got a lot of unfinished business to do."

> DRUMMOND: THE IMPORTANT THING IS THAT YOUR UNFIN-
> ISHED BUSINESS IS IN THE HANDS OF EXCELLENT PEO-
> PLE WHO CAN MANAGE THINGS BEAUTIFULLY
> WITHOUT YOU UNTIL PROJECT SAPPHIRE ENTERS ITS
> NEXT STAGE. AND I PROMISE YOU'LL BE BACK IN
> PLENTY OF TIME FOR THAT.

Rocked back in my chair. He was right, of course. I just hadn't thought of it that way before. I couldn't personally have led the Otnar'at mission unless those teams of people I'd put in charge with Williams's help were capable of running themselves for a while. And of course, Williams himself. Shuddered for a moment wondering where I'd be right now without him.

DRUMMOND: YOU STILL THERE?

"Yeah. I'm thinking."

DRUMMOND: DANGEROUS STUFF, THINKING. HAVE A CARE.

"Same to you, Drummond." Thought for a while more about leaving the base under Williams's command. No problem with Williams—he just wasn't a Helmsman. Of course, he had Burton LaSalle to handle *that* part of the job. And Barbousse would be around to keep track of things in my absence. . . .

DRUMMOND: WELL? EITHER YOU DID A GOOD JOB AND CAN LEAVE FOR A WHILE, OR YOU DIDN'T.

And probably it wouldn't be a bad idea if Claudia and I did give things a rest for a while. We both knew where we were heading on our present course. Made sense. . . .

DRUMMOND: HEY, BRIM.

"All right, I'll go! How soon?"

DRUMMOND: I CAN HAVE A TYPE 327 THERE IN TWO STANDARD DAYS. LET'S SEE, WHERE YOU ARE, THAT'S DAY AFTER TOMORROW—IN THE MORNING. CAN YOU BE READY?

This really wasn't happening, of course—except it *was*. "Yeah. Sure," I blurted out. "I'll be packed and waiting on the dock."

DRUMMOND: SEE YOU IN FOUR DAYS OR SO, BRIM. HAVE A
        GOOD TRIP.

"Right," I replied, wondering what in xaxt I'd just signed
up for now and feeling kind of disgusted that I'd done it in
the first place. But I was a whole lot too late thinking about
that now.

ADMIRALTY: SIGNING OFF.

I touched DISCONNECT, and the display faded. Sat there in
silence a few moments, thinking about what I'd just
promised—and how very little information I had about it.
Then I shrugged. Someday, I promised myself, I'd finally
learn to say "no." Meanwhile ... "Ah ... Jim," I called,
limping away from my cluttered desk, "all of a sudden,
we've got a lot to talk about on the way home!"

Next morning, our incoming Gontor convoy needed no announcement on the local media, even to a city long ac-
quainted with the resounding thunder of starships lifting and
settling to landfall. This arrival shook the very ground we
walked on, intruded on our personal spaces with no mitiga-
tion. Ships simply began to appear through the clouds—then
simply kept coming ... and coming ... and coming. Now
and again throughout the morning, I studied them from the
roof of Headquarters as they rumbled overhead, clumsily—
to the eye of killer-ship Helmsman—maneuvering in the
tight constraints of a *very* crowded airspace. There were all
shapes and sizes of starships: transports, mammoth liners,
humpbacked livestock packets, store ships of every descrip-
tion, many small ships—mostly tramps—that would have
been better off plying the trade within planetary systems than

trying the hazards of an interstellar passage. Every starship was deep-laden and moving with the uncertainty of precariously thin useful-lift ratios.

I must admit the sight of that great fleet stirred me deeply. For all its diversity, yes, and occasional disorganization, it had a sense of purpose after its hazardous passage the long way 'round past Braltar from Avalon. It was a sense the convoy would need for the second leg of its voyage, this time, through much more treacherous space. This was especially true considering its long-distance escort, which was *much* less impressive than the convoy itself—and reflected perfectly the pinched circumstances of our badly stretched Imperial Fleet at this point of the war. To shepherd these ninety-six ships through potentially the most treacherous interstellar space in the galaxy, our Admiralty had been able to provide the ancient battlecruiser *Celeron* (Voot knew from what backwater they'd resurrected that old ship, pride of another era); four disruptor monitors, one of crude, prewar design; and a pair of armed rescue tugs. Seven military starships—more like six and a half—to guard ninety-six heavily laden, virtually irreplaceable merchantmen. Not a reassuring show of strength, and yet there it was. In the long void between the umbrella of Starfuries we would launch from this base and the much thinner umbrella of Starfuries Delacroix had managed to land at the other side on Gontor, this was the best that could be done. Luck and skill would have to fill the gap. All I could do was quietly thank Voot and his greasy beard for the success of our mission to Otnar'at. If ever the forfeiture of human lives seemed worth the cost, now was the time. . . .

As the last ships were thundering down into the harbor, I transferred some last-cycle data to Jim Williams's account, then shut down my workstation and prepared to make an of-

ficial appearance at the harbor to welcome Count, (the Hon.)
Vice Admiral Basal Zakharoff. Earlier, Barbousse had
fetched me a respectable uniform. These days, I spent most
of my time in blue flight coveralls and a Helmsman's jacket.
As I dressed, I felt unusually stuffy in the starched fabrics
that, previously, I had considered quite the norm for non-
combat situations. How very little time I required to establish
bad habits! Wrestled a xaxtdamned pair of white gloves over
my hands—why is it white gloves are *always* too small? Do
they thraggling *make* them that way? Somehow fastened the
xaxtdamned buttons while thinking that people who regu-
larly fly all over a xaxtdamned galaxy have little need for
xaxtdamned white gloves that attract every xaxtdamned
speck of dirt within five hundred xaxtdamned light-years
whether the wearer touches anything or not! Hate the
xaxtdamned things! Got a thorough, perceptible, check from
Cottshall—only my collar needed adjusting. A second check,
this one much more stringent but totally unobservable to the
inexperienced eye, from Barbousse earned me a wink.

"You look extremely military, Admiral," he allowed.
From Barbousse, this was an endorsement half the Fleet
would gladly die for, especially since I still had a black eye
that would make a professional Kanz'u champion blush with
envy. Made me feel pretty good about myself as I half
limped through the headquarters lobby; hoped I wouldn't trip
and fall flat on my face.

Outside, Petty Officer First Class Joe Russo waited at the
open door of the great, elegant limousine skimmer he'd been
shining that day I met him—complete with my two-star flag
flying from a jack staff at the bow. Hador's reflection from
the trim alone was enough to blind a man. "Mr. Russo," I
said, "I thought you'd sent *that* to salvage."

Russo saluted and grinned proudly. "Almost did, Admiral," he said. "But when Master Chief Barbousse took over as ranking NCO, he told me t' belay that 'cause we might need it someday. Grand-lookin'limo, isn't she?"

Glanced at Barbousse, who appeared to be studying something on the roof of the building next door. Chuckled. "Best-looking limo I've seen in a long time, Mr. Russo," I said. Couldn't argue with the truth. . . .

When he arrived at the dockyards, Atalanta's harbor had descended into a noisy, teeming chaos with provisions lighters and bristling maintenance barges speeding everywhere—in every conceivable direction—all at the same time. Zakharoff's ominous, gray flagship *Celeron* was moored to one of the city's largest piers, where she appeared to loom over every ship in the harbor. A frowning, humpbacked mammoth from an earlier age, *Celeron*'s massive, asymmetric hull was originally conceived as a platform for the type of enormous, antiship disruptors that had been the final arbiters in space-power struggles for a millennium or more. These colossal weapons could destroy other battlecruisers, huge asteroids—even cities. But they could neither fire rapidly nor traverse swiftly, and were next to useless against new attack ships developed over the past ten years. In an attempt to bolster this weakness—unseen by her original designers—at least seventy new, rapid-firing disruptor barbettes had been let-in to her massive hull, and she now bristled like an oversize hedgehog.

Russo picked his way through the teeming surface traffic and brought us to the foot of her brow, where four Imperial Marines stood at parade rest, blast pikes at their sides. As our skimmer drew to a hover, the Marines came to rigid attention and one of them called out, "Alongside!"

Startled me. A long time had passed since I'd had much to

do with the old capital ships; we don't stand on much ceremony dodging aboard Starfuries. Glanced up to the other end
of the brow, where an officer, a boatswain's mate, and ten
ratings had just come to rigid attention on a small, retractable
platform I guessed was deployed for the express purpose of
honors and ceremonies. "Alongside!" the officer echoed.

Russo opened my door smartly. "Need a hand, Admiral?"
he whispered without moving his lips or changing his expression.

I winked an appreciative "no," then struggled to the pavement and limped a little shakily to the brow, allowing Barbousse to hand me onto the treads, which whisked us to the
platform with no further discomfort on my part.

At the precise moment I arrived on the honors platform,
the officer—a full Commander, no less—called out, "Over
the side!" Instantly, the boatswain hammered two traditional
"clear tones" from his golden tocsins and we saluted.

"Permission to board I.F.S. *Celeron,*" I said.

"Permission granted, Admiral," the Commander said with
a steely look. "Admiral Zakharoff sends his compliments and
requests your presence in the ship's wardroom—first hatch
to your left past the boarding lobby."

"Thank you, Commander," I replied, and stepped into the
old warship's elegant, paneled boarding lobby, where another two rows of perfectly outfitted Imperial Marines came
to attention as Barbousse and I passed between them. Wondered what they did when they weren't honoring something.
Haven't noticed us capturing many enemy ships by boarding
these days. Inside, we made our way quietly through a long
'midships alleyway traversing what I guessed was the ship's
main deck. By the first hatch to the right, two more Imperial
Marines stood at attention on either side of an open hatch or-
namented with a huge, gilded Imperial comet. From the

sounds coming from inside—and a strong odor of drinking spirits—I knew I'd located the wardroom.

Barbousse stopped short of the door. "Officers' country, Admiral," he said. "I'm wearing my summoner—just signal when you need me."

I looked him in the eye and nodded thoughtfully. Here was a man who was a hundred times more talented than most of the flag officers in the Fleet. Yet he was not permitted inside the wardroom of an Imperial warship, no matter how mean and insignificant she might be. We'd been through this a thousand times over the years. By his firm wishes, he remained an enlisted man in history. "I'll signal," I assured him. Then I stepped into the wardroom, all dark wood paneling, deep carpets, potted greenery, and soft lighting—a perfect clone of all the fine old men's clubs I'd visited—but as a Carescrian never been permitted to join—in Avalon.

"Rear Admiral Wilf Ansor Brim, Imperial Fleet, Military Commandant, Atalanta Fleet Base!" a white-uniformed steward announced while I stripped off my right glove and folded it under my left shoulder strap. Perhaps twenty officers—including two Rear Admirals like myself—were gathered in full uniform at the far wall before a massive bar, behind which four more stewards stood at watchful attention. The room suddenly became quiet, and a large man with a florrid countenance—wearing one more stripe on his sleeve than I did—turned to face me. Had to fight off a smile wondering what he thought of the black eye.

"My dear Brim," he rumbled in a deep, soggy bass, extending his hand, "how good of you to pay us a call. Come refresh yourself in our humble wardroom." He was tall and portly, with a uniform that must have cost at least half the Empire's original outlay for the *Celeron*. His face was lined and creased by what appeared to be a lifetime of unrestraint, and you could park a Starfury in the bags under his liverish eyes. But aside from the obvious deterioration, there was *something* very substantial to this fat old reprobate. Perhaps it was that aura of power the nobility always seems to emit. Perhaps it was even a vision of wickedness—his mustache combined with a small goatee and pendulous veined cheeks gave him a look I'd always associated with the Gradgroat-Norchelite church's "Evil One." Whatever it might be, Zakharoff was an imposing, impressive person. I decided to reserve judgment until I'd had time to more accurately take the man's measure. "Basal Zakharoff," he said as I grasped his hand—a surprisingly firm, masculine handshake. Don't know why it surprised me.

"I am honored," I countered, looking the man square in the eye. "Welcome to Atalanta."

Zakharoff made a curt, little military nod. "Gentlemen," he said, indicating me with a casual wave of the hand, "may I present our host, Admiral Brim?" With a hand in the center of my back, he ushered me toward the bar. "I believe you're an appreciator of Logish Meem, aren't you, Brim?" he asked. "At least that is the impression Onrad gives."

I nodded—name droppers don't much impress me. "I've been known to sample a bottle now and then," I conceded.

"Miller," he said, signaling the bar steward, "Admiral Brim will have a goblet of our Tamrhone oh-five."

The steward fixed me with a glance, then nodded, and Zakharoff began introducing me to the other officers. Two of them—the Rear Admirals, both senior to me—I now recognized as classmates of mine at the Helmsman's Academy; they seemed mildly interested that I had managed to become an Admiral, too. "You've been most fortunate, Brim," one of them, David Lynch, allowed in patrician articulation. "Especially considering your origins."

Felt my hackles rise. He hadn't changed. Remembered him as such a poor Helmsman that he'd graduated without the tiny winged comet to wear on his left breast. I'd read in a recent issue of the Academy's alumni publication, *Helm,* that he'd just finished a tour as Chief of the Navigation Aids Bureau in Avalon. Wondered what sort of cock-up he'd committed there to wind up as part of this suicide squadron. "Thanks," I said, reaching for my goblet of meem. "Sometimes Dame Fortune smiles for the strangest of reasons."

"I dare say she does, the old whore," Lynch roared, raising his glass in a chuckling toast to the other Rear Admiral, one Bill Liddle—who'd also failed to complete flight school, if I remembered correctly.

I mumbled something inane, then busied myself sampling the meem. Wasn't half bad. Lamentable to waste it on these insolent bastards! Continued along the bar with Zakharoff, meeting the kind of people I'd encountered when I'd entered the Fleet during a war whose ashes had been cold for more than a decade. Found quickly that I *still* didn't have much to talk to them about. My world is filled with starships and weaponry, not the latest social intrigues at Court.

Aside from my black eye, one topic that did interest them all was the Carescrian reinforcements that would soon be added to our Imperial forces. They'd heard about *that.* Of course, I didn't know much more than they did about the subject. But since I *was* a Carescrian, they expected I would be a font of information, and I suppose I came off like a dunce, at least in their eyes. Kind of wondered how a busy officer was supposed to keep up with such trivia in the first place, but mentally threw up my hands. These men had little to do with today's fast-evolving Imperial Fleet. They still lived in an era that had gone by the boards ten years ago. Like the grand old ship they inhabited, they were doomed, either from the deadly, new combat that was closing in around them—or from the equally lethal peace that would follow.

After less than a metacycle of this drivel, I found myself glancing about, wondering how I could make an early escape without incurring Zakharoff's wrath. Stuffed shirt or no, he *was* a force to be reckoned with. Like it or not, one doesn't irritate the big guns whenever one pleases. Nevertheless, I desperately needed something—anything—to get me back to reality, no matter how crazy Atalanta's reality might have become in the past few metacycles.

Just as I was about to make a lame excuse and bolt for a door regardless of the consequences, a rating from the ship's COMM center showed up carrying a red envelope prominently marked MOST SECRET-IMMEDIATE/FLASH. He spoke with one of the stewards, who quickly struck a tiny chime and announced, "Message for Admiral Brim!"

The room went stone-cold silent as I limped across the floor to sign for it. Every eye seemed to follow me as I hobbled to a private corner of the wardroom, sat in a gloriously comfortable easy chair, then applied my thumb to the envelope's seal. After the opening sequence, I peered inside and withdrew a KA'PPA message form:

DFLKJHBQWIOT3456JLKV SOIEYWRTLKU
[TOP SECRET]

FROM:
U. BARBOUSSE, MCPO, I.F.S. CELERON, ATALANTA, HADOR-HAELIC

TO:
WILF A. BRIM, RADM, I.F.S. CELERON, ATALANTA,
HADOR-HAELIC

IF I AM TO TRUST MILLER, THE BAR STEWARD, YOU
LOOK BORED NEARLY TO DISTRACTION. SHOULD
YOU WISH AN ESCAPE, USE THIS AS YOUR TICKET TO
FREEDOM. YOUR SUMMONER WILL BRING ME TO THE
WARDROOM DOOR IN LESS THAN A CYCLE. RUSSO
HAS THE LIMO IDLING AT THE FOOT OF THE BROW.

[END TOP SECRET]
DFLKJHBQWIOT3456JLKV SOIEYWRTLKU

Managed to contain the c'lenytwide grin that threatened to
spread across my face. Wheezed a couple of times stuffing
the message back in its envelope, then got to my feet as Zakharoff strode to my chair. "Sensitive business, my dear
Brim?" he asked.

"Sensitive, indeed, Admiral," I replied with as serious a
demeanor as I could produce, considering the circumstances.
"It seems as if I must return to headquarters immediately."
As I activated my summoner, I discovered that everyone at
the bar was staring at me in utter astonishment. They must
not know many Carescrians who receive MOST SECRET-
IMMEDIATE/FLASH messages.

"One hopes the situation is not so serious as to prohibit
your appearance at the ball this evening," Zakharoff offered.

"One can only hope, Admiral," I said gravely as Barbousse appeared at the doorway. "One can only hope." Turning my attention to the surprised officers, I made one of
Zakharoff's curt, little military nods. "Good day, gentlemen," I said, then clicked my heels. "Admiral Zakharoff."

"Admiral Brim," he said, looking down his long, bulbous
nose in dismissal.

Turning on my heel, I joined Barbousse in the alleyway. Russo had us back at Headquarters before another half metacycle had passed.

Couldn't get better than a "military" rating from Barbousse when I left for Cottshall's soiree that night. My black eye and pronounced limp gave me the look of an alley cat who has lost control of his alley. Actually, I think I looked worse in my formal uniform than I might have in my fatigues and flight jacket. Kind of like a new white carpet shows up every bit of dirt, no matter how insignificant. Nevertheless, here I was, back in the limousine, dressed in full soup and fish—ceremonial cape, cutaway jacket, epaulettes, ruffled shirt—and on my way to our Officers' Club, which in a metacycle or so would be strained to the very limits of its capacity. The receiving line was scheduled to begin in less than half a metacycle. "How's your transport pool holding up?" I asked Russo.

"We're doin' fine, Admiral," Russo replied. "But I've never seen so many VIPs in my life."

"They'll be gone after tomorrow," I promised.

"Better be," Russo chuckled. "Couple of my drivers are threatenin' to defect to the League if they have to haul many more uppity bigwigs."

"Tell 'em to pick me up if they leave before this little bash is over," I said with a laugh. "I think I want out, too." Ahead, the circular driveway to the Club's main entrance was a miniature traffic nightmare, with SPs gesturing and whistling in a vain attempt to keep early guests and last-moment commercial traffic moving. Voot only knew what it would be like when people *really* began to arrive.

"Beggin' the Admiral's pardon," Russo interjected, "but I've often wondered how you manage to put up with what you do." He reached over the windshield and touched a button that began to pulse. "It's all over the base the way you got treated aboard *Celeron* this afternoon—an' none of the scuttlebutt came from Chief Barbousse."

Sat speechless for a moment. Clearly, the ratings had a grapevine nearly as efficient as the Chiefs'. "Don't quote me, Russo," I warned, "but after all these years, garbage like that doesn't bother me much. Kind of like scar tissue—hasn't a lot of nerves in it."

"An' besides, you showed 'em all, didn't you, Admiral?"

"Thanks," I said. "I did what I needed to do." Ahead, traffic in the driveway was simply dissolving as we approached. "Russo," I asked, "how'd you do *that?*"

"Had the boys install a little VIP switch up there," he said, pointing to the pulsing switch over the windshield. "Lets the SPs know you're on the way. They simply stop traffic everywhere until I give 'em the word."

"Mister," I grumbled as we drew up unimpeded before the Club's main entrance, "you're going to spoil me—turn me into another Summers."

"Can't hear you, Admiral," he said as he jumped out and opened the door for me. "Whenever you want the limo, just let Mr. Cottshall know. I'll be here before you know it."

I grabbed his arm to steady myself as I got out. The leg still ached with dull pain, especially when I'd been sitting for a while. "Thanks, Russo," I said with a chuckle. "I'll count on that." Cottshall had stationed four of our SPs in their best uniforms on either side of the door. One, with at least a million hash marks on his sleeve, moved quietly to my side.

"Er, can I offer some help, Admiral?" he asked.

"Thanks, Chief," I said. "I've got a metacycle of receiving line ahead of me. Might as well get used to it now."

"If you need anything at all this evening . . ."

"I'll yell," I called over my shoulder. "Keep an ear posted."

"You bet I will, Admiral," he said with a big grin.

Two more SPs yanked the doors open, and I made my way through clouds of mu'occo cigarette smoke, perfume, and the odor of spirits into an already-crowded lobby, where I handed my cape to a steward and tried to field greetings from people whose names I should have remembered, but didn't. Cottshall had stationed himself to one side of the ballroom at a small lectern, directing operations with all the precision of a dancing master conducting an elaborate ballet. He looked up as I came alongside and grinned. "Ah, welcome, Admiral," he said with obvious pride of accomplishment, and nodded to the crowded lobby. "Quite a turnout already."

"Quite a turnout, indeed, Mr. Cottshall," I said, grinning. "Congratulations."

"It's not even started yet," he said. "I'll let you know about congratulations tomorrow."

Squeezed his arm. "I'm willing to make a few predictions."

"Thank you, Admiral," he said. "By the by, Ms. Valemont-Nesterio is already inside the ballroom preparing for the reception line. You might wish to join her."

"Good idea," I said, hoping I didn't look too eager, and slipped through the doors into . . . what *used* to be the Officers' Club ballroom. Cottshall had transformed it. In the center of the room, a huge table groaned beneath a princely expanse of hors d'oeuvres arranged around two huge ice sculptures of climbing Starfuries. In the far corner, a chamber orchestra was setting up at the bandstand, which itself had been transformed into a giant opened mollusk shell. *Five* temporary bars would soon be in operation, one at each wall and another at an angle near the door to assist in traffic control. Beside them, a small army of white-coated stewards—had Cottshall hired *all* the ratings on the base?—were loading additional tables with hors d'oeuvres. Stanchions connected by a thick golden rope led into the room from the main doors and designated space for our reception line. Everything in place except . . . Claudia. Where was she? Cottshall *had* said she'd be here.

Suddenly, I caught the sensuous odor of perfume and felt a hand on my arm. "Good evening, Admiral," she said, proffering a goblet of meem with one hand while she held a flute of E'lande—nearly consumed—in the other. Almost gasped—she wasn't just beautiful this evening, she was glorious! She'd chosen white for the occasion, a color that revealed her tawny complexion at its best. And she'd dressed in the hugely fashionable *costume antique* style that had shocked—as well as thoroughly charmed—Avalonian society during the past few months. Her gown was extremely low-bosomed and concealed little of those ample, clearly unrestrained, breasts I loved so. With a high waistline, and a very narrow, slit-to-the-thigh skirt that carried sheer down to tiny, high-heeled shoes, it was clear to me that she was destined to be extremely popular among our male guests tonight. All I could do was stare—when I dared.

"Great shiner you've got there," she said, with a grin and a sidelong look of amusement.

"Like that, eh?" I asked, trying to keep my gaze where it ought to be—she was *gorgeous.*

"Gives you that sexy look of the streets," she replied, with a faux-serious countenance.

"Speaking of sexy," I countered, "that gown of yours is positively erotic—and beautiful."

"Like it?" she asked, twirling to give me a better view.

"Mother of Voot," I swore under my breath. "You must have had it made specially for me."

She made a sidelong glance. "I did, you know."

"Right," I said, "and Nergol Triannic is about to sue for peace."

"Sometimes, Wilf Brim," she said, rolling her eyes, "I could stick your xaxtdamned modesty somewhere that isn't your ear."

"Sorry," I replied.

"You ought to be," she retorted. "And now you're staring."

"Damned right I'm staring," I said. "If you got that gown for me, then I don't intend to miss even a square milli-iral of skin."

She grinned and glanced at the door. "Cm'on, you," she said, taking my arm. "Here's Captain Williams, and look who he's got with him. Adele! Isn't she the crafty one? What a *lovely* gown!"

At that moment—and not *until* that moment—did I realize that I hadn't given even a single thought to bringing an escort of my own. And clearly, neither had Claudia. . . .

By Twilight and twenty, the noise from the lobby had become deafening, and our little reception line was braced for the onslaught. Closest to the door was Jill Tompkins, Chief of Operations, squired by one of the Helmsmen who'd survived the Otnar'at raid with me. What Jill did for a formal uniform more than made up for the unsightliness I brought to the party tonight. Next was Burt LaSalle, our senior Space Officer with a gorgeous blonde he'd met in the city (who couldn't hold a candle to Claudia, even though her gown showed *acres* more skin). Next, Jim Williams and Adele Hough, Claudia's secretary, looking exquisite in a gown designed for a royal princess. Then Claudia, and finally me. Felt like we were waiting at the wrong end of a firing squad.

At Twilight and a half sharp, a grinning Cottshall stuck his head through the double doors. "Ready everyone?" he asked in an excited voice.

I turned to Claudia and rolled my eyes, while reluctant bleats of, "Yeah," and "Guess so," struggled from the lips of we sacrificial offerings to the gods of polite society.

"Then brace yourselves," Cottshall warned, and both doors swung open.

Actually, it was even *worse* than I'd expected, but that could serve as another story altogether. . . .

There had been dancing in the ballroom upstairs for nearly half a metacycle now, however I was content to wedge myself into one of the club's dimly lit, basement bars, nursing two very numb feet and a greatly ill-treated right hand, the latter victim of more than two hundred crushing handshakes. For some lunatic reason, nearly every male who had come through the receiving line felt compelled to declare personal dedication to the Empire's ultimate victory by earnestly— painfully—wringing my hand as if it were something to be killed by strangulation. Doubtlessly a testosterone thing, I mused—Voot knew I'd probably done the same idiotic thing myself on occasion. But now, with the actual ball successfully under way upstairs, I found it terribly nice to hide for a few moments and lick my wounds, so to speak. Oh, sooner or later I'd have to return to the ballroom and mingle. Like it or not, the job of Base Commander *does* come with certain political strings attached; Voot knew that I'd already palmed most of it off to Cottshall and Williams.

And after all, it was *still* little more than two days since they'd dragged me half-dead from the LifeGlobe. . . .

"Hey, StarSailor," Claudia's soft voice whispered caressingly in my ear. "Don't suppose you'd like to dance, would you?"

"How about a drink now and a promise for later?" I suggested, getting to my feet a little less painfully now and offering my barstool.

She grinned. "I've already had a couple drinks tonight. You could make me tipsy—and you know what that means."

"You go to sleep," I chuckled. "Right?"

"Well, yes," she said, her cheeks reddening slightly, "that, too."

"Sorry," I said. "However," I added, *"this* time, I might just take advantage of you."

"That a promise?"

"Absolutely."

"In that case," she said, perching daintily on my barstool—and completely ignoring the fact that her skirt had ridden most of the way up her thighs in the near darkness beneath the bar—"I'll have another E'lande, if you please."

I grinned and wedged in between her and a great, buxom redhead on the next barstool who was chatting up one of the captains from the convoy. The redhead didn't seem to notice me at all—great padding. "An E'lande for the lady, please," I called to the steward, then returned my gaze to Claudia. "Do I get to stare a little now?" I asked.

"Oh yes, definitely," she said in a little whisper. ". . . I'd like that."

"What do I get to stare at?"

"Whatever you'd like to stare at," she said, grinning. "Within reason, of course."

"Does that include legs that might have escaped your skirt?"

"Well," she said, frowning as the steward delivered her drink, "I suppose."

I paused till the steward busied himself with another order, then glanced down appraisingly. "Great legs," I said.

"You think so, eh?" she asked, stretching them out a bit for a critical look.

"Of course," I replied, putting my arm around her waist for a stealthy hug. "Always have; always will."

"Yeah," she whispered, half closing her eyes. "Oh how I have treasured that over the years, Wilf Brim."

"Nothing to treasure," I said, sipping my meem and conspicuously returning my gaze to her legs. "Merely doing what comes naturally."

She punched me playfully on the arm and retracted her legs. "Is that *all* you intend to stare at, then?"

"It's all right to ogle your boobs, too?" I whispered with a chuckle. "I'd really like that."

After a long, thoughtful pause for a sip of her E'lande, she nodded. "My boobs," she said with a certain gravity, "are customarily . . . sacrosanct. But in your case, I shall make an exception." She slowly rolled her shoulders forward and peered circumspectly into the much-slackened top of her gown. "Is that better?" she asked, moving her head to one side.

I didn't know what the person behind me could see—and didn't particularly care—but I suddenly got a view that started my heart pounding like a jackhammer. "Voot's beard," I whispered reverently, "they're—you're—exquisite, Claudia."

"Actually," she said, with a little glance my way, "I rather enjoy the way they look, myself."

At that juncture, I suddenly jettisoned the last tattered shreds of my self-restraint. "Claudia," I groaned, putting my arm around her waist again, "do you suppose that we could, well, go somewhere afterward and ah . . . ?"

"Ah, *what* afterward?" she asked.

"Well," I said, as the whole Universe went whirling away out of control. "Well . . . Voot take it . . . Claudia, will you—*please*—go to bed with me tonight?"

She closed her eyes with a little sigh. "Oh, Wilf—yes, I will go to bed with you tonight," she said, taking my hand. "For a while there, I was afraid you weren't going to ask." She glanced around and giggled. "Finally! No more 'Phones. No more teenagers sneaking a kiss. Gorgas doesn't expect me home until tomorrow, so I want it *all* before you run off to Avalon. What do you say to that?"

Felt my legs shaking. "Thank the gods," I whispered more to myself than anyone else. I could hardly believe my good fortune. "You must know I've wanted you for years, now," I stammered, "and . . ." Suddenly I ran out of words—very probably the best idea at such a time.

"Come on, Wilf Brim," she whispered, placing a perfumed finger to my lips. "We've got to do a bit more palm-pressing upstairs before we start in on our own pleasures. Let's get it over with before my feet give up and die."

That brought me back to the surface quickly enough. We did, of course—both of us—need to do a lot more palm-pressing before the night was over. "Yeah," I grumped, "just so long as my hand holds out."

She'd started to slide off the barstool when—abruptly—she stopped and snapped her fingers with a troubled look in her eyes. "Probably this is going to sound a little strange," she said, squirming back onto the cushion, "but I've been running on here in my usual, totally self-assured manner, assuming that *you've* got a wonderfully private place we can go and get naked together. Was that a . . . well, a . . . viable supposition?"

"W-e-l-l," I admitted with a grimace—suddenly very much concerned about the subject myself—"now that you *mention* it . . . ah . . . *no.* I don't suppose you've ah . . . ?"

"Not me. I'm married, remember?"

"Yeah, I've noticed," I grumbled. "Otherwise, we'd be old hands at this by now."

She giggled for a moment and shook her head. "It's sure not like the old days when we had my apartment whenever we wanted to romp, is it?"

Had to chuckle myself. "Not quite, Claudia," I replied, "but by Voot's greasy beard, we can't just let something like *this* get in our way."

"It's been a long time since I've hiked my skirt and rutted on the grass, Wilf Brim," she said with another giggle. "In fact, the last time I tried that kind of kid stuff, I think was with you, wasn't I?"

"Don't have any idea," I protested. "But you certainly had a lot of boyfriends in those days. I'll bet any of 'em would have been more than glad to . . ."

"Well, *tonight,*" she interrupted quickly, "you're all I've got left in the way of boyfriends. And in my dignified, middle-aged capacity as Atalanta's Harbor Master, I now require a bed to roll around in when I'm making love." She grinned and took my hand again. "Especially if I've got the dignified Base Commander rolling around on top of me."

"Sounds like good thinking to me," I agreed. "But where? Seriously. Nice as my suite in the Officers' Quarters is, it's got thin walls. And as I recall, you tend to, well . . . be a little noisy once you work up to lift-off speed."

"Mother of Voot," she whispered poking a finger in my sternum. "The pot calling the kettle black! You ought to hear yourself when you've reached your short strokes. Talk about noise. You'd wake the dead."

"Or an entire Bachelor Officers' Quarters," I admitted. "All right . . . think, Brim. Where?" Then I glanced at her from the corner of my eye. "Well, this is *your* town, after all. Don't you know some place?"

"I suppose we could check into a hotel," she said, lighting a mu'occo. "Before I got married, I was pretty good at looking like an innocent housewife."

"Of course nobody in town would ever recognize *us* as the Harbor Master and the Base Commander," I said mordantly. "Especially since we're hardly noticeable in these formal outfits."

"Yeah. Guess we wouldn't blend very well, would we?" she said, then giggled. "By the way, you're staring at my boobs again."

I grinned. "If I don't come up with someplace to take you pretty soon, this might be everything I get to see tonight."

"That *would* indeed be distressing," she said, finishing her E'lande, "because I'm really in the mood for showing them off a little more than I've done so far."

I thought about that for a moment, then shakily finished my meem. I'd done a lot of fantasizing about those boobs over the years. Think, Brim, xaxtdamnit. Think! Then, out of the blue it came to me. "Mother of Voot," I exclaimed, rolling my eyes to the ceiling. "Where'd you tell Gorgas you were going to spend the night?"

She shrugged. "In that little roomette off my office," she said. "Since you put the base back on its feet, I've had to spend lots of nights there. Managing a harbor like this one is damn near a six-watch job—you certainly know that. And I can't just hop a gravcycle to the Bachelor Officers' Quarters when *I* want to turn in."

"Yeah," I said, backing down quickly. "I understand."

"So why'd you want to know about . . . ?" she began, then got a funny little grin on her face. "Oh my God, Wilf, of course! Why didn't I think of that?"

"Would it work?"

"Xaxt—of course it would. Everybody's *here,* tonight."

"Got to be a few security people over there."

She laughed. "Wilf," she said, "there's probably nowhere on this whole *planet* you and I can go together that at least someone isn't going to guess what we're up to."

"Yeah," I agreed, thinking back to my afternoon aboard *Celeron.*

"At least locked in my office we'll have some privacy. Besides, it's got a great bed—for a foldaway."

"Is it a great bed for doing what *we* want to do?" I asked.

"Certainly ought to be," she said, slipping down from the barstool again, this time with a contented grin. "But it will take *both* of us to make a really valid decision, don't you think?"

"Absolutely," I agreed as we pushed our way through the noisy throng. "Just as soon as we put a few political finishing touches in place upstairs. . . ."

Chapter 7

◆

Operation Eppeid

19-21 Octad, 52014

Somewhere in Effer'wyckean Interstellar Space,
En Route to Avalon

I'd flown in a Type 327 only once before—during my recent assignment to the Sodeskayan front. But this second ride impressed me even more than the first. With urbane Lieutenant Commander Jim Payne and his freckled co-Helmsman Lieutenant Nedda Green at the controls, we'd been streaking toward the galactic center for little more than a day and a half now, but already distant brilliance from the gleaming trinary star we called the Triad of Asterious was streaming through our forward Hyperscreens.

A more impressive aspect of our journey, however, was

the fact that we'd been highballing through *enemy-held* interstellar space since a few metacycles after we departed Hador-Haelic. Hadn't much worried about that as we raced through the star systems of The Torond—we'd given them enough trouble to keep them occupied for a while. But I'd expected all xaxt to break out when we started across the ancient civilizations of League-occupied Effer'wyck.

Somehow, it didn't, although passive sensors on our outer hull indicated that we'd been briefly tracked by every BKAEW site along our route. Seemed strange at the time—we'd be painted with BKAEW energy for only a moment, just enough for them to get a quick position reading. Then the site would shut down again. With the war going so solidly their way, it almost seemed that they simply couldn't be bothered with a single intruder—especially one our size. So, hearts in our mouths, we'd continued on course unopposed.

Until we started past Yanrepé, that is, when suddenly, we were painted by a *markedly* more powerful source of BKAEW energy, enough to send our warning sensors screaming into overload. Hadn't encountered anything like that before. Anywhere. And to all indications, it was beamed from a *long* way off—as far as the great star system of Bax, on the far side of Effer'wyck. Somebody with one xaxt of a new BKAEW had just become very interested in our little ship. Wondered why—what did this new BKAEW reveal to its operators that the others did not?

No answers—but in any case, it was the end of our free ride. Moments later, Candlewax, a chubby, round-faced sensors rating at the proximity console, reported we'd just been jumped by a pair of killer ships—apparently Gorn-Hoff 262s from their high rate of speed. Most probably they'd lifted off from Ni'rapp, the fortified starport on the planet of Yanrepé captured by the Leaguers on their savage march through the Effer'wyckean star systems—a point of interest only, under the circumstances.

I watched Payne chew his lower lip as he and Green poured more and more energy to the eight Krasni-Paych Wizard Drives in streamlined pods on either side of our hull. After a time, we'd exceeded the ship's velocity-gauging instruments and could only guess what our actual transspace velocity was. But it was *just* enough to keep the Leaguers out of range to our rear—so far.

Unfortunately, because of that same protective high velocity, we had also become *quite* visible against the darkness of interstellar space. At maximum power settings, Wizard Drives tend to generate vivid yellow-green Drive plumes, often approaching two hundred c'lenyts in length. Most Wizard-powered starships, like our Starfuries, are equipped with diffusers to prevent this very phenomenon; Type 327s are not. However, without them we had been squeezing out an extra seven percent velocity gradient. Had we lacked this thin margin, the Gorn-Hoffs long ago would have reduced us to a rapidly thinning cloud of subatomic particles. As it was, we were managing—*just* managing—to stay ahead, while we put on a show like a small comet streaking across the skies, visible to every ship within half a Standard Light-Day.

"They've broken off, Commander!" Candlewax reported in a tight voice.

"Have they now?" Payne replied, without taking his eyes off the instruments. "Well now, I believe we can start to breathe again, Admiral."

"You can say that again," I whispered fervently.

"No, that's not what I mean," Payne said, pointing out through the forward Hyperscreens. "Look."

Half-standing, I peered over the 'Screen cowlings and felt

a genuine surge of relief. "Talk about your average beautiful sights," I whispered devoutly. Ahead, the stars simply ended along an irregular periphery that extended across our line of flight as far in either direction as the eye could see—the 'Wyckean Void. Light-years ahead, where shoals of stars began again in the far distance, lay the relative safety of home. Within the metacycle, we'd coasted back to normal cruising speed and been joined by an escort of twelve new-looking Starfuries. It was almost as if nothing had happened, which, when one considers events in a certain light, was really the way things turned out anyway. Or seemed to be. . . .

The Triad of Asterious: three great stars serving as orbital mooring for (arguably) the five most influential planets in the known Universe. Asterious-Proteus, dedicated to basic research, and foundation of the Empire's technological commerce for more than a thousand years; Asterious-Melia, mercantile hub of a trade cooperative that spanned the whole galaxy, and beyond; Asterious-Ariel, communications center for a network of clients and servers so vast the actual numbers were no longer comprehensible; Asterious-Helios, pan-galactic center of transportation and shipping; and Asterious-Avalon, historic, hoary capital of Onrad IV's Grand Galactic Empire. None of the five was my natural home; I'd simply adopted them all somewhere along the way, often in the face of stubborn resistance. But each time I returned after any sort of absence, I did so with tears of emotion in my eyes.

Now, we were flying over the great streets and byways of Avalon City herself. On the way to our assigned landing vector on Lake Mersin, we'd descended out of thin cloud layers over the long, park-lined Boulevard of the Cosmos, instantly recognizable by the colorful, towerlike palaces it bisected every four c'lentys as it split the Austral environs of the city center.

Below, near its intersection with Emrys' Memorial Parkway, I spied the huge Lordglen House of State where I'd stayed—actually was *supposed* to stay—during my first official visit to the capital as a commissioned officer. It was from that house that I'd launched an outlandish, impossible romance with Margot Effer'wyck, a love affair that *still* dogged my life—and, in the end, was probably responsible in part for Claudia's marriage to Nesterio.

For a long moment, I let my mind race backward through nearly twenty years to the night I'd met Her Serene Majesty, Margot Effer'wyck, Princess of the Effer'wyck Dominions and first cousin to Onrad, the present Imperial ruler. It had been a routine wardroom party aboard little I.F.S. *Truculent*, my first ship. Margot was there as an ordinary Lieutenant—a hardworking one at that, I'd quickly discovered. And if the tall, amply built woman had not been the most beautiful I'd ever encountered, she'd still appealed to me in a most fundamental manner. Even after all these years, I could picture her that evening: artfully tousled golden curls and soft, expressive blue eyes, flashing with nimble intelligence. Skin almost painfully fair, brushed lightly with pink high in the cheeks. And when she'd smiled, her brow formed the most engaging frown he could imagine. Moist lips, long, shapely legs, small breasts, and . . . I bit my lip.

We'd become lovers not long after we'd met. She a princess of Effer'wyck, the Empire's most influential dominion—I a commoner from the shabbiest sector imaginable. For a while, the desperate absurdity of galactic war had canceled out that awesome gap in status. But reality intervened soon enough, forcing a marriage between Margot and Rogan LaKarn, Baron of The Torond—a union designated to cement the bond that existed in those days between his massive palatinate and the Empire under our now-abdicated Emperor Greyfin IV.

Afterward, Margot and I had continued as best we could, carrying on a tawdry affair filled with endless stretches of longing punctuated by brilliant flashes of our own, special passion—and, not so incidentally, blinding me to the future I *might* have won myself with a glorious woman from Atalanta named Claudia Valemont.

For a while the affair had worked—even after ersatz peace forced a return to "normal" canons of class and status. But eventually distance, her child by LaKarn, and her onetime addiction to the Leaguers' devastating narcotic TimeWeed ate away our ties until only longing remained, buried deep within my very psyche to mask the pain it brought. Eventually, LaKarn's zeal to impress his League masters had turned what remained of Margot's sense of duty against him, and she'd escaped into the League-occupied Effer'wyckean star system with her young son to help lead the growing partisan movement there. But now, after LaKarn's successful kidnapping of young Prince Rodyard more than a year ago, I wasn't certain if she was even still alive. Or that anything remained of our relationship but memories. . . .

Willed myself back to the present as we thundered over the squat, glass-walled Estorial Library where Hobina Kopp first presented her startling Korsten Manifesto on Rights and Responsibilities more than two hundred Standard Years ago. Less than a c'lenyt farther, I spied Courtland Plaza and the great Huntingdon Gate. From there, I followed Coregium Boulevard the short distance to the Imperial Palace—one wing of which was still enclosed by builder's scaffolding after the Leaguer hit that had killed Hope's mother during the Battle of Avalon. At least Hope had survived to pass her mother's almond-eyed beauty on to future generations—in spite of the rather plain Carescrian heritage of her father.

Many memories here—perhaps *too* many. Again I fought myself back into the present. Lake Mersin was coming visible ahead now as Payne prepared the Type 327 for landing. Off to the right, I spied Kimber Castle where Cago JaHall composed *Solemn Universe* and his other classics of the same idiom. There: the silver-and-gold-domed Tower of Marva with its fluted sides and curious winding concourse. Soon the Grand Achtite Canal passed rapidly astern as we continued our descent to the boreal of Desterio Monument. More reminders of war here—many great craters, yawning foundations, and masses of rubble marked the Leaguers' continued attempts to punish the city that so far managed to withstand its worst onslaughts. Abruptly, Verecker Boulevard and the lake were coming at us at better than one seventy-five c'lenyts per. Off to the left, Grand Imperial Terminal dominated all else at the end of Palidan Causeway. Then, moments later we were down in one of those silk-smooth landings I quite understood were nearly impossible to obtain from this fast, tricky starship. "Beautiful!" I exclaimed to Payne.

For better or worse, I was home.

Drummond sent a skimmer to meet me at the Fleet Base. Nice touch, considering how difficult it was to get transportation anywhere these days. Gave Payne and Green a lift to the Officers' Quarters before the driver—a freckled young rating named Cowper—started out for the Admiralty. Told him to take the long way 'round while I got my head screwed on again after our pell-mell flight across half a galaxy.

En route, I simply gave up trying to get Claudia out of my head and let my mind roam where I knew it would. That marvelous night I'd spent in her office was intruding on my every thought—as it had all the way from Atalanta. Closed my eyes for a moment to rest them and found myself racing backward in time until I was mentally back at the Officers' Club that night. . . .

After our lunatic arrangement in the bar, Claudia and I had returned upstairs to finish our politicking—separately and together—in the most expeditious manner we could. Hadn't been easy, either. Everyone had been anxious to be noticed at what was sure to be an historic event—especially Zakharoff, who'd *also* had eyes for Claudia (as had most of the senior officers on the base).

Dutifully, I'd spent precious—frustrating!—moments in prolonged, largely one-way exchanges with the convoy captains, listening to their prides, peeves, and (all-too-often-lame) jokes. In nearly any other circumstances, of course, I'd have found these dialogues fascinating—fun, too. Helmsmen naturally enjoy talking to Helmsmen, and normally I'm no exception. But Voot's greasy beard, *not* when the most desirable woman in the galaxy is waiting for me to take off her clothes and make love to her! *Thought I would lose my thraggling mind.* If nothing else, the frustration had served as anesthetic to my aching hand, which was by that time going through a second session of exquisite torture.

First, Claudia would work herself free and set course for the door, making little signals at me with her eyes. However, every time she managed to do that, *I'd* find myself unable to break away from whoever had corralled me. Of course, just as soon as I could finally rush off to meet her, *she'd* have been waylaid again—sometimes by two and three persons, all intent on making points with the powerful Harbor Master—or covertly aspiring to the same favors she'd promised me!

Again and again and again we'd found ourselves frustrated, until in desperation we'd fled to a cloakroom, where she suggested that she simply should leave for her offices *alone* the first chance she got. I could then accomplish my separate escape the moment I was certain hers was successful.

Trust Claudia! Simple plan—and, by Voot, it had worked.

I'd 'Phoned the transport pool immediately to release a surprised Russo and his limousine for the remainder of the evening; from the Club, I could walk to Claudia's office in only a few cycles and save everyone trouble (plus buy us a few more shreds of privacy). Then, at once trapped in the lobby again—this time by two overweight civilian dignitaries from Atalanta City Hall—I'd forced one more laugh at one more tired joke while I'd watched Claudia's lanky chauffeur help her into the backseat of a staff skimmer and drive off into the early-morning darkness. After that, it had taken me only moments to break free and signal for my cape.

Once I congratulated Cottshall—couldn't forget *that;* he richly deserved a pat on the back—I'd stepped through the doors into the cool, crisp night and *freedom.* Nodded to a few partygoers leaving at the same time; turned down offers of rides, then drew in a welcome draught of fresh air while I peered up at the stars winking bright and clear through the night air. Watched a flight of four Starfuries soar up from the harbor and thunder overhead in perfect formation, running lights gleaming red and green through the heavens. My hand had ached as well as my feet, I'd been more than a little bit tipsy, and I'd never wanted to *see* another reception line again. But I'd hardly touched the pavement as I strode the quarter c'lenyt to the Civilian Headquarters building. Not every night a man had the most beautiful woman of his life waiting for him the way she was waiting for me!

My pulse had thumped like a nervous schoolboy's when I'd flashed my ID to the civilian guard, signed the visitors' register, and—*finally*—made my way through half-lighted hallways to Claudia's office, heels clicking hollowly through the silence.

As I'd rounded a last corner—the office was at the end of a darkened corridor—her door had opened, and I'd seen her waiting for me, white gown nearly luminous against the dim light coming from her office. At that point, it had seemed as if I were floating over the floor, absurdly fearful that I'd waken and find it was all a dream. But she'd reached out her arms for me, and at our first touch, I'd known she was entirely real.

We'd stood there embraced in perfumed silence for what must have been an eternity while I delighted in the sensation of her breasts pressing my chest. Then, without further ado, I'd simply shut the door behind us and locked it from the inside. . . .

"Admiral Brim?" Cowper called, making me jump.

"Er . . . yes?" I said, dragging myself back to a distastefully passionless now. Glanced out the window and . . . there we were in Locorno Square, gazing up at the great statue of Gondor Bemus on its high, impossibly slender pedestal. Miraculously, young Cowper had managed to survive the frenzied traffic—without disturbing me—and pulled to a stop at the curb before the grand rococo mass of the Imperial Admiralty. I was impressed, both by young Cowper and—as always—the edifice itself.

Throughout the great metropolis of Avalon, it seems as if the very laws of mutation often find themselves mysteriously suspended. Staid, gray buildings and monuments whose stones *should* have been replaced centuries in the past remain

proudly on useful duty, even though their original purpose
has been lost in the mists of time. Great domed temples built
to accommodate half-forgotten deities still loom royally
above their more contemporary, more practical inferiors—
and they are often filled by babbling tourists. Magnificent
palaces and residences still raise outlandishly decorated,
many-windowed facades to the very skies. But even among
these antiquated, obsolete monstrosities our staid—but ad-
mittedly beloved—Admiralty building stands out like a sore
thumb.

Illegally, I passed Cowper a handful of credits as I got out
of the staff skimmer—well, even drivers ought to buy themselves nice suppers once in a while—and headed across the
busy sidewalk for the infamous Admiralty staircase. As the
story goes, years, perhaps centuries in the past, a single flock
of itinerant gray pidwings—fat, squabbly birds the size of
small dogs—lighted in the ancient trees that had been
planted on either side of the staircase. Voracious scavengers
that consume virtually anything in the way of garbage (while
depositing byproducts just as voraciously) they became instantly enamored of the location. In spite of heroic efforts to
the contrary by Admiralty Groundskeepers, they took up permanent residence. And they prospered—heroically. Each
time the Groundskeepers invented a new pidwing repellent,
one or more environmentalist groups would rush out of the
woodwork and forbid its use in the name of Dame Nature.
Over the years, the rapidly multiplying birds, as well as their
even more rapidly multiplying byproducts, had ultimately
become part and parcel of the Admiralty itself.

I hurried up the marble treads, carefully—but unsuccessfully—attempting to avoid the droppings. Then, stamping
my feet, I strode onto the wide entry plaza, returned the
salute of ceremonial guards dressed in parade uniform, and

strode without breaking step through the doors—which were, by tradition opened for me no more than an iral in front of my nose. Only old-timers made it successfully through without balking—but I'd mastered the process early in my career.

Inside the majestic domed lobby—filled with musty odors from a thousand years of cheerless government drudgery—I pushed my way through crowds of milling Blue Capes to the directory, so I could look up Drummond's office—rumor had it that the office movers were busy these days of quickening war effort. I was running my finger along the "D" column when I felt a hand on my shoulder. "You again?"

I turned, then broke out in a helpless grin. "Bosporous Gallsworthy!" I exclaimed, taking a proffered hand in mine. The man before me was short and thin, with a pockmarked face and bushy eyebrows that always failed to hide the cold intelligence of his eyes. No way could I forget the extra-tough Principal Helmsman aboard my first ship, I.F.S. *Truculent*. At one time, I considered him the Fleet's greatest starship driver, and to this day seldom fly anywhere that I'm not reminded of the valuable lessons he taught me during those early months of my fledgling career. Years ago, at a low point in my life, the same man even risked his position as Commissioner of Civilian Spaceflight in Atalanta to secure me a job. Now, as a Vice Admiral, he'd risen to Chief of Defense Command, one of the highest offices in the Fleet, with a permanent position on Onrad's War Cabinet. And he still remembered me. "Good to see you, Admiral!" I said.

He laughed and slapped me on the back. "Brim," he said, "it's always a real treat talking to you after you've been reported missing and presumed dead. Great shiner you've got there."

"You should see the other fellas," I muttered defensively.

"So I hear," Gallsworthy said. "Understand you really raised havoc at Otnar'at."

"Shot 'em up a bit," I said modestly.

"Shot *you* up a bit, too."

"Yeah," I winced. "Lost some good people, too."

He nodded thoughtfully. "We always do, don't we?" Then he shook his head. "Well, since you didn't get yourself killed on that raid, we've got another—better—opportunity on tap."

"Thought that might be the case," I said. "Drummond's setting it up."

"Yeah," Gallsworthy said. "He's expecting you. Fourth floor, Suite 432."

"Thanks," I said. "Saves me from looking it up."

"Saves you going to twelve first," he said, pointing to the directory. "He moved to the new fourth-floor offices yesterday."

"You going to be there?" I asked.

"Probably not," Gallsworthy said, rolling his eyes. "Got a meeting with the Home Defense League right now—bunch of wealthy patriots ready to repel all invaders with star yachts and sporting blasters—but I'll be up if I can get rid of 'em soon enough."

I chuckled as he pushed his way into the crowd, then made my way to the lifts vowing to cadge a continuing succession of field assignments as long as I could possibly carry them out. . . .

Drummond's comfortably statuesque secretary was primed for my arrival. "Good afternoon, Admiral Brim," she cooed, as if we'd known each other for years—intimately, even. "General Drummond's expecting you."

"Thanks," I said, and took a chair. Drummond usually kept the latest HoloNews edition in his outer office.

"Oh, no, Admiral," she said. "You can go right in."

"Sorry," I said, striding across the room to knock discreetly on the door to his inner office.

"It's unlocked," a voice called through the thick paneling.

I opened the door and smiled. Relaxed behind a massive, antique desk that must have cost more than a squadron of Starfuries, Drummond looked as though he'd certainly come up in the world. Canny eyes and prematurely white hair gave him rather the look of a religious zealot, but I knew from long experience that his one and only faith was the Empire. Small in stature with a long, narrow face and prominent nose, he was a deliberately unpretentious man—something I've admired since the day we met between wars in the Leaguer capital of Tarrott. As always, he wore a comfortable Expeditionary Officer's service uniform with none of his many decorations: brown street shoes, dark olive trousers, and a matching olive reefer jacket with an Imperial comet on the left breast and two rows of five brass buttons down the front. The three stars of a Major General adorned each shoulder. His vast new office was decorated with exquisite HoloPortraits of idyllic prewar Effer'wyck, and twelve tasteful-looking easy chairs were set around a massive, inlaid cvceese' table. Deep, gray carpet covered the floor.

Smiling, he folded a late edition of the *Avalon Times* he'd been reading and placed it among the precisely ordered stacks of documents that surrounded the large blotter on his desk. Then he moved to one of the chairs, indicating its immediate neighbor for me. "Good to see you, Brim," he said with a frown. "You had us worried for a time."

"Had *me* worried, too, General," I said.

"Yes," he said with a quiet laugh, "I suppose it did." He

glanced out the window for a moment, then returned his ever-thoughtful gaze to me. "You look like a man who has only *just* avoided death, Admiral," he said presently. "And you retain the pronounced limp that was reported to me from your infirmary in Atalanta. One wonders if your report of availability for combat was all that accurate."

Don't know why Drummond always made me feel like an errant schoolboy; he only ranked me by a single star. Nevertheless, as usual I merely shrugged. "I didn't sign up to do any *marching*, General," I said, calmly as possible. "I fly starships."

"So I understand," he said, steepling his long fingers with a little grin of resignation. "But so I *do* hear it with my own ears, assure me that you are, at this moment, an able-bodied Helmsman."

"*Any* starship current on my ticket, *anywhere, anytime*," I replied firmly.

He nodded. "Good," he said, "because I've got a commando mission going out within a week's time. Needs an escort leader—Starfuries, of course. Mark Nines."

"One week?"

"*Next* week."

"You don't give much advance notice, do you?"

"Actually," he said, "we do . . . did, that is. The original escort commander was killed during training exercises. Captain David Norwyck; I assume you remember him from your Academy days."

I nodded. Tall, handsome, many friends. Not a bad sort— for one of the beautiful people. He'd been tolerant enough of my Carescrian background to ignore me completely.

"So, you'll take the job?"

"Why me?"

"It's a critical raid that must absolutely go off on schedule.

Your name came up because of some *very* special qualifications."

"But I'll only be escorting, right?"

"More or less," he said. "It's why you'll be in one of the new Mark Nines. You'll get lots of opposition on this one. We're going after a new BKAEW they're just now putting on line. Want to bring the first production model back home for a closer look."

That rang a bell. "Wouldn't be on one of the Bax planets, would it?" I asked. "On the way in from Atalanta, we got caught by a big one that seemed to be coming from the edge of the 'Wyckean Void."

He nodded. "Bax-Lavenurb, in fact. Thought it might have picked you up on the way here. Powerful."

"Powerful indeed," I agreed. "They must have been testing it. Every run-of-the-mill BKAEW site from here to Atalanta picked us up, too, but nobody stayed on the beam long enough to do any more than that."

"Sent up some Gorn-Hoffs to hurry you along home, did they?"

Nodded.

"Standard procedure these days," he said. "Our operatives in the field tell us we can expect to see a lot more of that in the near future." He shook his head. "Bad for many of the operations we plan to launch in the near future. *Sapphire,* for one."

I raised an eyebrow.

Drummond smiled sardonically. "With BKAEWs like that installed at Otnar'at, they'll be able to home in on our Gontor convoys at great distances. And they'll cut 'em to ribbons— rather like your man LaSalle did to them, recently."

"Thought I'd taken care of Otnar'at for a while," I protested.

"You certainly did," Drummond said with a frown. "Un-

fortunately, you seem to have done somewhat *too* good a job
of it."

"I don't understand."

"You put the Toronders so *thoroughly* out of business at
Otnar'at that it appears you frightened the Leaguers themselves. *They're* gathering together what they call an 'Assistance Force' to beef up what's left of the base with first-line
squadrons direct from the Sodeskayan front. Amounts to an
invasion of sovereign Torond turf, but that never bothered
Triannic in the past. And my guess is that LaKarn's too
much of a bootlicker to complain much about the whole
thing."

Covered my eyes. Leaguers. Xaxtdamned Leaguers!
"WON-der-ful," I swore under my breath. "Simply thraggling WON-der-ful. That means we've got worse convoy escort problems than if we hadn't attacked at all."

Drummond nodded. "You couldn't have predicted that,"
he said.

I shrugged, too upset for appropriate comments. What in
xaxt was I going to do? Until one of our starship manufactur-
ers came up with a long-range escort . . . "Hey," I exclaimed,
"what about the Carescrian squadrons I was promised?
They're supposed to have long-range escorts."

"You're on the right track, now," Drummond said with a
significant look. "Except that this new BKAEW the Leaguers are starting to ship all over the galaxy will make it a lot
easier to deal with long-range escorts, too."

Sat there for a few moments letting the facts sort themselves out. "So what's my part in this commando raid of
yours?"

Drummond looked thoughtful for a moment. "Actually,
it's not *my* raid at all," he said. "Our BKAEW enterprise is
no more than a small part of another operation—an assault

by the Imperial Expeditionary Forces against a huge starship maintenance facility located on a neighboring planet. Only a few persons—you alone among the actual combatants—have any idea that the larger operation is only a feint, albeit a mighty important feint."

"That still doesn't tell me what part I play in the mission."

"Oh, you're officially in charge of the escorts," Drummond said breezily.

I nodded; that seemed normal enough. "But if it's not your operation, then whom do I work for?"

"Good question," Drummond said. "For the most part, you'll be taking direction from operation's commander, Major General Megan Trafford, Imperial Expeditionary Forces," Drummond explained. "She's good," he said. "You'll like her. But you will secretly remain under my direct command—by orders of Grand Admiral Calhoun." He rubbed his chin. "If any conflicts occur—either before or *during* the actual operation, I shall expect you to ensure that Sapphire's objectives are met first. A disagreeable assignment in a number of ways—but the primary reason we needed someone who trusts *me.*"

Closed my eyes for a moment. Not just disagreeable; more like downright ugly. I knew nothing about General Trafford, but if I were forced to act in direct contravention of her orders, she could have me shot, or at least put in prison for the remainder of my life. Only someone who had absolute confidence in Drummond—and in turn Calhoun, then Prince Onrad—could possibly be trusted to carry out the secret protocol to my orders. "All right," I said after a long pause, "I'm game."

"I already knew that," Drummond said with a little smile.

"Thanks, General," I said. "Now, what about these escorts I'm supposed to lead?"

"Good bunch of StarSailors," Drummond assured me. "They've been practicing with the landing force for a month, now. Everything's pretty well under control, but if there are any last-moment decisions, they'll probably call on you."

"Great," I grumbled. "Well, with what I know about the overall operation, I can certainly give them information that's as bad as anyone else's."

"You've got a few days to catch up, you know."

"Thought you said a *week.*"

"*You* thought I said a week," he corrected, "*I* said *next* week."

Thraggling wonderful. "All right, General," I said hoping I didn't sound as exasperated as I felt. "How do I get started?"

"Easy," he said—a warning flag if ever there was one. "Tomorrow, at Morning plus one and a half, take a shuttle to one of the orbiting FleetPorts"—he peered into a workstation built into his desk—"yes, FleetPort 19. They'll help you check out a new Starfury Mark Nineteen and crew. Then, report back to me. By that time, I'll have everybody in one spot to start briefing you. All right?"

"All right," I said, standing. "What about the rest of today?"

"Yours," he said. "I'd imagine you'll want to stop by the palace to see Hope. Onrad's tied up tonight with a state dinner—his annual Ambassadorial Ball, I think—but he sends his regards and expects to see you sometime while you're here."

"How about transportation?"

"Your driver's waiting in the basement garage. He's all right, isn't he."

"Cowper? He's fine," I said. "How about someplace to stay?"

"Got you a room at the Fleet Base VOQ."

"Mother of Voot!" I exclaimed, fluttering a hand on my chest. "Not sure I can survive all that luxury."

"Try," Drummond said, getting to his feet in dismissal. "I shall expect to see you late tomorrow afternoon."

"Yeah," I grumbled on my way out the door. "Late tomorrow afternoon." Looked at my timepiece—it was already into Evening Watch. Didn't know what I'd do with all the thraggling time on my hands. . . .

First things first. Hope's bedtime was coming up fast, and I had no idea whether I'd find time to see her again before I was on my way back to Atalanta—or otherwise, after the raid. "Imperial castle," I said to Cowper. "Use the Huntingdon Gate."

He hesitated a moment, then chuckled uncertainly, as if I were pulling his leg. "Oh, right, Admiral," he said. "And should I announce you to the Emperor?"

"That won't be necessary," I replied. "When you get to the Huntingdon Gate, just pull up beside the guard station. They'll tell us what to do next."

"You're serious, aren't you, Admiral?"

"Very serious, Cowper."

"Yessir. We're on our way, sir . . . !"

Traffic was *horrible.* All the skimmers in the galaxy seemed to have arrived at *this* end of Coregium Boulevard, and Huntingdon Gate was at the *other.* Nothing do but sit back in the seat and relax. *This* was Cowper's problem for the moment. My mind's eye was freed for a return to Atalanta—and Claudia. . . .

I'd peered around her office for only a moment that night. In the dim light, it seemed softer, but hardly transformed from the efficient, businesslike room I remembered. Not much of a place to make love. I couldn't find the bed she'd mentioned, either—even a couch. On the far wall, however, a door I'd earlier taken for a supply closet radiated a rosy, feminine glow. "What's in there?" I'd asked.

She'd taken my hands and nodded. "Come see," she whispered.

A sitting room of sorts—comfortable—with white, multi-paned windows and soft, yellow-gold-colored draperies. The floors were golden oak, partially covered by a pink-and-saffron carpet. A canopied bed, a chiffonier with large ornate mirror, and four chairs done in pale azure and dusty rose were the room's only furniture, save a daintily carved coffee table before the chairs. Two glorious paintings I swore were genuine Tanurés hung on the walls as a perfect accent to the room's colors. She'd closed the door softly behind us and locked it. "I have the only key to this one," she'd said with a little smile. "Amazing how often I've lain alone here dreaming of you."

Hadn't any words for that; hadn't words for anything. I'd simply pulled her close and placed my lips on hers. The perfume she wore was strong and erotic. At first, we'd kissed gently, but in spite of everything I could do to rein in my runaway desire, my breathing had quickly gone shallow. So—thank Voot—had hers. Slowly, her mouth had opened, and I'd found my lips pressing wet, inner tissues. "Oh, Claudia," I'd stammered before I could stop myself, "I've wanted you so much over the years."

"Yes," she'd murmured, her voice urgent and strangely breathless. "God knows I've wanted you. How did we manage to miss each other so completely?"

"My fault," I'd whispered. "For years, I couldn't see any farther than . . ." Words failed me.

"Margot?"

"Yeah . . . Margot."

"Guess it doesn't matter anymore, does it?" she'd said.

"Not anymore," I'd replied. "Nor, I suppose, do the futures into which each of us has locked ourself. Nothing we can do about them."

She made a little sigh. "We've managed to lose the past as well as the future, you and I. So I guess only the present matters now," she'd said a little wistfully.

"The present and one other consideration," I'd said, drawing her close again. "Something I never found the courage to say before—not even tonight."

She'd drawn away slightly to look into my eyes with a little frown. "What's that, Wilf?" she'd asked.

"The fact that I love you, Claudia," I'd said fervently. "I loved you years ago, too—and I've never stopped." Shook my head sadly. "It's clearly too late to make any difference, but at least I've finally said it—if that matters anymore."

Gently, she'd drawn me to her lips and smothered my mouth with kisses. "It matters, Wilf," she'd murmured. "Oh *God* how it matters."

Then my whole being had gone spinning off and I'd lost myself in her lips and arms and breasts and breath and . . . "Claudia," I'd whispered nearly out of my mind, "I need you. Now."

She'd nodded. "Now," she'd repeated with half-closed eyes, then moved toward the bed.

Instead, I'd taken her arm; led her gently to the mirror.

"What *are* you doing?" she'd demanded, looking doubtfully at our reflection in the mirror.

"Thinking I ought to share this with you," I'd explained, sweeping her long hair aside to kiss her ears and the back of her neck.

"S-sharing what?" she'd asked with a little quiver.

"Sharing how beautiful you are," I'd replied, carefully

opening the back of her gown. "Let me show you . . ." With
that, I'd lifted the bodice of her gown away from her bosom
and let it drop. "Couldn't possibly keep all this to myself,"
I'd said. "Remarkable how your breasts have become even
more gorgeous over the years."

She'd pushed the gown gradually to the floor while she
peered at herself from different angles. The perfume had become even stronger now—and infinitely more exciting. "So
you like them, then," she'd said appraisingly. "You don't
think they sag a little?"

"They're magnificent," I'd whispered, cupping the heavy
fullness in my hands while great dark nipples pouted stiff beneath my caressing thumbs.

She'd sighed as I nuzzled the back of her neck. "I-I *am*
beautiful, then, aren't I?" she'd whispered with a pleased little smile. "I was so afraid you wouldn't think so anymore."

"I don't understand," I'd said.

"You never will, you wonderful, masculine imbecile,"
she'd replied, leaning her head back on my shoulder with a
happy little laugh, "—and thank heaven for it."

After that, I'd lost myself fondling those glorious breasts
while she purred into my ear and gazed with pleasure at her
own lovely body. Finally, with a long sigh, she'd skimmed
her briefs to the floor—some time earlier, she'd evidently
disposed of the sheer stockings I remembered she was wearing at the bar. "Now," she'd said, "we can enjoy looking at
everything."

Completely aroused by this time, I'd begun to caress the
growth of stiff thatch that began spottily beneath the swelling
of her stomach and ended in a luxurious, wooly tangle where
my trembling fingers probed deeper and deeper between her
legs. At length, she'd made a sharp little gasp.

"Hurt you?" I'd asked in a shaky voice.

"Sh-h-h," she'd whispered, rhythmically thrusting her hips while she followed my hands in the mirror with half-closed eyes. Then, abruptly she'd thrown her head back to nibble my ear. "Is that what I think it is, poking my behind?" she'd demanded.

No longer daring to speak, I'd pressed closer and nodded in the mirror, my heart pounding as if it would escape my chest.

"You're ready, then, aren't you?" she'd asked, sounding a little out of breath now.

"Y-yes," I'd whispered.

She'd slipped out of my arms and turned to face me. "So am I," she'd breathed, ever so deftly opening my trousers and skimming them to the floor. Warm, soft hands had probed beneath my briefs, then slid lower until, "Oh, Wilf!" she'd exclaimed while an urgent surge of delight swept my loins, "my God, you *are* ready, aren't you?"

I'd stepped out of my boots and trousers, placed one arm around her shoulders, the other beneath her knees, and carried her gently to the bed. Seemed as if she weighed nothing at all.

She'd watched languidly while I stripped off the remainder of my clothes and lingered for a few more moments, drinking in the startling beauty of this woman who had been the object of my dreams for so many years.

At last, when I could no longer check the mounting tension in my loins, I'd knelt on the silken sheets between her drawn-up knees, and we'd hungrily nibbled each other's lips while I plunged myself into a great pool of warm, viscous liquid that carried me all the way to another Universe—then far, *far* beyond. . . .

By the time we arrived, Huntingdon Gate was a madhouse of limousine skimmers. Guests for Ornad's ball were all arriving at the same time. Somehow, the palace guards seemed to be managing things in stride, but so far as I could see, only by the use of supernatural powers. Through the years, I learned—mostly by observation—that nobody can cause problems as well as ambassadors. "What should I do now, Admiral?" Cowper asked as he slowed our dingy, maltreated little staff car just shy of the great entrance road. His voice was tight with dread; probably it was the first time he'd been this close to the palace.

"Just make a sharp right turn, as I told you," I explained. "Then drive to the rightmost arch—the one that's reserved for emergency traffic."

"But Voot's beard, Admiral, they'll have my bloody head for this."

"Not with this red card I have in my hand," I assured him for the eleven millionth time. "Really. We'll both survive this—and I'll see you get something to eat."

"From the Royal Kitchens?" he whispered in a reverent voice.

"Probably from the royal vending machines," I corrected. "But we'll see. First, we need to get through the gate."

"Aye, Admiral."

At the barrier, a huge Royal Marine corporal stooped nearly in half so he could look into the back window at me. "Admiral?" he asked imperiously.

I handed him my ID and the special red card.

He shoved my ID into the reader, then frowned as he turned to card over. "What is this?" he demanded, as if I'd handed him something spoiled.

"What's this, *Admiral*," I corrected.

"Er, yes . . . *Admiral*," he added reluctantly.

"This, Corporal," I explained, "goes into your ID reader with my badge. Put it there now."

"But it is not an ID card," he sniffled, as Cowper began to cringe and slide beneath the front seat.

"Admiral," I prompted.

"Admiral," with a scowl.

"Corporal, does it look as if the badge might harm your machine?" I demanded.

He looked at both sides again. "Er, no . . . Admiral."

"Then put it in the thraggling machine."

Grumbling, he put it into the reader slot. Immediately, a globular display materialized above the machine. In it was the head and shoulders of Tazmir Adam, Imperial Secret Service Chief. He peered at me through the window for a moment, then grinned. "Admiral Brim!" he exclaimed. "Here to see Hope?"

"You bet. If she's still awake, that is?"

"You vouch for your driver?" he asked.

"I'll vouch for him personally," I said. Any other combination of words would have set off every security device on the grounds.

"Come on in, then," Adam said. "Corporal, pass these people through."

"Thanks, Taz," I said, then checked the Corporal, who now had a look of utter dismay on his face.

"S-sorry, Admiral," he said as he handed back my badges.

Looked out the window at him. "You wouldn't be if you weren't such a grouch, Mister," I said.

"Bloody right you are, Admiral," he admitted with a grimace.

"Then do something about it," I said. "Expect me back sometime to check."

"I'll be waitin', Admiral," he said as a clearly stunned Cowper drove through the gate, and was passed moments later by a huge limousine skimmer flying the flag of Sodeskaya. "V-voot's b-beard," he stammered as he drove along the concourse toward the great palace courtyard, where at least a hundred pages in crimson holiday uniforms and white wigs mingled with harried chauffeurs in a snarled effort to escort the celebrity guests inside and remove their oversize skimmers to a parking lot. "Where do I go now, Admiral?" he asked. "Isn't as if I drive on these streets every day."

I grinned. "Take the next left turn," I said. "It'll bring us to the kitchen entrance where I'll bet they'll give you something to eat—and I'll visit a most beautiful young woman."

"Er, you'll be stayin' the night then, Admiral?" Cowper asked.

"No," I replied with a chuckle, "she's a close, er . . . friend—and kind of young for that, anyway."

"I see, Admiral," Cowper said—I assumed he didn't.

"Park it over there, please," I directed, pointing to an open space between two more staff cars.

Only moments later, we marched into the Royal Kitchens, where—somehow not surprisingly—Onrad IV, Grand Galactic Emperor, Prince of the Reggio Star Cluster, and Rightful Protector of the Heavens, was standing on a carton of preserved goods, sampling a delicious-smelling sauce from a huge cook's ladle. A portly man who nonetheless carried himself with great natural dignity, he was dressed in the formal uniform of an Imperial Fleet Admiral with the crimson Ribbon of State across his chest. One of the chefs was holding an apron protectively across His Majesty's ruffled shirt. "Excellent!" the Emperor pronounced, wiping his lips elegantly with the bottom of the apron. "Too xaxtdamned bad we've got to share it with that bunch of stuffed shirts upstairs." As he was stepping off the carton, he glanced my way. "There you are, Brim!" he exclaimed, stepping forward to offer his hand. "Taz said you'd just arrived. Thought I'd try to catch you here."

"I'm honored, Your Majesty," I said, taking his hand while Cowper cringed into a corner.

"Oh, Gorksroar," Onrad exclaimed, clapping me on the back. "I wanted to tell you what a great job you did at Otnar'at. Guess that'll hold the bastards for a while."

"Well," I began . . .

"Well, xaxt," Onrad said. "I heard all about the xaxtdamned Leaguers. Don't think anything about it. Had to happen sometime, anyway."

"Thank you, Your Majesty," I said.

"No thanks due, Brim," he said. "I meant what I said." Then he put his hands on his hips. "Drummond says you're willing to take over the raid."

"Yessir," I replied.

"In spite of the other business? Could be messy."

Looked him directly in the eye. "I'll admit I don't like it all that much, Your Majesty," I said. "But I only have to trust three people in the matter—General Drummond, Admiral Calhoun, and *you*. Don't see how I can go wrong."

"We won't let you down, Brim," he said.

Somewhere in the back of my mind, a faint voice warned something about, ". . . put not thy trust in princes," or something. I battled it to a standstill. "Thank you, Your Majesty," I said, understanding all too well that if it came to a choice of the Empire or me, well, bye-bye, Brim. . . . Then I shrugged. It was the best anyone could ask for.

"From the looks of the black eye, you took quite a beating in that LifeGlobe," Onrad said with a look of concern. "You going to be all right?"

I nodded, then managed a grin. "Didn't tell Drummond I'd

take *two* missions for some helm time in one of those new Mark Nines, Your Majesty," I replied.

Onrad broke into a roaring laugh. "I promise I'll never tell," he said, and clapped me on the shoulder again.

At that moment, a harried-looking page came fighting his way through the confusion of cooks. "Your Majesty!" he yelped importantly. "You were due in the ballroom five cycles ago!"

"Tell 'em I'll be there directly," he said, rolling his eyes. Then he fixed me with a *most* imperial look. "There's nobody else to send on this mission, Brim," he said, "and it's got to come off on schedule. Otherwise, all our plans are up in smoke."

"That's what Drummond told me, Your Majesty," I replied.

"What he *didn't* tell you was that in my opinion you're too damned valuable to send. You almost got yourself killed less than a week ago, and now we're dispatching you on a job that's *even more* dangerous." He glowered. "The fact is that nobody else could do the job you've done so far in Atalanta—and you'll be needed there even more when the Carescrians get there. So for the love of Voot, don't get thraggling killed. All right?"

"I'll do everything I can to prevent it, Your Majesty," I assured him with a grin.

"See that you do, Brim," he said. "And for once, my highly valued Carescrian subject, I mean every single word."

"Thank you, Your Majesty," I said, feeling my cheeks go red.

Onrad clapped me on the back once more. "Don't thank me," he said. "I simply need you back here in one piece. Understand?"

"I understand, Your Majesty," I said.

He smiled. "That's better," he said, then stepped around me to put a hand on Cowper's arm. "Cowper," he said, as if he'd known the man's name forever, "I want you to take good care of the Admiral while he's here. Right?"

The blood drained from Cowper's face, and I thought for a moment he was going to faint. Somehow he seemed to rally. "C-count on it, Y-Your Majesty," he stuttered.

Onrad grinned and turned to a very senior-looking chef. "LeGrande," he said, "see to it that these men dine *at least* as well as the snobs you're serving upstairs." Then, with a wink in my direction, he pushed his way into the kitchen and was gone.

Never did get to see much of Hope. By the time I made my way to the nursery, Nurse Tutti allowed me barely a metacycle for my visit. Said the little girl was always getting visits late in the day—and *yes,* she realized I was the father. But since Hope couldn't know that, it didn't make all *that* much difference in the first place, did it? Had to agree, Voot take it. Tutti's rarely wrong; perhaps that's why Barbousse loves her so. Passed her a stash of written letters and a jewelry box from Atalanta, then got a last kiss (a bit sticky with candy I'd brought) from Hope and a stack of written letters from Tutti going the other way. When I returned to the kitchen, seemed like it took the whole kitchen staff to feed me supper while Cowper sat across from me, slowly eating a third dessert. He still had a stunned look in his eyes, but later he recovered sufficiently to return me to the VOQ—where I was asleep before my head touched the pillow.

Next morning, long before the Triad lifted above Avalon's horizon, reports of terrible raids began to come in from Atalanta. Drummond woke me with the bad news, and I joined him in the COMM Center immediately. Only after nearly a metacycle did things being to sort themselves out well enough that the attackers could be identified as Leaguers. The bastards were flying huge formations of Gantheisser GA 87 Zachtwagers (precision shooters), as well as Gantheisser GA 88s, Gorn-Hoff 111s, and Trodler 17s—their deadliest attack ships. I ground my teeth as more and more reports of terrible destruction crowded the KA'PPA channels. I knew who'd ultimately caused those raids—*me*. Summers had been right! But then, what other choices had I been given? I've noticed there aren't a lot of alternatives when it comes to waging war. Couldn't let it stop me, even though Claudia was in the thick of it and I was worried sick about her. Before I could go back and do anything about it—*her*—personally, I had a mission to run. So I soldiered on with a heavy heart. Certainly went a long way toward proving the old adage that love and war should never, *ever* be mixed.

Later in the morning, Cowper drove me to the military shuttle terminal, and I was soon on my way to FleetPort 19. Constructed in stationary orbit approximately 150 c'lentys above spinward Avalon, the huge defense base was shaped like a flattened globe nearly three-quarters of a c'lenyt in diameter. It was ringed about the middle by a transparent mooring tube and pressurized to the standard atmosphere on the surface below. Complex antenna fields on both "poles" of the huge structure furnished clear communications throughout the galaxy; the mooring tube provided forty-five docking portals spaced equally around its margin, each equipped with its own optical mooring system and retractable brow. Both the interior of the structure and its moored ships were supplied with locally generated gravity distributed evenly on every level with "down focus" toward the center of the planet itself. As my shuttle approached, I saw that a number of the portals were occupied by new-looking Starfuries, while other surface shuttles and transient ships were distributed among the others.

Spent most of the day wringing out TG 39, the new Starfury MK 9 I would fly on the mission—helped me forget my worries. Its crew, mostly survivors of Norwyck's disastrous crash, treated me pretty well, considering I was taking over from their late, clearly much-respected commander. Felt pretty good about everything in the spaceflight department by the time I'd packed up my battlesuit and caught the next down shuttle for Avalon.

Got back to the base in time to catch a quick supper in the Officers' Club, then Cowper drove me through the snarled traffic of rush hour to the Admiralty, where—after more bad news from Atalanta—I got my first briefings on the actual mission. Someone had named it Operation Eppeid. General Trafford, herself, was presenting the briefing, and had included a number of fairly high-level people from both the Fleet and the Imperial Expeditionary Forces in the audience. From that, I quickly determined that this evening's presentation would be a lot more than just an overall, touch-only-the-high-spots introduction to the operation.

Trafford was a hefty but—to me—very attractive blonde who carried herself like a proper general officer. She'd dressed in a comfortable Expeditionary Officer's service uniform: a tight, dark olive miniskirt that revealed sturdy, well-shaped legs; brown pumps with high heels; and—like Drummond—a matching olive reefer jacket with an Imperial comet on the left breast, two rows of five brass buttons down the front, and the two stars of a Major General on each shoulder. Unlike Drummond, however, she also wore four rows of decorations and campaign ribbons. She had straight, black hair cut short at the shoulders; an oval face with low cheekbones; large eyes and even larger, old-fashioned eyeglasses; a narrow nose with prominent nostrils; and a mouth with pouting, generous lips. As I'd expected, she started things precisely on time, clearing her throat imperiously and lowering the room lights until the only illumination was a stark spotlight beamed directly at her lectern. If nothing else, I decided with a grin, the woman exhibited a superb sense of theater.

"Good evening, people," she began, clearly long accustomed to making high-level presentations. "I am Major General Megan Trafford, and as you know, this will be a detailed overview of a mission we have code-named Operation Eppeid." She paused to scan the audience. "You are all warned that this briefing will contain operational information at the level of Top Secret, as defined in Section Nineteen of the Joint Services Security Manual. If anyone is not cleared at that level, will you please leave now."

Another pause, during which no one left. Then she nodded and activated a huge holographic display behind her with a general view of the galaxy. "A considerable number of Imperial troops have by now been specially trained in the Command camps for Space-to-Surface Assault, or SSA warfare," she began. "During the past year, we have secretly conducted several small landings on the far side of the 'Wyckean Void by a few of these specially trained soldiers using two or three of our latest reentry landing craft. And we've obtained spectacular success." She adjusted her glasses for effect. "We've kept these raids small enough to avoid unduly upsetting the occupying Leaguers—while going after nothing of a spectacular nature. But," she emphasized with noticeable pride in her voice, "on each of these feints, we have learned a great deal about such specialized operations while sustaining minimal casualties—although," she hastened to add, "*no* casualties are really ever minimal."

At that point, she stopped and peered around the silent

room as if she were about to reveal a great, lost truth. "The time has now arrived," she declared dramatically, "to put these lessons to the test!" I yawned. Trafford was a high-level, political lecturer indeed. Her presentation so far augured a *long* evening. . . .

Had to chuckle as the plan unfolded. If anything, Gallsworthy's comments on the mission as a "better opportunity" for getting myself killed appeared as if they might be conservative, to say the least.

Fleet Command had cobbled together for the General a small assault armada consisting of eight light cruisers, six Free Effer'wyckean disruptor monitors, sixteen surface bombardment ships, two flotillas of tiny Electronic Warfare trawlers, a number of the latest armored landing craft, and I.F.S. *Montroyal*, a brand-new medium transport. Trafford had secretly assembled them all—along with nearly three hundred battle-ready commandos—near two uninhabited planets located less than a light-year from our side of the 'Wyckean Void.

Fleet Command had likewise provided me with six squadrons of sixteen Starfury MK 9s each to fight off defending starships plus another four squadrons of Type 327 attack ships, whose job it would be to smother defensive fire from the surface. Considering that a large percentage of the Starfuries were almost brand-new and could therefore be depended to fly nearly anytime we needed them, the numbers seemed adequate for the job—at least early in the mission, when we'd face only local opposition. But once the attack had been under way for a few metacycles, we could have a lot of unwelcome company in *very* short order. To my knowledge, fat Leaguer Marshal Hoth Orgoth commanded nearly fifteen hundred attack and killer ships in Effer'wyck. And—to my recollection—he'd never been shy about using them!

According to Trafford, the main thrust of her incursion was

to destroy the Bax-Emithrnéy Gravity Docks, a massive starship repair complex—vast enough to service the largest starships in the known Universe and sufficiently impregnable to withstand poundings from our most powerful disruptors. The Effer'wyckean government had constructed it at enormous cost before the invasion, and it was now serving as a furtherance to Nergol Triannic's ambition of taking over the entire Home Galaxy. A worthy target indeed, opined Trafford.

However, another, less-important objective of the huge raid was to capture a new BKAEW apparatus that League engineers had just finished installing on Bax-Lavenurb, next planet out from Bax-Emithrnéy. That, she continued, was why the Admiralty had decided to risk their new *Montroyal.* Wouldn't do much good to simply destroy the new Leaguer equipment; research boffins on Proteus needed to find out what made it tick. And doing that required it be taken home.

Clearly, arrival of all those ships off Bax-Emithrnéy at their appointed station in the assault plan, exactly at zero hour would require no less than a miracle of spacemanship. Trafford had timed everything to commence just before Emithrnéy rotated Bax's first rays over her horizon near the gravity docks. The first groups of SSA Commandos to arrive would silence huge disruptor batteries that ringed the complex, then the main force would arrive with special demolition charges designed to disable the facility for the remainder of the war—without rendering it completely nonrepairable during postwar years. I had a feeling she might possibly be counting unhatched chickens at *this* rather disconcerting point in the conflict, but one *does* need to plan for the best outcomes, after all—or defeat becomes a virtual certainty.

While all this raiding and demolishing was taking place on Bax-Emithrnéy, Trafford continued, a much smaller force of SSA Commandos and Royal Engineers would be landing on

Bax-Lavenurb, near the new BKAEW site. I noticed from the General's large collection of HoloPics, that it was located atop a high, sheer precipice at the edge of a small lake in what appeared to be rocky, barren terrain interrupted by great upwellings of the planet's crust, some more than a c'lenyt in height. It was going to take a steady hand to operate something the size of *Montroyal* in and out of that location. Little wonder, I thought, that the Effer'wyckeans never bothered to populate Lavenurb.

Once Trafford's commandos had the BKAEW site under control, Royal Engineers would disassemble the BKAEW equipment (including all special antennas we could see on the reconnaissance HoloPics), bundle them aboard *Montroyal*, then withdraw as quickly as possible to our own side of the Void with no regard to the larger operation.

On the surface, Trafford made things look smooth and well planned—an operation by, as well as for—the textbooks of interstellar warfare, carrying with it the potential for vast damage to the enemy and prodigious profit for our Empire. But with all the literally *zillions* of things that could go awry during such a large, complex operation, I could see that Operation Eppeid *also* carried with it the quite-viable seeds of disaster. And, significantly, Trafford had made no plans whatsoever for that kind of eventuality. . . .

Chapter 8

The Raid

22–25 Octad, 52014

Avalon City, Asterious-Avalon

More bad news from Atalanta in the morning. Williams's reports described terrific battles in space around Hador and more Leaguer raids against both the Fleet Base and Atalanta City proper. Many casualties, much damage. Word must have gotten around rapidly concerning Claudia and me—especially our tryst in her office. Nothing specific in Williams's report, of course, but a subtly written portion of one section made a *most* distinct point about the safety of Ms. Harbor Master.

Made me stop and consider that magnificent woman, and *friend,* for quite a long time—more than I could really spare at the moment. What would become of *us* now that we'd finally admitted so much to each other? Clearly, we'd again become an "item" around the base, but would we ever again risk baring the long-smoldering emotions we'd experienced that night? Even more important, had we learned how to live in the moment—for as many "moments" as life might send our way—or would this be the one and only time we found courage to seize the present and run with it? During those long moments, I wanted—needed—her more than I wanted to breathe. But half a galaxy separated us in distance—and a whole cosmos in fate. . . .

Spent the next metacycles at FleetPort 19 conferring with the ten squadron leaders who would do most of my work during the raid. Wasn't surprised to find they already had everything concerning the mission well in hand. Got the distinct impression they'd welcome a return to normal squadron duties; assignments like these are dismally boring during practice phases—although they *do* liven up considerably in execution!

During the late afternoon—Avalon's afternoon, that is—Trafford sent us in formation out to a restricted star system for a full-dress rehearsal at two simulated sites where our "success" in the exercise could be judged by a bank of scoring engines her people were operating.

With Drummond's support I'd earlier commandeered a volunteer Starfury from FleetPort 30, the orbital base I'd commanded two years previously during the Battle of Avalon. Without someone to fly wing on me, I'd be forced to stay out of the action—and *that* was totally unacceptable. Just so happened that the FleetPort's present commander was an old friend on whom I'd depended for support and friendship since my days flying racers in the Mitchell Trophy Races—Toby Moulding, who in fact had set the present absolute-velocity speed record in 52009. Made things a lot easier when I asked him for a good ship and crew to fly my wing during the mission—nobody likes to place his own people in extra danger unless he absolutely has to. But he came through, with a smile, even. And I departed in company with one of his best ships, its crew captained by Lt. Commander Hazel Watters, another canny veteran-survivor of the Battle of Avalon.

Remarkably, all elements of Trafford's little armada managed to arrive at the initial point, some million c'lenyts from the primary planet, precisely on time, only a few clicks before dawn lighted the faked support facility. The E-W trawlers immediately blanked all BKAEW and KA'PPA traffic around *both* the primary and secondary planets, leaving a few secretly chosen channels open for our own communications. At the same time, light cruisers and disruptor monitors moved in to surround the surface perimeter of the mocked-up gravity docks—all without the scoring simulators calling for a single shot to be fired. Simultaneously, my four squadrons of attack ships dived for the surface while the Starfuries fanned out to establish regular patrols of the whole star system. Exactly twelve cycles following our initial deployment—*still* without the need for a single disruptor shot—two armored landing craft disembarked one hundred sixty SSA Commandos, whose job it would be, were this the actual assault, to silence huge surface batteries protecting the gravity docks. Seventeen cycles after this—when the scoring simulators indicated all surface batteries were indeed silenced—the main landing force deorbited and went about rehearsing its business of destruction.

A perfect assault drill, so far. Of course, it *ought* to have been perfect—after all, nobody was shooting back!

At this point, Watters and I flew to the secondary planet, where the fake BKAEW had been secured by a detachment of SSA Commandos. Our high-speed transport was at the site as advertised, and the Royal Engineers already had much of the imitation antenna dismantled and ready for loading operations. Clearly, Trafford expected no opposition here! I'd earlier noticed, with some concern, that she'd neglected to assign any escorts to this part of the operation. I didn't want to raise any issues so late in the game—a bad move, and I *knew* it—but I resolved that I'd check the situation out soon as I could during the actual raid. Watters and I hung around while I got a handle on what was *supposed* to transpire, then returned to the primary planet just in time for the whole exercise to be completed. From her headquarters in I.F.S. *Glorious,* the operation's flagship, Trafford broadcast her smiling blond countenance to each of our globular displays with a "Well done, people! Well done!" Then, we returned to our various assembly areas to rest and wait for the real thing—call-up on twelve-metacycle notice. I knew it wouldn't be long.

Watched a lot of people celebrating at FleetPort 19. Had a few drinks with Watters and the crew to be sociable, then caught myself a down shuttle to Avalon. Couldn't quite nudge myself into the mood to celebrate *this* particular success. Everything had been a little too easy today for my tastes. And after spending a lot of my life as a combat Star-Sailor, I knew for a fact that war was *never* easy. . . .

Sometime toward morning, I came awake in the lonesome stillness with a crystal-clear head and Claudia on my mind—almost as if we could have reached out and touched. Saw her as she was that morning that I'd departed for Avalon. We'd made intense love a number of times during that miraculous night, and I'd been left with the kind of gut physical satisfaction that only comes when the sex has been especially good and hormones are still running strong. Couldn't remember feeling that way for years—probably not since the two of us were fifteen years younger and only just discovering what a magnificent pair we made together in bed.

I'd gazed for a long time as she slept, lying on her back, head tilted my way and lighted by a gentle radiance that came streaming through the window from one of Haelic's satellites. That long hair I so delighted in was completely disheveled and strewn all over the pillow. One arm and a great, glorious breast were free of the stained satin sheet we'd pulled over us when we'd satisfied our latest cravings for each other.

Watching her sleep there, I'd wondered seriously about this mysterious element of being we called love—and all the million or so times I thought I'd found it. Perhaps the only time I *hadn't* thought I'd fallen in love was when this magnificent woman and I had been lovers.

Back then, she'd simply been a close, very close, friend and coworker—as well as the most exhilarating, innovative sexual partner I'd encountered to date. And Voot knew she'd had more suitors at the time than most Rothcats have fleas! Her evenings had been so booked up it seemed as if every man on Haelic was after her. I'd thought many of them—possibly most—shared a bed with her on occasion, and felt quite privileged to be one of them. Now, as I'd begun to appreciate the mature Claudia as a person, I sometimes questioned how many of them actually *did.* Perhaps I had meant a great deal more to her than I'd thought at the time. But then, after all these years, was I even capable of recognizing love—in *either* of us?

I'd reached no conclusions that early morning, other than soberly recognizing that the woman sleeping beside me had—many years later—produced a most profound effect on the inner man that was now Wilf Brim. An effect much different, and much deeper, than anything I had yet encountered.

Then it had been time to go—the Type 327 they'd sent was due to lift for Avalon within three metacycles, and I hadn't even begun to pack! Remembering that Claudia became a very light sleeper toward morning; I gingerly got out of bed and began collecting clothes we'd scattered all over the room. Arranged a sorrowfully wrinkled gown over one of the chairs and folded her undergarments neatly on her couch. Then I'd donned the wreckage of my own uniform—looked as if I'd spent the night wrestling Sodeskayan Bears. Wasn't going to be much question what either of us had been doing after the ball! Probably should have thought of that the night before, but we'd clearly been concerned with other, more compelling matters.

To say that departing that morning was merely painful would be the understatement of the year. I'd remained beside her bed for the longest time, simply gazing at her face, captured by a kind of emotion I'd never before experienced. Stronger, *much* stronger, than simply desire—though that was certainly a component, too. Then, just as I'd knelt to kiss her good-bye, she'd wakened, blinked a few times, then held out her arms to me. "Guess it's that time, isn't it, Wilf," she'd said sleepily.

I'd taken her in my arms, and when our lips met, it was just as if we were starting over again. Her breath, the perfume, the sharp, erotic odors that lingered on my face and cheeks. Somehow, I'd managed to bring myself under a modicum of control, and we'd remained locked in each other's arms until my breathing and thudding heart subsided once more. At last, when I dared to speak again, I'd whispered, "Claudia, I love you," in her ear.

"I love you, too, Wilf," she'd answered dreamily. "It's nice to say that after all these years."

"What are we going to do?" I'd asked, in a kind of bewildered frenzy. Wasn't used to that sort of thing—I'm calmer in a dogfight when people are trying to *kill* me!

"Do about what, Wilf?" she'd asked.

"About us," I'd said, drawing back to sit beside her on the bed. "Where do we go from here?"

"Questions like that need a future, my love," she'd said, "and we don't have one. Even the little bit of present we so bravely seized last night is just about all turned to past."

"But we love each other," I'd protested.

She'd smiled and nodded. "Yes, I suppose we do, don't we?" she'd said with half-closed eyes. "How nice. Perhaps even nicer for the waiting."

"Then we can't just . . . forget everything and go on as if nothing happened," I'd stammered.

"Without a future," she'd said, "that's about *all* we can do." Then she'd smiled languidly. "I don't know what I'm talking about, Wilf," she'd said gently, kicking the sheet aside and looking into my eyes. "Maybe there is still some sort of chance for us—I simply don't know right now. This body of mine is much too awash in hormones for me to make any kind of judgments—especially about you." She bit her lip a little, then put my hand on her breast. "If you didn't have to go right away, well . . ."

Needed all my willpower, but I took one more kiss, then got back on my feet.

She'd swung her legs to the floor and walked quietly beside me as I made my way to the door and cracked it open so I could peek cautiously into her office.

"My desk lamp's on!" she exclaimed in a distressed voice

as she drew back from the door. "It wasn't when we came in here."

Nervously, I shouldered my way into her office and quickly discovered that the outer door to Adele's lobby was still securely locked. I was alone—the room was likewise empty. But Claudia's 'Phone had been switched from STANDBY to DISCONNECT. "Automatic switch, perhaps?" I asked, nodding to her desk.

"Absolutely not," she said, then padded into the room with me and peered around in the dim light. This time, the sight of her lush nakedness was simply more than I could take— *mother of Voot,* what a goddess! To xaxt with the Type 327—I'd just opened my arms to her when she'd made a little gasp and pointed to the coat rack.

Heart pounding, I turned and felt my jaw drop. There, hanging from the main rod was a fresh woman's business suit in a clear plastic cover, a white blouse, and a lacy slip. Beside the business suit hung a pair of flight coveralls and my battered leather Helmsman's jacket—with a folded garrison cap hanging from its pocket, two stars prominently visible. In the rack below were a small feminine valise and a pair of Claudia's tiny street shoes. Beside them, stacked atop a packed duffel bag, were my flight boots, my razor, and a change of clean underwear, complete with rolled-up socks. Attached to a third—clearly empty—duffel bag was a printed note that read simply. "Deposit formal uniform here for later pickup." Couldn't determine where to place the blame: Barbousse, Russo, or Williams. Probably it was a concerted effort of all three with the active assistance of Adele. Didn't really care at the time—only that Claudia and I owed a real debt of gratitude to some wonderfully furtive "busybodies." Then, in the course of my shaving and changing clothes, we'd found ourselves mutually compelled to withdraw to her bed, where we'd made gentle love for nearly half a metacycle before at length we'd bid each other a last—somewhat perplexed—farewell. . . .

After everything else that morning, it had come as no particular surprise when Russo "just happened" to be passing outside Civilian Headquarters—with an extra mug of steaming cvceese' in the staff skimmer!—at the very moment I stepped onto the sidewalk. So in spite of what I'd considered to be rather a late start, I'd arrived in plenty of time for Drummond's Type 327 to depart for Avalon on schedule. . . .

At the beginning of Dawn Watch, the message board on the inside of my VOQ door buzzed me awake—couldn't remember falling asleep again. Trafford's mission was on immediately and my squadrons were scheduled to move out from their respective FleetPorts in twelve metacycles.

Pressed the ACCEPT and ACKNOWLEDGE buttons, then dressed in clean coveralls and hurried out into the lobby, where Cowper was gulping the last from a plastic cup of cvceese'.

"Shuttle port, Admiral?" he asked.

"That's right," I said, pouring myself a cup of scalding cvceese' on the way. "Who told you, anyway?"

"Nobody, Admiral," he said, opening the door for me, "but just about Dawn Watch, everything started to go crazy at the transport pool. Didn't take much of a guess to figure you were probably in on it, so I brought the skimmer."

I grinned as he climbed into the front seat and accelerated into the early-morning traffic. "Something tells me you've got a future in the Fleet, Mister," I said, sipping my cvceese'.

"Yes sir, Admiral," he replied, glancing at me over his shoulder. "I'm going to be a Helmsman someday. I've already completed the first three prep courses for The Academy."

Thought of myself five hundred thousand years ago, battling my way through that era's sequence of mental challenges until I thought my head would explode—even began to doubt my ability to qualify toward the end. Somehow, I'd persevered . . . *just so I can fly out and get myself killed today,* I considered cynically. "You know there's a trick to those prep courses," I said at length.

"There is?" he asked, his voice filled with amazement. I liked the fact that he was too proud to ask.

"I'll tell you what it is," I volunteered.

"S-should I write it down?" he asked excitedly.

"No," I replied. "It's simple . . . but not easy."

"Neither are the preps, Admiral."

"I understand," I said. "But there's only one basic you need remember in order to blast your way through to The Academy. And that's simply to *never* give up—no matter how frazzled and confused the preps make you. Keep at them; eventually, you'll win. After that," I added with a chuckle, "things will be so tough you'll look back at them almost fondly. But by that time, you'll *know* there's nothing that can lick you anymore. Ever . . ."

Cowper dropped me at the shuttle port; I caught the next up-run to FleetPort 19. Got me there a metacycle early, so I borrowed an office and collected my messages. Neither Williams's official compilation of the previous day's events nor Barbousse's personal account sounded particularly good. The Leaguer attacks were continuing unabated and causing tremendous damage (as well as suffering) in the city. They were also rapidly wearing down our defenses by the simple process of attrition. We'd lost seven Starfuries so far (two had been salvaged and might fly again) and three Defiants—

plus most of their crews. Ground my teeth as I sat there helplessly in the FleetPort. Not a xaxtdamned thing I could do until I'd finished this thraggling mission!

At least Claudia was still safe—or had been at the time the messages were sent. The only other good news was that Delacroix and his crew had managed a last-moment escape before the Leaguers really got down to business. Nobody seemed to know where he'd gone, but I was certain we'd need him—and *Yellow Bird*—again before this awful war was over. Bit my lip as I finished my messages—mostly junk except for a few interesting dispatches from Sodeskaya. Regardless of the logic behind these vicious attacks—LaSalle's destruction of the Toronder invasion convoy *or* my raid on Otnar'at—the Leaguers had now turned their full fury on Atalanta. And I wasn't there to do anything about it!

The last message had been an announcement from a famous Avalon haberdashery announcing a special bargain sale of Fleet uniforms. Wondered what sort of StarSailor had time to *care* about custom uniforms in the midst of this desperate war, but shrugged in resignation. Our old Empire needed *everyone's* efforts to win this war—even politicians'!

For a second time in less than three days, the diverse ships of our tiny assault flotilla slowed through Hyperspeed to arrive at an initial point, this time the real one, off Bax-Emithrnéy, within moments of zero hour—another genuine triumph of spacemanship in all respects.

My squadrons were flying superbly; the late Captain Norwyck would have been proud of them—Voot knew *I* was, also. To my left, impeccably spaced, the forty-eight Starfuries of Group Red from 81, 93, and 74 Squadrons; to my right, the additional forty-eight Starfuries of Group Green from 83, 87, and 91 Squadrons. Half a c'lenyt farther away to port—and a quarter c'lenyt lower—sixty-four speedy Type 327 attack ships from 35, 19, 38, and 24 Squadrons, group call sign Blue, cruised in perfect formations, ready to proceed toward the surface.

This close to Bax—only a few light-metacycles distant over my left shoulder—the high vault of space had taken on that odd, hazy aspect that one finds only in near proximity to a powerful light source. My ships appeared as if they were traveling behind a huge scrim. Nearby, a collection of fast-drifting asteroids seemed to pass beneath us at nearly a sharp angle—dangerous, those! For a moment, I had the peculiar impression of hanging motionless between an infinite sheet of perforated gauze and a vague flat disk made of crushed velvet. Surreal! But peaceful—so far. The longer that tranquility could persevere, the better I liked the whole operation.

I checked the proximity indicator—nothing—then calmly and methodically scanned the great sphere of space around me; dividing the arced starscape into neat strips by upward and downward movement of my head. Still nothing.

Nothing below on Emithrnéy, either—no disruptor bursts, at any rate. Here and there, small settlements glimmered against its huge, dark disk. And near the top like a jewel on a ring, the port city of Eppeid and its famous gravity docks. Thought about the people down there—the occupied Effer'wyckeans as well as the Leaguer tyrants who held them in thrall. They'd be waking together soon—the Effer'wyckeans detesting their subjection, the Leaguers indifferent—and merciless—in the role of vanquishers.

My KA'PPA repeater clicked for a moment, then a red indicator glowed unsteadily, lighting the word JAMMING. A moment later, the active-mode proximity indicator also reported itself jammed. Our E-W trawlers had gone to work, and only two—highly secret—emergency KA'PPA channels remained unblocked for emergency use. Quickly the Star-furies in Group Red fanned out to encircle the target planets. Group Blue and the four squadrons of attack ships headed down for an orbital holding pattern. In my mind's eye I could see the light cruisers and monitors descending slowly through the atmosphere to secure the gravity-dock perimeter—if, indeed, that would even be necessary. So far, everything appeared to be going at least as well as the practice run.

Checked my timepiece: five cycles into the operation: our first two armored landing craft would be headed for the surface now, charged with silencing the massive disruptor batteries that protected the great maintenance yard. If all went well, they'd make landfall in precisely seven cycles. . . .

Suddenly, a confused irregular sparkling appeared in the distance ahead—just short of Eppeid. Disruptor fire! I jumped, surprised as the sparkling quickly intensified. The radio began to ring with yells and curses, then, quickly, with cries for help—not all in Avalonian.

Tried to determine what was going on. The first two landing ships couldn't have reached the surface yet. I ordered the attack ships to the area by radio quickly as they could deorbit; asked tiny Kempton Winter, the balding commander of 38 Squadron, to report the situation. Then Watters and I waited for the bad news—bound to be trouble now, whatever had caused this premature flare-up. It came only cycles later, a *colossal* disruptor began to fire. One of the surface batteries clearly had just gone into action; within moments, it was joined by a second, then a third and forth. Each was to have been silenced by the first-wave SSA Commandos. Biting my lip, I was tempted to demand a report, but sooner or later, someone would remember that he or she was supposed to periodically keep me informed. Moments later, I got my first coherent information from Burt Winter.

"Hello, Tempo," he gasped, using my personal call sign. "Payoff, here—looks like one of those first two deorbiting landing craft ran afoul of an escorted merchant transport going the other way! Xaxt of a firefight—and now everyone's blasting away at anything that moves."

Just then, I saw two of the big disruptors fire simultaneously, followed immediately by a powerful explosion that darkened our Hyperscreens for a moment.

"Mother of Voot!" Winter swore. "They just blasted *Furious* out of the sky! Better 'n eight hundred people on board that old . . ."

"What about the other landing craft, Paycheck?" I interrupted, grinding my teeth.

"The other SSA lander got in all right . . . I think," he said. His words were punctuated by a terrific blue-green explosion—much more powerful than the last big one. Kept the Hyperscreens dark for nearly a click.

"What was that?" I demanded.

"One of the League's xaxtdamned disruptor sites!" Winter answered excitedly. "By Voot, *some* of the commandos must have made it."

"How about our main landing force?"

"A moment, Tempo," he said. I could hear a salvo of rapid-fire disruptors in my helmet speakers. The firing stopped for a moment, followed shortly by another, longer salvo. Then, *"That* ought to discourage the zukeeds!" Winter shouted. "Now, Tempo, what was that?"

"What was *that?"* I demanded.

"A line of battle crawlers—looked like Mark Nineteens. They *were* going after the main landing force."

"So, the main force is on the surface?" I asked.

"Barely, Tempo," he replied. "They're just now debarking—into a lot of trouble."

"What can I do to help?" I asked.

"Not much right now," Winter said. "Just watch out for the Gorn-Hoffs so we can concentrate on ground targets. We—" His voice ended abruptly in a long burst of static.

"Paycheck!" I yelled. "Paycheck!"

"Sorry, Tempo," a different voice reported, "Paycheck's caught a packet. This is Paycheck Two. Can we help you?"

"Thanks, Paycheck Two," I said. "Keep your eyes open; I'll need to know what's going on. And call me if some of us need to come down and help."

"Got you, Tempo."

Didn't even remember Paycheck Two's real name—she sounded shaken. I'd have been, too! Called Watters on the radio. "Tempo to Tempo Two," I said. "Let's have a look next door at Lavenurb."

"Lead on Tem—" Watters begun, but was abruptly cut off by another voice that interrupted with:

"*Look out,* Tempo! Gorn-Hoffs—yellow apex!"

Glanced over my right shoulder—there they were. Leaguers! Led by a sleek, wicked-looking Gorn-Hoff 262 that glistened scarlet in Bax's strong light, six of the killer ships were coming at us from less than a half c'lenyt distant. Switched on the radio again. "Tempo to all Red, Blue, and Green!" I yelled into the helmet microphone. "Gorn-Hoffs in the area. I repeat, Gorn-Hoffs in the area! Keep an eye out!" The first ones were already passing on our right and turning toward us.

Didn't really have time to be frightened. Pulled the Star-fury into a tight turn and climbed toward them, firing the three disruptors that I controlled, even though the Leaguers were still out of range. Missed, of course, but made them break off their turns—too soon. I yanked the Starfury over on her back, did a half-roll, and before they could recover, there we were—Watters and I both—within easy range. Aimed for the first in line—the gleaming red one. Slight pressure on the steering engine and he was in my sights at close range! Let fly with my disruptors; so did my Gunnery Officer, Crenshaw. We both got him first time—hits all over the fuselage.

Tongues of radiation fire escaped immediately from the Gorn-Hoff's hull as its collapsium hullmetal un-collapsed in the torrent of energy from our disruptors. The Leaguer Helmsman threw his killer ship into a desperate turn—could see two slender streams of gravitons twisting from his steering engine. Then, he simply . . . exploded like a bomb, with a great flash followed by a rolling puffball of flamelike energy and a cloud of debris. The heavier Drive chambers and Spin-Gravs continued on course, trailing vivid smears of radiation fire. Parts of the hull torn off by the explosion followed more slowly, fluttering along like dead leaves while they flashed intermittently in Bax's streaming brilliance. Confetti, almost . . . No, LifeGlobes.

Now the sky was full of Gorn-Hoffs. The bastards arrived a xaxt of a lot earlier than we'd been promised. Somebody in Intelligence would pay for this blunder! Disruptor beams just missed me as I made a brutal turn and Crenshaw got off a couple of high-deflection shots. *Just* missed!

Defending us as best I could. Crenshaw blasted away at another Gorn-Hoff. Out of range . . . suddenly we came out of a half-loop immediately over another Gorn-Hoff silhouetted against the planet. Rolled and dived for him vertically. Saw the Leaguer's tapering fuselage in outline—the short, winglike fins that steadied it in close atmospheric maneuvering, the yellow disruptor turrets . . . lifting toward me. Could see the bridge crew craning their necks up at us.

Poor Leaguers never got off a shot. We hit them with all twelve disruptors. The whole bridge simply disintegrated in glittering shards of Hyperscreen and escaping atmosphere. Heard people screaming behind me. Didn't blame them! Looked as if we were going to collide with the wreckage. Voot's B-E-A-R-D! Dragged the controls back and *just* managed to pass over him. Looked back and saw the Gorn-Hoff planing down toward the planet upside down, with a thin, bright streamer of radiation fire trailing from the power chambers. A number of LifeGlobes popped open in its wake, quickly slowing until they seemed suspended in space while the Gorn-Hoff continued its last descent.

Then all the Gorn-Hoffs were gone! Had enough? Doubted it. More would be on the way. Where was Watters? We'd been separated in the dogfighting. Looked up at sudden movement overhead: one Starfury—Watters's probably—and a Gorn-Hoff. Couldn't get there in time to help, so I watched, both horrified and fascinated. Magnificent display of space acrobatics by both ships: flick turns, snap rolls, reversements. Neither seemed able to gain an iral on the other. Suddenly, as if by agreement, they turned and faced each other. Insanity! The Starfury and the Gorn-Hoff firing every disruptor while they charged head-on. The first to break would be lost, for he—or she—would expose their hull to the other's fire without fail.

Nothing on the intercom but labored breathing—everyone afraid to breathe. At the very moment when collision seemed inevitable—the Gorn-Hoff visibly shuddered, shaken by disruptor hits, then disintegrated. Held my breath, while the Starfury continued—miraculously—through a shower of radiation fire and debris falling slowly toward the surface.

Moments later, Watters pulled back in place beside me. "Gutsy, that!" I sent.

"Thanks, Tempo," she said as if nothing exceptional had occurred, and we raced off at full speed to Lavenurb while all the radio channels began to fill with sounds of dogfighting.

Leaguer killer ships were arriving from somewhere in full force. Called for a surface report from Paycheck Two. Nothing—probably caught a packet like his number one. "Tempo to any Blue," I yelled into my mircophone. "Need a situation report from down there!"

"KettleDrum One to Tempo," a strained voice crackled in my helmet speakers. "A bit dicey down here right now. Trying to help the poor SSA sods on the surface. Low-level stuff. Lost a few 327s—don't know how many, but the Leaguers have got a lot of firepower."

"Tell me about the ground, KettleDrum. What about the 'poor sods'?"

"Sorry, Tempo. Even dicier down there. No surprise to protect 'em at all. Pretty badly pinned down. Don't seem able to fight their way anywhere near the gravity docks. Need battle crawlers for this type of work, I think!"

"Anybody pulling 'em back, KettleDrum?"

"Haven't heard a thing from General Trafford, Tempo."

"Thanks, KettleDrum. Keep me posted."

A short squirt of Drive and we were over Lavenurb, boring down through the atmosphere as we decelerated. The target BKAEW site was under heavy cloud, but our radios were picking up a lot of battle talk. Sounded as if the SSA troops had run into some unexpected trouble over here, too. Our two Starfuries plunged into dark, swirling clouds only a few thousand irals from the surface and came out in driving rain some thirty c'lenyts to spinward of the fighting. Went all the way to surface level with the visibility getting worse. Barren, rock-strewn terrain with huge, pillarlike upwellings of rock. Simply WON-der-ful conditions for flying on the deck at high speed. In the distance, a few vague bursts of disruptor fire. We thundered over a line of battle crawlers. Didn't expect *that!* Then a number of structures burning furiously, and suddenly a huge BKAEW was directly ahead of us, half-dismantled. Could see groups of SSA Commandos firing anti-crawler missiles, but weapons that could be carried by hand wouldn't keep the big Leaguer machines at bay forever! Past the antenna, I could see I.F.S. *Montroyal,* our fast transport, pulled up at the bottom of the precipice with its cargo doors open. Circled for a moment to judge the progress. As the Royal Engineers separated a component from the BKAEW, loadmasters hurried it to the precipice aboard rough-terrain vehicles, then lowered it to the waiting transport. They appeared to be making extraordinary progress, and had there been no threat from crawlers they would have finished in plenty of time. But *again* our Intelligence had failed us. Wasn't necessary to widen my circling much at all before it became clear that the site was ringed by Leaguers, and the commandos certainly would be wiped out in less than a metacycle. Behind us, I watched a blue signal rocket go up, followed by an eruption of ground fire that rocked the ship and dimmed the Hyperscreens. Dived for the deck again. Needed to call in support *fast,* or this part of the mission was about to come a cropper, too. Switched to one of the secret unjammed KA'PPA channels. "Tempo to all Blue-35 and Green-87," I called. "Tempo to all Blue-35 and Green-87. Report immediately to secondary target. Highest priority."

"Bouncer One and Bouncer Two on the way, Tempo."

"Bandanna One and Two on the way, Tempo."

"Setscrew Two on the way, Tempo; Setscrew One's had it."

"PawnShop and Tappet, all four on the way, Tempo. Hang on. . . ."

Hot damn, horse cavalry to the rescue—just like the old books! Listened with a growing sense that we might just bring this BKAEW theft off. Couldn't wait for them to get here. "Come on, Watters," I yelled, "we're going in to do what we can down below!"

A thick pall of smoke—and probably chemical fog—was beginning to form around the BKAEW, that was still disappearing piece-by-piece into *Montroyal* at a steady—if not very reassuring—rate. So far, no Gorn-Hoffs had appeared overhead; probably all busy dicing with Starfuries at the primary target. But we'd eventually attract their attention! Count on that!

The two of us came down to roof level with our twenty-four disruptors spitting fire at everything that moved. Gray-uniformed Leaguers and their light weapons flew in every direction. I burned two lorries carrying troops—bastards never heard us coming. Fired a few blasts at a crawler—didn't make it stop, but I knew I'd made it mighty hot inside. Two staff skimmers blew up nearby just as someone launched a stick of missiles at us. Blew most of them of the sky—one burst nearby, *bang!* tore a mooring point from our right pontoon! Circled over a squad of Leaguers manhandling a disruptor caisson into place. They heard me coming and scattered. Sent their disruptor at least thirty irals in the air.

Abruptly: "PuppetMaster to all Blue-35," Trafford's voice boomed over the KA'PPA combat traffic—she was Puppet-Master—"belay Tempo's request. Repeat, belay Tempo's request. All Blue-35 ships are ordered to remain with the primary target until released."

Messages from Blue-35 stopped abruptly while Watters and I shot up a whole squad of missile-equipped Leaguers quick-stepping toward the BKAEW site. Did lots of damage, but we were only a drop in the bucket, and we couldn't *touch* the crawlers that were fighting their way closer and closer to the Royal Engineers—as well as closer to a position from which they could fire directly down at the transport (if the Gorn-Hoffs didn't beat them to it).

Somehow, I'd hoped things wouldn't come to this, but they *had*. Nothing was proceeding according to plan anymore, and she didn't need as many starships to cover a withdrawal as she might during a successful attack when her forces were deployed over a larger area.

Speeding over still another smashed disruptor caisson—Watters must have blasted it. By the light of her disruptor blasts, I could see gray-suited figures running 'round in twos and threes, and five perfectly monstrous battle crawlers moving forward toward the BKAEW. Voot's beard. No stopping them at all. I had to do something—*fast*—or the mission was a *double* failure.

Think, Brim! Think! I could argue with Trafford all day about her orders, but since both of us had two stars, we were stalemated. However, since, ultimately, mine came direct from Emperor Onrad, himself, I had an obligation to carry them out, no matter what. And if they didn't agree with Trafford's, well . . . we'd sort that all out later. How to break the stalemate . . . ?

Suddenly it came to me! Of course! We both might have two-star rank, but *I* had a special card I could play. Hated to use it, but . . . "Tempo to all Blue-35 and Green-87," I radioed again. "Tempo to all Blue-35 and Green-87. This order supersedes PuppetMaster by authority of same-service prerogative. Fleet units 35 and 87 Squadrons will report immediately—I repeat report immediately—to secondary target for independent action by twos. Highest priority. All other Fleet units to continue as before."

Moments later, messages began to arrive again.

"Comin' fast as we can, Tempo."

"We're on our way, again, Tempo."

"Five Type 327s heading toward you, Tempo."

"Ten Starfuries at your service, Tempo!"

Laughed grimly in spite of myself (while plastering still another disruptor caisson). Clearly, no one wanted to be named as part of a controversy between two flag officers. But by the same token, no one was willing to ignore a direct, same-service order, either. I was back in the war! Abruptly, the first Type 327s with their heavy firepower appeared overhead, and the situation began to change radically. Before long, smashed and blasted battle crawlers were aflame all over the stormy landscape, each marked by a black pillar of smoke that reached into the low clouds.

Were the reinforcements in time? As I circled the site, the last parts of its BKAEW appeared to be waiting for the ticklish process of easing them over the precipice and into the transport. Couldn't be *that* much longer before I could release the Type 327s back to . . . *Wham!*

Mother of Voot. *Here* came the thraggling Gorn-Hoffs!

Luckily, for the most part, many were already busy fighting off the first flights of Starfuries to arrive, but more were arriving every cycle. Visibility had by now gotten even worse—which did nothing to prevent two Leaguers from making a frontal attack on me—so close I actually jumped in my seat. At this point, my chief concern was to avoid getting Watters and me involved in a collision in the gloom.

Suddenly, the radio blared, "Look out, Tempo! Break left!"
Reflexively—I didn't have time to realize the shout was
meant for me—I cranked the Starfury into a vertical climb.
Somehow, Watters followed—superb Helmsman, that
woman! We were almost too late. A near miss exploded beneath me with such violence that my feet jumped off the rudder controls. A square pseudo-wing bearing the ebony
Leaguer chevrons swept past in a flash only a few irals away:
the Gorn-Hoff's slipstream in the atmosphere was so violent
that this time the controls were ripped away from my hands.
Instinctively, I completed a roll and leveled out just above the
treetops, so frightened I could hardly catch my breath. *Bang!
Bang!* Two more near misses nearly threw my Starfury on her
back. Caught sight of Watters fighting for control off to my
right as I hurled over into a violent skid that nearly overpow-
ered the gravity system—red lights all over the "G" panel!
People screaming behind me on the bridge. At the same time,
some of the 'Gravs stuttered—more red lights. I hauled back
on the thrust damper to smooth things out, then gingerly
opened up again. The red lights flickered out and the ship
seemed to respond normally. Waited for Watters to tuck herself in beside me, then I climbed for the cloud base. Everywhere I looked there were Gorn-Hoffs—and thank Voot, a
few Starfuries—blasting away as fast as they could shoot.

In the driving rain, another Gorn-Hoff turned toward me,
rapidly wiggled its stubby pseudo-wings, and engaged me. As
I swerved immediately to face him, both Crenshaw and I
opened up at him at the same time. Fully eight of our disruptors could bear, but we both missed, passing like a whirlwind
only a few irals below him. I dragged the Starfury into a tight
loop and threw the steering engine hard over to the left. For a
moment, we trembled on the verge of an energy stall, but
somehow completed an astonishingly tight turn with thin

streams of gravitons pouring from the right pontoon—a surprised Watters went shooting off to the right. The Gorn-Hoff's Helmsman seemed even more surprised and began a turn to starboard, skidded, righted himself, then turned to port—directly into my field of fire at close range! Before he had time to complete his maneuver—whatever it might have been—I quickly corrected to give a better shot to Crenshaw, then we both let go with a long burst from eight disruptors again. Flashes appeared all along his fuselage and pseudo-wings. The bridge Hyperscreens disintegrated in a shower of glittering crystal shards and atmospheric blowout. A couple of LifeGlobes popped out into the wake, then the Gorn-Hoff veered sideways at less than 150 irals altitude, righted itself for a moment, mowed down one of the peculiar stone columns in a shower of sparks and flames, and finally crashed into a deep crease in the rocky surface with a terrific explosion that momentarily lighted the whole arena in an evil glow.

At this point, the weather seemed to be clearing a bit. Gaps appeared in the walls of rain and mist and . . . Voot's greasy, rancid beard! To my left, a fire was raging near the foot of the precipice—alarmingly near *Montroyal,* which appeared to be just about loaded. Had she been hit? Atop the cliff, a shrinking half-circle of Royal Engineers was sewing a dense minefield while others were rappelling down ropes to a dozen or so armored landing barges parked helter-skelter on the narrow strand below. A couple of the engineers looked up from their perilous work and waved bravely. I certainly didn't envy them down there.

"Hallo, Tempo," someone radioed, "can you hear me?"

Checked my tail—reasonably clear, for a change—then cranked the Starfury into another tight circle above *Montroyal.* "Tempo is circling overhead," I said.

"Finally," someone said in a scolding tone. "We've serious trouble down here, Tempo—both *Montroyal*'s Helmsmen have just been killed by snipers, and I have issued orders to evacuate all personnel in the landing barges!"

"Thraggling WON-derful," I whispered to myself. Now what? But I already knew. "Who is this?" I demanded.

"Colonel Ryan Cromer, Royal Marines," came back in a deep voice.

"What shape's the transport in, Colonel?" I demanded.

"No apparent damage, Tempo," Cromer reported. "I've spoken to the crew. However, since we've no one to fly it, I've ordered everyone into the armored landing craft. We have no time to lose at all."

"The transport crew's already in the landing craft?"

"Of course. I've thoroughly mined the *Montroyal* herself. No danger of her falling into the wrong hands."

"I want to speak to *Montroyal*'s crew," I said. "Ranking man or woman."

"We are in the process of evacuating this site, Tempo," Cromer growled in a frightened voice. "If you delay anyone's departure, I may be forced to order my landing craft aloft without them."

"I want *Montroyal*'s ranking crew member *now*, Colonel," I growled. "Your men haven't even finished evacuating the top of the cliff."

"I shall see if I can find someone," Cromer sniffed and the radio fell silent except for commotion from the dogfight that continued to swirl around me while I circled endlessly. Now, the last few Marines were rappelling toward the strand. At the final moment before I demanded someone's attention with a disruptor salvo: "Lieutenant Commander Alan Jennings, here, Tempo," an unruffled voice said. "I'm *Montroyal*'s Systems Officer. Can I be of service?"

"Will she fly?" I demanded.

"I believe she will, Tempo," Jennings replied, as if he were standing on a street corner of Avalon. "All systems were turning over when this oddball Cromer ordered me aboard a barge."

"Everything's *still* turning over?" I asked. "Nothing shut down?"

"Not to my knowledge, Tempo. I doubt these SSA people know enough about the ship to shut things down. But I hear they have her mined so she isn't captured."

A Gorn-Hoff thundered past me in the driving rain, on fire from stem to stern. Crashed in a tremendous explosion a half c'lenyt out in the wind-roiled lake. "Can you get the crew back on board?" I asked.

"Certainly can, Tempo," Jennings said, still as if his situation were perfectly natural. "We're all in the same lander, but I don't think we've anyone left who can fly her."

"What do *you* know about the flight systems?" I demanded, watching the last few SSA Commandos start down the ropes. "Can you identify the controls at the helm?"

"I can, Tempo," Jennings said, at last sounding just a little excited. "I've spent the last month testing them."

Not much more time now. Alone now at the top of precipice, the Leaguers were starting through the minefield—taking disastrous casualties, but making steady progress. "You can show me the flight controls I need to fly her, then?" I asked.

You could almost hear the smile on Jennings's face. "You bet I can, Admiral . . . er, Tempo!"

Glanced at the Leaguers again. They'd be through the minefield in only cycles. Going to be *close!* "Get the *Montroyal* crew back to their stations, Jennings, and meet me on the bridge! I'm coming down." Switched on the blower. "All hands prepare for immediate landfall," I shouted. "All hands prepare for immediate landfall. Demolition hands fuse your scuttling charges now!" Then, "Tempo to Tempo Two. We're going to land. Don't follow—this releases you as number two to this ship. Acknowledge, please."

"Tempo Two to Tempo. Acknowledge. Need help driving that rig home?"

"Negative, Tempo Two," I said, lining up a quick approach on the lake, "—unless you want to stick around and escort."

"Sounds like a plan to me, Tempo," she said. "I'll stick around."

"Thanks, Tempo Two," I said. Eased into a downwind leg smartly. Cut the power, curving around crosswind-to-downwind in a tight, continuous turn that allowed me to watch the sky behind—everyone's a sitting duck on the landing circuit. Trimmed her up . . . lift-enhancers deployed. Into the wind now. Plenty of height . . . perhaps a little too much. Right roll to opposite left rudder on the steering engine . . . plunged vertically . . . so! Neutralize. Thrust damper closed—eased back on the steering engine to check her. Sinking gently, now. Steering engine right back and . . . we were down in great cascades of water, heading for the strand at high speed. Too fast! Gravity brakes—*quick!* Streams of gravitons thundered forward from our pontoons. I could feel the deceleration, even through the ship's local gravity. Slowing . . . There! Stopped her just as the pontoons ruined themselves on the rocky strand with great scraping shrieks of hullmetal as we beached some two hundred irals from the transport. Switched off the ship's local gravity—bleah! No time to feel sick. "Demolition hands arm all scuttling charges and report to me aboard *Montroyal* with remote detonators!" I yelled into the blower. "All other hands to board *Montroyal* directly—on the double! Now!"

Threw off my restraints and followed the bridge crew down the companionway, then onto a slippery, wet pontoon and finally onto the rocky strand. The armored landing craft were buttoning up and lifting in great apparent haste, even as the fifteen of us made our way toward *Montroyal.*

As we approached the ship, somebody—Jennings, of course!—started the big SpinGravs. Good man. The few moments he saved by that thoughtful action might ransom all our lives. Have to walk on the damned pebbly strand. Turned an ankle and my whole damned hurt leg went to xaxt. Gorksroar!

Suddenly, the rocky beach erupted in fiery spouts of pebbles. Glanced over my shoulder to the top of the precipice, where a few gray-suited Leaguers were firing at us with blast pikes. They'd be joined by more momentarily. "Run, xaxtdamnit!" I yelled at the StarSailors. "That's real stuff they're shooting up there." Saw a Drive mate go down with a shrill scream, clutching her hip. Two others scooped her up and dragged her to the transport. Hobbling along for all I was worth now, but my bad leg was getting in the way. *Didn't sign up to do any marching, General,* I'd bragged to Drummond. Gorksroar! More shots! More cries of pain. Beach was alive with fiery spouts of pebbles—soon everyone had passed me! *Run,* xaxtdamnit!

Without warning, I was nearly blinded by a terrific brilliance strobing out over the lake, then the top of the precipice simply erupted in towering, thunderclaps of explosions as a trio of huge forms—blurred by sheer speed—raced in from the lake, just cleared the precipice, then arced off into the sky, followed by the thunder of wide-open SpinGravs. Two Type 327s flanking a lone Starfury. I grinned as I hobbled to the relative safety of *Montroyal*'s beached prow and climbed inside a hatch in the nose. Watters hadn't forgotten us!

Turned to check the strand for latecomers. Three still,

crumpled bodies remained on the beach. Ground my teeth—
three more deaths I could blame directly on myself! The
xaxtdamned BKAEW in the hold had better be awfully valuable. Listened to the rumble of the power chambers. "Which
way's the bridge?" I asked one of the hands closing the
hatch. She pointed to a companionway. "Up two levels, Admiral," she said. "Come on, I'll take you there."

Dragged my bad leg up the steep ladder behind her and
got there eventually. Had a lot of encouragement from the
din outside. Someone was giving a *real* war up there on the
precipice now—couldn't be much more time before somebody reached the edge with enough firepower to stop us.

A man with a walrus mustache was in the Flight Engineer's
seat to the right of the big ship's single Helm—a lot of the
newer transports had similar bridge layouts—lots of room to
move about. Two navigator's stations aft. Load master station
at the bulkhead. Pretty good visibility through the Hyperscreens. "Good to see you, Admiral," the man said with no
more emotion than if we were parked at the Avalon Fleet
Base. "I'm Jennings." He was slender, medium in height, with
short brown hair that he brushed forward, eyeglasses (which
probably had prevented him from becoming a Helmsman), a
crooked smiled, and a twinkle of intelligence in his eyes.

"I'm Brim," I said, vaulting into the Helmsman's seat and
plugging in my battlesuit—thank Voot for standard fittings!
"Mighty obliged to find the 'Gravs turning over."

"No problem, Admiral," Jennings said. "I used AutoStart."

"Whatever that is," I said with a grin and busied myself
scanning the controls. Four sets of Drive readouts, eight sets
for the SpinGravs—normal readings from what I could see.
Decided to let Jennings worry about them. Four verniers for
the thrust dampers running two 'Gravs each . . . pretty much

as I'd expected. Gravity brakes near the foot controls. Looked over at Jennings. "Anything weird I ought to know about?"

"Pretty regular bus, *Montroyal,*" he said. "At least that's what Morrison and Peters used to say."

"The Helmsmen?"

"Yeah."

I nodded. Nothing to say about *that.* "D'you know the takeoff velocities?" I asked, hoping against hope he'd have heard. Otherwise, I'd have to make some critical guesses.

"Vee-one's about 125 cpm, vee-R's 129, and she'll come unstuck at 137," Jennings replied without hesitation. "But she'll tell you when she's ready."

Right. Most large transports *did* talk to their Helmsmen. "Gravity brakes for reverse thrust?" I asked, watching out the window as six Type 327s blasted the top of the precipice again. Must be getting hot up there.

"Affirmative," Jennings replied. "Simple foot pressure acts like a throttle."

Checked my panel—nothing about the ship's hatches. "All buttoned up?" I asked.

"Hatches are green light, Admiral."

"Where's the blower?"

"Switch by your hand on the armrest."

Yeah. Should have seen it. Selected ALL STATIONS, then, SPEAK. "Hands to stations for lift-off," I called. "All hands to stations for lift-off; prepare for internal gravity." I choked back my gorge as I flicked the "G" switch, then checked in the aft-view screens. All clear. Finally—I couldn't think of anything else—I shrugged, placed my feet on the sensors, and gently pressed. A deep growl issued from deep in the ship's belly as we began to move backward off the strand. No scraping noises on *this* ship; she was meant to be run aground. "Here we go," I mumbled.

By now, growing numbers of gray-suited Leaguers had discovered *Montroyal* wasn't returning their fire and had been rappelling down the cliff on the ropes that remained from the Royal Engineers. At least fifty of them were crowded around my TG 39, and some had evidently gotten enough nerve to enter some of the hatches—I could see movement in the bridge. Sad to see the elegant little killer ship sitting forlornly on the strand with all her hatches open. Except for the ruined pontoons, she was in tiptop shape, but now she was doomed. Nobody likes to destroy a perfectly good starship—especially a Helmsman. Unfortunately, I had no choice. Seemed as if I was killing everything today, people, starships. Glumly, I pushed SPEAK again. "Attention Starfury demolition hands," I said. "Attention Starfury demolition hands. Activate your remote detonators immediately. I repeat, activate your remote detonators immediately." A moment later, the brand-new Starfury was wracked by six blinding explosions that instantly transformed her sleek main hull and pontoons into spherical clouds of hullmetal fragments and Drive crystal shards expanding outward from glowing puffballs of fire and raw energy. I shrugged. What a tragic waste—but then tragic waste *was* the very essence of war, wasn't it? If nothing else, the little killer ship had taken a few score Leaguers with her when she ceased to exist; that was the reason she'd been created in the first place. . . .

Back to business. More Leaguers were rappelling down the wires every moment, and the ones who hadn't gone up in the explosion were picking themselves off the strand and shooting at us with everything they had. This lot had only blast pikes—I could hear the shots *pinging* and *zipping* against the stout hullmetal outside. But it wouldn't be much longer before somebody else showed up with *a lot* more firepower.

I advanced the thrust dampers gingerly and found to my

delight that *Montroyal* didn't need a lot of thrust to break away and begin to taxi forward. After we started to move, I actually pulled the thrust dampers back to IDLE, and there was still plenty of power to carry us through a 180-degree turn. "Nice," I said, even though the forward pivot point was at least thirty irals aft of my seat.

"That's what they all say," Jennings replied with a grin. It wasn't difficult to see I had the controls of an engineer's machine. She was certainly no Starfury, but she felt pretty good for all the extra bulk.

I continued out toward deep water, while a furious air battle went on above our heads. Starfuries and Gorn-Hoffs everywhere—and a number of streamers on their way down. Vicious up there. The bastard Leaguers were out to get us or learn the reason why!

At last, the center of the lake—or at least that part that offered the longest takeoff run. I had no mortal idea how much room she'd need to get into the air. Glanced at my instruments for a moment—nearly useless. Although I recognized every readout on the panels, I didn't know what the values meant. Jennings probably didn't realize it—and I certainly wasn't going to frighten him with the information—but he'd *really* be the one flying takeoff. I could contribute little more than steady and experienced pressure on the controls. . . .

Time to do it! Swung the bow toward the far end of the lake—a bit of a crosswind, but after I got this much mass moving along, we'd need a *serious* gust to deflect us. Standing on the gravity brakes now, I turned to Jennings. "What do we need for takeoff power?"

"One point four EPR ought to be plenty, Admiral?" he said.

"One point four," I acknowledged, and moved the thrust dampers forward until that value appeared in the readouts.

The huge SpinGravs deep in the hull built quickly to a majestic thunder—aft, we were soon throwing great clouds of spray and gravitons hundreds of irals into the air. "Whadda you think, Jennings?" I asked.

"She's ready to go, Admiral," he said—with that big, unconcerned grin plastered across his face again.

"Then here goes nothing," I yelled and released the brakes. Glanced at a readout showing we weighed about forty-four milstons as we slowly—at least to a Starfury driver—accelerated down lake, pushing aside gray, white-capped rollers that angled against our bow like ranks of marching Leaguers. No trouble keeping her on course, even with the crosswind. Faster and faster—heavy spray slamming against the forward Hyperscreens—bumping, rumbling. Big 'Gravs were working damned hard to move all this weight. End of the lake coming up, now—a lot faster than I liked. Forced myself calm—or something that passed for calm. Still accelerating. Would have to do something pretty quick—speed was nearly 125 CPM! Getting ready to *yank* her into the air if necessary, when suddenly, a woman's voice came from my readout panel: "Vee-one."

"Rotate," Jennings prompted a moment later—calmly as ever. I eased back on the controls and the big ship smoothly rotated nose up, then *really* began to pick up speed. As advertised, she thundered sublimely into the air at 137 on the nose and cleared the first stone pillars at the end of the lake by at least fifty irals.

"Y-you transport people aren't used to lots of clearance, are you?" I stammered, glancing at Jennings while fighting my breath under control. Starfuries are usually in vertical flight only clicks after leaving the water.

He smiled and shrugged. "Don't *need* any more than that, Admiral," he said matter-of-factly.

I rolled my eyes. Jennings had a point, there—it all had to do with one's personal definition of "normal." Glad to see Watters thunder past the port Hyperscreens (Starfuries won't stay aloft at the speed we were moving). We were climbing toward a fierce air battle that could very well extend all the way out into interstellar space—and beyond.

"Gradual pitch change to seventeen degrees," the woman's voice directed from the console.

I glanced at Jennings.

He nodded.

Gradually, I raised the nose until the inclinometers read seventeen degrees, then the AutoHelm reduced power to a climb of ten thousand irals per cycle and I heard a change in the 'Grav noise.

"You'll want to bring up the lift-enhancers about halfway to five as we go through fifteen thousand irals," Jennings said, eyes glued to his instruments.

"Five on the lifts," I acknowledged.

Soon we had rumbled through twenty-five thousand irals and I brought the lift enhancers to zero. Speed was building nicely now. Tremendous battle all around us. Gorn-Hoffs and Starfuries—with the odd Type 327 that was sticking around to see us home. *Montroyal* had no real speed, no acceleration, no maneuverability, no disruptors. All I could do was keep flying a steady course and trust to Lady Fortune. Felt kind of helpless in the big, unarmed transport. Easy for someone like me to forget this kind of flying, where doughty Helmsmen and crews have only their own skill and courage to get them through the perilous wartime skies. I laughed ironically to myself—they called *me* brave. . . .

Chapter 9

Atalanta

26–32 Octad, 52014

Interstellar Space—nearing Asterious, aboard I.F.S. *Montroyal*

Jennings and I had managed to fly *Montroyal* almost all the way back to the KA'PPA Institute Research Labs on Asterious-Proteus when the light cruiser I.F.S. *Glorious* hove abreast of us, regally edging aside our escorting Starfuries as if she were a full-fledged battleship. Moments later, Trafford's blond countenance appeared in a global display—she didn't look happy. "Brim, you xaxtdamned traitor," she snarled, her face contorting with anger. "I will have your head for what you did to me this afternoon. As of this moment, I am officially charging you with the failure of the entire mission."

Felt my eyebrows rise. "What?" I demanded.

"You heard me, Admiral Wilf A. Brim, you worthless coward," she growled, her face reddening more as she spoke.

"I don't think I did hear you, General," I said, slipping the AutoHelm to AUTOMATIC/FULL-AUTHORITY. "What I thought I heard was that you were blaming the failure of your mission on *me.*"

"You heard correctly, Brim," she said, "and I'm going to make you pay dearly for it."

"Pay for *what,* General?"

"You know xaxtdamned well, you bastard Carescrian."

"General," I said, glancing at Jennings, who was trying to look anywhere but at *me,* "I strongly suggest you calm down, immediately—you have neither cause, nor call to make such a statement. And I don't particularly care for your choice of language, either."

"You haven't begun to hear the abuse I plan to heap on you, Brim," she said. "Your absolutely craven desire to pull those squadrons to a secondary mission where you would *personally* come under less fire disgusts me. All the dead and wounded . . ." She allowed her voice to trail off dramatically—it was my first clue to what was *really* on her mind.

"General," I said calmly as I could under the circumstances. "Your mission had already gone awry by the time I called those two squadrons to the secondary target."

"How do you know?" she asked with fire in her eyes. "You weren't anywhere near the main target when you countermanded my orders."

"Wait a moment, General," I protested. "As I recall, it was *you* countermanding *my* orders."

"You had no claim to issuing any order *at all*—except those that had to do with directing the Combat Space Patrol,

Brim," she said. "This operation was under *my* command, not yours."

"Directing the CSP is precisely what I was doing, General," I replied through clenched teeth.

"You were shifting forces, Brim," she protested.

"As I saw fit to carry out both primary and secondary operations," I said, keeping myself only *just* under control. "You may recall, General, that you assigned no escorts to the secondary target at all—killer *or* attack ships. Had I not acted as I did, *that* part of the operation would have surely failed."

"You deprived my primary operation of the very ships that could have turned the tide of battle," she growled. "It is clear that *I* did what I could to ensure success only to have you sabotage my carefully laid plans."

She was putting on a skilled performance, and no doubt recording it with care. A cold shudder of trouble swept me for a moment. Courts-martials are constructed on just such statements!

"General," I said carefully, "it is my opinion that you are in no condition to carry on a rational conversation at this time."

"Oh, it is, is it, you coward?"

"It is, General," I replied. "I am no follower of the psychological arts, but at the present time, you neither appear nor sound rational. After you have had a chance to relax for a day or so and assess the actual mission results, I shall accept your apologies, both professional *and* personal."

Trafford's eyes suddenly became wide with anger and she clenched her teeth. "Apologies?" she screamed in a strangled voice, "I will have your career for this Brim—if not your *life!*" With that, the display went dark. . . .

With substantial assistance from the unflappable Jennings, I managed to wrestle *Montroyal* to a three-bounce (but who's counting?) landfall in one piece on Asterious-Proteus's Lake Manchester and even succeeded in bringing her alongside one of the KA'PPA Institute piers while punching only a single dent in her pristine hullmetal. Ashore, I set up rides back to FleetPort 19 for the crew of poor TG 39 and placed Jennings in temporary command of *Montroyal* until Transport Command could send out a couple of Helmsmen to take over. Then I raced to the COMM Center for the latest news from Atalanta.

Still *bad!* Both Barbousse and Williams reported that the Leaguers were almost constantly overhead, and the city was in flames—as was much of the above-ground base. The crews in LaSalle's Starfuries and Defiants were giving admirable account of themselves, but the number of ships available was dwindling rapidly. Tom Carpenter, the Base Engineering Officer, had been reduced to salvaging wrecks from the bottom of the harbor for parts to keep the others in space. And without adequate escorts, the next Gontor Convoy had been cut to ribbons. Only Delacroix and *Yellow Bird* were getting supplies through to the nearly isolated space bastion. According to Williams, unless something happened immediately to change the status of the base and its ability to protect future convoys, the Gontor portion of Sapphire was in *real* danger of collapsing.

And this female jackass Trafford had time to blame me for the failure of her mission! Mother of Voot!

At least Claudia was still safe (as of nearly eight metacycles previously, when Barbousse's message had been sent). She'd been living on base since her home was destroyed the previous day. Nesterio had moved in with her. Don't know why I resented him in the same bed where his wife and I had so recently proclaimed our love for one another. Testosterone clearly induces male insanity. So does love. . . .

I needed to get myself back to Atalanta as soon as possible! But first, there was something I might be able to do in Avalon that would have a direct and almost-immediate effect on the situation in Atalanta. Checked my timepiece—middle of Night Watch there; everybody I needed to see would be asleep. But, thanks to orders from Moulding, Watters and her crew had checked into overnight quarters, so they could provide me transportation to Avalon in the morning.

I picked up some clean socks and underclothes at the terminal, then caught a ride to the Visiting Officers' Quarters, where the desk clerk handed me a small envelope; said it had been hand delivered for me earlier in the day. Frowning, I left a message for Watters requesting a Dawn plus two departure in the morning, then opened the envelope and extracted a note scribbled in familiar handwriting.

Skipper:

Heard you were here on Proteus. How convenient—so am I. Let's meet! As I remember, you owe me drinks—I paid the *yamshchik* for our Sodeskayan *troika* ride. 'Phone me at my new bender, I.F.S. *Narwhale.* Tonight or nothing—I leave in the morning; I'll bet you do, too. The Officers' Club's open all watches, and I'm thirsty.

                                        Nadia Tissuard

I grinned—small galaxy! After today, I needed some cheering up, and couldn't think of many people who could do quite so thorough a job! Years ago, before the war—*this* war, that is—she'd been my First Lieutenant aboard the original I.F.S. *Starfury,* where she'd proven herself an exceptional Helmsman who could carry out a myriad of duties with the cheerful willingness of a GradyGroat saint. She'd also been utterly candid about life in general and, off duty, quite extraordinarily sensual. We'd formed a special sort of bond in those days, she and I, and on more than one occasion had been at pains to remain on the safe side of professionalism. To this day, she still called me "Skipper" and I called her "Number One."

When she was promoted as Captain of the bender, I.F.S. *Nord,* however, we allowed our friendship to gradually expand into one of a more intimate nature, though Dame Fortune seemed resolved to prevent us from anything but a few hurried—if increasingly determined—gropings. Had to chuckle as I remembered the *troika.* We'd actually *connected* for one brief moment . . . before the Sodeskayan secret police broke us up like a couple of groping kids! But that's part of another story entirely. . . .

Went to my rooms and washed up, then put in a 'Phone call to *Narwhale;* got through to a very young Duty Officer—an Ensign clearly fresh from training school—whose image stared back at me for a moment from the globular display, then demanded to know on what priority I was calling his skipper. Couldn't blame him; it *was* pretty late in the day, and I was wearing my coveralls with no indication of rank. "Is she alone?" I asked.

"What?"

"I said 'Is she alone?' If she's alone, then my priority is 'Flash'; otherwise, I'll call back tomorrow."

"Who is this?" he demanded.

"It's a personal call, Ensign," I said, "—and I'm 'Phoning by *her* request. Now, is she alone or shall I call back later?"

"Listen you," the Ensign screeched, "I have no idea if the Captain is alone or not. It's not any of my business."

"Neither is this thraggling call, Mister," I said with growing irritation. "Now you put me through to your Captain—immediately."

Suddenly I heard another voice come through the background, followed by a stuttered "Y-yes, C-captain," in anxious inflection. Next, Tissuard's saucy, round face was goggling at me in the display. Wide-spaced, candid eyes, a pug nose, and full, sensuous lips—with prematurely salt-and-pepper hair—gave the aspect of a middle-aged pixie.

"Mother of Voot!" she exclaimed. "Skipper!"

"Bet your pretty backside, Number One," I assured her.

"WON-der-ful!" she growled, rolling her eyes. "Oh, just *thraggling* WON-der-ful." Immediately, the video went off as I heard, "Just a moment, Wilf." Then, the voice channel went silent as well. A few moments later, the phone came back to life as Tissuard reappeared, cheeks glowing. "New man on the crew," she muttered. "He'll be flogged within an inch of his life . . . just as soon as I can get through some of my flogging backlog." Then she giggled and threw up her hands. "But he's now *first* on the list!"

"Maybe I've got a better idea," I said.

"Than flogging?"

"Well . . ."

"Skipper," she giggled, "remember this is the *duty* phone."

"You *said* you were thirsty."

"I am," she replied with a grin. "But what does that have to do with . . . you know . . . flogging?"

"Depends on what kind of flogging."

"You tell me."

"Thought we might flog a few drinks, then," I said.

"Maybe *first*," she said with a laugh, then, "Where are you—at the VOQ?"

"Yeah."

"D'you have a car?"

"Xaxt no," I said. "I hardly have a ride home."

She frowned a moment. "Just stay where you are, then," she said. "I'll come get you."

"All right," I said. "What are you wearing?"

"Now or when I pick you up?"

"The latter."

"Casual," she said.

"What does *that* mean?"

"Something as brief as I possibly can get away with," she whispered, cupping her hand to the 'Phone. "I like to watch your eyes get big."

"I'm sure they will," I said with a chuckle. "But I didn't bring any civvies on the mission. This is about all I have to wear."

"What you've got on is fine," she said. "Helmsman's jacket, and a garrison cap. Otherwise, I won't recognize you."

"You're a dream," I sighed.

"Fifteen cycles," she said. "Meet you out front. All right?"

"Fifteen cycles," I said, as the 'Phone went dark. In spite of everything else, I grinned to myself while I pulled on my boots. At least I wouldn't spend much time tonight worrying about Trafford. . . .

True to her word, Tissuard pulled up before the Visiting Officers' Quarters within fifteen cycles. Well, perhaps twenty-five cycles, but who's counting? She looked wonderful, sitting there in a staff car wearing a tiny skirt riding even farther above her knees than Claudia's. She had a compact figure with largish hands and feet—and a prominent bosom that rarely failed to attract male attention, even when mostly concealed by a Fleet Cloak.

As I got in and closed the door she frowned. "Your eyes

aren't very big, Skipper," she said, looking at me thoughtfully. "Here, see what this does to you." With that, she drew her blouse open. She had nothing on beneath, and those huge breasts stood out like those of a woman half her age, tipped by small, dark-brown nipples. She was absolutely gorgeous, and she knew it. "Well," she said as—indeed—I felt my eyes widen, "that's a little better." She giggled. "For a moment there, I thought perhaps that Valemont woman had completely stolen those gonads of yours."

I grinned as she closed her blouse and started off along the roadway. "Word travels fast, doesn't it?"

"The *right* kind of word," she said. "She making you happy?"

"Yeah," I said.

"And you've spent only one night with her . . . aside from years ago?"

"Hey, cm'on, Nadia," I objected with a grin. "She wouldn't ask about *you*."

Nadia laughed. "Until you and I get a decent roll in the hay going—one that lasts more than fifteen clicks *and* deposits some tangible results right *here*—she'll have nothing to ask about."

"True," I admitted, putting my hand on her shoulder, "but it's not that I haven't tried. You've got to give me credit for that."

"Oh, I do," she said, glancing at me with a smile. "The fact is, however, that I've already been waiting a couple of years now. I could be *old* before we finally get it on."

I laughed. "Open that blouse again," I said.

"Huh?"

"I said, 'open that blouse again.' I want to feel your boobs."

Grinning, she pulled open her blouse. "Well?" she demanded presently.

I turned in the seat to weigh each of her heavy breasts in my hand with a professional bearing. "The way these stand up by themselves, they don't look as if they're going to grow old very soon," I said. "Even if we have a lengthy wait, they're going to look wonderful to me."

"Kiss 'em," she said.

I did.

"Longer."

I did again—much longer, this time.

"Let me see your lap, now."

I did.

"Come on, Skipper, sit up. No slouching—let me see your lap."

I grumbled.

"Yeah. That's *much* better. Now I believe you. . . ."

The Officers' Club bar was small and intimate—fitting for a research planet, where almost everyone was a civilian. Tissuard and I had found a private spot at the end of the counter and were halfway through a first round of meems when abruptly she switched the subject from her new bender. "I think you're in deep Gorksroar, Skipper," she said looking up from her drink as if she were angry.

I frowned. "Deep Gorksroar?"

"You know what I mean."

"I know what 'deep Gorksroar' means," I answered. "But why am I in it—this Trafford thing?"

"Damn straight," she said. "That woman's out after you ass, Skipper, and in an entirely different way than I usually am."

"Were *you* part of her operation?" I asked carefully. The whole thing was *supposed* to be top secret.

"No," she said. "I didn't even know about the operation till this afternoon. But there's this Old Girls' network that would make your friend Barbousse blush with envy. And when I got wind of what that bitch has on her mind, I figured I'd better get with you—in spite of the fact that I'd promised to stay out of Valemont's way for a while." She laughed and lit a Mu'occo cigarette. "I like what I hear about her, in spite of being a bit jealous."

"Thanks, Number One," I said, squeezing her hand. "I really appreciate that."

Tissuard nodded, then became *very* serious. "You won't appreciate what I'm going to tell you next," she said, exhaling a long plume of spicy smoke.

"I'll damn well appreciate the *telling* of it," I said.

She squeezed my hand back. "Thanks," she said. "Trafford must have caused quite a cock-up at Emithrnéy."

I nodded and sipped my drink. "Looked like it, anyway," I said. "But from what I could see, she didn't really *cause* it. Her plans were certainly adequate for the mission, although we might have practiced them a little more realistically."

"Then what happened?"

"Bad luck more than anything else. She'd simply made no contingency plans and got caught flat-footed when things went to xaxt in a handbasket."

"Interesting," Tissuard said. "That's what I'd heard too. She's in pretty serious trouble for that—a lot of people got killed." She took a thoughtful draught of her cigarette and looked at me with a frown. "So what was your part in the mission?"

"I was in charge of the escorts."

"Makes sense," she said. "Then what in xaxt did you *do* to earn that much anger?"

I shrugged. "There was a secondary objective to the mission on a nearby planet," I said. "I took a couple of squadrons over to make certain *that* came off."

"I take it you were successful?"

"Had to fly a transport home, but, yeah, I'd say that part of the mission was successful."

"Her secondary objective was aboard the transport, I suppose?"

I nodded.

"Skipper, you don't know the first thing about flying transports. How in xaxt did . . . ?"

"Long story; don't ask."

She nodded, then sucked her lip for a moment thoughtfully while she stubbed out the cigarette in a cloud of spiced smoke. "All right," she said presently. "That gives me enough information to make some sense out of what I'd heard."

"I'm listening," I said.

"All right—this is what I make of it. First and foremost, Trafford's rear end is in a big sling because of the contingency plans she bungled—and she knows it. In turn, she's looking for someone to dump the blame on before her career goes into the life-support system for recycling. The best thing she can come up with is that everything went to xaxt because there weren't enough escorts, so that involves the escort commander. Pretty simple so far," she observed.

I grimaced as Trafford's words rang in my ears. First the countermand to my orders for cover at Lavenurb—which I countermanded in turn—then her midspace tirade. "She's quick," I groaned. "I didn't suspect anything until she started yelling at me on the way home."

"Which she recorded," Tissuard added, shaking her head sorrowfully. "Voot's beard, what a thraggling politician!"

"Better than me," I observed.

"Brother Brim," Tissuard said, "compared to that woman, you don't even qualify as an *amateur* politician." Then she laughed caustically. "Thank the gods."

"Well," I countered, "there *is* a little more to everything than meets the eye, Number One."

Tissuard cocked her head and peered at me through one eye, then ground her teeth. "Oh Gorksroar!" she exclaimed under her breath. "Don't tell me that capturing the Lavenurb BKAEW was *really* the primary. Of course. Why didn't I think of it myself? Blowing up the Emithrnéy gravity docks mission didn't make all that much sense."

"I didn't think you *knew* about the targets," I protested.

Tissuard rolled her eyes and finished her drink. "When *you're* in trouble, Skipper, I find out everything I can—legally or otherwise." She signaled the steward. "Two more of these please! And damn lucky for you that I do," she added.

"Yeah, I know," I admitted. "Thanks."

"You're welcome." She grimaced. "I suppose somebody in a high place gave you secret orders to make certain that big Lavenurb BKAEW was delivered here, no matter what— *and* guaranteed you'd be taken care of in case . . ."

"That's about the size of it."

"How high a place?"

I looked into her eyes. "High as it can go," I said.

"WON-der-ful," she groaned, "just thraggling WON-der-ful. I suppose you've never heard anybody say, 'Put not your trust in princes'?"

"Once or twice."

"So you trust him?"

"If I can't trust *him*, who in xaxt can I trust?"

"Wilf, Wilf, Wilf. For Voot's sake, even you must know that the higher you go, the *more* people are controlled by politics—especially big credits."

"So what else don't I know?" I grumped.

"About Trafford's political clout, probably," she said.

"I knew she was pretty powerful," I said.

"Not *pretty* powerful—*very* powerful. Do you have any idea who her daddy is?"

I shut my eyes. "Oh no," I groaned, "not Count Tal Confisse-Trafford."

"You've got it, Skipper. Sole owner of Confisse Mining, Ltd., the biggest operation of its kind in the known Universe. He's got more thraggling money than Onrad himself."

"I've heard that," I said, "but I certainly didn't know whose father he is. Besides, I wouldn't have done anything differently, even if I *had* known."

Tissuard sighed. "That's probably true, isn't it?" she muttered.

"Anyway," I added, "that BKAEW was about to impact Atalanta—as well as some operations we've got in the works. *Big* operations, Number One—got a stake in one of them, myself. I didn't have a xaxt of a lot of choice."

Tissuard finished her second drink in silence, then signaled for a third. "All right," she said, "here's what I think's going on. Somebody big in the Admiralty who's *also* one of your mentors—probably Drummond or maybe that handsome bastard Calhoun himself . . . laid the assignment on you. Then the Big Boy later blessed it himself. Right?"

"Close enough for government work."

"Well, right now, Daddy Trafford has got all your mentors—including the Big Boy himself—by the gonads. And believe me, he's not treating 'em the same fun way I treated yours in the troika that evening. Confisse Trafford's *squeez-*

ing. You can damn near hear those boys yelping from here. His dear little Megan is about to have a promising career shoved somewhere it won't produce an orgasm—*as well as* besmirch the family reputation for excellence. Perhaps *that* will give you an idea how much you can count on your friends in high places."

Made sense, the way she put it. "So what do you suggest?" I asked.

"Don't know," she said, stroking her chin. She lit another cigarette. "Probably the best thing you can do is make yourself scarce—get back to Atalanta the quickest way you can and . . . well, you'll *never* lie low, so probably the next best thing is to get yourself so involved with what's going on there—like Sapphire—that they can't do much to you.

"What the xaxt do *you* know about . . . ?"

"As much as I could learn on my back under a fairly big wheel—after an expensive lunch, Skipper," she said with a laugh. "Don't worry, nothing's compromised. I've got more clearances than *he* has, and, well, you've had some experience yourself with my personal need-to-know."

I grabbed her hand again. "I think I love you, Number One," I said.

"Right now, it's not the kind of love I'm looking for," she said. "But it's damn well appreciated, anyway."

"So are you."

"Going to cost you only a kiss this time," she said, grinning. "Next time, you'll have to thank me with your trousers off." Then she frowned. "Now, my lovable Skipper, here's what you are going to do tomorrow morning when Watters—that's her name isn't it?—sets you down in Avalon. . . ."

Watters dropped me off at the Fleet Base on Lake Mersin a little after Dawn plus three. Cowper was waiting; had me at

the Admiralty just prior to Morning and a half, where I managed to snare a tired-looking Drummond—was it luck or was
he waiting for me?—before his early staff meeting. Whatever the case, his statuesque secretary wordlessly ushered me
into the inner office the moment I showed up at his door.

"Come in and sit down, Brim," he said with a dour aspect,
indicating a chair in front of his desk. "Quite a cock-up yesterday at Emithrnéy, I understand."

"Looked like one to me, General," I said as I sank into the
comfortable chair.

"A miracle you managed to bring your part off at the secondary target—in spite of everything," he said with a frown.
"A real miracle." He shook his head somberly. "When in xaxt
did you learn to fly transports?"

"I didn't," I said. "Fellow named Jennings did most of it; I
just handled the controls while he supplied all the right information."

"Gorksroar, as usual," Drummond said with one of his little smiles. "You wouldn't admit to doing anything special
even to save your life, would you, Brim?"

Ignored him—didn't need that. "Jennings deserves the Imperial comet for what he did," I said. "That's an official recommendation, General."

Drummond made an entry at his workstation. "Noted," he
said. "He works for Transport Command?"

"Yeah."

"I'll take care of it."

"Thanks."

He looked at me a long time while he stroked his chin. "I
can't imagine you don't have some inkling of what's going
on behind your back," he said at least.

"I've heard a few rumors," I said noncommittally, and
waited for him to pick up the ball again.

"Well, she *did* talk to you by radio yesterday before you landed, didn't she?"

"General Trafford?"

"Nergol thraggling Triannic."

I laughed. "They both do appear to be out after my rear end," I said. "But Trafford seems to feel that I'm personally to blame for her troubles yesterday. I get the impression she believes the ships I took to Lavenurb would have saved her bacon on Emithrnéy."

"Nothing would have saved her bacon," Drummond growled firmly. "Trafford's an excellent field commander, but she simply ran into bad luck yesterday when one of her landing craft blundered into an armed transport with an escort. Without that surprise, her whole operation was doomed—and she had no contingency plans in place. Believe me, I know. I've been up all night going over the results." He grimaced. "Don't see how *you* accomplished what you did with only one squadron apiece."

"Good people," I suggested.

"Yeah," Drummond said, "good people like *you*. Onrad wants to promote you for what you did—*after* you get your fourth Imperial comet." Then he sat back in his chair. "Unfortunately," he said, "in spite of all your good work, we've—and specifically *you've*—got serious trouble this morning."

I only nodded in silence. He didn't know how much I knew, and it couldn't hurt to hear what he might add to Tissuard's information.

"The look on your face suggests you've already heard something," Drummond replied.

"About Daddy Confisse-Trafford?" I asked with great innocence.

He nodded silently while he nervously chewed his lip. "He's bound and determined that daughter Megan's lily white battle record will *not* be blemished. Ergo, he wants a scapegoat."

"Me."

Drummond shrugged. "That's about the size of it. You are the only one who did anything directly in contravention of her—'must-be-perfect'—orders."

"Understood," I said. "What kind of support can I expect from you and Calhoun?"

"Everything we can do to help," Drummond said.

"How about Onrad?"

"The same—I talked to him in the middle of the night."

"So how much trouble can I be in?" I asked, but I already knew the answer—and thanks to Tissuard, I was ready to pounce.

"In our own, very ordinary, day-to-day world, *no* trouble," Drummond said. "But Confisse-Trafford doesn't operate in our world. People with that kind of money, power, and above all arrogance, they operate in a completely different Universe. And in that one, he throws a *lot* of weight, too." He glanced out the window for a moment and took a deep breath. "It's not certain that even Onrad will prevail in this one."

I smiled. Nice of Drummond—must have hurt 'fessing up to that kind of truth. "Thanks," I said. "So what do I do now?"

"You've got two immediate choices, the way I see things this morning. You can remain here and try to fight this thing from the beginning—we'll supply the best legal help in the Fleet. Or, I'll fly you out of here immediately—before the bastards can get their claws on you. I've Jim Payne and his Type 327 waiting right now at the Fleet Base to take you back to Atalanta."

"Thanks again," I said—and meant it. "What's your advice?"

"Go back to Atalanta," he said. "The best legal help in the Fleet will be absolutely powerless against the kind of talent Trafford can bring in to prove her case."

"So I'm doomed, eh?"

Usually, Drummond would have used that opening for some kind of joke. This time, he simply shook his head. "No, Brim," he said. "She won't be able to hang you or have you shot—though Daddy *could* pull that off if she really wanted it. But, well, realistically, your career is in real jeopardy."

I took a deep breath. Thank the gods Tissuard had prepared me for this! I'd had time to think everything over, and knew what I had to do without making shoot-from the-hip decisions that were usually bad. "All right," I said. "I'll go back to Atalanta with Payne. But if I'm about to take a fall to save your necks—when you *asked* me here to help you out of a bad spot—then you owe me *big time.* Especially since I managed to bring off your mission while I ruined myself."

"No doubt about that," Drummond said, looking at me unhappily. "We owe you an immense debt."

Had him just where I wanted him! "Then there are two things I want you to promise me," I said.

"Name them," Drummond said. "If they're humanly possible, they're yours."

"Good," I said. "First, I need those Carescrians and their long-range escort ships assigned to—and departing *for*—Atalanta *immediately*—not almost a month from now, as poor Ambrose promised just before he was murdered. Otherwise, we can kiss Project Sapphire good-bye—plus waste a xaxt of a lot of lives, time, and matérial we've already invested. . . ."

Drummond looked me in the eye. "Done," he said. "You'll have those Carescrian units in Atalanta day after tomorrow."

"Thanks, General," I said. "The second thing may be a bit harder."

"What is it?"

"I've a job to finish in Atalanta, General," I said, "and also in Gontor. I've worked hard to set things up the way they are. See if you can put off this courts-martial Gorksroar until I get a chance to make it all happen, I'm still your best chance for bringing off Sapphire."

Drummond folded his hands and nodded. "I know you are, Brim," he said. "We'll do everything we can to delay things— all three of us. But even in the best of circumstances, I'm afraid you'll have very little time. Confisse-Trafford doesn't brook waiting for anything—and right now, he's in a hurry. He brings newer and deeper meaning to the word arrogant."

I shrugged, then stood and extended my hand. Drummond was a good man, perhaps one of the Empire's best—and this was *hard* on him. "Been good working with you over the years, General," I said. "I assume I'll hear from you."

Drummond took my hand without looking me in the eye. "I'll be in touch, Brim," he said.

Then, I simply turned and walked from his office. I knew things were going to be bad when I heard him begin to weep softly.

On my arrival in Atalanta, it was clear that things were—if that were possible—even worse than I'd been told. Williams and I stood at the entrance to the underground hangars, shading our eyes from Hador's strong midday light and looking out across Grand Harbor, where a tiny launch was pulling a rusty barge three times its size toward the half-dismantled ruins of starship swarming with salvage workers. What a horrible change! Wrecked starships now littered the filthy water everywhere, and great columns of smoke rose from the huge expanse of gravity docks that lined the civilian portions of the harbor. Out in the gulf, a once-clear horizon was now turned

to reddish brown haze from countless fires that burned out of
control above us on the base and throughout the city behind
us. The whole atmosphere was one of destruction; even the
still air smelled strongly of burning buildings and scorched
metal. Close by, the bridge of a shattered Gorn-Hoff pro-
truded just above the water, its Hyperscreen frames twisted
and empty as water splashed in and out of a great blackened
hole aft of the Helmsman's station. Farther on—bent into a
rumpled "V"—what was once the hull of S.S. *Mandakai,* a
fast transport, lay against a blackened portion of the rocky
breakwater. She'd been carrying spare Krasni-Peych Spin-
Gravs, desperately needed by overworked maintenance crews
who were trying to keep the few surviving Starfuries in space.
Only half her cargo had been salvaged.

It had looked like that all the way in from space. Smoke,
wreckage, and craters once again defiled the terraced slopes
of City Mount Hill and the close-packed, haphazard collection of fanciful, sun-baked structures that covered them.
Spires and minarets lay toppled across the narrow streets.
Once-gleaming domes yawned shattered like fantastic broken
eggs. Blocks-long colonnades with their once-graceful arches
had been reduced to rubble. The huge GradyGroat monastery
seemed mostly whole, but *this* time, the Leaguers were making certain it would not lift off for space as it had during the
crucial battle of the last war. As Payne's Type 327 had passed
overhead on final, I saw that no tree remained standing in the
famous tiered gardens, and every outbuilding had been flattened. Even the great flame-shaped spire had been shattered
in a number of places.

"Hard to believe they could do this much damage so
quickly," I said gloomily, glancing at a rating who was carrying the few packages of hard-to-get indulgences I'd had time
to pick up in Avalon.

Williams shook his head. "Always been a hardworkin' bunch, those Leaguers," he commented with a straight face.

"Yeah," I said bleakly. "And getting better with practice, evidently. Want to give me a nonofficial summary?"

"We're holding our own, more or less," he said with a grimace. "Convoys to Gontor are still getting through, but our losses are mounting rapidly in that day-long part of the trip where the ships have no modern escorts. I assume you heard that Zakharoff was killed when I.F.S. *Celeron* took a brace of HyperTorps and blew up on the way back from Gontor."

"Ouch," I said, with sudden, bleak empathy. "Hadn't heard about old Zakharoff." Felt sorry for the fat old reprobate and everybody else on his old ship—including his double-arrogant officers. They might not have been very nice, but whatever one might say about them, they were undeniably brave. Most of the men and women on board must have known it well in advance of their own, untimely, deaths. Damned antique battle cruiser: without escorts, she'd been nothing but a sacrifice (along with Voot only knew how many cases of that fine old Tamrhone '05 meem).

"Unless we get those long-range escorts soon," Williams continued, "Sapphire is in real trouble. With all the losses we're taking from those convoys, we're not landing enough goods on Gontor to do any good."

I put my hand on his shoulder. "That's the good news I've brought. Got a confirmation message from Drummond while I was on my way here. We'll get our long-range escorts tomorrow—along with crews, spares, and maintenance people. The whole shooting match. All you've got to do is find some place to put 'em up." I peered around the cavern; the great expanses of piers was still mostly empty. "I assume we still have room."

Williams laughed. "If the worst of my troubles today were finding room for reinforcements," he said with a grin, "then I'd have a pretty plush job, wouldn't I, Admiral?"

I was about to carry on with the banter, but the "wouldn't I, *Admiral*" reminded me of my other concerns—specifically what Trafford was about to spring on me. Couldn't let poor Williams be sandbagged when that happened. I grabbed his forearm and looked him in the eye. "Jim," I said, "let's you and me take a short ride in your staff skimmer. We need to have a little talk about the future. . . ."

Most of the above-ground buildings on base had been damaged in one or another of the many Leaguer raids. My offices were now located in what had been a basement records storage area of Military Headquarters; the original Commander's suite in the spinward wing lay crushed beneath milstons of rubble—luckily most everyone had made it to the shelters, but *just* in the nick of time.

A long time passed that afternoon and early evening— along with two Leaguer raids—before I could finally close the door to my office and 'Phone Claudia. Thank Voot, the Civilian Headquarters building remained untouched—so far. Adele put me through immediately.

"Wilf," she said in a whisper, "I've been hoping I'd hear from you all day. Thought you might be too busy to take a personal call." She was *so* beautiful, even in the display.

Made a quiet laugh. "I'd have taken a call from you in a moment, Claudia," I said, "but I couldn't have said what's on my mind very easily with all those other folks around."

"What *is* on your mind?" she asked.

"Mostly you," I replied. "Mostly saying 'I love you.' "

"That's awfully nice to know," she said. "I've been hearing

your voice say that every time I listen to my mind. I guess now you know I love you, too."

"When can I see you?" I asked, with a sudden urgency. Promised myself I'd get some sort of control over these emotions—I was acting like a xaxtdamned schoolboy.

"How about tonight?"

"Hoped you'd say that," I replied. "Where?"

She made a little laugh, then looked me directly in my eyes from the display. "Somewhere I can keep my clothes on," she said. "We need to do some serious talking."

I grimaced; my brains had evidently been hanging between my legs again. "Sorry," I said. "Did I look like that?"

She smiled softly. "I couldn't tell, Wilf," she said in what was a bald-faced, but otherwise much appreciated prevarication.

Glanced at my timepiece—it was already well into Evening Watch. "How about late supper at the Officers' Club?"

"Strange," she said. "I had the same idea myself. Except . . ."

"Except what?"

"Well, I'd almost forgotten that the Officers' Club is pretty well flattened."

Xaxtdamned Leaguers, they always pick the very best targets. "Got any other ideas?"

"Well, there's the hangar cafeteria."

I grinned; couldn't think of a less romantic spot in the Home Galaxy—but when you're under constant attack, places for having a quiet, romantic rendezvous become fairly scarce. "Sounds like a plan to me," I said. "And there's probably not much chance I'll make a pass at you there, either. Of course," I added, glancing theatrically at my timepiece, "shouldn't be all *that* many people eating right now, come to think of it."

"Wilf Brim!"

"See you in fifteen cycles?"

"Fifteen cycles."

I made it in less than ten cycles; she showed up after nearly thirty. Somehow the lateness made her all the more appealing because I knew that, as Madame Harbor Master, she had a reputation for implacable punctuality. And she was even more beautiful for our recent separation. Wanted to take her in my arms and smother those lips in kisses, but—"Claudia, how nice to see you again!"—we made a good show of shaking hands for the staff at the steam tables and the few, lonely diners at that hour. Wondered to myself how many of them believed us. . . .

If not exactly the finest Effer'wyckean cuisine, our suppers were surprisingly good, considering the vicious attacks that were going on above us. Even so, I dined without paying much attention to the food. I suppose she did, too, because we seemed to sit there forever, talking rather than eating—long after our half-finished main courses were cold and unappetizing. We seemed to have a million things to discuss. However, despite our relative privacy, we kept skirting the subject we'd come to talk about—until, at length, she looked me in the eye and whispered, "Wilf Brim, that was a wonderful evening I had with you."

"Thought it was pretty wonderful, myself," I replied.

"You made me feel so beautiful," she whispered, her face coloring.

"You are beautiful, Claudia," I assured her "But then, the way I feel about you, I probably wouldn't notice if you weren't."

"We need to talk about the way you feel," she said.

"Yeah," I said, "I know. This has to be giving you a lot of trouble."

She looked into my eyes again. "It has, a little, Wilf," she said, "—especially after I accepted the fact that I'd let myself fall in love with you again."

Somehow I reined in my galloping emotions enough to croak out, "I love you, too, Claudia," even though things weren't going to be quite that simple. At our ages, there was a lot more to this thing we call "love" than simply soiling bed sheets with our lovemaking. "*Still* giving you trouble?" I asked.

She shook her head and smiled a little. "Not anymore," she whispered.

"Tell me about it, then," I said, frightened almost to death by what she might say. "Anything's fine except sending me out of your life."

"Got to admit I considered that," she said thoughtfully, "—but no more than a couple of moments. Losing you a second time would simply be unacceptable."

"Thank you," I murmured, ready now for anything she might decide—including running away together.

"Will you still thank me if I tell you I'm not going to leave Gorgas?" she asked.

I'd been afraid she might decide something like that, but it was infinitely better than losing her completely. "I can handle it," I said, "just so long as I've still got *some* access to you," I said. "But how are you and Gorgas going to manage?"

She smiled. "I shall be fine. And Gorgas, well, he simply won't hear about us, so he'll be fine, too. Our relationship, Wilf—the love part—is simply none of his business, and that's the way it will remain." Suddenly, she frowned. "You don't look very happy," she said.

"Terrible face for playing cre'el," I said. "Everybody knows what I've been dealt." Then I simply reached across the table to take her hand, and to xaxt with the rest of the Universe, including everyone in the cafeteria. "Guess I'd thought of us running away together or something stupid like that—but even touching your hand is pretty wonderful after all these years."

"Oh, Wilf," she said, firmly removing her hand and placing it safely in her lap under the table. "You'll soon have a lot more than this hand to hold; you certainly know that." Then she blushed and gave a little laugh. "For now, my impatient lover, listen to what I'm trying to say. I realize that sometimes our moments together will be few and far between. But when we *do* get together—and I promise that will be as often as either of us can meet—we'll be like the other night all over again. Wonderful, special, extraordinary. New! We'll never get used to each other because we'll always be in that miraculous time of mutual discovering. Wilf," she said, her eyes fairly drilling mine, "you have no idea how I hate the word 'perfunctory.' "

"You'll never use it about us," I promised, suddenly realizing that her life may not have been all *that* pleasant over the years—in spite of her professed native alter ego. Maybe it explained the hard-edged furnishings in her home that had nothing to do with the Claudia I knew. Then, suddenly the word "home" I'd used yanked me back again to a very painful reality: *Trafford.* Wasn't much chance I'd be living anywhere even remotely near Atalanta much longer. Ground my teeth—I'd have to tell her soon. But not now. "Claudia," I blurted out, forgetting everything else, "d'you think we could go somewhere and be alone for a few moments?"

"Can't think of anything nicer," she said, "—especially since we're past the serious stuff. And, well, if I wasn't in the mood before, I'll admit I'm rapidly getting that way now."

Had to laugh. "In the mood for *what?*" I asked.

She gave me a big grin. "Think about it for a while," she said.

"Let me see," I said, fingers to the bridge of my nose. "Is it something we can do together?"

"Absolutely," she replied with a mock-serious look. "If you do it alone too often, you go blind. Mother warned me about that."

"Hmm," I said, fighting back a sudden laugh. "Well, that gives me a pretty accurate idea of what you're in the mood for."

"Thought it might. All right?"

"I've only been dreaming about the same thing since I left your office that morning," I said. "But if what I hear about Gorgas is true, we're back to our old problem of 'where?' As I remember, you weren't all that enamored about hitching up your skirt and . . ."

"No," she said quickly. "And I'm still not." She gave a little laugh. "By the way, the last time in the grass *was* with you. I'm quite certain."

"How are you certain?" I demanded.

"Diary," she replied.

"I'll be damned," I said. "Did you note down if it was good?"

"Except for the grass stains."

"That pretty well eliminates everything but one of our skimmers, then," I said.

"Or a LifeGlobe."

"A *what*?"

She grinned. "A LifeGlobe," she said. "I'm certain you remember how comfortable they are for certain activities. I do."

I nodded.

"Well, I happen to know where there's a whole storage chamber full of LifeGlobes. And I've got the door combination. Give you any ideas?"

It did. And oddly enough, once we had the thing deployed,

I managed to talk her out of all *her* clothes again. This time, however, we didn't get caught. . . .

Halfway through the next morning, Williams appeared at my office door with a big grin. "A few visitors have just arrived," he announced.

Looked up from a report I was writing—one of many I'd need on hand if I was going to effect a clean transition to the next Commander once Avalon called for my head. "I thought the xaxtdamned Leaguers just bombed us half a metacycle ago," I said irritably.

"*These* visitors are friendly," he said. "At least they appear to be."

"*Who,* then?"

"How about a couple of squadrons of those Carescrian hunter-killer ships?" he asked.

With everything else going on, I'd almost forgotten the Carescrians; certainly took care of any gloom I might have worked up. "When?" I asked.

"Now," Williams said.

I checked my timepiece, frowned. "What's this 'now' business?" I demanded. "Thought they weren't due till this evening."

"Well," Williams said, "they misjudged—so sue them." Pursing his lips, he peered at his communicator. "Actually," he said after a few moments, "they're already out of orbit and lining up on the harbor. Wouldn't want to watch 'em land, would you?"

"You *bet* I would," I replied. "You've got a skimmer?"

"In the lot," he said. "Come on."

We sprinted to the parking lot like a couple of children. On the way to the underground lift, I shook my head in near disbelief as Williams dodged the skimmer around enormous new piles of rubble—some still blazing. Damn Leaguers could do a *lot* of damage in a very short time, these days. "Lucky for us someone decided to relocate part of the base underground," I commented bleakly. "If we were mostly on the surface the way we were years ago, we'd be using open-air offices—those of us lucky enough to have survived."

Nodding grimly, Williams pulled into the hangar lift, and we plunged downward through the hundred or so irals of solid granite that protected so much of the base's present essence. When we reached bottom, the roadbed looked as if it had been scrubbed spotless—a xaxtdamned big change from the first time I'd seen the concourse.

"You really built a fire under the Ops people," I commented. "Place looks like a Fleet Base now instead of a junk yard."

"Down here, at least," Williams said grimly. "But I don't deserve any credit for it—Jill Tompkins pretty much pulled everything off by herself. All I had to do was get rid of her predecessor—which I did with *great* pleasure, the CIGA bastard."

We stopped in a rush of gravitons near the great armored harbor doors and hurried outside onto a maintenance platform cut into the massive entrance arch a few irals above high tide. I'd been so busy I hadn't noticed what a beautiful morning it was—cool breeze off the water, couple of puffy clouds, water birds nagging each other. Out in the harbor, two Starfuries were just lifting clear of the water at the end of soaring white wakes. Lacking the general air of destruction everywhere—and the dozens of burning, half-sunken hulks in the harbor—it might have been one of those moments a person could easily forget we had a war on. Unfortunately, I had too many problems for the mood to last. "What do *you* know about these people," I said.

"Nothing," Williams said with a chuckle. "Except that I'm damned glad they're here. The way I *expected* things to happen, they'd take a Standard Year to show up and we'd have a couple months to get ready for 'em."

"Yeah," I agreed. "That's what I'd figured, too."

"Well, whatever you did back in Avalon sure sped 'em up," he said. "First thing I knew, one of the clerks from the KA'PPA shack came runnin' with a message from this Colonel Anderson—you mentioned him in your briefing—then, wham, two squadrons of ships from what they call the Fifty-Sixth Hunter-Killer Group—plus a transport full of spares—are half a day out and comin' fast." He laughed. "Let me tell you, we did some scurryin'. Had to prepare thirty-three moorings—that's *sixteen* piers. Evidently, their doggone ships are so big, you can only moor two at a pier—and their 'light transport' needs one all by itself."

"Sort of wondered why they call the hunter-killers 'Basilisks,' " I said, frowning. "And another thing, who's this *Colonel* Anderson, I wonder? Why's somebody from the surface forces involved with starships?"

"I did ask about that," Williams explained. "Seems the Carescrians don't have a *fleet*, as such—something about the Empire having only one Fleet and them wanting to be independent. So they set themselves up in the Expeditionary Forces." He laughed. "Supposedly that puts 'em under old General Hagbut in Avalon, but since he can't tell a Drive crystal from a helm, they pretty much run themselves."

Rolled my eyes, I'd been crossing paths with General (the Hon.) Gastudgon Z' Hagbut, Xce, N.B.E., Q.O.C. since my earliest days in the Fleet. Hoped we could stay clear of him, but . . . Well, maybe I'd get lucky this time. Then I heard the damnedest rumble in the sky. . . .

"Holy mother of Voot!" Williams exclaimed.

I couldn't even get that much out. Two by two, the damnedest ships I'd ever gawked at started thundering out of the sky and across the harbor like great, flat-bottomed teardrops: bold, husky, noisy machines, completely unlike the elegant, needle-slim Starfuries we flew—or the nimble ships of the League or The Torond they would fight. *Had* to be the Basilisks, and they were *huge*. Broad, scowling bridges creased lofty, beetlelike brows; massive disruptor turrets blistered flanks and underbellies. They reminded me of lorries, somehow, and looked as if they'd maneuver with much the same grace. If they taxed even *multiple* steering engines as much as I guessed (nothing that big could possibly operate on just one), they'd simply *have* to mush on turns and pullouts. Yet for all their gruff, belligerent menace, the big silver ships turned onto final and settled toward the water with a grace that belied their apparent mass—as well as the reputed inexperience of their crews. If nothing else, these Carescrians had certainly mastered formation flying!

Last one down was the supply ship—another blunt, businesslike machine brutally optimized for efficiency. As it rolled out and came to a halt above its gravity foot, I turned to Williams. "What do you think?"

Williams shrugged. "I'm no Helmsman," he said, "but those Basilisks of theirs look big enough to be attack ships. How's that going to play in a dogfight?"

"Don't know," I replied, looking back out in the harbor where the Carescrians were picking up their taxi vectors and starting toward us in ranks of four. "But they'd better have some *powerful* maneuverability if they hope to mix it up with the Leaguers . . . and live to tell the tale."

As the first four taxied toward our hangar doors, we watched businesslike docking crews scrambling over the steep, slippery decks in their huge, insulated mittens and attractor boots, popping open optical cleat doors and preparing their ships for mooring in a most professional manner. Williams spoke into his communicator, and presently a great rolling thunder swept over the harbor as our defense barrage boomed out a fifteen-disruptor salute specified for the rank of colonel. Moments later, the four leading Basilisks swiveled their topside turrets to vertical and fired the twenty-disruptor salutes due a Rear Admiral.

"Certainly impressive on the surface," Williams allowed.

"Let's hope they're just as impressive when the chips are down," I said.

In moments, the first four ships were abreast of us, the Carescrian emblem—our Imperial comet imposed on a banner of red-and-white stripes—boldly applied to each flank, just abaft the 'midships turret. Holding my ears, I peered up into their lofty bridges, where a veritable *crowd* of people were seated. One of them waved to us as they passed. I couldn't see below the Hyperscreens, of course, but it looked as if the bridge crew lived in palatial abundance compared to the snug flight bridges of our Starfuries. Of course, comfort was a relative matter in the midst of a dogfight. The *real* comfort was inflicting a lot of damage to one's adversary while getting home with all tail feathers intact.

Half-deafened, we watched until all thirty-two ships passed inside the doors, followed by the big, new freighter. Then we returned to what remained of Headquarters—and the million headaches that were waiting there. Now we had a million and *thirty-two. . . .*

Chapter 10

Gontor

32 Octad–10 Decad, 52014

Imperial Fleet Base, Atalanta, Hador-Haelic

That evening, I met Colonel Anderson, the Carescrian commander. Cottshall showed him and Williams into my tiny—by now *very* disordered—interim office. "Welcome to the base dump," I said, indicating a couple of chairs I'd had installed for the occasion.

Anderson glanced around, then chuckled as he and Williams settled into the chairs. "Looks like the office of someone who's got his hands full," he said. "Hope we can take some of that work off your back." He was small and wiry with thinning gray hair, a florid complexion, and blue eyes so mesmerizing it wasn't difficult to see why he'd succeeded in cobbling together the first operational squadron from Carescria. Unless I missed my guess, he was both a visionary and a man of infinite patience.

"Work, as in escorting convoys?" I asked.

"That's what we're here for," Anderson said.

"When d'you suppose you'll be ready to start?"

Anderson grinned. "Captain Williams, here, warned me you wouldn't be shy about asking that," he said.

"Told him we're in the middle of a war around here," Williams said with a chuckle. "He allowed as he'd already noticed."

"Jim's not entirely correct," I said. "We're *up to our necks* in war, and won't have much time to spare your crews for training."

"General Drummond pretty much gave me that same idea when he rang me up with our transspace movement orders."

"So?"

"Admiral," Anderson said grimly, "I'll tell you the same thing I told Drummond: we're as ready as we can make ourselves without someone actually shooting at us. Does that answer your question?"

"Except for one thing," I said.

"Yes sir?"

"How do you *feel* about people shooting at you?" I asked.

Anderson looked me directly in the eye. "The sooner the better, Admiral. The sooner the better."

I nodded. "We'll begin getting you oriented tomorrow, then," I said, "soon as your crews have some sleep. We'll meet in the hangar at Dawn plus two and a half—about the time Hador's above the horizon and the Leaguers have finished their morning raid. I'll have some veteran Helmsman and Gunnery Officers there to go up in your ships for evaluation rides. Then we'll get together and discuss things. All right?"

"Dawn plus two and a half," Anderson acknowledged. "How many ships would you like?"

"All of 'em," I said. "I'll have at least ten of our Helmsmen there—and we'll provide some escort Starfuries just in case the Leaguers decide to crash our party."

"Sounds like a plan to me," Anderson said. Then he winked. "I think all of us will appreciate the escort, though none will probably admit it."

I grinned. "I understand," I said. "But if it were me, I'd admit it."

Everyone who'd made landfall with the Fifty-Sixth was in the hangar when I arrived the next morning: every Basilisk Helmsman and crew dog, every fitter and rigger, even the transport gang. Clearly, none had ever been in a combat zone, for they were all eyes, peering at everything with real fascination—especially our Starfuries. Must have been a shock. The differences between our elegant little interceptors and the massive Basilisks were astonishing. Starfuries were *so* much smaller, sleeker, and lighter-looking—as agile and lithe as they flew. But the differences were much deeper than mere design. Our Starfuries were also well broken to combat. Their disruptors were seared and scarred from constant firing; their once-perfect hulls were dulled and streaked from constant use—most were chalk-marked for repairs of holes and tears from disruptor hits. In contrast, the powerful-looking Basilisks were spanking new, clean, tested only by their recent flight from Carescria—and by their Helmsmen's ability to hurl them about in space in mock battles. They were as unproved in combat as the battered Starfuries were tried.

I'd brought sixteen of our Helmsmen from 71 Group with

me and as many Gunnery Officers, each of us as anxious for a first flight in these huge, unwieldy-looking killer ships. As I'd rather expected, a grinning Colonel Anderson signaled me from an open Hyperscreen on the bridge of his own ship, E 73, *Anderson's Folly*. "Come on up, Admiral," he called through the open visor of his battlesuit—grayish green rather than our traditional Fleet blue. "Cvceese's on—home style!"

"I'll have *two*," I answered as I hurried across the brow. Carescria might be—or *have* been—the most maligned portion of the Empire, but even Emperors drank Carescrian cvceese' (and rode in ships made of hullmetal from Carescrian asteroid mines). Inside—the giant boasted a small boarding lobby!—a brace of ratings saluted and pointed me to a *moving* companionway. And even after staring at the big ship for considerable time the previous afternoon, I *still* was unprepared for the spread of real estate on the bridge. When we shoehorned ourselves into the flight bridge of a Starfury, we—the Helmsman, Gunnery Officer, Systems Officer, and Navigator—felt snug and quite part of the starship. The Basilisk's flight bridge, on the other hand, was nearly as large as that of Delacroix's *Yellow Bird*, and the first row of consoles seated two Helmsmen and one of the three Systems Officers. Two other rows seated the other Systems Officers, the two Gunnery Officers, and a Navigator! A thraggling battleship! I was suddenly horrified at the thought of going to war in such an outlandish machine: we'd had trouble enough with the Leaguer's Gorn-Hoffs in our nimble Starfuries; now this lumbering, nearly five-hundred-iral-long monster seemed infinitely worse—a true flying crypt. I tried not to let my feelings show as the grinning Anderson proudly thrust a steaming mug of the aromatic cvceese' in my hand and introduced me 'round the bridge crew; perhaps bridge "crowd" was a better term, I opined grimly. The co-Helmsman had generously given up his seat for me. Seemed like Onrad's throne when I climbed in and connected my battlesuit; at my left—a thraggling c'lenyt distant!—Anderson appeared to be perfectly at home in the palatial splendor. "All set, Admiral?" he asked.

What the xaxt, I'd been up in the occasional battleship. "Ready, Colonel," I said through a big grin I really didn't feel. Thank Voot I'd sent half a squadron of Starfuries up ahead of us. If the Leaguers attacked, I didn't want to be caught in this great, hulking death trap—I still had a couple of evenings with Claudia before I cashed in!

While Anderson busied himself with the systems check-out, I attempted to adjust my seat. Just couldn't make it feel right—too much spare room. Ended up making the restraints too tight—comforting, if uncomfortable. Closed and sealed my helmet visor, prepared myself for the worst. At least I knew they really flew—I'd *seen* that yesterday.

In the corner of my eye, I saw Anderson hit a switch. Deep inside *Folly*'s hull a whine started, a straining whine like some massive dynamo starting to turn. On my console, a red light began to strobe, rising in pitch and amplification until it was abruptly replaced by a tremendous, throaty roar of power that shook the monstrous starframe itself before smoothing into a bass rumble I could hear through my battle-suit and literally *feel* in the deck. Sounded like a muffled version of a Sodeskayan battle crawler thundering across the snow at flank speed, or the noise an express tram makes when it comes through an underground station without stopping. I glanced in apprehension at Anderson, but he was busily doing the same thing *again*—another whine that turned to a frame-shaking roar and smoothed to blend with the original rumbling, making the noise even louder. Then he did the same thing again *four* more times!

By the time the sixth mammoth SpinGrav had added its rumble to the overall cacophony, I was awfully glad for the ear protection my battlesuit afforded. Nevertheless, if raw noise were any measurement, this particular Basilisk was ready for space. I scanned the readouts; for all the size, sound, and fury, nothing seemed out of the ordinary. At least from her instrument panel, *Folly* was a rather normal starship.

I looked up to see Anderson looking at me with an air of anticipation. "With your permission, Admiral."

Xaxt, I thought I was only a passenger. I smiled. "Please," I said.

"All hands to lift-off stations," Anderson said into the blower. "All hands to stations for lift-off. Switching to local gravity *now.*"

Somehow, in the midst of all this newness, I'd nearly forgotten that. Almost lost the breakfast I'd shared with Williams less than a metacycle ago. Somehow—miraculously—everything stayed where it was. Ahead, the armored doors were open to the harbor. Listened to Anderson talking to the other ships, then suddenly the mooring beams winked out and we began to move smoothly away from our berth. Moments later, we started along one of the main canals toward daylight.

Don't know when it was that I actually started feeling comfortable about everything. Probably it was just after I heard the harbor controller say, "All right, Army E 73, you are cleared for lift-off when ready." Anderson moved his thrust damper all the way to MAXIMUM POWER—it registered on my helm—and I felt as well as heard the tremendous bellowing of the six monstrous TTarp & Yentihw SpinGravs, as acceleration shoved me back in the seat despite our local gravity. The Basilisk didn't merely start off along the vector, she *hurtled* herself forward, a great, silver juggernaut, thrusting aside the early morning combers in clouds of spray. Beside us, three other Basilisks thundered along in perfect echelon while, aft, half the harbor had disappeared behind towering billows of spray and mist that completely hid the city from view.

Soon my Helmsman's sense told me the big ship was getting ready to fly; I could feel the water beginning to drop away, the waves softer under the hull. Anderson eased back on the steering engines. Abruptly, the rumble and vibration of the choppy harbor disappeared, leaving only the deep, singing roar of the 'Gravs. The Basilisk raised her nose; the powerhouses deep in the hull thundered their song, and we howled our way toward space with surprising acceleration— but not before two Starfuries passed us in a vertical climb, and from the looks of their graviton trails, they weren't in a maximum-effort ascent. I shivered. Those same Starfuries were only *marginally* better in acceleration than the Gorn-Hoffs they diced with every day. Clearly, if the Basilisks and their drivers were going to be effective against the Leaguers, they would need an entirely different fighting strategy from anything we used.

For the next metacycle, the Carescrian Helmsman put the big ships through their paces. In deep space, they turned out to be amazingly powerful ships, and very fast once they'd overcome their own terrible momentum. These were not ships made to mix it with the enemy; their technique would be to pounce at high speed, using the terrific firepower the Carescrian designers had provided: roughly a third more than a Starfury Mark Nine. And should any Leaguer Helmsman try to escape from a Basilisk by running in the same direction, he (or she) was cold meat. Even more important, however, we now had a killer ship with the range to escort convoys deep into the enemy starspace—where the action was about to relocate as our battered old Empire finally began shifting to offensive strategies.

I don't know any Helmsman who finds it particularly exciting to ride in somebody else's flight bridge, and just as I was developing a slight case of boredom, out of the blue, so to speak, we were attacked! White flashes appeared magically all around our Basilisk, uncomfortably close. I recognized them for what they were—disruptor fire—but I wasn't sure about the Colonel beside me. "Anderson!" I shouted, glancing aft where a Gorn-Hoff was taking long-range potshots at us. "Break!"

Anderson did—almost explosively—yanking the big starship over on her back, then streaking off at a sharp angle to our original track. I watched in terrified fascination while the lead Leaguer arced over in a beautifully coordinated maneuver and started after us; his partner continued straight ahead, snapping out bursts of disruptor fire as he, too, closed the distance between our two ships. Got ready to take to my Life Globe for second time—*if* I managed to survive!—when suddenly two huge forms charged out of the stars below us.

Basilisks!

They were moving at such tremendous speed toward the Gorn-Hoffs that—fast as the Leaguers might hope to accelerate—they had no chance at all to escape. The Basilisks opened fire almost at the same time, sending long, accurate blasts tearing into the enemy ships from stem to stern. Radiation fire boiled out of the Leaguer on our tail for only a moment before it was simply replaced by a bright flash, then a reddish puffball expanding slowly outward as it receded astern. No LifeGlobes I could see. Off to starboard, the second Gorn-Hoff seemed to stumble in its flight, then began to tumble violently, trapping everyone inside, before it, too, showed a thin smear of radiation fire beneath its belly near the power chambers, then disappeared in its own blossoming explosion.

When I looked again, the two Basilisks had disappeared, bringing to mind words uttered by Grand Admiral Calhoun—another Carescrian—during the days when a number of us had "borrowed" the very first Starfuries (under Onrad's secret orders) and taken them to Fluvanna to fight the Leaguers as mercenaries—another story altogether. "Slash and run," Calhoun had always told us. "When you're outnumbered"—as we'd been every day of that campaign—"just slash and run. Don't stick around for a kill, or they'll get you every time; damaging the bastards is almost as effective— sometimes more. And *your* butts will remain where they've been growing all these years." I grinned as I thought about it. The Basilisk drivers had used their famous countryman's tactics to great avail, except that with their devastating firepower, they'd actually gotten clean kills—something we'd seen very little of those days in Fluvanna!

Moments later, two of the escorting Starfuries I'd sent out in advance arrived—rather too late—to rescue us. They milled about for a few passes, but there didn't seem to be any more Gorn-Hoffs in the area, so they wiggled their pontoons and flew off—almost in embarrassment.

"You were decoying the Gorn-Hoffs for the other Basilisks, weren't you?" I asked Anderson.

"Of course," he replied, turning to me with a great smile behind his visor.

"Nice teamwork," I said.

"Thanks," he replied. "Voot knows we've been practicing long enough. And worrying."

"Worrying?"

"Damn straight," Anderson said. "We've known since the

beginning our Basilisks are too big and heavy to mix it up with ships like Gorn-Hoffs and Oiggaips. So we've had to develop tactics to take advantage of our own strong points—tremendous speed from these big 'Gravs as well as battleship firepower. And, of course, you'll notice that we're nowhere near the surface, where we'd have to overcome gravity as well as drag all this weight along when we climbed back to the stars. Seems to work."

I nodded happily. "Does seem to," I said. It did.

Actually, it worked for nearly three Standard Weeks—and three large convoys—that arrived nearly unscathed at Gontor under Carescrian escort. Because of the long distances between Atalanta and Gontor, our convoys could effect tremendous changes in midcourse locus—magnitudes of light years—by simply zigzagging, thereby making it nearly impossible for the Leaguers to find them while concentrating sufficient forces to *both* ward off the Basilisks and wreak worthwhile damage on the convoys.

Then, reports of tremendously powerful beams of BKAEW energy started coming in from both the convoys and their Carescrian escorts, beams powerful enough to send everyone's warning sensors into overload, the kind I remembered from my recent trip to Avalon. The Leaguers had finally installed a few of their new BKAEW in The Torond, and now they could track our convoys at truly outlandish distances. It let them pinpoint our transports no matter where they were, then focus their attacks like never before. Within two days, half a squadron of Basilisks had been badly damaged and the convoy they guarded torn to shreds—in spite of destroying nineteen Gorn-Hoffs and damaging twenty-five more during the long battle. Of an original thirty-five transport ships that set out from Atalanta, only seventeen managed to unload at Gontor.

The savaged Basilisks arrived back in Atalanta two Standard Days later. Williams and I went to the armored doors with Anderson when they made landfall. The big Carescrian ships were rugged, all right, I had to give them that—and a lot more. As I held my ears against the awful noise of their 'Gravs, I found it difficult to understand how some of them made it back to the base at all, so terrible were their wounds. One's bridge no longer existed; someone was steering her from a jury-rigged station cut raggedly into the nose with a torch. She must have come down from orbit slowly because of it; otherwise, the doughty Helmsman would have been burned to a crisp. Another ship's midsection looked like some sort of coarse sieve, holed by what must have been more than a hundred rents and tears. Only Voot knew how a few of her 'Gravs had been spared from the holocaust of disruptor fire she'd suffered, but there she was, taxiing in as if nothing out of the ordinary had occurred. Someone had even jury-rigged a flag staff near the stern, from which they'd flown the old Imperial battle ensign. Still another Basilisk was glowing red from within and trailing a reeking pall of black smoke behind her, listing and tottering as she moved, yet somehow grinding onward toward the safety of our underground hangars and the expert firefighters who could save her.

I suppose Williams and I had seen so many tormented ships in our day that—more than anything else—we were only trying to estimate how soon we could expect to get them in service again (those that would *go* into service again, that is, rather than into the scrap heap for parts).

Anderson, however, was a different story entirely. Except for those early raids during the previous war, when I'd lost most of my family, Carescria had been attacked rather infrequently. Except for the most infamous asteroid mines—which themselves were reasonably assault-proof, at least from disruptor and missile attacks—there hadn't been much worth attacking in that poorest section of the Empire. Moreover, the new factories that were now turning out Starfuries and the new classes of Carescrian ships had been located on planets so far distant from Leaguer bases that Nergol Triannic had yet to develop attack ships with enough range to mount an effective assault—provided his reconnaissance ships could locate them in the first place.

As a consequence, Anderson had seen few shot-up ships of any kind before, and certainly no shot-up Basilisks. Now, he stood shocked, at the stiffest military attention, literally welded in place by the ghastly parade of wrecked starships—*his* starships; his flesh. Tears streamed along his cheeks as he silently touched the fingers of his right hand to his temple in salute and kept it there until the last Basilisk had thundered deafeningly into the hangar. . . .

We spent a long time that night in the little Officers' Club we'd cobbled together in the wardroom of a wrecked transport. After I'd downed sufficient meem and E'lande, I found that I really didn't mind the slightly listing floor, nor the fact that I'd volunteered to fly co-helm in Anderson's Basilisk on the next convoy. . . .

Sometime after the beginning of Night Watch, one of the stewards tapped me on the shoulder. "Admiral," he whispered, pointing to the door, "someone to see you." It was Barbousse.

Excusing myself, I walked unsteadily toward the door. "What's up, Chief?" I asked.

"General Drummond called on the KA'PPA phone from Avalon, Admiral," he said with a look of dislike—I'd already confided the Trafford business to him; didn't want him to get caught unawares. "I told the General a couple of times that you weren't in and I didn't know where you were. He said to go find you—direct order. So I've done that. If you want, I'll go back now and tell him the same thing again."

Put my hand on the big man's shoulder—solid as bedrock. "Thanks, Chief," I said. "Probably I'd better go see what he wants. It may have something to do with the shellacking that last convoy took, or . . ." Didn't want to finish that.

"That ungrateful gang could wait till tomorrow, Admiral," Barbousse suggested.

"Thanks, Chief," I said, fabricating a confident smile that I knew he wouldn't buy anyway, "but I'd better go face whatever music they're playing."

For a moment Barbousse contemplated me with a frown. "Er, how do you *feel*, Admiral," he asked uncertainly.

"I've got enough meem in me to tell the son of a capcloth what I really think of all this Trafford Gorksroar," I said with a grin, "—but *just* sober enough to keep it to myself."

"I've got a skimmer outside, then, Admiral," Barbousse said, saluting with a little smile.

Went back and said my good-nights, thumped Anderson on the shoulder—gave him a somber thumbs-up—then followed Barbousse out to the skimmer. I was back in my makeshift office within fifteen cycles. Asked the COMM Center to open a KA'PPA voice channel back to Avalon— MOST SECRET/EYES ONLY—FLASH—for General Drummond's office. Waited nearly half a metacycle before:

ADMIRALTY: PLEASE SIGNAL WHEN READY FOR GENERAL
DRUMMOND.

"Ready," I said.

DRUMMOND: HELLO, WILF. WORD IS THAT THE LAST
            GONTOR CONVOY GOT BLASTED BADLY. WHAT DO
            YOU KNOW ABOUT IT?

"Not too much, yet," I said. "The escorting Basilisks just got back a few metacycles ago—and you heard right; they're shredded."

DRUMMOND: HOW'D IT HAPPEN?

I thought for a moment. I'd talked to a number of the Helmsmen in the Officer's Club; they'd all seemed to agree what had happened. "From what I can piece together," I said, "the convoy was tracked by a long-range BKAEW. Sounds as if it might be like the one I helped pinch from Lavenurb. Whatever it was, it let the Leaguers concentrate their forces directly in the convoy's path. Before that, they'd had to spread out over a wide area searching."

DRUMMOND: THAT ALL?

"The Carescrians only got back a few metacycles ago. That's all I've got for now except that it wasn't exactly a banner day for the Gorn-Hoffs. Out in space where they can use their speed and firepower, those Basilisks are *deadly*. The Leaguers are licking a few wounds themselves, tonight," I said.

DRUMMOND: HOW MANY OF THE CONVOY TRANSPORTS
            MADE IT TO GONTOR?

"You'll know the official numbers as soon as I do," I said. "Unofficially, about two-thirds, according to the Helmsmen I talked to tonight in the Club, but they aren't exactly sober, either."

DRUMMOND: GOOD ENOUGH FOR ME.

"What else?"

DRUMMOND: I'VE GOT A SMALL SQUADRON OF SHIPS COM-
ING YOUR WAY. SIX OLD LINERS, ED-4S. YOU'VE
FLOWN THEM, I BELIEVE?

"A lot. But why?"

DRUMMOND: I'M COMING TO THAT. THEY'RE SCHEDULED
FOR LANDFALL IN ATALANTA DURING THE NEXT DAY
OR SO. YOU'LL NOTICE SOME UNUSUAL ANTENNAS ON
THESE. ALL RIGHT?

"All right." Wondered what the xaxt he was up to.

DRUMMOND: MAKE CERTAIN THEY'RE REGARDED AS ONLY
A COUPLE OF OLD TRANSPORTS—NO PUBLIC FUSS. WE
DON'T WANT THEM NOTICED. BUT WHOEVER JUGGLES
MAINTENANCE SCHEDULES MUST MAKE CERTAIN
THAT THOSE SHIPS RECEIVE THE HIGHEST PRIORITY
WHENEVER THEY'RE IN PORT, UNDERSTAND? WHAT-
EVER THEY WANT THEY GET, WHEN THEY WANT IT.
BUT QUIETLY. STILL WITH ME?

"Still with you, General," I said, feeling my temper begin
to fray a little. "By the way," I asked caustically, "are you
going to let me in on this little secret or am I losing my clearances in preparation for being sacrificed?"

DRUMMOND: SORRY, BRIM. NO, YOU'RE NOT LOSING YOUR
CLEARANCES. NOT YET. I JUST WANTED TO MAKE
CERTAIN YOU SET THINGS UP AT THE BASE SO THESE
SHIPS GET THE PRIORITY TREATMENT THEY NEED
WITHOUT REVEALING THEY'RE ANYTHING EXCEPT A
COUPLE OF OLD MILITARY TRANSPORTS ON UNIMPOR-
TANT MISSIONS.

"So what in xaxt *are* they, already?"

DRUMMOND: PROBABLY THEY OUGHT TO BE NAMED IN
HONOR OF YOU, BRIM. THEY'RE BKAEW-JAMMING
SHIPS EQUIPPED TO OPERATE AGAINST THE NEW LEA-
GUER BKAEW YOU BROUGHT OVER FROM LAVENURB.
A TEAM OF KA'PPA INSTITUTE BOFFINS ON ASTERI-
OUS-PROTEUS MADE SHORT WORK OF ITS PROTECTIVE
CIRCUITS, THEN DESIGNED WHAT THEY CALL
"JEROME/A," A SUPER JAMMER TO JAM THE SUPER
BKAEW. THOSE INNOCENT-LOOKING ED-4S I'M SEND-
ING HAVE THE FIRST SIX PRODUCTION MODELS OF
JEROME/A ON BOARD. THEY'LL SIMPLY CRUISE
AROUND SPACE, MAKING CERTAIN THE LEAGUERS'
NEW BKAEWS DON'T OPERATE WHEN WE'VE GOT
CONVOYS MOVING. IS THAT BETTER?

"Better," I said. "And you want them to look like harmless
transports so you don't have to escort *them*. Right?"

DRUMMOND: THAT'S IT.

"I'll make sure the right people are briefed," I assured
him. "Anything else?"

DRUMMOND: I'VE GOT TO ASSUME YOU WANT TO KNOW
THE LATEST ON THIS TRAFFORD DEBACLE.

"Fascinating subject—at least for me," I said. "What's the word?"

DRUMMOND: NOT GOOD, BRIM. CONFISSE-TRAFFORD'S
BRINGING TERRIFIC PRESSURE TO BEAR ON ONRAD.
THREATENING TO HOLD UP AN IMPORTANT MILITARY
APPROPRIATIONS BILL IN PARLIAMENT. I DON'T KNOW
HOW MUCH LONGER WE CAN STALL HIM.

"Specifically what's Trafford want—outside of my neck?
I still haven't heard."

DRUMMOND: A GENERAL COURTS-MARTIAL. WANTS YOU
THROWN OUT OF THE SERVICE. THINKS THAT OUGHT
TO CLEAR THE TRAFFORD NAME.

"Thought so." I paused, fighting desperately to quell the
anger building inside me. I was helpless, and I didn't like it
at all. Finally got myself under control. I still had a job to do
here that was a lot more important than me *or* my career.
"What's the status of Gontor," I asked. "How much more
stuff do you need there before the Sapphire invasion?"

DRUMMOND: MAYBE SIX MORE CONVOYS WITH AT LEAST
HALF THE TRANSPORTS INTACT; THEN WE CAN MOVE.

"So how much time do I have?"

DRUMMOND: I REALLY DON'T KNOW, BRIM. MAYBE A
WEEK, MAYBE A MONTH. THEN THEY'LL WANT YOU

HERE FOR THE COURTS-MARTIAL. COWARDLY BAS-
TARDS SURE WOULDN'T GO TO A DANGEROUS PLACE
LIKE ATALANTA TO HOLD IT.

I shrugged to myself. "Thanks," I said. "Anything else I
should know about?"

DRUMMOND: NOTHING I CAN THINK OF NOW, EXCEPT

"Except what?"

DRUMMOND: I'M EMBARRASSED TO SAY IT.

"Go ahead. You can't make things any worse for me than
they are now."

DRUMMOND: TRY THIS: ONRAD PERSONALLY REQUESTS
THAT YOU KEEP ON WORKING UNTIL THE MOMENT
YOU'RE ORDERED HOME FOR THE COURTS-MARTIAL.
HE'S AFRAID SAPPHIRE WON'T COME OFF WITHOUT
YOU.

"Thraggling nice of him."

DRUMMOND: HE REALLY MEANS IT. SO DO I, I GUESS. WE
NEED—THE EMPIRE NEEDS—YOUR KIND OF GRIT ON
STATION AS LONG AS POSSIBLE. CALHOUN WOULD
ASK YOU FOR THE SAME THING, BUT HE'S JUST GOT
MORE PRIDE THAN ONRAD AND ME.

Ground my teeth as I sat there at my workstation. The bastards meant to suck my juices absolutely dry before they
threw me away. But, then, I *had* taken that oath a number of

years ago when I was commissioned—and an assignment's an assignment, regardless. "All right," I said after a long pause. "I'll keep on working till the moment I'm relieved."

DRUMMOND: THANKS, BRIM. WE WON'T FORGET YOU, BE-LIEVE ME.

Big thraggling deal! "Anything else?" I asked.

DRUMMOND: YEAH. A BIT OF SCUTTLEBUTT I'LL BET YOU'LL FIND FASCINATING. YOU REMEMBER ONRAD'S COUSIN, MARGO LAKARN? USED TO BE PRINCESS MARGO EFFER'WYCK BEFORE THE WAR WHEN SHE MARRIED ROGAN LAKARN.

"I remember," I said—oh *how* I remembered.

DRUMMOND: THEN YOU KNOW SHE'S BECOME THE LEAD-ING PARTISAN LEADER IN EFFER'WYCK SINCE ROGAN DIVORCED HER AND SEIZED THEIR SON. HE'S PUT A PRICE ON HER HEAD NOW.

I'd heard. "What else is new with Margo?" I asked appre-hensively. She'd been living dangerously for a long time—with all the damage her partisans had done to the occupying Leaguers, her capture (or worse) must be one of their major goals. Every time I've heard her name over the last couple of years, I've expected a report of her death to follow.

DRUMMOND: KA'PPA FREE EFFER'WYCK REPORTED THAT SHE WAS MARRIED TODAY; THE WHOLE EFFER'WYCK-EAN RESISTANCE MOVEMENT'S CELEBRATING RIGHT UNDER THE LEAGUERS' COLLECTIVE NOSES.

Felt my jaw drop. *That* was a surprise! "Who's the lucky man?" I asked, once I'd regained my composure.

> DRUMMOND: SEEMS HE'S QUITE A MYSTERIOUS GENTLE-
> MAN WITH WHOM YOU'VE HAD SOME CLOSE CON-
> TACT, RECENTLY. WORD IS THAT HE AND MARGOT
> HAD BEEN SEEING EACH OTHER FOR A COUPLE OF
> STANDARD YEARS NOW. FELLOW'S NAME IS CAMERON
> DELACROIX; OWNS A FAST TRANSPORT CALLED YEL-
> LOW BIRD.

Our six ED-4s arrived a single day before the next convoy for Gontor was scheduled to depart—and within three days of Drummond's call. The old ships were once the most widely operated commercial space vessels of an era, designed with the snub-nosed bow and elongated, teardrop hull that characterized—actually *defined*—a whole generation of starships that followed. Helmsmen in their cramped flight bridges looked forward through old-fashioned V-shaped Hyperscreens. Two more Hyperscreens at each side of the bridge gave the ships their frowning, raptorlike countenance—a look that a whole generation of space travelers associated with the romance of starflight.

Maybe I was simply getting old, but in my estimation, those classic, teardrop lines were among the most beautiful sculptures ever fashioned by the hand of man—right up there with Starfuries, in fact. Somehow, the ships possess an elusive sort of timeless grace and beauty that had been literally wrung out of today's designs in the name of profit and production efficiency. They aren't large as modern starliners go, but after the First Great War they were perfect for every light-cargo hauler throughout the galaxy. And though larger, newer liners may have carried the glamorous payloads between major ports in our galaxy, at least a thousand times more commerce traveled elsewhere aboard little ships like ED-4s. Old, maybe, but damned useful nonetheless.

I made certain Jill Tompkins in Operations was briefed and ready to service them the moment they arrived. Had to smile when I saw them up close. The six old ships certainly didn't *look* like much of a threat to the League. Dented, scratched—even grimy in places—they looked a little unkempt as they rumbled into the hangar and pulled up to moor at the service wharves. The only things at all odd about them, and you had to look *carefully* to notice, were the unusual antenna arrays for Jerome/A along their flanks and the fact that the long row of passenger Hyperscreens on either side were now opaque—although the latter wasn't *terribly* uncommon, considering the old ships were generally no longer used for passenger traffic. I "casually" met with their six lead Helmsman during the next Standard Day. All were volunteers: retired Fleet officers risking their lives again for the Empire when they'd already survived a whole career of dangerous service. Hoped I'd be that way when I finally retired . . . then remembered that I probably wouldn't have to worry about *that* option anyway. Strange how that seemed to be playing on my mind so much these days. . . .

One by one, the ED-4s departed unobtrusively for deep space—less than a day before the next convoy lifted for Gontor. Alone at the seawall, I watched when the last thundered off the harbor to disappear into Atalanta's smoke-hazed sky. Made a quiet, private salute. Brave old ships crewed by brave men and women. . . .

"Break, Hotshot, Break!"

I heard the battle begin on the Basilisk's short-range KA'PPA. Astern, I could see disruptor flashes around the ships of convoy Element Two. The Leaguers had finally located us; but thanks to the ED-4s and Jerome/A, they'd taken nearly one and a half Standard Days of blindly feeling around space to do it. And because they'd had to scatter their forces so much even to find us, there really weren't enough of them to effectively counter our escorting Basilisks.

Nevertheless, "enough of them" also meant there were still a lot of Leaguer ships in space, each clearly determined to stop or at least cripple our convoy at all costs. Gorn-Hoffs, as usual, specially equipped, I guessed, with oversize Hyper-Torps to deal with the heavy transports we were shepherding. They'd be due here at convoy Element One any moment. I ground my teeth. Wanted to be at the helm of a Starfury; instead, I was sitting helplessly at the co-helm of Anderson's Basilisk as the Leaguers hove into view aft. Felt *terribly* useless; if I'd been in charge, we'd have been fighting those Leaguers right now instead of waiting for them to come to us. Instead, we were staying in visual range of the convoy element we were escorting—supposedly, it made the transport crews feel more secure.

There. The first dots appeared astern, growing rapidly to Gorn-Hoffs in the Basilisk's aft quarter Hyperscreens.

"Gorn-Hoffs, bearing green horizon," I warned. Jerome/A knocked out *our own* BKAEW-based warning systems, as well as those of the Leaguers.

"Gorn-Hoffs from green horizon," Anderson acknowledged, then—*finally*—slowed and moved out to the right behind Element One while Simpson, our Gunnery Officer, angled all our movable disruptors aft. Ship-to-ship combat at HyperLight velocities was a lot different than dogfighting near a planet. Not much room for maneuvering and no head-on shots at all. The only real firing positions were slightly abaft of the target or dead astern.

The Gorn-Hoffs had switched to line abreast, now, eight of them. Still beyond the range of our disruptors, they were about five c'lenyts away from the rearmost transports of our element when they fired their HyperTorps in bright, wicked-looking ripples of light. Moments later, the missiles began to explode amid the plodding transports with blinding pulses of light that dimmed our Hyperscreens but seemed to do little damage, because the big ships somehow continued unwaveringly on course.

The Leaguers were close enough to use their disruptors now, but since we'd stayed close to our element until the very last cycle, we were not. As we maneuvered ourselves into position, I watched the rearmost transport—an ancient, battered veteran of the starlanes—buck violently as it took immediate hits. Hullmetal plates flew off in pieces, flashing for a moment in the somber light of a star that raced past. Then the disruptor beams reached the ship's bridge, smashing, blazing forward in clouds of shattered Hyperscreen crystal and wisps of radiation fire. No one at the helm now; probably no helm left. Slowly the big ship swerved, rolling through its long axis until suddenly what remained of the bow reared up—clearly exceeding all structural limits—and the gigantic hull broke in half, streaming a wake of whirling, churning debris—cargo, people, wreckage—and pitifully few LifeGlobes—as the convoy steadily pulled away from the hulking remains.

At last, our Basilisks were in position to open fire—Anderson aimed for the closest Gorn-Hoff to us, whose Helmsman had been clearly concentrating too much on the transports ahead of him. At the same time, seven other Basilisks started moving in from positions in a half arc around the rear of the combat box—clearly, these Carescrian crews had become proficient at shooting in record time.

While I checked space in our immediate vicinity again—temporarily unoccupied by Leaguers—I felt a slight kick as Simpson fired our disruptors. Long, strobing beams angled sideways to erupt in flashing strobes of malignant brilliance against the Gorn-Hoff's fuselage. He staggered visibly, then rolled without warning and tried to speed off into space away from us. It was the last mistake the Leaguer Helmsman would ever make—at least in *that* Gorn-Hoff. Anderson was ready, and sent our massive Basilisk accelerating after it like a runaway asteroid. Once again, the strobing beams sprang forward from our disruptors, sparkling evilly all over the fleeing ship's tail section. Abruptly, three of its four Drive outlets dimmed, blinked, then went dark. The Leaguer yawed hard to the left, but Anderson fed in rudder, followed him around, while Simpson fired off short bursts that flashed angrily along the Gorn-Hoff's side. Suddenly, a number of hatches opened in the hull and a dozen or so LifeGlobes popped into the ship's wake. One caromed violently off the prominent bulge Gorn-Hoffs have ahead of the steering engine, shattering in a fog of gossamer shards from which two battlesuited figures appeared, flailing arms and legs as they passed overhead and disappeared into the distance.

The attacks continued steadily from that point. As we returned to the convoy, I watched nearly a dozen Gorn-Hoffs making determined assaults on the plodding cargo ships, but the Leaguers couldn't put together enough ships for the kind of devastating, coordinated attacks that had so ravaged earlier convoys, and our Basilisks were driving off individual Leaguers as quickly as they attacked.

Only metacycles later, the convoy moved within the defense sphere provided by Gontor's hard-pressed Starfuries. Once they showed up, the Leaguers finally abandoned the savaged transports. They were clearly under orders to avoid combat with effective concentrations of escorts—our cargo ships posed the real threat to the League.

A Standard Day later, as we slowed through HyperSpeed and Gontor hove into view in the forward Hyperscreens, I allowed myself to relax. Had to smile wryly while I walked aft for a last cup of good Carescrian cvceese'. Jerome/A was clearly a lifesaver—maybe even a Sapphire-saver. If capturing that prototype BKAEW on Lavenurb ultimately cost me my career, it was probably worth losing—at least so far as the Empire was concerned. Wasn't sure how happy I was about the result *personally,* but that xaxtdamned oath I took so many years ago didn't leave much room for personal considerations. . . .

Gontor had certainly changed from my last visit. As Anderson coasted in for a landing, I could see the surface of the huge asteroid now fairly bristled with antispace disruptors—as well as wrecked Leaguer starships. Later, below the surface, an even more impressive transformation had manifested itself. The once-dark and airless corridors, assembly rooms, warehouses, and barracks now teemed with activity. Colossal, vaultlike hangars were jammed with landing craft of every type—including whole chambers filled with a new class of lander, called an LSC, designed specifically to carry crawlers. Other rooms contained hundreds of new battle crawlers, these designed along Sodeskayan lines. If nothing else had been gained from the debacle of Operation Eppeid, it was the importance of large concentrations of heavy armor with massive disruptors firing *horizontally* (instead of vertically against sites specially hardened against attack from overhead) to support invading troops on the ground.

As I sped through the asteroid's network of tunnels aboard one of the base's ancient trams—brilliantly restored to use by our Royal Engineers—I found myself strangely relaxed. Very much at peace with myself; even somewhat detached—not exactly my normal state of mind. And inasmuch as the sensation persisted, I began to think I might be coming down with one of those rare viruses that still plague civilization from time to time. But during supper in one of the huge mess halls, with Gontor's newly arrived, fire-and-brimstone Commander—a General whose name I continued to forget all evening—I began to understand I probably wasn't ill at all. *Finished* was a better word. My work here in this mighty citadel, as well as in Atalanta, was complete. For me, the war was over—at least so far as any further contributions I might make. Soon, I wouldn't even be privileged to wear the uniform that had literally defined most of my adult life. And then . . . I kept trying to avoid the question each time it blundered into my mind, but couldn't . . . who would I be after that? I had no answer at all.

The Admiralty message was waiting when I made my late-afternoon return to Atalanta a few days later. I didn't need to see it to know it had arrived. Williams, Barbousse, and Russo were waiting when Anderson's Basilisk berthed; I could tell from the look in their eyes when they met me at the end of the brow. On the way to Headquarters, none of the three gave the slightest reference to anything amiss, but while they made their reports—nothing urgent anymore; Atalanta was once more an exemplary Fleet Base, capable of running itself—they didn't meet my eyes for more than a few moments at a time. Even old Cottshall greeted me in a strange, fatherly way as I paused by his desk before going to what passed for my private office (the new one underground would be finished just in time to house my replacement).

"Hold my calls for a while, will you, Hathaway?" I called out the door. Then, I allowed myself a glance at my desk.

It was sealed in the usual scarlet, CONFIDENTIAL/ PERSONAL plastic envelope used for personnel actions. Before it got to my desk, someone in the COMM Center necessarily had received it, run the translator, and read the translation before sealing it in the envelope—then simply *had* to tell a close friend who simply *had* to tell a close friend. . . . It wasn't *really* military information of any value to our enemies, and of course I could never prove that anybody I'd seen so far *really* knew what was in the envelope. But word was out—and the surprising thing was that I didn't particularly care about that part of the bloody muckup. Everybody was going to find out sooner or later, so who cared *when*?

I stood beside my desk for a long time just looking at the xaxtdamned thing. Didn't want to acknowledge to myself that it had—finally and irrevocably—arrived. Then, grudgingly, I applied my finger and thumb to the seal, waited a moment while the envelope checked, then saw it unlock. Picked it up as if it were dirty. Inside—in triplicate—was a terse set of orders.

SD-VF7AWEGKOHJAEORITUFGJVASDKJFG
[CONFIDENTIAL/PERSONAL]

FROM: JUDGE ADVOCATE-GENERAL
OFFICE OF THE JAG
ADMIRALTY
AVALON, ASTERIOUS-AVALON

TO; WILF A. BRIM, RADM, COMMANDER, ATALANTA, HADOR-HAELIC

INFO: BU FLEET PERSONNEL

1. EFFECTIVE 1 DECAD, 52014, THIS DOCUMENT
TEMPORARILY RELIEVES YOU FROM COMMAND, OF
FLEET BASE, ATALANTA (REF STD REG 6783426-SDAF,
PARAS 5328-5365, AS AMENDED).

2. YOU ARE ORDERED TO REPORT FOR TEMPORARY
DUTY THIS OFFICE AS SOON AS PRACTICABLE BUT
NO LATER THAN 20 DECAD, 52014, AS DEFENDANT IN
COURTS-MARTIAL PROCEEDINGS FQWG098956/DSFG
(SUBJECT CLASSIFIED), INSTITUTED 1 DECAD, 52014.

3. TRANSPORTATION AS BEFITS RANK OF RADM (REF
FLEET TRAVEL REG 6783426-SDAF, PARAS 4234-
5198/B&C) WILL BE FURNISHED WITHIN THREE
STANDARD DAYS YOUR REQUEST.

4. APPOINTED COUNSEL WILL CONTACT YOU BY 22
DECAD, 52014.

FOR THE JUDGE ADVOCATE/GENERAL:
HERSHAL KIMTU, CAPTAIN, I.F.

[END CONFIDENTIAL/PERSONAL]
SD-VF7AWEGKOHJAEORITUFGJVASDKJFG

Took a long time till I realized I wasn't breathing. Suppose I should have been ready for the DAMNED thing—
Voot knows I'd had enough warning. Somehow, though,
since my return from Avalon I'd remained in a sort of unbe-
lieving denial, hoping against hope a miracle would occur.
Instead, *it* had happened, and I was stunned—heart racing,
short of breath—worse than any of the many times I'd been
wounded. I'd already been told I wouldn't be permitted to
win, even with the best counsel (and I'd have the best, I
trusted Onrad for that). For me, it was a death sentence—end
of my Universe. Years ago, after my first tour of duty in Atalanta, I'd been the victim of a CIGA-driven RIF, or Reduc-

tion In Force, and I'd taken that with a great deal more equanimity. But I'd been a lot younger then, too; had a whole lot of future ahead of me—wasn't so spoiled—corrupted, probably—by the trappings of power and office as I am now. Grinding my teeth, I forced myself to sit while I read the message a second time, then a third. The impassive sentences of governmentese plunged into my very soul like daggers. At last, I put it down and closed my eyes, holding on to the edges of my desk as if its weight could somehow protect me.

Must have been sitting there for half a metacycle when the 'Phone beeped. Was about to raise xaxt with Cottshall for letting the call through when I opened my eyes and saw Claudia in the global display. She had a look on her face that told me she knew, too. "Hello, Wilf," she said softly. "Good to see that you . . . got back safely."

In spite of everything, I felt myself smile. Love might make a man crazy, but . . . I discovered on the instant—it's also a very soothing analgesic in times of anguish. Thought of a billion things to say while I sat there like a blockhead, but finally settled on the brilliant repartee of, "Hello, Claudia. Good to see you, too." We sat in uncomfortable silence for a moment before I simply lifted the orders and shrugged. "You've heard about these, haven't you?"

She nodded. "Y-yes," she stammered.

"I assume it's all over the base, then?"

"Pretty much—at least among those of us who really care for you."

"Figures. Thanks."

"What are you going to do, Wilf?" she asked suddenly.

"Pretty easy question, at least for the immediate future," I said numbly. "I'm going back to Avalon to face a courts-martial that I'm not allowed to win."

"I know," she replied as a tear rolled down her cheek. "And after that?"

"Your guess is as good as mine," I said. "I suppose I'll burn that bridge when I come to it."

She laughed a little. "Wilf Brim," she said, "you will always be impossible, won't you?"

Felt myself smile again. "As long as I can manage it," I said. Then, "When can I see you?"

"Now," she said. "Hurry."

"Where?" I asked.

"I don't particularly care," she said. "We'll find someplace. The only thing that's important is that we be together every moment the gods give us."

At that moment, I couldn't think of anything in the entire Universe to refute her words. . . .

A Standard Week later, I'd tied up all the loose ends I was going to tie—except Claudia, that is, but *that* particular loose end wasn't ever going to tie neatly, not in my lifetime, at least. I'd turned everything on the base over to Williams, after which a little pressure on Drummond got the man promoted to flag rank as well as named "Temporary" Base Commander . . . until such time as the lynch mob they'd rigged for me in Avalon could do its dirty work. After that he'd take over officially. Other than Claudia, Barbousse had posed the biggest problem. He'd been so angry that he'd actually submitted his resignation from the Fleet until Drummond had it quietly squelched, and I'd had time to reason with the man.

For me, however, it was all over but the shouting, as they say. Tomorrow morning, Jim Payne and his Type 327—he complained he was beginning to feel rather like a jitney driver —would take me to Avalon where, following a short period of profound unpleasantness, I would be handed a new, well *different*, life. I'd managed to avoid a farewell banquet tentatively scheduled for tonight by invoking the "temporary" nature of my orders, even though everyone knew it was only a ruse. Somehow, the thought of all those people trying to be cheerful would have sent me screaming for shelter; funerals give me the creeps. I was going home under a cloud from which there would be no escape, and *that* was bloody *that*. Besides, Claudia and I had plans to spend the night together, somewhere. No amount of partying could possibly measure up to being alone with her; besides, it would be a long time before we were afforded that kind of opportunity again. Perhaps forever. . . .

In the late afternoon, with all but a few good-byes done with, I'd ridden my gravcycle here to the GradyGroat monastery atop City Mount Hill. Didn't know when—or whether—I'd see Atalanta again, and the monastery had by far the best view of the city. Below sprawled the Old Town's disorderly confusion of whitewashed buildings dappled everywhere by tiny, flower-filled gardens that were wedged into every nook and cranny. Streets here were for the most part twisting to some random pattern and so narrow that the balconies almost touched. All too often, though, these peaceful, urban vistas were interrupted by burned-out, roofless buildings, abandoned and gaping at the sky, streets blocked by piles of tumbled brick and stone. Closer to the bottom of the hill—and the base—whole blocks of the more modern districts had been leveled.

Some down there blamed me directly for the devastation; however, not even the craven Summers could have saved them from this particular fate. War is simply not kind to strategically important cities like Atalanta. But then, war is not particularly kind to anybody, victors or losers alike.

Here and there I caught glimpses of toylike trolley cars laboring up—or racing down—the hillside like crimson beetles equipped with shrieking, ear-piercing whistles that could be heard all the way back in Avalon; I'd loved to ride them once, in a younger life. Out in the harbor—relatively quiet now a metacycle after the last ships of the latest convoy had lifted for Gontor—a flight of Starfuries thundered across the water at the end of long, white wakes, then soared effortlessly into deep blue vault of space. Probably I'd also spent my last metacycles at the controls of one of those, too.

I'd pushed on as far as they'd allow. Now, the war was going forward without me. Pretty much a new war, at that—I'd had a hand in making it so. Since the fall of Fluvanna three years ago, our old Empire had been on the defensive—defiant, but powerless. Our preparations at Gontor and my raid at Otnar'at were changing all that. Now, we were not only defiant, but for the first time, we were about to go to an aggressive standing. Our first offensive, the invasion of Fluvanna from Gontor—Sapphire—had only this morning been moved up three Standard Weeks.

And this new Imperial aggressiveness was being felt throughout our Home Galaxy. The failure of LaKarn's Torond to bring off a secondary invasion of the Free Fluvannian planets—and our preparations to liberate the part that had been lost originally—had caused the League High Command to "temporarily" shift troops and equipment into occupied Fluvanna from active campaigns elsewhere. A case in point: absent ground forces that had been transferred from the Sodeskayan campaign, they were beginning to lose ground to the defending Bears. Once this process truly established itself, the Bears would make it literally irreversible. And soon, we would launch our own offensive—a second front that, ultimately, would prove to be the beginning of the end for Triannic and his jackbooted minions. . . .

For me, however, the war was over. I'd carried out my orders the best I could—not perfectly every time, but always to the very best of my abilities. And, I'd survived, when others with the same skills but less luck, had not. I'd been to the heights, made a difference when I was able, and taken my wounds with the rest, when it came to that. Somehow, it hadn't been enough. I'd soon be sacrificed to the gods of politics, wealth, and power—on my own side! Oh, anyone who cared to learn the truth would know what really happened. But in the larger scope of things, my passing would be little more than a ripple on a breezy lake. My courts-martial would be discussed for a day or two in the Officer's Clubs, then quickly forgotten in the sweep of total galactic war—and our coming triumph over the League. But no matter what my subsequent fate, I knew I would always feel a tremendous pride for what I'd done to help bring that victory about—and be prouder still of serving with the men and women of the Imperial Fleet.

Epilogue

11 Decad, 52014

Imperial Fleet base, Atalanta, Hador-Haelic

I was seated next to Jim Payne at the co-Helmsman's console of his Type 327 as we taxied through Atalanta's underground hangar toward the open doors and the harbor beyond. On either side of the canal, Starfuries and Basilisks were lined up smartly as if they were on inspection—which I assumed they'd been, shortly before we departed. Crews and maintenance people stood in neat formations next to each ship, waving as we passed. Behind us—in spite of my requests for an inconspicuous departure—the underground wharf had been crammed by people: Claudia, Barbousse, Williams, Cottshall, LaSalle, Tompkins, Russo, and so many of the others who'd made my brief stay in Atalanta enormously worthwhile from a personal point of view. I'd run out of words early that morning when Claudia and I parted outside the tiny room we'd shared during our last night together. So at the land side of the brow, I'd simply paused, turned to the silent throng, and saluted in silence, grinding my teeth to stifle an outburst of emotion that would have shamed me for the remainder of my life. Then, I'd turned on my heel and marched into the ship.

Once past the armored doors, we were joined by a whole squadron of Starfuries: sixteen ships in an arrowhead formation with our Type 327 at the tip, escorting us out to the windy harbor, hurling clouds of spray that glistened on their flanks in Hador's gleam, and started the problems with my tear ducts again. Not many objects made by the hand of man are as beautiful as a Starfury. After what seemed like a thousand years, we turned onto the takeoff vector and began to skim along the surface as if our nine starships were joined by hullmetal cables. Moments later, we were airborne, streaking almost vertically for outer space as I glued my face to the Hyperscreens for a last glimpse behind our tail of the city—and a lot of people—I'd grown to love. Embarrassed, Payne turned his head the other way until we reached the blackness of space and the Starfuries had turned back for home.

After he'd politely allowed me enough time to compose myself, Payne turned in his seat with a large envelope in his hand—and not just any old envelope. I'd sometimes flown missions before the war, carrying messengers who bore purple envelopes like this—special ones embellished by a wide crimson ribbon and sealed with Onrad's personal crest. "General Drummond and a Royal Courier delivered this just before I took off in Avalon," Payne explained, handling the envelope as if it were still in Onrad's possession. "The General ordered me to wait till after we were in space before giving this to you."

"Er, thanks," I stammered in surprise. From Onrad—now what? Shaking my head, I took the envelope and placed it on my lap, then stared out the Hyperscreens at the flowing spaceman's tunnel until I no longer felt like throwing it across the flight bridge. Finally, I placed my thumb and forefinger on the sensors outlined just below the seal. The logic took its own sweet time thoroughly verifying my fingerprints, but at last the seal split in two with a quiet *tink*—the kind you get when you break a thin crystal pane. Inside the envelope was a single sheet of . . . well, it felt like—it *was*—parchment when I drew it out, with real pen-and-ink writing on its surface. At the bottom was more ribbon and three more seals, real ones in old-fashioned wax, like the ones that royalty use when signing important documents like treaties.

Imperial Proclamation and Decree.

Know ye by these presents that I, Onrad the Fifth, Grand Galactic Emperor, Prince of the Reggio Star Cluster, and Rightful Protector of the Heavens do make and seal this proclamation by all powers and endowments vested in me at my coronation. From this day onward, Our loyal subject, Wilf Ansor Brim, will be known throughout all the civilized Universe as Lord Brim, 1st Duke of Grayson. With this title, I also assign, from Royal Land Holdings, the five habitable planets and two nonhabitable planets of the star Grayson, and all properties, minerals, rents, leases, and income pertaining from them to his sole ownership. Decreed this first Standard Day of Decad in the Standard Imperial Year 52014.

Onrad V

Attached to the surface of the proclamation was a simple yellow stick-on note with the following scrawled on it in ink:

Brim:

Perhaps this title I have created will make the necessary enduring of an unfair courts-martial—and all the attendant unpleasantness—more palatable. Be assured the undeserved black mark on your name will someday be removed. That I guarantee personally.

By the by, my friend and subject, in case you perceive this is the end of the war for you, don't. Your next assignment will come directly from me, and believe me, it will curl your ears.

Onrad

Handy Reference to Imperial Units of Measurements

Prepared for visitors to the Home Galaxy
by
THE GALACTIC ALMANAC
(AND HANDY ENCYCLOPEDIA)

Dates:

The Standard Imperial Calendar in use throughout most of the Home Galaxy is based upon the Avalonian local calendar and consists of four-hundred-day years, divided into ten months: Unad, Diad, Triad, Tetrad, Pentad, Hexad, Heptad, Octad, Nonad, and Decad, each with forty days, grouped into four, ten-day weeks. Dates are expressed either as

<day>/<year>, as in 131/52013, or <day><month>, <year>, as in 11 Triad, 52013.

Units of Time Measurement:

Standard	Multiple	Historic
Click =		1.5 x human eye blink
Cycle =	50 clicks	
Metacycle =	50 Cycles	

Time of Day Measurement:

Time of day throughout the Home Galaxy is based upon the Avalonian local day and is fixed by six, four-metacycle "Watches:" Dawn, Morning, Brightness, Evening, Twilight, and Night. These are adjusted to local time, whenever possible; however, where local rotation time is either too short or too long, partial or multiple Standard Days are implemented. Time of day is normally written as: <watch initial>:<metacycle>:<cycle>:<click>, truncated as desired. Example: D:3:45 or B:00:15. Verbally, time of day is expressed by speaking the watch name followed optionally by, "plus" and a one-, two-, or three-metacycle offset toward the next watch. This may optionally be followed by, "and" with a one-, to forty-nine-cycle offset toward the next watch. Examples: Dawn plus one and twenty-five, Evening and forty, Twilight plus three. In casual speech, the use of "and a half" indicates twenty-five cycles past a meta-cycle, as in, "Dawn and a half," or "Dawn plus three and a half."

One Standard Day anywhere in the galaxy is based on the six-watch Avalonian Day.

One Standard Week is ten Avalonian Days.

Other units of measurement:

mmi	One-thousandth of an iral.
thumb =	One-tenth the length of a human foot (see below).
iral =	derived from ancient measurements of an "average" human foot.
c'lenyt =	5,500 irals.
milston =	mass of approximately one Standard Mill Stone (see Imperial Museum, Avalon).

Surface Directions:

Lightward =	Facing planetary rotation.
Nightward =	Opposite direction from planetary rotation.
Boreal =	Left-hand planetary pole, facing Lightward.
Austral =	Right-hand planetary pole, facing Lightward.

Bearings in Space:

Bearings are based on a four-hundred-degree circle with the zero-degree mark at the nose of the starship, also known as "Red." Other "color" points are Orange (approx 66.6 degrees), Yellow (approx. 133.2 degrees), Green (approx. 199.8 degrees), Blue (approx. 266.4 degrees) and Purple (330 degrees). Bearings are expressed in relation to the ship and generally followed by the words "apex" or "nadir" to indicate "high" or "low" in relation to orientation with the ship's internal gravity system.

A starship approaching from 330 degrees "high" would be on a relative bearing of "blue apex." A starship approaching "low" from 390 degrees would be on a relative bearing of "red red purple nadir."

BILL BALDWIN, the author of *The Helmsman* series, is a graduate of the Mercerburg Academy and the University of Pittsburgh, where he earned a B.A. in journalism and a Masters of Letters degree. He served in the U.S. Air Force at Cape Canaveral supporting Project Mercury. He also managed astronaut public relations during the Gemini and early Apollo programs. He has worked as a computer programmer for Burroughs Corporation (now UNISYS) and Xerox Corporation. Bill lives in Dallas, Texas with his wife Pat and two cats.